Praise for

Secrets of the Sands

and

Guardians of the Desert

"The final product put me in awe of where the world-building skills of Wisoker are at this early stage of her career . . . reminiscent of something out of an Ursula K. LeGuin novel in detail and complexity. Wisoker, like the best authors of this genre, has created a completely original society upon which to tell her story."
—*SF Site*

"intriguing . . . engaging."
—*Publishers Weekly*

"An absorbing story, a unique world, and fascinating characters. Leona Wisoker is definitely a writer to watch!"
—Tamora Pierce

". . . a lushly visual and highly detailed world of desert tribes, a language of beads, and a unique way of viewing the world."
—*Library Journal*

"Leona Wisoker is a gifted storyteller and in *Secrets of the Sands* she has succeeded in crafting a refreshingly unpredictable tale set in a stunningly rich and detailed world."
—Michael J. Sullivan, author of the Riyria Revelations series

"For its complexity, intriguing story, and (as in the first volume) for its characters I find totally fascinating, I heartily recommend *Guardians of the Desert*."
—*SF Revu*

"A storyteller with a good deal of promise. Give this one a try."
— CJ Cherryh

"Sturdy, engaging, confidently-written—*Guardians of the Desert* is all any fan could have hoped for in a sequel. The delightful Ms. Wisoker is now two for two."
—C.J. Henderson

"With a flair for evoking exotic locales and an eye for detail, Leona Wisoker has crafted a first novel peopled by characters who are more than they first seem. From the orphaned street-thief who possesses an uncanny ability to read situations and people, to the impetuous noblewoman thrust into a world of political intrigue, Wisoker weaves a colourful tapestry of desert tribes, honour, revenge, and an ancient, supernatural race."
—Janine Cross, author of the Dragon Temple Saga

"Wisoker makes a praiseworthy work when it comes to world building, creating with care and without haste a strong world, one piece at a time...another unique element of the story which . . . certainly will be developed more in the series' next novels."
—*Dark Wolf's Fantasy Reviews*

Children of the Desert

series

by Leona Wisoker

Book One: Secrets of the Sands

Book Two: Guardians of the Desert

Book Three: Bells of the Kingdom

Bells of the Kingdom

Leona Wisoker

FOR THE WINDSOR
LIBRARY –
THANKS FOR
ALL THE HARD
WORK!

Leona Wisoker

Copyright © 2012 by Leona Wisoker
Interior map by Ari Warner Copyright © 2009
Cover illustration Copyright © 2012 by Aaron Miller
Cover design by Rachael Murasaki Ish

First Trade Edition—published 2013
Printed in the United States and the United Kingdom

ISBN 978-1-936427-22-2

MERCURY RETROGRADE PRESS
6025 Sandy Springs Circle
Suite 320
Atlanta, Georgia 30328

www.MercuryRetrogradePress.com

Library of Congress Cataloging-in-Publication Data

Wisoker, Leona.
  Bells of the kingdom / Leona Wisoker. -- 1st trade ed.
     p. cm. -- (Children of the desert ; 3)
  ISBN 978-1-936427-22-2 (trade paper : alk. paper) 1. Fantasy fiction. 2. Epic fiction. I. Title.
  PS3623.I847B45 2013
  813'.6--dc23
                        2012039078

Dedication

This book is dedicated to all the "silent" survivors out there: of childhood abuse, of drug and alcohol addiction, of PTSD, of bipolar disorder, of chronic depression . . . . The list seems endless at times, and is always heartbreaking. I could not have written this book without the incredible generosity and trust of so many survivors who have shared their stories with me; I thank you, one and all, and bow before the incredible strength that most of you don't even understand you possess.

May you find healing and peace; may your families and loved ones find healing and peace; may your neighbors and countryfolk find healing and peace; may the world, in the end, find healing and peace.

Namaste.

Acknowledgments

I'm very grateful for the support and encouragement of so many people, most of whom have been named already in the Acknowledgments of my previous books. I am especially grateful, this time around, for the wonderful patience of all the people who waited an extra year for this book; I truly hope it proves worth the wait!

One of the most momentous events for me, during the final round of revisions and editing of this particular book, was the rapid decline and passing of my father in 2012. Dealing with his death shook me far more than I could ever have foreseen, and while there is absolutely no direct parallel between my relationship with my father and the child-parent storyline featured in this particular book, the experience definitely affected the clarity with which I wrote about certain emotional moments.

This has been, by far, the hardest book I have ever written; in part because I did have to travel to some very emotionally dark places in order to understand why the various characters acted as they did.

There were many, many people who held me up, encouraged me, and kept me going over the past few months, who served as my light in the darkness, and who deserve a mention here, even if they have been pointed out in former books: my husband Earl, my mother Renate, my siblings Steve, Tanya, and Sue; my friends Patrick, Todd, Russell, and Rick; the incredible trio of Chris, Amy, and Ame; and of course my publisher and editor, Barbara Friend Ish, and her wonderful family. Aaron Miller also deserves an extra round of applause for the fabulous cover, as does Ari Warner for the continuing excellence of the maps.

I thank you all, and bow to you all, and can never repay any of you adequately for the support. All I can do is offer my best effort to the next book, and the next, and the next, to repay in some small measure your faith in me . . . and because I believe that would have made my father prouder than anything else I could possibly do in this life.

Contents

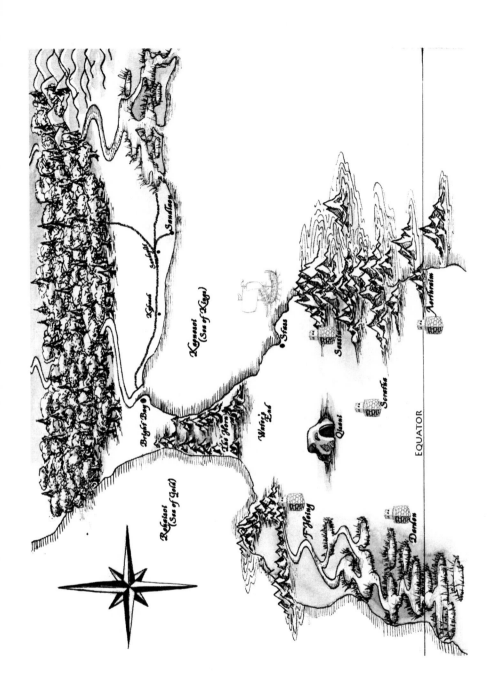

Royal Library Map no. 123:
The Southlands and Southern Kingdom

Prologue

Start with the bells. There were always the bells.

Late summer air, heat-hazed, thick, and sticky, clung to Kolan's skin. Through the wide, arched window the Arason Church gardens spread out in shades of green, white, and gold: there a row of midseason peas; over further, lines of summerbeans; another, taller section was corn tasselling into a frayed, delicious mess.

His mouth watered as he looked out at that last item.

The resonant *braummm* of the Arason Church bells, marking two hours before noon, jarred him out of his drowsy survey of the gardens. It was hard to keep a contented contemplation of anything going for long, with those things sounding off seemingly every time one relaxed. It hadn't been so bad out on the edges of town, where Kolan had grown up; but here, especially in this room, the bells always made his teeth vibrate fit to fall out of his mouth. Not relaxing at *all*.

But then, as *sio* Dernhain would have said, Kolan wasn't *supposed* to be relaxing. He was supposed to be working at learning to write clean copy. Reluctantly, he brought his attention back to the parchment in front of him. *An Accounting of the Life of Tenedal*, it read. *Head Priest of the Arason Branch of the Northern Church, d.1090-1111*. He studied the graceful writing without enthusiasm, then reached for the quill.

With delicate care, he copied the line, his writing stark and clumsy compared to the sample above it. A large blot marked every other letter. He sighed, set the quill aside again, and looked out at the pale blue sky. A large horsefly rattled by, circling, searching for a place to settle; Kolan sent it spinning back out the window with a well-aimed slap and a silent apology to the Four.

Harm no living creature, from beetle to boy: one of the Holy Creeds that Kolan recited, alongside a dozen other novices, every morning. *All have their places and purposes in the eyes of the gods.*

What purpose a horsefly or tick had, Kolan couldn't begin to guess. Even *sio* Ense, the gentlest of the Arason Church *siopes*, had admitted to difficulty with that one.

"Perhaps," he'd said thoughtfully, "it's enough to merely *understand* that one is doing wrong, and be as gentle as possible in removing the offending creature from one's person. It's very difficult not to slap a stinging insect away from one, and it's very difficult to avoid harm to the insect when removing a tick or mosquito."

Solian, on the other hand, laughed at Kolan for being concerned over insects.

"They're *bugs*," he always said, usually as he was squashing a beetle underfoot. "There are hundreds and hundreds of them, Kolan! They give birth to dozens more every few days. We'll be *overrun* if all we do is shoo them gently outside. The gods don't care about *bugs*. They care about *us*. Otherwise the bugs would be running the world, not humans."

Even though Solian was only a novice, like Kolan himself, and *sio* Ense a full senior priest, Kolan couldn't quite decide who was more right.

The heavy tramp of many booted feet on stone echoed through the window to Kolan's left, the one that looked out over the main courtyard. Kolan wavered, biting his lip, but stayed stubbornly put. Curiosity wasn't any part of his duties at the moment. *Sio* Dernhain had been specific: *Not for anything less than a fire do you leave that seat and stop your practicing*, he'd said. *When you can write a line without a blot, you can get up. Until then, you* sleep *at that desk!*

Sio Dernhain wasn't particularly noted for his kindness, compassion, or patience.

Kolan looked at the blotchy copy line and grimaced. This was going to be a long day.

A thin, wavering shriek floated up from the courtyard. People began shouting. Kolan stood, then sat, then stood again. He made two steps toward the courtyard window, then retreated to the stool, clenching his hands in frustration.

Another of the Creeds came to mind: *Obedience to the gods requires a clean heart and a dedication to one's given tasks. Seek not the chaos of the world outside, but be content with the inner truth and strength the gods will always give to those who truly seek it.*

Kolan sighed deeply and picked up the quill. His next attempt only had four blotches, which counted in his mind as encouraging progress.

Outside, people shouted and bellowed. He resolutely shut his ears to everything and bent over his work. *Seek not the chaos of the world outside.*

Two blotches. Maybe he could produce a clean line before the commotion died down, and sneak a look out the window as a reward.

The next line had so many blotches as to be nearly illegible. *Dedication to one's given tasks.* He scowled at the paper and forced himself to slow down. Pay attention. Focus. *Dedication.*

Each slight curve seemed to take forever, each loop an eternity of care. Nothing existed except the quill, the paper, the ink, the motion.

He put the final stop at the end and sat back, blinking: *perfect.* He'd done it. Not a single smear or blot. He put the quill aside and looked toward the courtyard window, but didn't climb from the stool. The air hung heavy and silent; whatever had happened, it had finished already. There wouldn't be anything to see.

Seek not the chaos of the world outside. He studied his copy line, compared it to the original; his version was distinctly clumsier. He reached for the quill, cleaned it carefully, then dipped it back into the ink and began again.

Some time later, Dernhain said, from a scant step behind him, "Not bad, *sannio.*"

Kolan jerked, startled from a near-trance. He barely managed to avoid knocking the ink pot over, but the quill flew from his hand and clattered onto the floor.

Dernhain covered his broad face with one hand and sighed heavily as Kolan scrambled to retrieve the quill.

"Never mind," he said in answer to Kolan's stammered apologies. "*Sionno* Hagair wants to see you. Now."

"Now?" Kolan looked down at his inkstained fingers.

"Now," Dernhain said. "Hurry up. There's someone in his office that wants to talk to you."

Kolan stared, bewildered. Dernhain's glare left no room for questions. "*Go!*"

He ran.

Sionno Hagair's office always seemed, to Kolan, far too small to accommodate not only the man himself, but the massive piles of *stuff* that accumulated on the black oak desk. Bound books and piles of precious paper formed one thick tower; bags of mysterious powders and granular substances another tall, sloppy heap. One handwoven mesh bag held what had to be over a hundred glass balls, variously colored and sized.

Kolan tried to avoid looking at that bag. They *had* been his marbles, the only thing from home he'd been allowed to retain when he entered the novitiate. *Sio* Dernhain had objected that the small glass toys were far too valuable and constituted a novice holding unacceptable wealth; *sionno* Hagair, after some thought, and to Kolan's everlasting gratitude, had firmly overridden Dernhain.

Seeing his marbles here still sent a dull, embarrassed ache through his chest. What had happened to *sionno* Arenin hadn't been his *fault*—but he carried the guilt all the same. *Harm no living creature, from beetle to boy.*

The tall man standing beside Hagair's desk coughed and said, impatiently, "Well, boy?"

Kolan darted a quick, nervous glance at the Head Priest's stern, unsmiling face. Hagair dipped his head in a barely visible nod, granting permission to speak. Kolan gulped and looked back at the tall stranger, who cut an imposing figure even in travel-stained clothing.

The man had introduced himself without waiting for *sionno* Hagair to do so. "Captain Kullag of Bright Bay," he'd said curtly. "Here to investigate word of witches in Arason. Do you know any, boy?"

Kolan had opened his mouth, shut it again, and stared at Hagair's desk to give himself time to think. At the captain's impatient prompt, he gathered his wits and said, "No, Captain, I don't."

A quick glance at Hagair showed the man's expression held the faintest hint of a frown, but the Head Priest made no open protest.

"I'm told you do," Kullag said heavily. "I'm *assured* you do. By a friend of yours. Solian."

Kolan shot the head priest another, more startled look. Hagair now looked thunderously grim.

"S-Solian?" Kolan stammered. "But he's in Jion!"

"He was *supposed* to go to Jion," *sionno* Hagair said. "Apparently he decided to travel south instead of north."

"Solian told me of a witch you're *familiar* with," Kullag interrupted, insinuation heavy in his tone. "Ellemoa."

Kolan felt color cresting into his face, betraying any blander statement he might have tried. Kullag nodded, his hard face creasing into a satisfied smirk.

"So you *do* know this witch," Kullag said.

"Witch isn't an accurate term, Captain, as I've already tried to explain," Hagair said, scowling.

"Lake-born or witch, it all adds up the same for me," Kullag retorted. "Under your own Church's edict, she's a damned creature, and I'm tasked to capture her and bring her to Bright Bay to face the holy judgment of the new *n'sion.*"

"The edicts from Bright Bay don't always apply to the northern branches, Captain," Hagair said promptly. "We do have a certain autonomy—"

"Take that up with the *n'sion,*" Kullag said. "I'm doing the job given me by King and Church." He turned a glare on Kolan. "Where is she?"

Gone, thank the gods. "I don't know, Captain," Kolan said aloud, quite honestly. "I haven't been allowed to leave the grounds since becoming a novice here. I haven't seen her in—" He glanced at the Head Priest.

"Almost two years," *sionno* Hagair supplied.

Kullag's scowl now rivaled Dernhain at his most impatient. "Where does she *live*, boy?"

"Captain, the proper term is *sannio,*" Hagair said. "Novice. *Boy* is disrespectful."

Kullag ignored the interruption, his attention fixed on Kolan.

Kolan gulped, his composure wavering. "I—I don't know, Captain," he said.

He *couldn't* tell this man where to find Ellemoa's cottage. Even empty and abandoned, it was *hers*. And since nobody knew why the lake-born had left, there was nothing saying she mightn't return one day.

She *wasn't* a witch. She *wasn't*.

He tried not to think about flames dancing on the tips of her fingers without burning the flesh beneath, and kept his gaze stubbornly on the corner of the head priest's desk.

"You don't *know*?"

"I always met her somewhere," Kolan said, not looking up. A fine sweat broke out on his forehead, and he didn't dare look at the head priest. *Seek not the chaos of the world outside. Dedication to one's given tasks. Harm no living creature, from beetle to boy.*

Lies harm one's soul, each one a tiny rip, hard to mend, each one a scar forever.

He'd take the hurt of a lie if it protected Ellemoa from this man.

Hagair shifted his weight restlessly but once more made no open protest.

"I see," the captain said, his tone black with disapproval and doubt. "Solian seemed quite certain that you would know how to guide us to her."

Kolan's heartbeat thudded in his ears.

"Captain," the Head Priest cut in, "Solian exaggerates. He also lies. He seems to find it amusing. There's a very good reason he was being sent to *Jion* for a long meditational retreat."

Kolan's gaze slid inexorably sideways to the bag of marbles.

"Since you seem to know Solian so well," *sionno* Hagair continued, "perhaps you can tell me what happened to his companions? He was sent north with a senior priest, *sio* Ense, and another novice named Asrain. Did he happen to mention them at all?"

"Missing priests aren't my concern," Kullag snapped. "*Witches* are my concern. And Solian struck *me* as surprisingly trustworthy, *sionno*. All things considered. I've gotten quite *good* at spotting liars."

Kolan could feel the captain's glare boring into him.

"Not as good as you think, apparently," the Head Priest said. "Since Kolan seems unable to help you, is there anything *else* I can do for you, Captain? It's almost time for noon services."

Kullag grunted. The air suddenly felt thick and dry; Kolan glanced up and found the two men glaring at one another with searing intensity.

"No," Kullag said at last, and with the barest sketch of a bow turned and stormed from the room.

"Gods hold your soul gently, Captain," *sionno* Hagair said without the least trace of irony. As the heavy tread of the captain's booted feet faded along the hallway, he sighed again, rubbing his hands over his face.

"*Sannio* Kolan, shut the door and sit down. Check that he's really gone first."

The hallway was empty. Kolan pushed the heavy wooden door shut, dread coiling in his stomach, and returned to perch on the single chair in front of the head priest's desk.

"I'm sorry, *sionno*," he said, deciding that he might as well get the scolding over with and receive his punishment allotment of Recitations.

To his surprise, Hagair grimaced and settled into his own rather sturdier chair without answering right away. At last he said, "There are gradations to morality in the real world that aren't always covered in the Creeds, Kolan. You've just tripped over one of those, I'm afraid."

Kolan glanced up, startled. "You're not angry?"

"I'm furious. But not at you. You handled that very well." Hagair pinched the bridge of his nose and squeezed his eyes shut for a moment, then dropped his hand to the desk and looked at Kolan again. "Now you tell *me* the real truth. *Do* you know where she lives?"

"Yes, *sionno*," Kolan said promptly. "But she's gone, with all the other lake-born." He caught himself and added, hastily, "Isn't she?"

Hagair's eyes creased as though he were restraining a smile.

"No," he said. "She stayed behind when they left. I spoke to her once or twice in the following months."

Kolan's mouth dropped open. "But her cottage was emp-hhmmphm." He bit his tongue and shut his eyes, feeling hot color flooding into his face again.

Hagair coughed a few times, then said, "I don't know about that. I haven't seen her in some time, myself. Perhaps she left and followed her people after all. I don't know why she stayed, so I don't know why she would leave."

I know why she stayed, Kolan thought dismally. He rubbed the fingertips of his right hand against the palm of his left without really thinking about it; glanced up to find the head priest watching him with a canny, perceptive stare.

"I think that perhaps if Ellemoa is indeed still in the area," Hagair said in an abstracted, distant tone, "someone ought to warn her that this captain is hunting her. Don't you think?"

Kolan nodded fervently and hoped that Hagair wouldn't send *sio* Dern-hain. Ellemoa would hide from most of the senior priests, and then there would be no warning given.

In fact, Kolan couldn't think of *anyone* that Ellemoa, if she was still present, *wouldn't* run from–except himself. He met Hagair's mild gaze, watched the man's right eyebrow arch slowly, and felt a jolt of breathless excitement slam through his stomach.

"*Sionno?*" he said, hardly daring to believe the hint he saw before him. Novices–*sannio*–weren't allowed to leave the grounds. Only junior priests–*sio-lle*–and above could leave the grounds. Was the head priest going to break *that* rule? Was this another one of the *gradations of morality* he'd mentioned?

"Sio Dernhain has you training as a scribe, I believe?" Hagair said. "Tedious work, that. Why don't you take the afternoon off and take a walk to clear your mind, *siolle* Kolan?"

Kolan opened his mouth to correct the head priest, then stopped. He blinked once, then again, his eyes feeling larger each time. He thought his stomach might turn inside out from sheer excitement. *Siolle.* Hagair hadn't said that by mistake. Kolan had just been promoted to junior priest.

Dedication. The gods were rewarding him for his dedication. *Praise the Four, praise them loud.* He would be sure to sing with more attentiveness during the next service, to let them know his gratitude.

"You're still here, *siolle* Kolan?" Hagair said mildly.

Caught out of his dazed wonder, Kolan jolted to his feet. "Thank you, *si-onno!* Thank you, thank you, thank you," he blurted, and fled on the wings of the man's laughter.

As he ran, the church bells embarked on their hourly, doleful announcement of time passing.

Start with the breath. There is always the breath.

The infant smelled like peaches and slightly sour milk, although Ellemoa couldn't remember having fed it recently. She couldn't remember anything beyond the warm grey mist around her and the thin whistling sound of her firstborn breathing. Something had happened, something terrible and frightening, out beyond the mist, but she didn't need to remember that now.

She wasn't alone any longer. She would never be alone again. That was the only thing that mattered. *I have a son.* He would stay with her forever. He would never abandon her without warning. He would never betray her.

You must leave the lake, Ellemoa, her lover said. She felt the mist stir around her, lifting her hair in a gentle caress. *It is not good for you to stay here so long. It is not good for the child.*

"I want to stay with you," she said absently, her attention on the infant. "He wants to stay with you. We love you. Don't you love us? Don't you want us to stay?"

The mist swirled in a subtle sigh, currents of heat threading across her skin. *You do not hear me,* her lover said. *You cannot stay with me. You must go back to the air, to the human side of the world.*

The word *cannot* caught her attention. She looked up, frowning; in her arms, the infant stirred restlessly, whimpering a little. A vague dread settled thickly into her chest.

"Of course we can stay," she said. "We're ha'ra'hain. We belong here, with you. You love us. You want us here."

No, her lover said. *You are far, far from the place where I live, Ellemoa. To me, this place is cold and unpleasant. You could not endure my true bed, and the child is too tender yet to even try. You only endure this much because of my support, and I grow tired. I am old, Ellemoa. I must rest. You must seek out lessers for your support for a time. You must go back to the air.*

"No," she said, dread spidering through her entire body. The infant burped, then began whimpering more loudly. "No, I can't. They left me. They abandoned me! I only have the humans now, and they hate me. They'll hurt me. You can't send me back!"

You must go back, her lover said, unrelenting, and the warm haze thinned rapidly.

"No! *No!*"

Protect the child, her lover said. *It will be my last. I do not have the strength for another. It will be the one to come after me, in time. Protect the child, Ellemoa, so that it may protect this area.*

Before she could protest again, the mists disappeared under a flood of sunlight. She staggered, throwing up one arm to shield her dazzled eyes. The infant, jolted into a less secure hold, wailed furiously.

Eerie mist lapped like iridescent water along the improbably thin strip of pebble-sand shore. Icy air slapped against her skin. She adjusted internal temperatures reflexively, and the shivering stopped.

How could you? she railed, glaring at the diaphanous waters. *How dare you? To leave me alone again, alone with the humans—I trusted you!*

There was no response. She could sense her lover sinking further into the scalding depths of the lake, indifferent to her rage.

The child's wail abruptly took on a more startled pitch. Moments later, a hard grip closed around each of Ellemoa's upper arms.

"Here she is, Captain!" a coarse voice crowed. "With a witch whelp, no less!"

Humans. Rage frothed through her instantly. They were threatening her child. Herself. *No!* She would kill them all, squash them like the rude insects they really were—

Something struck the back of her head, and she pitched forward to her knees, hovering on the fringes of a hazy near-darkness. A moment later a rough hand pulled her head back and a stinging, gritty powder drifted onto her face. The very touch of it felt obscene.

She tried to shake it off, but it clung, searing like tiny drops of acid. Her screams of protest drew laughter from the humans around her, then another voice joined hers: "You're *hurting* her! Stop it! She hasn't done anything wrong!"

Kolan. *Kolan.* She opened her eyes, blinking; for a moment she saw him, hands bound, on his knees as well, shouting at the men around them. Then the grit blew into her eyes, and she screamed, her vision blurring into agonized, fractured shapes.

"We don't have orders about a child," someone said. "Damned if I'm hauling a witch-brat back to Bright Bay."

"How can you do this to me?" she shrieked. "How can you do this to my child?"

"It's demon-spawn!" a man yelled back.

"Burn it!" someone else shouted.

"Drown it!" a third voice suggested.

"It's a *child*! How can you harm a child?"

"It's a damned creature," said a voice much closer to hand. "You'll be joining it in due time, woman, never fear!"

Her temper snapped. *Humans.* They were all insane. "The hells you say!" she shouted in his general direction. "No! You won't lay a hand on either one of us!"

She tried to surge to her feet, calling on the strength she'd been cautioned never to reveal to the humans—and found herself unable to rise from her knees. Her vision and senses were too blurred from that noxious powder to allow direct attack; she screamed again, incensed and, finally, frightened.

Focusing her attention on the lake, on her lover, she threw all the power she had into a desperate, silent scream: *Help me!* A few of the men around her swore and shuffled back a few hasty steps. Kolan cried out in pain; he'd felt the call more clearly than the soldiers. Not surprising. She'd given him more than he would probably ever realize before his choice to abandon her in favor of the hypocrites he called holy men.

Pity she couldn't take back any of the deeper aspects of what she'd given him. She could have used the extra strength at the moment.

Far away, far below, something rolled and shifted uneasily, then subsided to silence: refusing to answer the call.

Her child wailed again, preternaturally aware that it was helpless in a very dangerous situation. *Protect the child.* Her lover might not return for her–*faithless monster*–but he would for the child. She reached out to the child, slid inside its awareness, and channeled her demand through its cries.

The child's shrieks held agonizing pain this time, as the last of her strength tore through it and forced connections that wouldn't have formed naturally for a dozen years at least.

The vast bulk of her lover's awareness rolled and grumbled, then began ascending rapidly.

Ellemoa threw her head back and began to laugh, high and shrill: sheer relief from the fear, and a savage satisfaction that now these humans would pay for their aggression.

The men backed away, their own fear cascading from them like a waterfall. Kolan's shrieks seemed to fall into a strange rhythm with those of her child, as though he'd somehow locked onto or into the infant's pain.

My child. Mine! Not yours. Without moving a muscle, she thrust between them, severing the tenuous connection; felt Kolan fall sideways, convulsing and gagging. Her child's now razor-edged wails sliced into her. She forced herself to endure the noise only because binding it silent risked losing her lover's attention.

"Captain," someone said, voice thick with alarm. "The lake–look!"

Ellemoa bared her teeth and shrieked, "You will all *die* for daring to threaten us!"

"Ellemoa, no," Kolan hollered. "Don't do this to yourself! *Harm none, harm none!*"

She spat in his direction and laughed again.

The air changed: pressure whomped across her in a great, molten shock. *You are not protecting the child well,* her lover said disapprovingly, a great presence even to her blurred vision. Around her, humans screamed.

They're hurting us! Kill them! Kill them!

She felt the massive regard turn from her to the soldiers, felt her lover sorting swiftly through their minds, assessing the situation. *No,* he said at last. His words flickered in the not-space between moments, taking less than a human blink to convey. *If I kill these, humans will send more to damage this area that I protect. They will harm those who have done nothing to earn that hurt. I cannot kill these men for you.*

Unable to believe his refusal, she let out a wordless howl of protest. He was siding with the *humans*?

I will send you to safety instead, he said. *I will send you to a place where a younger relative has the strength to protect you while my last child grows to replace me. My relative will keep you safe and teach the child, as I lack the strength to do. You will return here when it is safe.*

"No!" she screamed aloud. "Kill them, gods damn you, kill them!"

Men shouted around her, dim animal noises she ignored as pointless–they were merely screaming and running about in stunned confusion.

There are many ways to do a thing, her lover said, *and not all of them require violence to a lesser form of life. You are too young yet. You will learn.* He paused; she felt him examining those around her again. *I will send this young human with you,* he decided. *He understands the way of things already. He can teach you. Let him help you with the child. Let him teach it restraint and discipline, and learn from him yourself.*

"Noooooooo!"

Heat built and thundered around her. Men screamed. Her child screamed. Kolan screamed. There came the sharp scent of urine, the bitter musk of sweat, and a twisting that threatened to rip her apart.

Something dark and rancid filled her senses. Threads of green and gold whipped through the not-space and twined around her in an unbreakable grip. *Mine,* a thin, slippery voice whispered. *Mine now. Mine!*

No, her lover said, sounding startled. *Who are you? You are not my cousin! Who are you?*

MINE. MINE now! Give! GIVE!

The threads tightened and sharpened around her.

Help me! she screamed. *My love, help me!*

She sensed a horrible, wrenching hesitation. Abruptly, her child's screams redoubled, then inverted to a resounding silence.

I cannot save you this time, her lover said.

My child! My child! Where is he?

The darkness whispered angry echo: *Where did you send it? It is mine. Mine! Bring it back, give it to me, mine!*

I am sorry, Ellemoa, her lover said. *I failed you. The child is safe. The child is safe. I am sorry. I love–*

The word trailed into a broken silence.

She hung in fetid darkness, unable even to thrash against the cocoon of bindings, and listened to Kolan's agonized howls with a savage sense of satisfaction.

This is all your fault, she told him. *Yours. All yours.*

He was too busy screaming to answer.

Chapter One

The south was a land filled with music, from the graceful language to the low whistles of servants moving about their work. At night, Scratha Fortress seemed to pulse with an underlying beat: the rhythmic sound had carried Idisio through a night of troubled dreams and out into the still air of pre-dawn.

A monstrous headache descended a bare breath after his eyes opened. Instinct drove him back into a more focused, escape-driven slumber.

It's a drinking contest, Azni said in his memory, and then Riss chimed in: *I thought you knew the game.*

He hadn't. He didn't drink; losing awareness of his surroundings had always been far too dangerous to risk. He hadn't even known what the changing taste of the acrid coffee meant until Riss explained–far too late, as it turned out.

As he recalled, she'd found his ignorance highly amusing. The hangover had been *far* from amusing, and he'd been having flashes of it at erratic intervals ever since, as though his body simply refused to let go of reliving that experience.

He descended further into stillness, letting the pain wrack through his surface nerves while he retreated to the deep place where pain was a barely noticeable tremor.

Music followed him into the stillness, and memory: *There is a lake, a ghosty lake*, someone sang, and laughed a big, rich, salty laugh. Red. The talkative sailor had sung so many shocking and funny songs, including one about a northern lake made of mist in which, supposedly, lived a horrendous demon . . . .

Scratha's voice floated through the void of memory: *I think you have Ghost Lake blood . . . You have too much northern in your face for anything else.*
A demon.
My father.
Idisio shuddered without moving a muscle, a comprehensive tremor that threatened to shake his brain from his skull. He forced himself deeper still, into a silence free of any memory at all.

Another sort of music woke him after a time: a complex array of whistles and the laughter of servants passing by his room. He lay still, awareness clarifying, and listened to the patterns. It wasn't simple music. They were *talking.*

With that awareness, his concept of the entire fortress around him shifted. The servants here sang, laughed, and spoke in codes that passed right under the noses of those in charge. They showed little to no fear of their masters, despite the awesome powers of the several desert lords present—and two visiting ha'ra'hain, the other of whom was rather older than Idisio himself.

A tart, minty scent filled his nose. A moment later, a damp cloth covered his face from nose-tip to hairline.

"Are you awake?" Riss said in a bare murmur.

He held still and kept his breathing even. After a few moments, she sighed and went away. He could feel her *presence* fading from the room; when he was sure he was alone, he pushed the cloth aside and propped himself up on his elbows.

The servants weren't afraid here. That was important. Why? With masters who could kill them in a matter of a breath, with a creature far beneath their feet who would take less time than that, what gave them such a cheerful indifference to the danger?

More whistles wove together as the servants went back the other way. His room was in a small side hallway, one of five; he'd refused more opulent guest quarters, still deeply uncomfortable with the notion of *being important.*

Riss's room lay next to his. Scratha had murmured something about propriety, but he'd clearly caught Idisio's relief at the separation. Being around desert lords—and the even more perceptive Deiq—was turning out to be more than a little spooky at times.

Idisio could sense Riss brooding over a reading lesson Lord Azni had tasked her with. Her thoughts washed over him like a sullen current: *This is so pointless . . . I wish he'd wake up! I don't like being alone here . . .*

She'd been getting increasingly uneasy about being alone ever since their arrival. Maybe it had to do with her pregnancy. He carefully blocked off awareness of Riss and focused his attention on tracing other whistles. His hearing followed his intent, arcing like a thrown rock to a chosen target. *Servants,* he thought. *I want to hear servants.*

A discordant babble arose in his ears: kitchen arguments over seasoning, a baby crying, a man laughing, something sizzling, something else bubbling, and steady chopping and pounding sounds. Idisio pulled away before the chaos overwhelmed him and tried to focus more clearly: *Whistles,* he thought. *Servants whistle-talking. I want to hear more of that.*

Nothing happened. He tried again, and this time was rewarded with a restless golden haze.

I do not understand, Scratha ha'rethe said, sounding annoyed. *What do you wish?*

The servants are whistling. It's a language. I want to figure it out. I want to hear them whistling, so I can figure it out.

A moment of silence, laced with bewildered, blurry impatience. *The matters of the tharr do not concern us,* Scratha ha'rethe said at last, then decisively withdrew into blank silence once more.

Idisio opened his mouth, then slowly shut it again, shaking his head. The shift in his attention brought Riss's thoughts slipping back into his awareness: *He looked like he was getting ready to wake up. I should go see if he's awake. He needs to start getting ready for Conclave soon.* Reluctant duty held her in place: *One more page,* she decided. *Then I'll go see.*

Idisio rolled from the bed, staggering slightly as he came to his feet. He scrubbed his hands over his eyes to shake himself fully awake and grabbed for his clothes.

Why don't I want to talk to her? he thought as he dressed, and had no answer for that question. *I should be nicer to her. She's in love with me. I love her too. Don't I?*

He poked his head out, checking the hallway, then hurried to get clear of the area.

Afternoon sunlight striped the hallways and courtyards as he wandered aimlessly through the fortress. He finally settled on a stone bench in one of the side courtyards and sat, kicking bare feet idly through a thick layer of sand, brooding.

A flicker of movement caught his eye. He looked up to find Azni approaching, and scrambled to his feet. She offered him a formal bow, to his intense embarrassment, and motioned for him to sit back down. Taking a seat on the bench beside him, she turned to sit cross-legged, moving as gracefully as a girl his own age could hope to manage, and smiled at him.

"You're troubled," she said in a low voice. "Would you like to talk about it?"

He blinked, startled, and glanced at the floor reflexively. His face heated.

"In a desert fortress," Azni murmured, "you never do have much privacy. Cafad asked me to come talk to you."

Idisio shut his eyes for a moment, his throat too tight for speech, and wondered if he could sink through the floor and escape.

"Nobody's offended," Azni said. "You haven't done anything wrong, Idisio. Cafad doesn't know *what* you're troubled about, only that you're upset and anxious. He's bound to the fortress now; he can pick up on a servant farting in the middle of the night if he wants to. It's an adjustment for him as well, and you're a very important guest. He's anxious to keep you happy."

And Scratha had once belted him halfway across the room. More than once, actually, before he'd known about Idisio's heritage.

I'd be happier with him handing out bruises. I knew how to deal with that.

Azni's eyebrows tilted expressively; she'd caught the thought.

"I'm *nothing*," Idisio blurted, his face fiery hot now, and shut his eyes again. "I'm *nobody*."

She didn't say anything. After a while, he opened his eyes enough to peer at her. She was watching him without expression, her head tilted slightly.

He drew in a deep breath and straightened, feeling a sudden lightness roll through him. "That's stupid," he said, "isn't it?"

"I wouldn't use that word," she murmured. "*Incorrect*, perhaps. Or *misjudgement*. But reversing the beliefs of a lifetime is a difficult task."

After a few moments he said, "I'm–somebody. Here. But I'm leaving. I'm going back–there. Back to Bright Bay, and beyond."

"Without Riss," she noted.

His breath hitched in his throat. "I . . . yeah." He didn't know what to do with that odd turn to the conversation.

"Would the adjustment be easier if she went *with* you?"

"No, worse," he said without thinking, and felt his face flare back into hot embarrassment.

She smiled, as though something about that answer had been important, and stood. Dropping a light, friendly pat on his right shoulder, she said, "Without intending to sound dismissive, Idisio — you'll learn. And so will Riss." She bowed again and left the room as quietly and gracefully as she'd arrived.

Idisio stayed still, blinking hard, and tried to figure out if he was supposed to be crying.

Chapter Two

There was a king, a lovely king/Who loved a lady fair . . . .
Tank stood at the rail of the Deep Sea Lover and breathed it all in: the song, the air, the creaking of the ropes and the sails, the thunderous whiffling roar of the wind in his ears. Beside him–and *downwind*–another passenger gripped the railing with both hands, face as close to green as dark skin could get, and heaved his guts out in a yellow-grey spray.

Tank grinned and looked up at the rigging, where he'd often seen crew members swinging about with the agile grace of intelligent lizards, no matter the weather. At the moment the webbing of ropes stood empty, all the sailors occupied with deck or below-deck tasks. A mad impulse seized him.

For all Ossin's violent seasickness, this was the clearest weather Tank had yet seen on this voyage. There would never be a better or safer time to try the game for himself.

Four bounding steps put him up onto a box and from there to a series of handholds he'd watched the crew use. Moments later, harsh rope scraped under his hands and the wind buffeted his shoulders, whipping his hair into a rough red screen over his vision.

Should have tied it more securely–
He'd watched the sailors climbing, and the pattern stayed in his mind, like the memorizing-the-room exercises Allonin had so often set him. Set a hand *here*, and *reach* with the other–swing sideways *this* way–and another foothold *here*–

Startled shouts filtered up from below. The wind whipped the other way, freeing Tank's eyes; he took a fast glance up to confirm memory, then scooted rapidly through the requisite motions as the shouts grew louder.

"Get your effing arse back down here, you piece of shit northern fool!" someone bellowed; the volume and the phrasing could only have come from Rosy, the first mate.

Tank ignored it and swung up another few feet. The crow's nest lookout, a skinny boy with ebony skin and startlingly pale blue eyes, stared down at him, expression bemused. Tank reached up a hand, slapped it lightly across the boy's bare feet, and laughed.

The lookout shook his head and said, in a thickly accented version of the common northern tongue, "Northern, you're turning *striped* when Rosy grabs hold of you."

Tank laughed again, then looked out across the water.

"Gods," he said on an exhalation, staring, and forgot everything else for a moment. The Kingsea stretched around the ship in seemingly endless shades of blue and green; a distant curve of land was starting to show on the far northern horizon. The vast landmass of the southlands was a bumpy line against the western sky: thready, shrunken, flattened.

Tank squinted, tracing contours, thinking about the maps Allonin had trained him to read and trying to translate elevation lines to real shapes.

I grew up somewhere over there, he thought, and found his mood souring. The lookout had misunderstood: he wasn't northern, whatever his hair color might proclaim. Not by a long road.

He looked back to the north and east, letting the sparkling emerald and sapphire colors boost him back into laughter, then grinned one last time at the lookout and began picking his way back down.

Down turned out to be considerably more complicated than *up*. By the time he reached the deck again his hands, calves and shoulders burned, and multiple blisters made every new handhold a painful trial. He tore an already stubby fingernail back to the quick, jerked that hand free reflexively, and almost fell; caught himself just in time, but the effort sent fire coursing through his muscles and produced an uncomfortable popping sensation in his left shoulder.

The moment his feet touched the deck, heavy hands laid hold of him and jerked him over to sprawl across the deck. He tucked into a roll and rose to his feet, still grinning; it would take more than a rough toss to dim his exhilaration.

Rosy glared at him, his thick hands fisted and ready to use. "What the *hells* did y'think y'was doing?" he demanded. The thick red rash across his cheeks and nose had almost disappeared beneath the rage flooding color into his skin. "Effing northern redling fool!"

"I wanted to see if I could do it," Tank shrugged. "No harm done, was there?"

Rosy's eyes narrowed. He took a step forward.

"Passenger," someone else said, warning, reminding. *"Paying* passenger, Rosy."

Rosy cut a sharp glare at the woman who'd spoken–a tall woman everyone called Slick–then jerked a sullen nod at Tank and snapped, "Don't do it again."

"I won't," Tank said. "Promise."

Rosy snorted and stomped away, obviously unconvinced.

"He's right enough in calling you a fool," Slick said, not moving from her spot on a water barrel. She kicked her bare heels in a light rhythm against the thick wood and grinned amiably at Tank. "I'd have said *rude*, more than fool. Not good manners, what you did. What ships you worked on, that they didn't teach you to stay off another man's lookout walkway?"

"None," he admitted. "This is my first time on a ship."

Her dark eyebrows arched skeptically, her mouth drawing aside. The leaping fish tattooed on the left side of her face wriggled with the movement.

"Huh," she said. "Then I'll go back to *fool*."

He shrugged, watching her tattoo squinch and contort, and wondered if he ought to get one himself. The notion didn't particularly appeal. He had enough permanent marks of the past on his body already.

"Wasn't so hard," he said.

Slick shook her head. "Lemme see your hands." She motioned for him to turn his hands palm-up, then grinned. "You've got the hands of a shorewoman, for all that great silly sword you brought with you," she said. "Go see Tanfer. He'll need to pour some *roosh* over those scrapes, or you'll wind up with gangrene. Those ropes ain't exactly clean. And you'll need a salve for the blisters."

He shrugged again and crossed to stand at the rail. She joined him a moment later, her expression still darkly amused.

"It's a relief, actually," she said, "to know you're a fool. Thought you had the sea madness at first. Blisters are an easy fix."

"Sea madness?"

She pointed out over the water in a vague sweeping motion; a bracelet of leaping fish, similar to the one on her face, was tattooed below her elbow. "People stare out there too long, sometimes they get strange. Some start hearing voices, start wantin' to jump on out and swim to whatever they're hearing." She shot him a sideways glance, grinning slyly.

"Voices?" Tank said, uneasily. He glanced out at the ocean again, no longer quite so pleased with the sight. *Voices.* No, he didn't like that idea at all. He'd had enough of *that* game, as the saying went. He remembered, long ago, street thieves backing away, dirty faces white with suspicion, and Lifty shouting: *He's one of them as hears the voices, Blackie, you don't want to go up against him, do you? I'd run, if I was you . . .* and yelping laughter when the aggressors fled, leaving Tank alone with Lifty once more.

You're crap as a thief, Lifty said, some time later. *You're a decent scrapper, though. Ought to go talk to them over at the Freewarrior's Hall.*

That, at least, had proven a wise suggestion. Tank drew in a long breath, focusing on the water and the air and the clouds.

Just a mercenary, he thought. *I can do this. I can be ordinary. I can control my life. No more voices. No more visions. Just a mercenary . . .*

Slick green-gold tendrils laced, briefly, through vein and muscle; he tensed and fought the past comprehensively back into hiding.

"Not a tall tale, for all that you'd be a fun one to pull on. Nah, the voices are real. I hear 'em myself," Slick was saying, contemplative. "Especially after someone's jumped. That's when they *sing*, like a happy drunk in a vat of mountain lightning."

Tank backed three long steps away from the rail, not caring if she thought less of him. "Sing?"

She turned, rested her back against the rail, and grinned at him. Wisps of dark hair, freed from the triple-bound tail most of the crew used, flittered around her face. "Scared you, did I?"

"Yeah," he said flatly. "You pulling me or you straight? No games."

"Straight," she said. "But backing off the rail won't help you. I seen folk sleepwalk up from below and jump."

"You don't stop them?"

"Gotta see 'em going for the rail in the first place. Not easy in the dark of the moon, or middle of a busy day, for that matter. And someone hazed heads for the water, they move fast as you did going up the walk. Hard to catch someone moving that fast."

He hesitated, a vague tremor of disquiet in his muscles, then returned to the rail and looked down at the rippled, frothing water passing by the hull. "Why do you come out this far, if it's that dangerous? And what about the crew? What if you jump?"

"Profit," she said succinctly. "Faster travel out away from land, and we charge more for shipping through a dangerous area. You'd'a paid half the coin and taken three times as long for a shorehopper trip. And the crew–Nah. We're solid." She held out one arm, turning it to display the fish tattoos more clearly. "Each fish is a voyage over the deep. Captain does 'em himself. We hear the call an' walk away, is when we get our first fish and full crew status. I worked as slophand for two years before this one." She pointed to the one on her face. "I'm the only one as still hears it, no matter who it's calling."

Her motions drew his attention to her body overall; slender, muscled, with small breasts and narrow hips. Her face had the light almond cast of a upper southlands heritage and the lighter bone structure of a northern: she probably came from somewhere around Sessin or Stass port, at a guess.

To distract himself from staring, he said, "I saw someone with a tattoo of a chain wrapped around his arm. That mean something too?"

She sobered. "Yeah," she said. "I know who you mean. Chain means he's killed. Black for on board a ship, red for land. Three links each body, as he's southern. Northerns use four. Stay away from him, he don't mind adding to the total; prob'ly won't last long as crew, himself."

He glanced at her arms again: no chain, only fish.

She laughed at him, unbothered by his quick survey, and said, "Not feeling like a swim, are you?"

"No," he said. "Not even a little."

"Good. Then I can leave you be." She started to turn away, then came back to the rail, her thin face intent as she stared out at the waves. "Something . . ." she muttered. "*There.*"

Something swirled the surface a stone's throw from the ship. A dark shadow that could have been a huge fish rose briefly and sank from sight as fast. Green and gold flickered along the edges of Tank's vision, then cleared.

Slick swore, somewhere far away.

No, someone said, much closer to hand. *No. Leave him alone.*

Tank leaned forward against the rail, staring after the shadow. He knew that voice.

"Teilo?" he said aloud. "Is that you?"

Slick's hand closed around Tank's arm, hard. "Oh, no you don't," she said. "Let's get you away from the rail." She tugged him back, shoving him toward the steerage hatch. "Get down below."

Leave him alone, the voice said–definitely Teilo this time. He'd heard that voice often enough to have no doubt. Where was she? He started for the rail again.

Slick hissed through her teeth and blocked him, shouldering him back. "Get down the damn hatch," she snapped. "Do I got to hit you?"

She didn't understand, and he didn't have the time to explain. What was Teilo doing in the water, and who was she talking to? It didn't make sense. He wanted to understand. He needed to understand. To talk to her. But–

Wait–Why would I want to talk to her? She'll only lie to me again. She'll only use me again.

He slowed, frowning. Slick bulled him back several more steps.

"Idiot, fool, ass!" she shouted at him. "Get below!"

But he's so perfect . . . another voice this time, one with a too-smooth overlay: he knew that accent *far* too well. Fear jolted him backwards three more steps without protest. *So wonderful*, the second voice purred. *He is perfect, he is wonderful.*

"Oh, hells no," he said aloud. Green and gold tendrils laced through memory, turning salt air to rot in his nostrils, bringing a fiery itch to old scars throughout his body.

Impossible. It's dead *. . . I killed it! And Teilo is nowhere* near *here right now . . . is she?*

What's happening to me?

"Get below!" Slick hollered, right in his face. Her teeth had gaps and her breath was sweet from a peppermint chew.

Shivering and bewildered, he let her bully him down into the passenger hold. The chill of the metal ladder under his fingers came as a reassurance of reality: he wasn't *back there*, in any sense of the word. The hold, while dank, dark, and small, didn't match up to the overheated hell of his childhood or the colder, swamp-rot smelling hell of a more recent time: this was a ship, not land, and he was *safe*. Nothing could grab him here, not even a demon returned from the dead.

Overhead, the hatch slammed closed, outside latches ratcheting shut. The sound calmed him further. He couldn't answer that deadly call if he couldn't get out.

Wonderful you're wonderful . . . Come play . . . Come play . . . perfect . . .

No, Teilo cut in again. *No. Leave him alone.*

The voices faded away. Tank paced, restless, peering into the shadows.

"You're hearing the song now, huh?" Slick said as she settled atop a sturdy box. She snorted and spat to one side.

"Not a song," Tank said absently. "Words. They're talking . . . She's talking."

"Oy, you're an odd one, then," Slick said, unconcerned. "Don't listen, is my advice."

Don't listen? Did I listen, last time? I didn't mean to. No . . . I didn't listen, *back then, and that was the whole problem. It was all my fault. I should have listened to Allonin. It wouldn't have happened if I hadn't run away–all my fault, all my–*

Memory hazed the distance between past and present, pulling *was* into *now*: *Come play with me,* the creature said, presence resonating through the chill, underground dankness. *Rosin sent you to play with me. I like to play. I know what you like. You are human, and humans like pain. I can see what you like. Rosin taught me. Here–you like* this, *and so you will like* this–

Pain prickled ghost-agony over Tank's stomach, arms, and groin.

"No," he said aloud, flinging his arms up in protest. "No!"

He could feel Slick watching him with more curiosity than alarm, could see himself as she saw him: a broad-shouldered redhead with wiry muscles, spinning in place and flailing at the air like a madman.

He couldn't catch control, couldn't pull himself from the maelstrom of intersecting moments.

Rosin taught me to give this, because humans like this, the creature said, and lines of fire burned through old scars. *I see it in your mind, I see it in your flesh, this is what you are, this is what you like–*

Heat centered around his groin, pain and pleasure flaring together; Tank arched his back and screamed–in the now, in the then, he couldn't tell. An answering scream echoed through his mind, threading through memory of striking out with everything he had: with anger, pain, grief, hatred; with years upon years of bottled-up madness. The scream from the past mingled with the ones in the present, and he went to his knees as dank brine filtered into his nostrils and the hold came into focus once more.

"Damn," Slick said in his ear, laughing. "Never seen someone take it quite like this before. You look to need a distraction."

Everything paused, hanging in fragile, crystal silence as he looked up at her. A few vague stripes of light ghosted in through the slats of the hatch overhead, just enough to see her smiling as she looked down at him.

"What's happening to me?" he whispered.

"Don't know," she said, indifferent. "And not my never mind. I get paid to sit and wait this out with passengers as get hit. I always know who the song's aimed at." The words held no pride, only fact.

A massive *presence* stirred below. Green and gold began to flicker in Tank's vision again.

"Distraction," Tank said on an exhalation, shuddering, nearly gasping the word.

"Right here," she said, and knelt beside him, her hand reaching unerringly down.

He soon discovered that Slick had other tattoos . . . quite a few, in fact, and some in spots that must have hurt like all the hells combined; but that thought came later, with recollection, not in the moment's heat.

*Perfect–oh! Perfect, how do you know such–*The alien voice swirled away in a tempest of distraction. Somewhere, Teilo moaned. Slick cried out. Tank howled and let go of restraint, of awareness, of fear: his vision went black and empty for an endless moment of relief.

Whispers and moans alike slowly faded away. He lay in the near-dark, gasping for breath, plastered with sweat; reason returned, bringing along awareness and glowing shame.

"Oh gods," he said aloud. "I'm sorry–I shouldn't have–"

Slick rolled over and stood, staggering slightly.

"I'm not sorry at all," she said. "That was pretty good for once." She bent and scooped up her clothes.

"But–What?" He blinked up at her, bewildered and still dazed.

She pulled on leggings and shirt, then leaned to offer him a hand up. He let her help him to his feet, unsurprised–now–by her wiry strength.

"Never had a man apologize for enjoying himself before," she said. "Get dressed. You're safe; they never come back twice for the same person. You've maybe even earned a fish. I'll talk to the captain about it if you like."

"I thought you were *crew*," he said, unable to explain more clearly.

"I am," she said. "My job is to keep the passengers alive. That takes different forms." Her teeth flashed in the gloom. "I'd say this was a good day's work, myself."

He stood still, staring at her.

Her grin soured with her tone. "What are you," she said, "some kind of northern soapy?"

"Soapy?"

"Priest. S'iope," she said, drawing the word out into an exaggerated drawl. "Soapy. Obviously not, or you'd know that one."

"No," he said, "but I don't take–that–lightly. It–it should *mean* more."

"It means you're alive. Means you didn't try knocking me out and busting through the hatch to get back out to the water." She laid only the slightest emphasis on *try*.

"That's not what I–"

"It is what it is, and I'*m* not complaining. Get dressed and shut up about it already. And go see Tanfer about that damn salve. No point saving your life only to lose it to rot."

She climbed the ladder and banged a hand against the hatch. Bolts shot back, and she climbed out without a backwards glance.

Tank sat in the near-dark for some time, staring at the juncture between past and present–and trying to figure out what in the *hells* had just happened.

Chapter Three

Feelings like love are a vulnerability first generation ha'ra'hain do not have. Ever. For anyone.

Lord Scratha's words cycled through Idisio's mind as he walked back to his room, trying to decide why he was so disturbed by the conversation with Azni.

I have feelings. I have lots of feelings. Even feelings for other people. I cared about Red. I'm glad he's found his son. I'm sad that he seems happy that his son's been adopted by a southern desert Family, and doesn't want to go meet the boy in person.

But . . . maybe *sad* was too strong a word. *Disappointed* came closer. And had he really *cared* about the redheaded sailor—or had he seen in the man's quest for his son an inverse echo of his own long-standing fantasy of having his father come rescue him from a life on the streets?

I hate this. I never used to think like this. It's being around Deiq that's doing this to me. He's making me question everything, just by tilting an eyebrow when he looks at me. But I have feelings. I'm human enough for that. I love Riss. I love her because… because…she's nice. She's…she's sweet.

"Damnit," he muttered under his breath. "Damnit, damnit, damnit."

As he neared his room, he could feel Riss's anxiety, hear her tumbling, bouncing thoughts: *Should I look for him? Why did he leave without telling me? He could be anywhere; this place is enormous—Why did he leave?*

He hesitated on the verge of retreat, then made himself keep moving forward. She was in his room, pacing restlessly. As he came through the light door, she spun and took a wide, bounding step toward him; at his instinctive flinch, she stopped and backed up, biting her lip.

"Where did you *go?*" she said, her voice squeaky, then blushed a deep crimson and turned her back on him.

"Sorry," she muttered over her shoulder. "Conclave's soon. You ought to get ready."

"I know. I'll do that now."

She nodded and started for the door, then stopped, twisting her hands together. "I'm a little–" She hesitated, jaw working as though chewing on what to say. "A little lost. You're the only one I know. You and Lord Scratha. It's a little scary. This whole–" She paused again, biting her lip, and finally shook her head. "I get scared. I get worried if I don't know where you are. It's just– strange, here. I've been having these d-d-dr–" She stopped, one hand over her eyes, then dropped it back to her side and looked at him.

"You'll get used to it," he said lamely, not sure what else to say. "It's not so bad here."

She stared a moment, her expression somewhere between bewilderment and annoyance, then shook her head and left without further comment. He let out a long sigh, listening to her settle back into her reading practice, and tried to see her point.

He couldn't. He'd always relied on himself to survive. Friendly faces dropped in and out of one's life without warning. She'd grown up in a secure life, with parents, with family, with a community. While that had turned against her in the end, she'd *known* something he'd never dreamed of and still couldn't quite understand.

He had more sympathy for Lord Scratha at the moment. The man was dealing with people in his *place*, his territory; people he didn't entirely trust, people who would more than likely stab him in the back given sufficient profit from the move. And if one of those people turned Idisio against him, or Deiq, Scratha's life could get very unpleasant very fast.

He's anxious to keep you happy, Azni had said. That made more sense to Idisio, by far, than Riss's uncertainty.

Thank all the gods Riss won't be in Conclave with me.

He immediately felt guilty for the thought. Riss deserved better than that. But as he began cleaning himself up and picking out clothes from the pile Cafad had sent him, he couldn't convince himself to feel any other way.

"I declare this Conclave open," Lord Scratha said. His gaze tracked along the table, touching each face with an almost tangible heat. He regarded Idisio with the same baleful ferocity; with a slight shock, Idisio realized that Scratha considered him dangerous as any of the desert lords around them now.

No, Deiq said, expressionless, his gaze on the tall Scratha lord. *He has to look like he thinks of you as dangerous. He hasn't come round to really seeing you as what you are yet. Trust me–you'll know when he does.*

Idisio said nothing, not trusting himself to reply without being overheard. The etiquette and process of mindspeech still baffled him; safer to stay silent and avoid mistakes. Deiq had years of practice; Idisio had a little over a day.

He looked around the table, trying to be discreet in his survey, and caught a number of other sly glances going around. Most flinched when they saw him looking their way, or grew suddenly still and guarded.

They sure don't see me as an ex-street thief, he thought ruefully, and hoped that Scratha wouldn't ever look at him the way the gathered lords were now. It *hurt*, in a weird way, even more than the times of being spat on as a whore, beggar, and thief in Bright Bay.

Those times had been about what he *did*. The looks now were all about who he *was*. *What* he was. He glanced at Deiq and found the elder ha'ra'ha's dark face lined with bitterness.

Get used to it, Deiq said; then his expression smoothed out to blank indifference again.

The massive metal doors began clanging shut, one by one. The echoing noise made Idisio think of prisons and cages, and he repressed a strong urge to bolt from his chair and out the last door before it closed.

To distract himself from his growing anxiety, Idisio studied the desert lords around the table. Scratha wore the most elaborate outfit, a loose silk shirt and pants in severe shades of grey and black, laced throughout with complicated embroidery; Azni wore the simplest, a rippling, unadorned dress of blue and crimson. The colors made the one look simpler than it was and the other more elaborate: *peacock and gravekeeper,* someone thought just then, and Deiq coughed into his hand, the corners of his eyes crinkling briefly.

Idisio blinked hard and looked elsewhere, unwilling to find amusement in that comparison.

Evkit stared directly back at him. His cold, cold eyes held no hint of flinch or guarding. A moment later, Deiq's elbow dug painfully into Idisio's side, jolting his attention away from that hypnotic gaze.

"Thanks," Idisio muttered, rubbing his ribs. Deiq slanted an unforgiving stare at him and went back to watching the proceedings. Idisio tried to follow suit, but his attention kept drifting to the banners around the table. Voices rose and fell around him, unheeded, as he found himself tracking common patterns, colors, and themes; not simply pretty pictures. It was another language, like the whistling.

"*Pay attention,*" Deiq said in his ear, his voice as close to a growl as a human throat could manage. Idisio blinked hard and sat up straighter.

"This Conclave has already begun on something of an...unusual note," Lord Scratha said, his gaze settling on Lord Evkit. Tension arced through the air like a silent whipcrack, then faded as quickly. Scratha turned his stare on Lord Alyea; she stiffened and glared back at him.

Prickly as a cactus, someone thought. *Can't wait to see* her *hit the change.*

Deiq raised his head and sent a hard glare down the table. Lord Irrio blanched and dipped his head in awkward apology.

What was *the change*? Idisio caught Deiq's eye and lifted an eyebrow in a tiny, inquiring twitch, hoping nobody else would see it. Deiq stared at him for a moment, as though deciding whether to answer, then said, curtly, *Later.*

"A Conclave begun with a plot revealed and a death chosen isn't what I expected when I called you all together," Lord Scratha said. "Normally that sort of thing happens at the end of a Conclave."

Idisio stared. Had the man actually made a *joke*? Idisio hadn't known Cafad had it in him.

As Cafad went on with the opening formalities, Idisio found his gaze drifting to Gria, newly discovered heir to Scratha. She sat rigid and grim, the white and ruby silks she wore only accenting the underlying paleness of her face. Underneath the mass of elaborate beadwork and jewelry they'd draped her in for the Conclave, she looked more like a child than ever. Her voice, when she spoke, came out steady and far more confident than Idisio could tell she actually felt; like Riss, she found this entire situation terrifyingly alien.

Her fear surfaced openly for a heartbeat when she glanced down the table at Lord Evkit. In response, Evkit's mouth twitched in the slightest, tiniest smirk.

Idisio, don't look at Evkit, Deiq said irritably.

Why not?

Just. Don't.

The elder ha'ra'ha's flat delivery reminded Idisio of Cafad just before the man lost his temper; he wisely shut up and kept his gaze away from Evkit after that.

"The ways have been shut," Cafad declared. "You may not travel to or from my lands using the hidden ways unless I permit it. And I will not grant that permission to any of you."

He glared at Evkit.

Idisio glanced at Deiq and found the elder ha'ra'ha suspiciously devoid of expression. A moment later, Evkit jerked to his feet and began shouting; Idisio felt an uneasy tremor run through the room. Cafad's eyes took on the all-too-familiar dark glitter of temper rising fast.

A burning wave of pain swamped over Idisio's entire body. Time distorted, voices blurring into incoherent waves; dimly, he heard Scratha began bellowing.

A hard slap to the side of the head shocked Idisio out of the pain and the haze all at once. As he blinked vision back into the moment, Deiq bounded atop the table, stamping his booted feet hard.

The table shook. The shouts cut off dead. Everyone stared up at Deiq as though he'd lost his mind.

"Stop," Deiq snapped. "That's enough, my lords! With all due respect, that's enough. You cannot *afford* to lose your tempers with a full ha'rethe below you!"

An image of desiccated trees turning fully leafed, of a long-blocked well returned to full functionality, ran through Idisio's mind. A strong shiver worked down his back.

Stop, damn you, Deiq cut in, his voice taut and black. Abrupt panic urged Idisio to run screaming from the room. Blood seemed to haze the very air. Again, Deiq's voice lashed out: *Stop it! Use your aqeyva training, Idisio, this isn't the time for you to go vapid on me!*

Idisio sucked in a deep breath, heartbeat thudding in his ears, and struggled to turn his attention inwards. Slowly, too slowly, his heartbeat began to ease; without warning, Idisio felt a massive pressure, as though a giant hand had closed around his entire body.

Slow it down, Deiq ordered. *Slow. This beat. Listen: one. One. Two. Two. One. One. . . good.*

Idisio hung suspended in a strange half-world for a long, stretched moment, as Deiq forced the beat into vein, nerve, and flesh with brutal efficiency.

Don't flop around! Deiq snapped, his tone a feral snarl. *Pick up your end already!*

Idisio blinked and focused with every ounce of willpower he possessed. Panic and pain smoothed away in a heartbeat, and he clicked over into a glassy calm. Deiq let out a hard breath, settling back into his seat.

"What would Conclave be without everyone losing their tempers?" Lord Salo said, voice as wobbly as Idisio's knees felt.

"Other places, fine," Deiq said grimly. "But not *here*. Lord Scratha, if you cannot discuss that particular matter calmly, I suggest you drop it altogether."

Scratha glared. Deiq glared back. Tendrils of tension whipped through the room like snakes.

Snakes, red and black, writhing across the bed—Lord Scratha's arm swelling as he panted, fighting off the deadly venom—

Idisio, stop it! Deiq snarled. *Will you drop into a full aqeyva trance already? Block everything out. This isn't over yet. I'll pull you out when it's safe.*

What—

Deiq cut him off with a ferocious glare that might as well have been a Scratha-vicious slap. Swallowing hard, Idisio focused on his breath, as he'd done so often on the long journey south with Scratha and Riss; followed breath inwards and around into the tight inner coil where everything else disappeared. All sound vanished. Nothing moved in his mind but awareness of his breath and pulse. He hung suspended in a dark grey haze with darker grey walls, and let the world go on without him for a time.

The grey shifted, thinned, and broke apart.

It's over, Deiq said, tone considerably calmer, although still taut. *Come on—*

An ungentle tug unwound him, like a child's spinning toy, from his refuge. Idisio blinked several times, vaguely nauseated by the abrupt shift of perception. As his vision cleared, he saw that the expressions around the table had reverted to bland vagueness.

Ha'reye react badly to extreme human emotions, Deiq said curtly. *Scratha's never had to learn how to posture without getting genuinely emotional. I had to keep Scratha ha'rethe from reacting to his anger. You were pissing into the middle of it, without meaning to. You don't have the training to stay out of it, you're trained to think human, and you actually like Scratha, for some damn reason.*

Lord Scratha is a good man, Idisio said, more than a little defensively.

He's a human, Deiq answered. *Now shut up and pay attention. You might learn something.*

Idisio drew in another long, quiet breath, eased himself into a cool detachment, and went back to listening to the external arguments bouncing around the table; reflecting, very, very quietly, that at the least, he'd learned to be *damn* careful around Deiq.

Chapter Four

Tank stood at the rail of the *Deep Sea Lover*, his mood as bleak as the dappled grey clouds hanging low overhead. The frothed silver-green sea had lost its appeal for him. He wanted solid land under his feet and a *normal life* under his hands again.

For the first time, he considered joining Ossin in his daily ritual of throwing up over the side. Only pride stopped him: he *wouldn't* let any of them see him that weak. Especially–now–Slick.

Up in the rigging, one of the sailors called out, "Oy, hey, five hunner year!"

From the deck crew, another voice bellowed, "Oy, hey, hey, come the wind!"

The rest of the crew picked up the rough work chant, in a typical call/response form, each sailor providing a different rhyming line:

Oy, hey, five hundred year
Oy, hey, hey, come the wind
Oy, hey, hey, numb the sinned
Oy, hey, hey, dumb the dear
Oy, hey, hey, plumb it near–

None of it made any sense to Tank, but work chants weren't actually supposed to make sense. They were about keeping the mind busy while the hands did a job.

Someone yelled, "Oy, hey, hey, got nothing here!" Laughter ran round the deck; everyone chimed in on the chorus:

Oy, hey, five hundred year

Then they began passing the chant around again with a new rhyme:

Oy, hey, hey, some they say

Oy, hey, hey, come the day
Oy, hey, hey, drink the drop
Oy, hey, hey, sink the top–
"Awww, pass!" someone hollered. That was met with catcalls and whistles of derision, and the chant started over.

This round, Slick's clear alto stood out against the rougher male shouts.

Turning, he saw her sitting on a large crate, banging her bare feet cheerfully against the wood. As she belted out the chorus, she tilted her head back as though offering the words to the grey sky above. The fish tattoo on her face squinched and shifted with her mouth; Tank felt a flush of heat race through his body at the memory of what that mouth had done earlier.

Slick glanced his way. Catching his eye, she grinned and made a fluttering motion near her face with one hand. He put a hand up to his cheek and found it hot. With a small gasp, he whipped round to put his back to her and anyone else who might be looking his way.

"Damn," Ossin observed from beside Tank. He wiped a hand over his damp mouth. "Must have been good, if looking at her gets you fussed." He smiled knowingly, but his ghastly color and trembling hands turned it into a sickly leer.

Tank turned his head to stare Ossin down. Ossin's grin steadied slightly. He glanced out at the water, swallowed hard, then grinned at Tank again.

"Hell of a trip," he said. "Never come this way before. Always went overland. Nothing that nice in the waystops along the Horn, for sure."

Tank looked out over the churning water, his jaw tight, and didn't answer. His hands tightened around the rail.

"Oh, don't look so sour," Ossin said, slapping Tank on the shoulder. It was clearly intended as a hearty buffet, but Tank moved sideways a step as the man swung. Ossin's fingers barely brushed his sleeve. "What are you so sulky for?"

"Just shut up," Tank said through his teeth. "Leave me alone."

Ossin laughed, a braying sound undimmed by his days of seasickness. "Oh, *tell* me she wasn't your first, boy, that would be a real shame–"

Tank's fist cracked into the man's jaw. Ossin sprawled sideways across the deck, loose-limbed, and lay still. A passing sailor glanced at Tank, knelt to check on Ossin as briefly, then stood, commenting, "*He'll* have a headache." He grinned companionably at Tank, then walked on without looking back.

Tank stared down at the unconscious man, then looked up to find Slick watching him. Her expression sardonic, almost contemptuous, she lifted a hand in a mocking salute, then hopped off the crate and began to walk away.

The third passenger, a burly northerner whose name Tank couldn't remember, was stepping out from the galley round when Slick went by. He said something indistinct. Slick popped him a foul hand gesture and kept going without breaking stride or even glancing his way.

Oh, no, Tank thought, seeing the man's eyes narrow. He started forward. Before he made two steps the northern had grabbed Slick's wrist and tugged her round to face him.

Tank lengthened his stride and opened his mouth to yell *Leave her alone–*

Slick's fists and knees ran in rapid sequence across the large man's face, chest, stomach, and groin, each blow precisely placed at the weakest possible spot. The northern coughed out a spray of red spittle and went down with a sloppy thud. Slick stepped back, looked down at him with a remote, considering glance, then turned and went on her way without even a flick of the gaze towards Tank. Two bored-looking sailors moved in, hoisted the unconscious man, and carried him down the ladder to steerage.

Tank stood still, mouth open, unable to believe the speed and ferocity of her attack.

Behind him, Ossin groaned. Tank turned and found the man beginning to stir. Deciding to avoid a repeat confrontation, he walked away, crossing to the other rail, and stood there undisturbed for the rest of the day.

It was as good a place as any to work on the mindfulness exercises Allonin had insisted he practice daily; but by the time he gave up and went down into the dank stench of the hold to try for sleep, he'd gained precious little in the way of peace or clarity.

By the time they arrived in Bright Bay, great black clouds hung over the *Deep Sea Lover* like an omen of doom, and more water than Tank had ever seen coming down from the sky hammered against the deck. The sailors worked through it, wearing as little as possible, seeming indifferent to the blinding sheets of water. Tank stood in the recessed doorway of the galley round, water stippling his face and clothes, too fascinated not to watch.

Slick tossed and caught and tied ropes with everyone else. What already-minimal and now soaking wet clothes did to her figure made Tank forget the chill in the air every time he looked her way.

Now and again her gaze went past him, as she worked; as blank and indifferent as though looking at another coil of rope. She saw him, he could tell that much. She just didn't care.

Bright Bay looked like little more than a variegated haze of shapes as the ship tied up to the longest dock. Tank took advantage of a brief lull in the work around him and went to get his pack from steerage. Ossin and the other passenger, whose name Tank *still* couldn't remember, sat on crates in mutual sullen silence. They glared at him.

Ossin said, "Are we *there?*"

"Yes," Tank said. "They're tying off now."

"Thank the gods. I'm not setting *foot* on a ship again this side of the Aftertime. I haven't kept a meal down this whole trip." He seemed more upset over his seasickness than by the great bruise along his cheek where Tank had struck him.

"I won't be on *this* one again, that's for sure," the other man said savagely. "Captain wouldn't even scold that effing ship whore for what she did, nor refund any brass bit of my passage money." His face held several deep discolorations, visible even in the dim light, and he winced every time he moved.

Tank shrugged into his pack and put his rain cloak on over it.

"Raining hard out there," he said neutrally. "Put your high boots on if you have any." From above came the thudding rattle of the gangplank settling out.

"Effing sewers will be flooding again," the burly man said. He and Ossin began a discussion of the various architectural flaws of Bright Bay; Tank went up the ladder without bothering to bid them farewell.

He determinedly *didn't* look for Slick as he went towards the gangplank.

As he stepped onto the dock beyond, his nerves hummed with raw tension and unresolved, undefined guilt. Reporting in to the Bright Bay Freewarrior Hall could wait. He wanted a drink *badly*.

He slogged through the downpour and ducked into the first tavern he saw: its shabbiness was almost hidden under the downpour, and a large brass ring hung from the sign for those who couldn't read the name.

Brass Ring. That name tied into an southern fireside tale that Allonin had told him, not long ago; at the end of it, everyone was drunk out of their wits and a northern king had been roundly tricked.

That suited Tank. With or without the involvement of northern royalty, the idea of losing his wits appealed mightily at the moment.

The ill-lit, smoky interior smelled of rank seawater, old pipe-smoke, and foulness that might have been an ale spill or something worse. Tank breathed shallowly until his nose stopped registering the worst odors, and headed past a scattering of small tables toward the bar.

A thick trail of water dribbled along the floor behind him; a rough layer of grit and sawdust absorbed it without any trouble. By each stool, large, blunt hooks protruded from the bar. Tank stripped off his rain cloak and draped it over a hook, then dropped his pack on the floor in front of the stool and sat down.

He ran his hands through his hair, pushing damp tendrils from his face, and looked for the bartender. The man stood in the gloom at the other end of the bar, his stare fixed on Tank with disconcerting intensity.

The murmuring of background conversations had gone completely silent.

Tension crawled through Tank's muscles. He turned slowly to look at the room behind him.

All men. All staring directly at him. All in the coarse, ill-assorted garb of the roughest type of sailor, including a thick belt from which hung either a hooked knife, a claw-spike, or a sailor's hook. A variety of scars on every visible stretch of skin hinted that they used their weapons readily and well.

This only happens in fireside stories, Tank thought distantly. *This isn't happening.*

Allonin's training didn't allow for more than a moment of disbelief: *Face what is, not what you want to be,* his mentor had said repeatedly. Like it or not, Tank was twenty steps from the door, with as many men in the way if a fight broke out.

He reduced it to cold numbers. Based on their expressions, he'd be faced with seven, maybe eight against one if this exploded into violence. Not good odds, but not bad, either, with over twenty in the room. Hopefully the rest would stay clear, but even if they all piled on, there came a point where too many attackers tangled each other up and actually made the fight easier. Besides, they'd expect an outsider to be easy prey, and Allonin had taught him tricks they might not know.

One such trick was a good bluff. The next was knowing when to run, and how to run fast; that latter trick had come more from Lifty than Allonin. Lifty had been good at running. He'd even managed to outrun Tank a few times.

I ought to look for him. See if he's still on the streets. See if he survived . . . what happened.

But that was a question for tomorrow and a distraction for today. Tank straightened his back and directed a flat stare out at the sailors.

"There a problem?" he said, keeping his tone easy, not challenging.

A few gazes flickered as they looked at one another in clear astonishment.

"Damn," one man said. A tattoo of a thick chain wound, in faded red and black lines, around one of his thick forearms from wrist to elbow. "He even *sounds* like Red. What's yer name, boy?"

Tank reevaluated the stares: not angry. Not hostile. *Stunned,* as though a ghost had walked through the door in broad daylight.

"I'm Tank," he said after a moment. "Who's Red?"

"You're near to his spittin' image," another man said, shaking his head. "Less 'bout forty year. I'd almost put money on him bein' your father. Redlings aren't so common 'round here, they're all northern-bred."

"Largely Stecatr pups, at that," another man said, and spat into the sawdust near his feet.

Tank fought for breath, blinking hard.

"What—*Where?*" he managed.

"Huh," the first man said, apparently understanding the question. "You ain't seein' him anytime soon. He works the *Black Starfish,* an' they headed out southbound to Agyaer a while back, some pushy noble drivin' them hard, way I hear it. They won't be back another two tendays, best guess, with this pissy weather."

A murmur worked through the room, sailors nodding in sour discussion of the unusual weather and what it would do to the shipping routes.

"He's a . . . a sailor?" Tank said, unable to believe what he was hearing. *What ships you worked on? None . . .*

Was it possible for *sailor* to pass from father to son, like red hair?

"Yeah," the man with the chain said. "He's a damn good one too, if more than a bit of a loon. How old are you, boy?"

Tank cleared his throat. "Uhm," he said, hesitating.

"Don't know? Tuh." They seemed to dismiss that as unremarkable.

"Fifteen," Tank offered, the same answer he'd given the Bright Bay Free-warrior Hall some weeks before. The men studied him as skeptically as Captain Ash had done, then almost as one shrugged, accepting.

"Come on and sit, then, redling," the man with the chain said, kicking out a free chair at his table. "I'll buy you a drink in his name. One of these days, you meet up with him, he can pay me back, if'n' he's got the right coin for once."

The room erupted in laughter, as if this tied into an old joke. Tank saw a glitter in their regard now that sent an uncomfortable chill up his spine. Something had changed, and he didn't know what or why; but one thing was clear: *Time to get out.*

"No, thank you," he said, scooping up his cloak and standing. "Thank you, but I'd better go." He grabbed his pack with his free hand, watching the room with one eye.

"Unfriendly, too," someone commented.

Someone else said, "*Setaka, senaka.*" It sounded like a west-coast southern dialect, and Tank didn't have a good enough ear for that to work out the meaning of the words.

More laughter filled the room. The man with the chain on his arm began to stand up. Other chairs scraped through the gritty sawdust.

Tank slung his pack over one shoulder, put his head down, and bolted for the door. Startled shouts replaced laughter. The man with the chain tattoo took a long step into Tank's path, his expression turning grim. Tank skipped sideways and around without pausing; set shoulder to door and shoved through.

Rain drenched down around him, muffling the shouts from inside the tavern. If they were wasting breath on yelling, they probably wouldn't be following. He took a hasty moment to settle his pack across both shoulders and flip the cloak over it, then trotted off into the rain.

Chapter Five

Idisio's sense of smell seemed to have grown unendurably sharp over the last two days; then again, the stench that filled the Conclave chamber was enough to make a horse gag a bit. Servants had carried in a light meal, then, in due time, a set of large chamber-pots and screens.

Alyea's expression went from startlement to outright horror. She glanced around as though looking for a polite alternative. Idisio hastily fixed his gaze on the table to avoid grinning. He could sense Deiq doing much the same thing.

"That's why I didn't eat anything," Deiq murmured in Idisio's ear. "I notice you didn't, either."

"I had a feeling it wouldn't be wise," Idisio admitted, letting the grin escape briefly, and heard Deiq chuckle.

In short order, the room filled with horrible odors. Lord Faer, in particular, let out a thunderously foul series of farts. Deiq's expression turned slightly pained at that barrage, and he shut his eyes. Idisio groaned quietly and fought against the impulse to pinch his nose, afraid that would be seen as rude.

Without opening his eyes, Deiq said, as quietly as before, "There's a trick to deadening your nose somewhat. Works for all the senses. But it cuts you off from awareness, and that's dangerous. I wouldn't recommend it here. In a safer place, think of a thin layer of cotton spread over the inside of your nose, or your ears, or whatever needs to be blunted. Unfortunately, in this instance, you're going to have to endure it. You don't want to miss any cues, in a room filled with desert lords who'd love to–" He paused, his eyes cracking to slits, then finished, "Take advantage of any weakness."

Idisio shot Deiq a sour glare, wishing the elder ha'ra'ha hadn't said anything. Being told all in one breath both of a way to ease the agony and that he couldn't take advantage of it seemed terribly cruel.

Deiq's mouth twitched into a faint smile. "You're welcome," he murmured.

The desert lords began settling back into their seats, a few looking a little ill themselves. The servants cleared the foul receptacles from the room and waved sticks of lit incense throughout before retreating and closing the doors once more.

"Take a bath when we finish up here," Deiq said under cover of the subdued conversations. "You'll feel better for it. Go to the bathing rooms near the gardens. They have the big tubs there, and you won't have to wait for the hot water–the servants keep it ready during times like this."

"Are you taking one too?" The notion of being naked around Deiq sent strange shivers up Idisio's back–and not pleasant ones.

Deiq's eyebrows lowered into a faint frown. He glanced at Idisio sideways, seeming to consider; then said, "No. You'll have your privacy."

Idisio felt a flush climbing his cheeks. Deiq's frown relaxed into amusement, and he looked away.

"Between you and Alyea," he murmured. He didn't explain the comment, and Idisio didn't ask, fairly sure he could guess.

As Idisio filed out of the teuthin along with the assembled lords, he drew in a deep breath of relatively fresh air and found himself really grinning for the first time in two days. A moment later, a waft of citrus filled his nose and Riss's hand closed tightly around one of his arms. He pulled away reflexively, well aware of the sardonically amused glances being aimed his way.

"Easy, Riss," he said through his teeth; her expression grew strained and anxious. He jerked his head at the watching desert lords, trying to explain without words that this wasn't the time for her to be affectionate. She glanced around and straightened, her expression turning chill.

"Of course," she said thinly. "Sorry."

Before Idisio could figure out what *that* meant, Azni swept in with a heavy sigh and gathered up all of Riss's attention.

"You're supposed to be reading, as I recall," the Aerthraim lord said. "I did say I'd send for you when Conclave was over, didn't I? Come on, then, off we go–" She steered Riss away, her delicate, thin-skinned hand resting lightly on the girl's shoulder.

Idisio let out another, longer breath of relief and tried to avoid looking at anyone.

Deiq dropped a hand on Idisio's shoulder for a moment, then went on by without speaking. To Idisio's surprise, the touch held no sense of amusement or sarcasm; just a calming strength, as though to say: *I know. Never mind.*

I love her, Idisio thought. *I do. I need to talk to her, to explain that I wasn't snubbing her, exactly. But first–I* really *want that bath.*

The Scratha baths turned out to be a large, circular room with pale stone tiles for the floor and a patterning of yellow block in the sandy-colored walls. The baths themselves were half-sunken, great circular vats deep enough to need steps down into them; two of the tubs were large enough for four people, while four smaller baths looked suitable for two people to share. A long, wide stone bench stood within a step of each tub–two benches, for the larger tubs. Nobody was using buckets to fill these baths: each tub boasted a pump, the handle well-wrapped in insulating layers of fabric.

Servants wrapped in rather fewer layers of fabric also waited by each tub.

Idisio stopped inside the arched entranceway, trying not to gape. The air hung heavy with humid heat. Two of the smaller tubs were already full, the water within steaming. Water splashed in a nearly white stream from one of the pumps into one of the larger tubs, which looked to be approaching full.

A young woman with a bright blue head-kerchief over close-cropped black hair approached. "*Ha'inn,*" she said, bobbing her torso in a quick bow. "You bathe?"

"Uhm, yes," Idisio said; it came out sounding more questioning than he liked, and he hoped his blush would be taken as coming from the intense humidity in the room. "That water looks, uhm, awfully warm, though."

She stared at him, looking both startled and perplexed for a moment, then said, "We can cool the water to suit your desire, *ha'inn.* Which tub do you wish?"

He pointed rather awkwardly at one of the smaller tubs. She bobbed again and whistled to the attendant, who promptly went round to the back side of the bath and knelt to make some mysterious adjustment.

"It will not take long," the young woman assured Idisio. "How warm do you wish it?"

"Not scalding," he said. "Hot is fine."

She smiled and whistled again; the attendant whistled back, the sound muted in the thick air.

"That whistle," Idisio said, fascinated out of discomfort. "You're talking. Can you teach me?"

Her expression went utterly still. Glancing around, Idisio found all the servants staring at him.

"*Ha'inn,*" the girl said, very carefully, "I doubt you would find such a minor amusement worth your time. Our little whistles are but a crude trick, nothing for one of such worth to demean yourself with."

In other words, Idisio thought glumly, *stay out of our damn business.* A Bright Bay thief would have said much the same thing, if with less grace, to an outsider wanting to know the secret codes of the city.

"Of course," he said aloud, and barely stopped himself from apologizing.

She seemed to relax; the others went back to gazing blankly at nothing in particular. The attendant chirruped again, then rose to his feet and nodded to Idisio.

"The bath is ready, *ha'inn*," the young woman said, bobbing again. "May I take your clothes for cleaning while you refresh yourself?"

"Uhm . . ." Idisio glanced around again, his face as hot as the room, and saw no polite way out of it. "Yes." He stripped down, avoiding her gaze, and handed over his clothes.

"Will you wish a male or female kathain to join you, *ha'inn*?" she asked, her nose wrinkling slightly as she bundled his garments into a tighter ball.

"Uhm . . . kathain?"

"Personal servant, *ha'inn*," she said without blinking. "For whatever needs you may have."

He opened his mouth, shut it again, then managed to say, with reasonable calm, "I don't really need a servant. I'm used to doing for myself, *s'a*."

One of her eyebrows arched. She regarded him with clear disapproval and lowered her voice to a bare murmur. "With all due respect, *ha'inn*," she said, "I am informed of your unfamiliarity with southern custom. So I will tell you, and I pray you do not take offense, that it does your host a great dishonor if you refuse a kathain. They are honorable companions, not what a northern would think of as a whore; sex is not their only function." She cleared her throat and waited, both eyebrows up now, her head tilted in polite attentiveness.

He glanced over his shoulder, feeling trapped: she had all his clothes, and he had a feeling she wouldn't hand them over easily. His room lay on the other end of the fortress, making a clean escape beyond improbable.

And he *really* wanted a bath. Even with his aromatic clothes removed, he stank.

He looked back and found a wry amusement in her expression now. "What if I ordered you not to tell Lord Scratha that I refused a kathain?" he asked.

She shook her head and gestured around the room. "*Ha'inn*, I cannot keep everyone here silent forever. And others will be arriving soon, for their own baths; they will see you alone, and carry tales."

He swallowed hard, weighing alternatives; looked at the size of the tub, thought about his own past and his own fears, and finally said, "F-female. Please."

Please, gods, don't let Riss walk in, he added silently.

She bobbed and motioned him towards the tub, then left the room without further comment.

He settled into the still steaming water with a deep relief that only came in part from the heat soothing his muscles. It felt considerably less vulnerable to be at least this covered.

The young woman returned to the room a short while later, carrying a simple wooden tray laden with an assortment of soaps, small jars, and bath brushes. She hooked the tray on the side of the tub, studied the array of jars thoughtfully, then selected one and carefully unstoppered it. Holding it up before her face, she blew across the mouth of the jar, aiming toward Idisio.

A delicate scent reminiscent of mingled rosemary and lavender wafted past him. The servant studied Idisio's face for a moment, resting the tip of the stopper against the lip of the jar, then shook her head.

"No," she murmured. "Not quite." She replaced the stopper and selected another bottle. This time the aroma carried a distinct overtone of apples, cloves, and ginger; Idisio found himself smiling like a newborn fool.

The servant returned the smile, then shook two carefully measured drops into the tub. The air around Idisio turned into a fragrant orchard. He sagged back against the wall of the tub, groaning. His eyes slid shut. Dimly, he heard the clink of the glass stopper being replaced; then came a pleasant silence for a few moments.

Water shifted and swirled.

He opened his eyes as the young woman finished settling into the water across from him.

"Uhm," he said in vague protest, too relaxed to really care. "*You're* kathain?"

"We are all kathain, *ha'inn*," she said. "I judged myself the best suited to handle your needs. The others would not understand your northern bias, but I grew up in the north, and I understand."

He squinted, then let his eyes droop closed again. It took a moment to think of something polite to say; finally he tried: "Where in the northlands are you from?" Not that he actually cared, but it was the type of light social comment he'd heard others make in situations–well, not like *this*, but in casual conversation.

"That is from a life past, and not important," she said. "You need not concern yourself with that question, *ha'inn*. You need not be polite with me."

He twitched a shoulder in a shrug and let out a long sigh, surprised at his own relief.

"You may speak of anything you choose, or not," she said. "We are bound to silence, always. Ask what you will, I must answer."

He cracked an eye and regarded her thoughtfully, wondering what she would do this time if he asked about the whistle-language. But she'd given him a clear enough warning, and he understood it too well to press the matter.

"What's your name?" he said instead.

"Anada, *ha'inn*."

"Call me Idisio."

She dipped her head in a slight nod. "If I may, I will."

"Please. This is all–really new to me."

She stood, leaning to reach the tray; water streamed down high, firm breasts and a solid torso, far from skinny but nowhere near overly-plump, either.

"If you would like," she said as she selected a cake of soap, "I will bathe you now."

Idisio shut his eyes and let out a slight whimper.

"I really wish you wouldn't," he said. "I have–I'm with–there's a girl." He winced at his own idiotic stammering.

There came a long silence; at last he opened his eyes a slit and found Anada holding the bar of soap out to him, her expression patient.

"Others would be offended," she said when she saw him looking at her. "This is why I elected myself the most suitable. I understand."

He gulped, relieved, and tried not to actually *grab* the soap from her hand.

Anada settled back against the other side of the tub and watched him, not even pretending to avert her gaze, as he began scrubbing himself.

"This girl," she said after a moment. "She is staying here, I understand? And you are departing."

"Yeah." He didn't look at her.

"This girl," she said, with the same lack of inflection as before, "is pregnant. Is this your child she carries?"

He snapped a quick glance at her face, startled.

"No," she said, tilting her head slightly. "I see. Did you kill the father of her child?"

He stared, his mouth open in stunned protest of that assumption.

"Again, no," she said before he could answer, and nodded slowly. "With a prayer that you find no offense in the words: It's best you're leaving, *ha'inn*. The north has formed you, body and soul. It would be many years before you understood the first tenth of our ways, and they would be hard years, without peace."

"Why aren't you *afraid*?" he blurted, unable to come up with any other coherent response. "You all—you're *servants*, to *desert lords*—and, and—" He made a vague gesture with the hand not holding the soap; water sprayed across her face, but the closest she came to flinching was to shut her eyes. "You're not even the least bit nervous about saying—*anything*. You act like—like you're equal, if not superior, to everyone here. How can you not be *scared*?"

He stopped, breathing hard and feeling more than a little foolish. Anada waited a moment, as though to see if he had anything else to say, then said, "*Ha'inn*—Idisio—in the southlands—" She paused, frowning a little, then went on, more carefully, "Scratha Family, and most other desert Families, believe that even the lowest servant enters into a sacred covenant with their chosen master. And I am not a kitchen sweeper; I am *kathain*. I have considerable status of my own. Within the bounds of this sacred moment, in this place, I *am* your equal. This service cannot properly work any other way: would become nothing more than dishonorable slavery and whoring."

Movement at the entrance to the baths drew Idisio's attention away from trying to figure that one out. Lord Ondio of F'Heing strode into the room. He nodded briefly, seeing Idisio, then turned his attention to the young man approaching him.

"Two," Ondio said curtly, "one at a time. Female. I'll have company later; they'll want their own. I don't share."

The young man nodded and led the desert lord to one of the larger tubs.

Idisio choked back his initial outrage and looked at Anada. Her placid expression was unruffled. "He is bound by the customs of his host to be rather more restrained than he would be with his own kathain," she murmured. "He will do no lasting harm."

Idisio's jaw dropped. "You're *serious*?"

"Yes."

"He's going to—just—*here*? In front of—dear *gods*. I can't—" Idisio started to stand, then glanced down and hastily sank under the concealing line of soap film once more.

Anada's mouth twitched. "I *could* help with that, *ha'inn*," she said. "Idisio. If you wish."

Idisio let out a vaguely strangled sound. A woman emerged from a side room, carrying a wooden tray of bathing supplies. Her dark hair was shorn back as tightly as Anada's, her naked body rather leaner and less rounded. She walked steadily, gaze unwavering, towards the tub Lord Ondio had climbed into.

Idisio shut his eyes. He couldn't help wondering if Deiq had known this would happen; it seemed entirely likely. *Manipulative bastard.*

"Are my clothes clean yet?" he said through his teeth.

"That will take some considerable time," Anada said. He could *hear* the laughter in her voice. "We can offer you a robe, of course, or a waist-wrap–but neither of those do a very good job of, ah, *concealment* for certain matters. And they are very undignified garb for a long walk across the fortress."

"You're *enjoying* this," he accused, keeping his eyes firmly shut.

"Idisio," she said, her tone turning serious, "it is a signal honor to be your kathain, however briefly. I do not wish you any distress; that is no part of my job. I do wish you would relax and trust me."

"It's not *you*," he said. Somewhere to his right, a woman cried out softly–he couldn't tell whether in pain or pleasure.

She sighed. "I understand," she said. "Believe me, I understand. But to leave now–I'm truly sorry, *ha'inn*. Southern status is a very complicated thing. You must not appear to be fleeing something so simple."

"*Simple?*"

The woman cried out again–definitely pained this time. Idisio ground his teeth together, flickers of silver turning over behind his closed eyelids, a rank smell coating his nostrils; he inhaled deeply, focusing on the smell of apples and ginger, and made himself relax again.

"Yes. Simple. The kathain you hear is trained to handle such as Lord Ondio. She will not truly be harmed." Anada paused, sighed, then went on. "I take no joy from your distress over this, ha'inn. I understand you see this differently than we do. When I saw you arrive, I had hoped the gathered lords would wait rather longer before availing themselves of this room after Conclave, and that a gentler one would be first in. F'Heing lords are always a little–energetic. Their tastes and customs differ from Scratha–rather widely."

The sharp slap of a hand against wet skin echoed through the thick air. Idisio shivered, his stomach turning over. Deiq's dry parting comment came to mind: *Between you and Alyea . . .* Idisio had a feeling that Deiq wouldn't have any trouble with this situation at all. But Deiq didn't *know* . . . and had probably better never find out, either.

"What happened to that sacred bit you mentioned, that equality you told me about?" he demanded, pushing distress into anger to keep unpleasant memories from surfacing. "How does that allow for—*this?*"

"Customs differ," she said, no less serene. "If you will trust me, Idisio— there is already a screen set between; that is from Lord Ondio's own preference. You will see nothing, which may help, and if you will speak with me, the noises will soon be irrelevant."

Idisio swallowed hard and risked a glance; a simple folding screen of wooden panels blocked off the view, as promised. He couldn't help muttering, "She's *trained*?"

A faint smile flitted over Anada's face. "Tell me," she said gravely, "what the great city of Bright Bay is like. I am told you lived there for a time, and I suspect most of what I have heard is rather exaggerated or distorted. Is there truly a gate cast all about with gold and diamonds?"

"Yeah," Idisio said. "The gold, anyway. I didn't ever see any diamonds." He began to relax.

"What wastefulness," Anada said, a little wistfully. "There are more of these gates, is this true? I was told of one used only by the dead, which I do not understand."

"Oh, yeah, the Black Gate," Idisio said readily. "That one's not really a gate, I don't think. I mean, it *used* to always be open. . . ."

The sounds beyond the screen eased from pained yelps to more guttural growls of mutual pleasure; Idisio found his breath coming more easily, and Anada's smile brightened in response. She *was* very attractive, and her laugh was more — more *graceful*, somehow, than Riss's usual coarse guffaw. Idisio blinked hard and told raucous jokes to distract himself from thinking about the differences between Anada and Riss. She promptly matched him, bawdy for bawdy. His chest began to hurt from laughing, and the nearby noises altogether faded from his notice.

By the time the water cooled and Idisio stepped out for a towel-down, Lord Ondio–and his companions–had long since left.

Idisio scarcely remembered they'd been there at all.

Chapter Six

Rain pounded down as though Ishrai had decided to drown the world. The purpose of Bright Bay's high sidewalks became apparent as the streets steadily filled with water. Horses slogged through an ankle-deep slurry of liquefied street trash, their riders hidden under thick cloaks and hoods, while pedestrians kept their feet relatively dry on the walkways to either side.

Tank found himself welcoming the deluge. While thunder and lightning did make him markedly nervous, a simple downpour like this felt deeply cleansing. His childhood in a coastal village hadn't exactly lent itself to a day spent playing in the rain.

Coastal village. He considered the words, nodding to himself. That was a safe description. Far better than the only real translation for *katha village;* and the words were close enough that he could always stutter over to the better term during a careless moment.

Northerns wouldn't know the difference, anyway.

He lifted his face to the rain for a moment, as though that might wash away the grey stain that came across his vision every time he thought about his childhood. *Avin. Tan. Damn it, damn you, damn them*—but it was over, and didn't matter now. *Mercenary. Mercenary. Ordinary, normal life.*

Water streaked across his face, stinging his eyes and blurring his vision. He blinked his sight back to relatively clear and went on, tugging his hood lower on his forehead.

The water level in the street dropped as he crossed from the dock section of Bright Bay into the more affluent merchant and residential areas. He paused, squinting through the rain, and discovered a series of long, narrow drain slits along the lower edges of the high sidewalks, and a higher elevation in the center of the street than at the edges.

Tilting his head to listen more carefully, he could hear that part of the thundering roar around him came from beneath his feet, as water cascaded through the drains down into the catacombs and, presumably, out into the bay.

The skin on the back of his neck tightened. Someone was watching him.

He lifted his gaze from the street and saw someone, heavily cloaked and hooded against the rain, standing not far away. Something in the breadth of the shoulders and the stance indicated a man; the sense of intent regard and the man's stillness implied recognition.

He couldn't possibly see my face in this muck, and I'm not wearing anything with a mark on it. So what is he recognizing me by?

Desert lord. Has to be. Damnit, I didn't even get to the Hall—

Tank stood still, gathering every muscle into readiness, keeping his mind ferociously blank, and waited. The figure shifted back a half-step, then paused and came forward with slow, measured steps. He stopped just out of arm's reach and studied Tank without speaking. Just visible under the hood, southern features came clear, and black eyes; the rain obscured expression, but there probably wasn't much to begin with.

"You're Tanavin Aerthraim," the man said without any doubt in his voice.

Tank's heart thudded up into a higher rhythm for a panicked moment.

"No," he said. "I'm Tank, and I've never seen you before. Now piss off."

The man regarded Tank for another moment, inscrutable; then his head dipped in a faint nod and he turned away without another word.

Tank stood, breathing hard, his throat thick with things he wished he could have said, questions he dearly wanted to demand answers to: *How do you know who I am? Who the hells are you? How much do you know about me?*

Were you here when it happened?

Better not to ask. Better not to know.

Mercenary. Ordinary.

The stranger turned a corner out of sight. Tank looked around to get his bearings: two streets over from the Hall. Unwilling to risk slipping on the low pillars that allowed foot traffic to cross while allowing horses and wagons to pass, he splashed down into the street itself, hoisted himself up to the other sidewalk a few steps later, and ran.

He went up the fourteen white marble steps with considerably more care than he'd taken on the rougher, muddier streets along the way. Somewhere, there had to be a plainer entrance, but he hadn't taken the time to find it before and didn't feel he had the time now: the Freewarrior's Hall seemed more solid sanctuary than any church or temple might offer.

What he remembered of Captain Ash suggested the man would stand up even to an enraged desert lord, if the matter involved a Hall hire.

The massive double doors, at least, weren't necessary. Two smaller, plainer doors, one to each side of the main entry, were far more suitable for everyday use; especially for a shivering, soaked, and slightly muddy new hire trying to avoid drawing attention.

Inside, four windows, each one a match in size to the giant formal doors, let in grey streaks of light that barely shifted the edges of the shadows to a lighter hue. Multi-headed candelabra caught and absorbed the grey into a further mottling of silver; the thick white candles filling each holder had never been lit. Great axes, swords, shields, and suits of armor hung along each long wall, and tapestries with various red and gold designs filled in any blank spots available.

Lit by afternoon sunlight during Tank's first visit, the main hall had been a welcoming, safe, very nearly sacred space; at the moment, it resembled nothing so much as the anteroom to a torture chamber.

Tank moved forward a cautious pace, then another, listening for any sound. The hall seemed utterly deserted. *Dead.* Had Ninnic's Guard gotten to this place after Tank left? Had the death of that vile, mad creature not been *enough*, after all?

"Welcome back," a dry voice said behind him.

Tank shrieked like a child, spinning in place so fast he almost fell over his own feet.

Captain Ash's dour face creased in a broad smile for a moment, then sobered again. He moved forward from his spot beside the door–Tank had walked right past him and never noticed–and clapped Tank on the shoulder.

"At least you didn't piss yourself," he noted. "Last two new hires I startled like that wound up mopping the floor."

Tank gulped for breath, struggling to calm his racing heartbeat.

"Captain Ash," he said, and completely failed to find anything to add to that.

The man's dark hair looked to be growing out from a recent shearing, and his skin had a sallow hue further darkened by the dim light. His steel-grey eyes held as much warmth as the stone around them.

"About time you got back," he said. "I was about to cross you off the books."

"I said I'd be back."

"People say things. Doesn't mean they happen."

Tank shrugged, not inclined to disagree with *that*.

"You still need sworn in properly," Captain Ash said. "Rules and such. You didn't sit still long enough to hear them before, and they're more important than ever–since I can actually count on *enforcing* them now." He dug into a belt pouch and produced a thick wooden disc, about the size of a coin. "Here's your permanent marker. Don't lose it. Don't let it get stolen. You stamp anything you send us with this, it's good as a signature–half the hires couldn't use a pen right way round if their lives depended on it, anyway. Notice I don't ask if *you* can." He tossed the wooden disc to Tank.

Tank turned the marker over in his hands, his mouth quirking in a sour grimace. The crossed-swords symbol of the Bright Bay Freewarrior Hall had been burned onto one side, crossed feathers carved in high relief on the other.

He hadn't realized how much the sigil he'd chosen would resemble the typical Aerthraim Family symbol. No help for it now; he shrugged and dropped the marker into his belt pouch.

"Second room on the right is open," Captain Ash said, pointing to a door at the end of the main hall that led to hire quarters. "Go take a day to sleep, you look like hell. Take two, if you need it. You look like a half-dead and drowned redling rat; I can't take you seriously that way. Remember where my office is? Meet me there when you've cleaned up and rested." He paused, sniffing lightly, and wrinkled his nose. "Baths are downstairs. *Take* one. Take five, if you like. You stink of ship."

He stalked away without waiting for a reply.

"Yes, Captain," Tank said anyway, more than happy to obey that order, and hurried off.

Feeling, for the first time in days, *safe*.

Chapter Seven

The darkness seemed like a live thing, creeping into Ellemoa, filling her from toes to crown. Her only respite came when *teyhataerth* or Rosin visited. Both brought pain, but both also brought *light*; and she craved light the way she'd once craved love, the way she'd once felt hunger for physical food.

Pain wasn't so bad, measured against being alone in the darkness. Being alone was much worse than anything else. She'd had Kolan, for a while, but they'd taken him somewhere else and not brought him back. Maybe she'd killed him.

Memory hazed.

How long had she been here? Where was *here*, beyond *somewhere in Bright Bay*? *When* was *here*? She slapped her hands along cold, dank stone walls and found no answer to any of her questions.

She couldn't see the stars. Or the sun. Heard nothing, in the darkness, other than the hoarseness of her own breathing. The sound of bells drifted in, now and again; but human voices, whether screaming or pleading or singing their madness, had long since stopped.

Stars . . . She had lain out on the soft cool grass of Arason and counted the constellations with Kolan. She remembered. He had told her stories about Payti's Torch and Eki's Dagger. He'd made her laugh with stories about Payti's Trickster aspect, and awed her with tales of Syrta's boundless love. He'd treated her as an equal–as human.

He'd been *kind*. Not at all like Solian . . .

She slapped her hands against the walls until the pain drove all memory of vast speckled skies from her mind, then began walking. She paced in carefully measured circles; lost count at five thousand steps and started over again. When her legs gave out, she slid to the floor. When her legs stopped hurting, she stood and began pacing again. How many times had she done that? Usually it took a hundred iterations of five thousand steps before someone came, but now she'd lost count completely.

She probably had killed Kolan. He'd been her only friend, the only one who tried to help her, and she'd killed him. It would be just like her, because she liked pain. That's what both Rosin and *teyhataerth* said, anyway, and they knew her better than anyone. The screams did feel good . . . even when it was Kolan writhing. No, she wouldn't have let him die. He was too much fun. Rosin wouldn't have allowed it, either.

This was all Kolan's fault. The thought felt grey, dull, and worn. She couldn't even remember where that belief had begun.

They'd all abandoned her, in the end, as she'd expected. Even *teyhataerth* had left her. Rosin had left her. They'd found someone more interesting. She knew it. She'd *seen* him, as he passed within her limited range of other-vision, some time ago: a boy with red hair, bright blue eyes, a handsome rugged body. Rosin wouldn't let her near this new toy; no, this one had to go straight to *teyhataerth* for some reason.

Had it been because she couldn't give Rosin and *teyhataerth* a child? She'd tried. She'd *tried*; but whether the fault lay in herself or in them, somehow an essential connection hadn't ever quite been made. They'd abandoned her, and her only child was long gone into the darkness. Rosin said her son was dead. Said she *had* to give another child, had to, must, needed to–and she couldn't.

Kolan said her son was alive. Rosin said her son was dead. She didn't know who to believe.

She heard *teyhataerth* murmuring and singing in the other-darkness, enjoying the new toy.

No–that was past. That had been a thousand paces ago. Ten thousand sets of paces ago. She couldn't tell. She'd lost all count.

Rosin would come for her soon. He would. He had to. He wouldn't abandon her *completely*. He liked her too much. He said so. Said she was *best*, his favorite, his marvel. He never lost faith in her, that she'd provide a child one day, that she *could* if she really wanted to. He was the only one who could help her do that, he was the only one who truly understood her. He had said that, too, over and over, until she'd really seen the truth of it.

The boy didn't want to play with *teyhataerth*. He yelled and fought; and *teyhataerth*, instead of overpowering the boy, screamed as though hurt–but surely it was only playing, it wasn't *possible* to hurt *teyhataerth*.

Teyhataerth sent the boy away, and screamed and screamed and screamed. Something was terribly wrong.

They would come for her soon. Would come to bring her pain, and to give *teyhataerth* healing, and to bring her *light*.

She heard a scream, a ground-shaking, breath-stopping shriek that doubled and tripled and echoed. A million daggers wrenched through her heart. Everything went silent.

No–no! That was past, as well. That had happened already. She didn't know how long ago. A hundred steps, a thousand, a hundred thousand sets of five thousand–she couldn't tell. Time was only an illusion, something to separate the times of pain from the not-pain. There had been a lot of the not-pain since *teyhataerth* screamed. It had begun turning into an entirely different sort of pain–recently? She didn't know if that was the right term.

A pair of grey eyes opened, casting a brilliant light across her, like a hazy lantern. She stared, transfixed, as a face took form around those eyes: a slender, pale young face, so like her own–but he wasn't looking at her. He was near but not in the cell with her. He was following someone, some human, some *man*.

She screamed and reached out, slamming her whole body into unyielding stone in an effort to reach him. Only one creature could have those eyes, that face–he wasn't dead at all.

My son! My son, alive, and just out of reach–don't go, don't go, come back to me!

For a moment, she thought her cry might have reached him. He blinked and turned his head, looking almost at her. Then he blinked again, and the vision faded, leaving her alone in the dark once more.

Ellemoa lost control then, screaming and writhing and battering herself against the walls; uncaring if this was another of the torment-dreams *teyhataerth* so often sent to test her. The vision had split open her mind, cleared the mist, awakened a vast hunger for freedom.

She would escape and find her son. She *would*. And she would get them both free of this evil, stinking place, where humans turned ha'ra'hain into slaves and animals to torture; they would go home. To Arason. To the cottage by the lake. And they would be safe.

Darkness and silence answered. She had no idea how long she spent screaming. She collapsed, finally, and wept for a while more, then slept.

She awakened to the sound of a sledgehammer hitting the door of her prison: the sound of escape.

Chapter Eight

There was a servant waiting patiently outside Idisio's room when he returned from his bath. Idisio's first thought was: *Scratha must want to talk to me;* followed, dimly, by a habitual tickle of anxiety: *I didn't do anything wrong! Did I?* Maybe he was about to be taken to task over some impropriety during that bath after all. Anada had seemed perfectly serene and content as he left–but then, kathain were obviously trained to look happy even when–

He stopped *that* train of thought, fast. He really didn't want to get upset right now. The bath and the conversation had left him with a drowsy contentment he'd rarely felt before. He didn't want to lose that.

Two steps later, perspective shifted: the servant wasn't standing in front of his door, but Riss's, and was watching Idisio's approach with a quiet alertness that clarified the situation. Not messenger, but *watcher*–someone important was in Riss's room, and the servant was here to be sure that someone wasn't harmed or bothered.

The list of names that Riss would allow into her private quarters was short, in Idisio's considered opinion; and as he was standing in the hallway and Lord Scratha almost definitely occupied elsewhere, that left only one real possibility: Gria, heir to Scratha.

He nodded vaguely to the servant and went into his room, unwilling to test whether his status would get him past that direct, unafraid stare. No reason to try, anyway. Something about Gria always made him deeply uneasy.

He considered the book laid out on the small writing desk, then shook his head, stretched out on the low bed, and let drowsiness intensify into a light doze.

Some unmeasured stretch of time later, he opened his eyes to find Riss letting herself quietly into the room. He propped himself up on his elbows, smiling, more rested and relaxed than he could ever remember being before, and said, "Enjoy your talk with Gria?"

She shut the door behind her, slowly, then turned to face him. Some of his ease faded at the expression on her face.

"Enjoy *your* little visit with the kathain?" she said blackly.

He sat up the rest of the way. "What—"

"I *heard* her," she snapped. "They wouldn't let me in—they said the room was closed to all but the *chaal*—the important people. Desert lords. And you. But I heard plenty from outside. *Plenty*. I heard you laughing. I know you were in there! And I heard—her—*them*—I know what was going on."

Idisio drew in a long breath, shaking his head. Anada had told a series of lively jokes; he'd laughed without worry about volume or being overheard. He'd even planned to tell Riss a few of the jokes. That seemed like a bad idea now, given that he'd have to admit the provenance eventually.

"Riss, there were other desert lords in the room. Lord Ondio of F'Heing, and, and—" He paused, unable to remember, exactly, who else had come and gone. Anada had captured his attention, as promised, so thoroughly that the background noises hadn't even mattered.

"Of course," she said. "Right. Obviously." She crossed her arms and leaned against the wall by the door, her glare unrelenting. "I'm not *stupid*, Idisio! I hear the servants talking, you know. It's, it's like some, some *scheduling* matter to them—make sure there are two women available for this desert lord, make sure there are two boys for *that* one, oh, and we probably don't have *enough* to satisfy the ha'ra'hain, but we'll have to do our best and hope they forgive the *discourtesy* of the situation! *Discourtesy!*"

Idisio swung sideways and set his feet on the floor, rubbing his hands over his face. "Riss," he said, looking up at her, "I *didn't*. I promise. I swear. What you heard was those desert lords."

"You took a bath with a, a kathain, though, didn't you? That's *custom* here, isn't it?" Her lower lip trembled; she bit it hard and put her shoulders back a little more, defiantly. "And you were *laughing*."

Underneath her words, silent frustration swirled: *You never laugh like that around me.*

He decided to ignore the unspoken subtext.

"Yeah," he said, "but all we did was *talk*, Riss. I swear. It's not—I couldn't avoid having her around, it would have been—this place has some weird customs. But nothing happened. Come on, you know me better than that, right? I—" He intended to say *love you*, but his mouth and throat seemed to freeze. He cleared his throat and instead offered, "I wouldn't do that."

She stared at him, her dark frown easing a little. "No? I don't think you know yet what you'd do or wouldn't do, Idisio. You're going on the road with Deiq and Lord Alyea. I doubt Deiq particularly cares about morals or relationships—word has it he'll fuck anything that moves."

Idisio flinched, startled to hear such coarseness from her. Who had she been *listening* to, that she'd picked up that sort of language?

She went on without pausing: "And Lord Alyea's—well, she's a desert lord, so *she'll* be—like the others, northern upbringing or not. As I'm hearing it, it's not going to be a matter of *choice*." Her jaw tightened; he thought he could hear her teeth grinding together, but it might have been the sound of his own fingers digging into his palms. "With that sort of company guiding you around, you're not *going* to hold faithful to me. You won't be *able* to."

He opened his mouth, shut it again, helplessly. "Riss," he said. "Come on. Of course I will."

She turned and left the room without answering or looking back. A few moments later, he could *feel* her, hunched up on the bed in her room, on the edge of tears.

"Oh, *hells*," he muttered, his perfect calm perfectly shattered.

After a long moment of furious indecision, he sighed and went after her. It took rather longer to settle her down, and even more time for the inevitable, if enjoyable, tension-breaking follow-up.

Once Riss fell firmly asleep, Idisio slipped from the room and went to find Deiq: relieved, again, to be out of Riss's presence, and feeling as hauntingly guilty over it as before. Especially since she'd been *very* attentive; he'd actually been a little disappointed when she drifted off.

I wonder if Anada is still in the baths . . . I wonder if she's too busy to . . . talk . . . .

"Godsdamnit," he muttered under his breath, and quickened his step, forcing himself to think *only* about finding Deiq.

Chapter Nine

Racks of weapons and practice dummies had been shoved into every available alcove in Captain Ash's office. His desk was little more than a wide board across two sawhorses, and the inkwell–a sturdy blue glass jar that had originally seen another use entirely–had a crust around the rim of the seal, suggesting that the contents had long since dried out. The captain himself sat on a wobbly three-legged stool that would have been more suitable for a ten-year-old than a man of his size and weight.

Tank stood in front of the desk, habit prompting him to memorize his surroundings, and tried to avoid the Hall captain's gaze; not from fear, but out of an uneasy awareness that he needed to *visibly* treat Captain Ash as a superior.

"Huh," the captain said, watching Tank narrowly, then sighed. He pinched his nose, as though debating whether or not to say something, and finally shook his head. "Tank. Huh."

Tank risked a quick, puzzled glance at the man. "Captain?"

"Rested enough? You sleep like a damn rock, you know that?"

Tank's face heated rapidly. "Not normally," he said before he could think, then stuttered under the man's withering stare. "Sorry. I . . . didn't think I was that tired." He was afraid to ask how long he'd slept; he vaguely remembered sunlight in his face at least once, and moonlight coming through the open window another time, so it had been at least a day, maybe two.

It was *embarrassing*, and frightening, that he'd gone so solidly out; on the other hand, he felt more rested than he had in a *long* time.

"Sleep like that on the trail, you won't be a hire here long," Captain Ash said. "Or alive, come to that."

"I don't. Won't."

"Best not." The captain squinted a little, then said, unexpectedly, "Tank. You familiar with another name, maybe?"

Tank's blood turned to ice. "No, Captain," he said, staring straight ahead. "Just Tank."

"Huh," the man said again. "Well, rules first, questions later. Main points: you don't steal, rape, swindle, or bully. I get credible complaints, you get a mark against you and hauled in for a talk next time you're in town. I get proof, you're out, whether you've faced me or not. You don't like those rules, you try finding a hall that doesn't hold that line, and good luck with it. Or you turn unsworn and lose the protection of that marker.

"Once you go unsworn, it's damn unlikely you'll live long; that's a brutal life, that way, with your companions apt to stab you for your socks. Hall hires are bound to respect each other, help when they can, whatever hall you're from. They have *standards*. They carry the reputation of their hall with them. They carry the *protection* of their hall–of all the halls in the kingdom–with them. You've got definite refuge and resource and training chances in any town with a hall. Unsworn just kill for money, and they get *nothing* more than money–and damn little of that, compared to a Hall hire. Bits to the round.

"You can sign with who you want, long as you register the contract with the Hall first, but there's names I'd warn you against having anything to do with–so check with me before signing if an offer doesn't come through the Hall. Check any contract offer with the local hall, same reasoning. We clear so far?"

Tank nodded. Any other response seemed likely to provoke another lecture.

"Local law ain't the same as kingdom law, and that ain't the same as Hall law," Captain Ash went on; Tank nodded dutifully, hoping to speed things up, but the captain continued at the same deliberate pace. "Local custom gets into a tricky grey area between enforceable law and common courtesy. I'll send you to Ten, next, he's the expert on all of that. You listen to what he has to say. Other than his advice, stick to the basics, like I told you–no raping, stealing, swindling, bullying–and you shouldn't land in anything you can't get out of. I've got an even longer speech for the dullards, but you have more wits about you than most I've seen come through those doors."

In the following silence, the captain's eyes seemed to bore into Tank with unusual intensity.

"Thank you," Tank said awkwardly, looking away to keep the moment from becoming a confrontation, and prayed the man wasn't about to resume questioning him about his background.

The silence hung, dragged, stretched.

"Go see Ten," Captain Ash said abruptly. "He's in the room back of the library. Come back here when he's done talking to you, and I'll go over your options for contracts. Get."

"Yes, Captain," Tank said, and very nearly tripped over a small crate of rusted dagger blades as he backed up.

"Forgotten how to dance, have you?" the captain inquired sardonically as Tank staggered sideways, wobbling frantically off-balance.

Tank hopped back to solid footing. "Nah," he said, deciding *brash* was the best answer to give, "just practicing a new style." He grinned at Captain Ash and left before the man could throw the inkwell at him.

The "library" was so small as to very nearly be a corridor. Tank put his arms out to either side as he walked by the bookshelves, testing; his fingertips reached less than a handspan away from the neatly arranged shelves of bound books, scrolls, and stacks of paper. The air was dry here, and smelled of leather, glue, and dust.

He paused to read a few titles: *Histery of Swordemakin, Once Uppon A Blacesmith, Care of Weppens*. He smiled at the misspellings and resisted the impulse to check other titles for mistakes.

At the far end—although as the room barely measured longer than wide, "far" was a relative term—an archway led into a slightly larger room. This one had walls covered with maps that would have had Tank's former mentor Allonin on his knees in awe. The largest spread over one entire wall, and showed the lands from north of the Great Forest to the foothills of the Scarpane Mountains, and from the Stone Islands east to the beginning of the Wastelands.

It was a massive amount of land, and a stunning achievement, especially as it appeared to be drawn to scale. Tank could see faint lines and measurement symbols scattered across the map.

In the center of the room, at a desk more elaborate than Captain Ash's only in that it had legs instead of sawhorses, sat an impossibly thin man with unnaturally large eyes. He looked up at Tank without any sign of surprise, blinked slowly, and said, "Ah. Pleased to meet you, Tanavin. I'm Tendallen, better known as Ten."

Tank felt his throat close off and the blood drain from his face. He took a step backwards, hands up in front of him as though to ward off a blow.

"Oh!" Tendallen said, looking distressed now. He stood up, proving himself to be considerably taller than Tank; his narrow skull nearly reached the ceiling. "Oh, I'm sorry. It's Tank now. Of course. I'm so sorry."

"No," Tank said, barely audible even to himself. He was having trouble breathing. "No. Not here. No." The Freewarrior's Hall was supposed to be his haven, his place away from that name, that person he'd been. Now it was tainted.

He backed up another step, the fire to *run* surging through his muscles: held still after that single step only because he had nowhere to run *to*. One panicked, blind flight through Bright Bay had already landed him in enough trouble for a lifetime. He wouldn't do that again.

Tendallen stood still, watching Tank with a strange, bright stare. His eyes were a pale grey-blue, and the sunlight shafting in from high windows and ceiling tubes caught odd, golden glitters from the irises.

"If it helps," he said quietly, "Captain Ash doesn't know your . . . background."

"He knows my name isn't Tank," Tank said bitterly.

Tendallen shook his head. "Not from anything said by me. I don't speak to him often, I'm afraid, and I tell him . . . very little of what I know. It's safer that way, even now, for both of us." He paused. "It's something of an accident that *I* know that name. An unintentional eavesdropping incident. And I shouldn't have said anything, I really shouldn't have. It's simply not relevant to your contract with the Hall. So please, stay. I do need to tell you some things, or the captain won't let you go out on a contract."

He sat down again, folding onto his stool gracefully; laced his hands together on the desktop, then waited, his strange stare never leaving Tank's face.

"You're not human," Tank said flatly, not moving. A horrid shiver fought to work up his back. He held it back with iron determination not to show fear in front of this–creature.

"I'm quite human," Tendallen said. "Believe me. My appearance is something of a genetic accident. A throwback, if you will, to an ancestor who *wasn't* entirely human. And my knowledge of you comes from nothing mystical, simply a moment of unintended eavesdropping, as I said, and some obvious connections from there."

The pressure in Tank's throat eased a notch. He hesitated, doubting: it could all be a lie–

"I'm not lying," Tendallen said. "Oh, I've done it again. No, I didn't read your mind. I'm far better at reading facial expressions and small movements. Not that you're particularly challenging, in any case. A blind man could have figured *that* one out."

"What the hells are you *doing* here?" Tank burst out. A thoroughly educated, intelligent, and perceptive librarian wasn't what he had expected to find in a freewarrior's training hall.

"Well, who else would have me?" the strange man asked dryly, motioning to his face. "In recent years it was worth my life to walk out on the streets, given that something as minor as a visible wart could get one accused of witchcraft and executed in numerous horrible ways. Captain Ash was kind enough to let me stay here, and I've done what I could to repay that."

He waved one thin hand towards the library room behind Tank, and around at the maps plastering the walls.

"Speaking of which," he said, folding his hands together again, "may I please tell you what you need to know at this point? Then you can be free of my frightening company sooner than later."

Tank advanced a hesitant step, not at all sure he was doing the right thing, and felt a flush heating his face. "Sorry for the rudeness," he muttered.

"I expected it," Tendallen said, expressionless. His gaze cut over towards the left wall, where a large map of the coastal plains took up most of the available space. "Please look at that map. Go stand in front of it, in fact."

Tank was more relieved than worried to put his back to the man. He studied the map with care to distract his mind from the questions piling up.

"You see Bright Bay," Tendallen said. "You see, to the east, Kybeach. To the east of that lies Obein, then Sandsplit. To the southeast of Sandsplit is the only other port town of the southern coast, Sandlaen. To the northeast of Sandsplit runs the Forest Road, which is the only path through the Hackerwood. Due east of Sandsplit are Northern Church lands: they claim the marshes that produce the holy grey salt."

Tank glanced over his shoulder, searching for sarcasm; found only blankness.

"The Northern Church is extremely strong north of the Hackerwood," Tendallen said, pointing Tank's attention back to the map. "There are cities, such as Stecatr, in which trouble with the Church quickly takes you beyond any kingdom law's ability to save you. South of the Hackerwood has become rather more relaxed over the years, even with the recent troubles; Bright Bay is so close to hand that kingdom justice is easily enforced."

He paused. Tank turned to look again, and this time surprised a thoughtful expression on the man's thin face.

"I would suggest, as you are young and far from experienced in the ways of the Church, that you stick to working the southern coastlands for at least a year or two. Isata is probably about as far as it is safe for you to go, until you understand more about the northlands. We are very different from where you . . . grew up."

Tank turned round fully, his hands tightening into fists at the innuendo the man managed to put into that one, flatly said phrase.

Tendallen stared back without apparent concern. "Kybeach is extremely unfriendly to outsiders," he said. "If something goes wrong in Kybeach, I suggest you run first and defend your actions to Captain Ash later. It's an unusual town; he'll give you more rope there than anywhere else you might travel. Sandsplit has some people you ought to steer clear of, but no doubt you'll find out who they are without my advice, which I believe you've had more than enough of already. Tell Captain Ash this word: *bluebird*. Good day. "

Tank didn't wait for a second invitation to leave.

Chapter Ten

In those days . . . Telling stories always put Idisio in a pensive mood, and the one about the childless kaen and the ruined city in the desert had always bothered him more than most. *None shall drink from this well* . . . Deiq hadn't reacted at all the way Idisio had expected, either; he'd had the most *peculiar* look on his face the entire time, and then had more or less admitted to being there, himself, when the actual events took place. *That story's nowhere near accurate,* he'd said, mouth tight with evident irritation, but refused to talk about it any further.

What that implied about Deiq's age, and Idisio's potential, was as impossible to comprehend at the moment as the notion of any part of that story being true. And what part had Deiq played at the time? Had he been the fat old man who cursed the kaen? Hard to believe; but he certainly hadn't been the kaen himself. More than likely, he'd been an offstage character, manipulating events from a safe vantage point. That seemed much more his style than pronouncements of doom: *If you touch me, this well shall instantly go dry, and your entire lands, O kaen, will then go as dry as your loins.*

Idisio couldn't even imagine Deiq using the word *loins,* for one thing. Picturing the way Deiq's mouth would doubtless pucker around such a word brought a rueful grin to Idisio's face and made it easier to push the entire incident aside as yet another strange moment to simply accept and forget about.

Thankfully, the armory Deiq wanted to look at wasn't far from the balcony where Idisio had told the story; he didn't have much time to brood over possibilities and impossibilities. Deiq opened the worn wooden door and stood still for a moment, staring in. The blackness beyond seemed a fitting backdrop for his lean form, reflecting his cynical nature in some abstract fashion. Idisio rubbed his eyes and glanced away to clear his mind of that notion.

He was perfectly aware that Deiq had suggested going through the armory as a way of distracting them both, and had gone along with that more than willingly; but the darkness and the stifling, hot quiet only made his thoughts return to the story he'd just told.

The great central desert remains empty to this day, but for the restless ghost of the old kaen.

At least Scratha Fortress wasn't *haunted* . . .

At that thought, Idisio felt an odd chill slither along his back, and Deiq shot a sharp glance back at him.

"Sorry," Idisio muttered, and tried to pay attention to his surroundings rather than brood about superstitions. Or Riss. Deiq had been adamant in his refusal to discuss her misery–or Idisio's–beyond a brief dismissal: *You've known her less than a month. Tell her whatever will make her happy.*

In other words, Idisio thought, *lie. Leave her behind with empty promises and without looking back. She's only human, after all . . . .*

Deiq aimed another sour glare at Idisio. "You're too damn young for good sense," he said. Then, without explaining that comment, he moved aside a scant step and waved Idisio forward to the doorway. "Stand here. What do you see?"

Idisio took two reluctant steps forward and squinted into the room. He saw vague outlines, defined by the sun flooding through the hallway behind them: the squared-off shapes of lockers and chests.

"Stores," he said. "Lockers, chests."

"Close your eyes. Take three steps forward. Wait–"

Idisio heard Deiq moving behind him, and then the sound of the door closing. He shivered again, uneasy for no good reason–although being locked in a dark room with Deiq would probably send most people into instant panic.

Most *humans,* he corrected himself a little sourly. *I'm not human. I never was.* He still couldn't quite grasp that at times, and wasn't entirely sure that he ever *wanted* to be completely comfortable with being *other.*

"You'll get used to it," Deiq said, as he had during Conclave; less bleakness saturated his tone this time. "Open your eyes. What do you see?"

Utter blackness surrounded them. "Nothing. It's dark."

"Is it?"

Idisio blinked hard, frowning and not at all sure what Deiq was getting at. "Yes . . ."

"Are you *sure* it's dark?"

"I–" He blinked again, squinted a little, and started to shake his head, not understanding the game Deiq was playing this time. Abruptly, darkness cleared, lifting into the same dim murk he'd seen from the doorway. He let out a hiss of surprise, and heard Deiq's satisfied grunt in response.

"I can only see outlines," Idisio said, reaching out to touch a nearby cabinet.

"It's a start," Deiq remarked. "Close your eyes again. Now–there's one oil lamp in this room. Do you know where it is, without looking?"

Idisio sorted through the shapes he'd seen; nothing more complicated than observation, here, and he was reasonably good at *that.*

"At the far end," he said. "On a long table."

"Yes. It's not a table, but that's good for a first try. It's the same green-oil lamp you've seen elsewhere; you remember what those look like when lit?"

"Yes."

"Imagine this one lit. *See* it lit, *know* it's lit."

Idisio scowled, concentrating fiercely. A faint golden haze rose in his mind. Deiq sucked in a sharp breath. Scratha ha'rethe said, *You wish this lamp lit?*

I'm trying to do it myself, Idisio said, his heart hammering.

The ha'rethe seemed to blink in slow puzzlement, then the sense of a shrug passed through Idisio and the golden haze faded.

"I think you were trying a little too hard," Deiq said, a strange catch in his voice. "Try again. More *quietly.*"

Idisio opened his eyes briefly, found only the same darkness as before, and sighed. "I don't understand this," he said. "It doesn't even make sense. How can I know something that isn't true? That lamp *isn't* lit. I can't know it is!"

"It's a matter of willpower," Deiq said in a tone of strained patience. "Look– like this."

The lamp across the room flared into bright life. A moment later, it went out, leaving them in utter darkness again.

"Try again," Deiq said.

Idisio blinked hard and focused on believing the lamp was still lit, but the room remained resolutely dark. Frustration turned his breath rough. Finally, he said, "Forget it, Deiq. This isn't working."

Deiq sighed. The lamp flared to life again.

"It'll come," Deiq said, not sounding entirely convinced. "You're still developing, that's all. It's going to take time."

Idisio shrugged off the faint tinge of condescension in that statement and went to examine the nearest locker. It stood taller than Deiq and somewhat wider than both of them, and was fastened with a simple clasp-lock.

"Wonder what's in here," Idisio said, absently wrapping his hand around the metal lock. He'd left his picks behind in Bright Bay, and in any case picking an armory supply lock would probably get him in troub–

The lock *snicked* open, rolling sideways, and fell into his hand like a ripe apple. He almost dropped it, shocked.

Deiq laughed. "Apparently that one's simple enough for you."

Idisio turned the lock over in his hands, staring at it. "I did that?"

Deiq nudged him aside and pulled open the locker door, revealing shelves of helmets, throat-guards, and arm-guards, mostly crafted of leather and chain-link. Idisio supposed more comprehensive armor would be worse than useless in the smothering desert heat.

He glanced at the doorway nervously, half-expecting someone to come through and start shouting at them for looting. Deiq snorted and snapped a finger against Idisio's shoulder.

"Stop that," he said. "Nobody would say a word if we decided to walk out of here with every piece we could carry on our backs." He pulled a helmet from a shelf, turned it around a few times, and finally replaced it. He shut the locker door and moved on to another.

Idisio stood still, looking around the room with a mixture of awe and anxiety. "Really?"

"Really," Deiq said. He touched the lock. It sprang open, as the one Idisio still held had done.

"But that's stealing!"

Deiq turned and gave Idisio a bemused stare.

Idisio felt his face flushing. "Never mind," he muttered.

Deiq made a dry, amused sound and went back to looking through the locker. Idisio reset the lock on the one he'd opened and sat on a chest, watching. After a few moments, curiosity got the better of his intentions. He stood, then turned and knelt to pop the lock on the chest. It gave as easily as the first, and he grinned as he lifted the lid.

"Damn, this would have come in handy in Bright Bay," he muttered.

"It would have gotten you killed in Bright Bay," Deiq said without looking up. "That's why you never allowed it to surface."

Idisio sat back on his heels and stared at Deiq's back. The elder ha'ra'ha continued opening lockers and chests. "You're saying I blocked myself into—into being . . . normal . . . on purpose?"

"Being human," Deiq corrected dryly, aiming a quick glance over his shoulder. He pulled shut the locker he'd been examining, refastened the lock, and knelt to open a chest.

Idisio watched in silence, understanding that Deiq wasn't going to answer the question any more directly than that. The chest turned out to contain well over a hundred daggers, some almost long enough to be considered short swords.

Deiq lifted one and slid it partway out of the plain leather sheath, tilting it a bit; lantern light caught and striped over the Scratha Family sigil on blade and hilt alike.

"Made here," Deiq said, studying the dagger thoughtfully. "The armory fell out of use before Cafad was born. The Scratha smiths were damn good, but they bailed out early on in the crisis years. I think they went to F'Heing, actually." He slid the blade back into the sheath and handed it to Idisio. "Stick this in your pack. It's better quality than you'll find most places."

Idisio measured the dagger with his hands and decided it would–just–fit; he'd have to repack a bit to make room. Deiq shut the chest without taking anything for himself, reset the lock, then stood with a sigh.

"Good enough," he said, looking around. "Scratha's got supply yet. I was worried that someone would have looted the stores during the cleaning, but it seems solid. Now all he needs are some guards, but I expect that will take a bit longer than household staff. Nobody's going to donate guards they way they would servants." He slanted a sideways glance at Idisio, and a smile tugged at his mouth. "Or kathain," he added pointedly.

Idisio bit the inside of his cheek and just as pointedly ignored that comment. "During the cleaning?" he said instead.

Deiq turned and gave him a long, thoughtful look, then shook his head.

"I shouldn't have said anything," he said in an oddly muted voice. "Drop it for right now, please. I'll explain later." He took a step towards the door.

Cleaning went round in Idisio's head once, twice, then latched onto a connection. Scratha Family had been wiped out twenty years ago. That had always been an abstract story for him, even after meeting Cafad; but now, walking through the rooms and halls of Scratha Fortress, Idisio suddenly realized how *many* people must have been involved in that disaster.

How much *blood* there would have been.

"Idis–" Deiq began, tone a dire warning, but got no further.

Something wrenched sideways inside Idisio's mind, and vision unrolled with the force of a tidal wave:

Blood plastered the walls, the floor, even the ceiling; bits of grey matter, feces, urine . . . The stench was as grey and brown in the nose as the visual destruction was to the eyes . . . The screams echoed in the air as though they'd acquired a life of their own. . . .

Deiq's hand cracked sharply across Idisio's face, shocking him out of the moment.

"God*damn* you!" Deiq panted, and lurched back to lean against a nearby locker, his own face grey and taut. "You had to think on it, didn't you? Had to wonder–*damnit!*"

He shut his eyes and slid to a crouch with his back rigid against the locker; hands fisted against his eyes, shaking all over. Idisio, still dazed, instinctively stared at his hands, memorizing every crease and dirt spot and nail edge with manic intensity.

There hadn't been a golden haze: did that mean the memory wasn't from the ha'rethe this time, but from Deiq himself? Or was Idisio picking it up, the way he had opened the lock, from some unknown resource within himself?

He made himself *not think about it,* fairly sure that Deiq would get even more aggravated with *that* thread of thought.

After what felt like a small eternity, Deiq staggered to his feet, his expression as bleak as Idisio had ever seen it. He looked down at Idisio for a moment of ominous, Scratha-like silence, then turned and left the room. As he passed through the doorway, the lamp went out, leaving Idisio in darkness.

Idisio stayed still, blinking hard, both hands clenched around the sheathed dagger; feeling safer in the hot, empty blackness than standing anywhere near Deiq.

Chapter Eleven

"Bluebird."

Captain Ash studied Tank's face for a moment, his eyebrows drawing into a faint frown. "Didn't get along with him, then? Nobody does. He puts a shiver up my back, too." He rubbed a hand over his face and sighed. "Bluebird," he said, more quietly, and shook his head.

Tank hesitated, then made himself ask. "Captain? What does it mean?"

"Means you're trouble and I ought to tell you to find another place to lay your pack," Captain Ash said bluntly. "But Ten's a scholar, not a fighter, and doesn't understand that trouble's part of the territory. I don't count his warnings too highly, most times."

He cocked his head to one side and fixed a sharp stare on Tank's face.

"This is an instance that puts me in doubt, however. Just so chances to be that there's an odd one been sniffing round last day or two, asking for word of a northern-looking redling with a southern accent and manner. Description he's giving out matches you, Tank, all but the name–and the name he's mentioning alongside that is one as *doesn't* match with a mercenary life."

Tank blinked hard and didn't say anything.

Captain Ash looked at Tank's expression and nodded slowly. "We don't ask about previous lives here," the captain said. "Told you that. I don't put my people's neck into a noose, either, not for commoner or king. This one's a junior merchant–apprentice, damn near. I gave him that there's a redling signed here, he could get that anywhere; but not the name; nothing else. Not the name, not the face, not the whereabouts. That's your business to say."

Tank let out a shallow breath of relief. The captain nodded again, as if that confirmed his guesses.

He went on, as flatly as before: "Interesting slant to the matter is, this junior says to pass along if you're the one he's looking after, he'll guarantee your hire with the merchant *he* works for, name of Venepe. Ambitious promise. I'm not inclined to push you into his contract. There's two others available, with better pay than what I'm willing to bet Venepe will offer; man's known as cheap and sour. This is one of them outside jobs I was warning you of. Venepe's not a good name on my list."

"This . . . junior merchant asking after a–a redhead," Tank said, unwilling to use the derogatory version, even though the captain managed, somehow, to make it sound completely inoffensive. "Any description or name for him?"

"Skinny blond weasel," Captain Ash said promptly, and Tank's heart sank. "Washed-out eyes, twitchy sort. Called himself Dasin."

Tank shut his eyes. *Dasin.* Of all the people he *didn't* miss leaving behind– and yet, his discomfort held more than simple irritation. Dasin hadn't been *all* bad. Far from innocent or even good, by any measure Tank liked to use. But there were worse names that might have come to find him. Names he couldn't win against, if they decided to take issue with any of several aspects of his past.

Dasin was, comparatively, an easy matter to handle.

"I'll go see him," Tank said aloud. "I'll see about this contract. I'll let you know if I decide to take it."

Captain Ash shook his head, sternly disapproving. "Your choice," he said. "Caravan yards, northeastern side of the city. Long damn walk, so send word if you take the job; no point slogging all the way back here. I'll note the contract in the book for you. Bring your pack along, same thought. Do you ride?"

"Yes." He didn't add: *More or less.*

"Got your own horse?"

"No."

"That's going to cut your pay, wherever you go. Even so, don't accept an offer of less than a silver round a day for this one, payable each town you reach, after his selling is done for the day. You can haggle a little; start with two rounds and walk away if he won't give at least one. Keep the contract terms town-to-town, with Venepe, not calendar-based; and if his path takes you through the Forest, the pay goes up to four silver, minimum, for that leg of the trip and anything beyond. Coastlands is easy. Northlands is a lot more dangerous, and the Forest is its own monster's worth of trouble. You remember all that?"

"Yes. Thank you."

The captain dismissed him with a sharp, sour wave, and Tank backed out of the small office with considerably more care this time.

The hot sun turned the damp streets into a steam bath. Tank took his time walking over the rain-slick cobbles, looking around with interest. His previous visit, if it could be called that, to Bright Bay had passed in a mad rush of fear and pain; this was the first time he'd actually seen the city.

Buildings rose high here and hunched low there, with no apparent pattern. Most were whitewashed brick or granite, but he saw a few sturdy wooden buildings at random intervals. Pottery shops and soap makers, chandlers and tanneries, barrel-makers and blacksmiths filled the air with sound and aroma. Tank's eyes watered every time a breeze blew pungent whiffs his way. He quickened his step, eager to get out of the area.

The coastal village he'd grown up in had featured an entirely different set of aromas, but those had been just as foul. On sunny days, when he'd been allowed–sometimes forced–to walk out in the air for a bit, he'd been followed by an awareness of his own sweat and dirt; the ever-present rotten-salt sea air; the garbage that always seemed to pile up in every outside corner and niche.

Sailors didn't care what the ports they visited looked like. Those who came to the *coastal villages* cared even less. Few had asked that their *companions* bathe first. Fewer had, themselves, bathed any time in recent memory.

That's over, Tank told himself, trying not to think about that time: but Avin's face swam into memory. The boy had always managed to find something unusual during their outdoor time: a feather boasting a bizarre checkered pattern; a worn piece of wood shaped like a duck–if you held it just right and squinted, anyway; an old shoe, a woman's, high-heeled and expensive once upon a time.

He remembered that shoe more clearly than most of Avin's scavenged items. Squat old Banna had taken the shoe away and stared at it with a very strange expression for a few moments before shaking her head and throwing it into the nearest trash heap. Thinking back, Tank suspected she'd recognized the shoe, and that it had told her of an unhappy end to its previous owner's life.

Realization shocked through him: even Banna, perhaps, had lost friends along the way.

Good, came the instant, savage response. *I hope she–*

Tank stopped himself before the rage came flooding up. He breathed deeply to center himself in the moment, as Allonin had taught him.

Breathe and count: one breath, two breaths, three; turn it into a silly song, if that works, or a marching chant. Breathe. Breathe.

His mind slowly settled into a glassy stillness. *Over. It's over. Today, tomorrow, now: not yesterday.*

He opened his eyes, glanced around to be sure no pick-thieves had moved to take advantage of his momentary distraction, and found a skinny, waifish face peering around a nearby corner. As soon as Tank turned his head in that direction, the street rat disappeared.

Tank stood still, waiting. After a few moments, the tangle-haired street rat peeked out again; he studied Tank for a long moment, then sidled out of hiding and slowly approached.

She, Tank corrected himself. Even through the loose, patchworked clothes and malnutrition, the shape was wrong for a boy. He nodded, civil and carefully aware of his surroundings still, well aware that distraction was a game the local thieves played well and that most operated in teams.

"I 'member you," the skinny girl said, pausing a step out of easy grabbing range. Her eyes tracked Tank's every movement, as wary of him as he was of her.

"I don't remember *you*," he said flatly.

She tilted her head to the side, squinting, and backed up a step. "You were all tanked," she said. "Staggering round like a moonstruck. You walked straight out into the market square and asked for bread instead of tryin' to steal it like you was supposed to. Blackie 'bout split himself laughing at you."

His heart lurched into a hammering rhythm. "What do you want?"

She stared past him, her eyes narrowing. Even knowing the game, he chanced a glance back. Nobody behind him, of course, and nothing happening; when he jerked his attention to the front again, she was gone. He put a hand to his belt pouch, surprised to find it intact and untouched.

He sucked noisily on his teeth, turning in place to survey his surroundings. He wasn't too far from the road leading to the southeastern market, and on reflection that had been the direction the girl had stared: the same market where he'd walked blindly out to ask for bread. It seemed entirely possible she'd been trying to tell him something.

Or she might have been playing stupid games, getting him jumpy so he'd miss a real pickpocketing attempt when it came. Lifty had taught him a number of the more common tricks; Tank didn't underestimate the inventiveness of street thieves these days.

He looked southeast, thinking it over, then shrugged and went on toward the caravan yard, rather more briskly than before.

Chapter Twelve

Rain thundered down as though Wae had decided to flood the world. Eki's breath howled by. Syrta and Payti were present in the ground underneath Kolan's feet, in the heat flushing through his body; in the flowerbeds and in the lantern-flames. The gods were everywhere, always.

Even in the dark. Even in a scream.

People moved around him, their forms dim as fluttering shadows, speaking irrelevancies. He made no answer, offered no movement; allowed them to urge him up from his chair and to the bed, from the bed to the chamberpot, back to the chair, sometimes into a sunny courtyard.

None of it mattered. He remained in the dark, in the screaming, in the fire and cold.

The shadows around him spoke of the gods, prayed in a language he'd nearly forgotten, reminded him of a life without pain. Somewhere distant, bells tolled: not the deeper tones of the Church bells, but the lighter clamor of the Palace bells. He wasn't sure that the Church bells even functioned these days: vague memory spoke of someone removing the clappers, long ago, but that could have been another of his many, nightmarish illusions.

He retreated from all the sounds, unwilling to listen. To emerge would be to face the betrayal, the agony, the knowing that those of his own faith had unleashed a torrent of horror upon the world.

Better for the bells to be silent than to celebrate that. Better to live in the intersection of fire and ice than to turn from the shadows and see the stark outlines of truth.

The dim prayers continued, brushing against him, maddening, compelling. There was honesty in the grieving words. Kolan began, reluctantly, to listen. The protective shadows in his mind began to fade and shred. Questions rose, connecting him inexorably to the *normal*.

How did I get here? Where is here? How did I escape?
Who am I?

The name *Kolan* held no meaning. It was an abstraction, a tag to align himself with something he no longer remembered. It meant no more than *chair* or *foot*.

The smells of honeysuckle and lilac drifted past him. Sometimes rain thrummed on the simple, slanted roof. Other times, sunlight poured through wide, low windows, bathing him in the munificence of Payti's love.

A tremendous cracking sound, an unearthly scream, a shattering earth tremor: he fell, sprawling over the dirty floor, and a section of the wall where he had been standing simply collapsed, caving into a cascade of rubble that led into a new darkness.

Fresh air tumbled through that hole like a blow against his skin. He curled up in a corner as far from the collapse as he could get, shivering, whimpering, crying in utter terror of this new threat. It had to be a threat. There was nothing good in the world, nothing safe. Every attempt at escape had been a manipulated game that ended with screams. His. Hers. Theirs. He'd stopped trying, long ago. How long? Time didn't exist, in the dark. Nothing existed except the screams and the knowledge that he had always been here and always would be.

After a long, long, terribly long silence, he stopped shivering. After another stretch of nothingness, the faintest glimmer of light formed in the breach: sunlight, creeping down into the hellish pit. He stayed still, watching that painful glimmer until it faded away.

Then he began to crawl forward, until grit and dirt and chunks of stone cut his hands and knees and elbows. The sides of the opening tore at his shoulders. His toes shredded against sharp edges.

Kolan drew in a long, long breath and let it out, flexing his toes slowly. The pain was gone. His flesh had healed. The darkness was gone. Sunlight bathed him. The silence was gone. Voices murmured softly nearby.

He listened, and their words slowly began to make sense, a scattering of clarity against a background of indecipherable mumbles.

"Hasn't moved . . . days."

"Tried a book . . . didn't even . . . it."

"I don't think he'll ever . . . out . . . damage."

"We have to . . . trying . . . what . . . have there?"

The words descended back into mumbles as Kolan let go of focus; the effort had already exhausted him. He sat in his simple chair, sunlight warming his face, chest, and lap, and rested.

The scent of apples and lemons wafted past. Someone bent over him.

"Opal," a voice said. It was a male voice, a kind voice, one that matched the comforting smells. "Opal, I have something for you. Look–marbles. Aren't they lovely?"

Gentle fingers opened up one of Kolan's hands. Several slick, cool globes of glass pressed against his palm. The man folded Kolan's hand around the toys.

Marbles.
My marbles.

Glass marbles in a bag, always by my side. Then gone. Stolen. Fever dream. Didn't miss them at first, not until–

Sio Arenin thumping along in perpetual bad temper, always rushing, always looking to scold, especially Solian–

Solian! Where is he? Did I see him in the darkness? I did–

Vague images of laughter, of a voice: Not so smart now, are you? Not so perfect now, are you? And *you–*Here's what *you* deserve–

She screamed protest, fought without result, bound by a greater power. Kolan watched, helpless, raging–

Give us a child, someone said. Give us a child and the pain stops.

Kolan held her as she sobbed, terrified and frustrated: I can't, she wailed. I'm trying. I can't!

The screams began again, and again, and again . . . .

At some point it all became normal. At some point it stopped mattering.

The marbles shifted in his hand, clicking and grinding a little as they settled closer together.

Marbles. Sio Arenin. The stairs. Solian.

Ellemoa.

The warm sunlight in his face turned into a searing blanket of understanding.

Ellemoa. Solian. Sio Arenin falling, shrieking. The heavy crack of shattering bone, so like the wall of darkness collapsing. Fever dreams. All a fever dream.

The marbles rolled around in his hand as Kolan slowly worked his fingers. Not a dream.

Ellemoa. Solian.

Ellemoa.

Marbles.

"Marbles," he said aloud, and heard a fluttering of startled conversation break out around him. He couldn't help smiling: they wouldn't understand the joke, but he said it anyway. "I've found my marbles."

Laughter started to bubble out. Before it reached his throat, the warmth turned to a terrible cold, the searing touch of Wae and Eki at their worst digging through his flesh and his soul alike.

Ellemoa. Oh, dear gods, Ellemoa.

He threw his head back and screamed with the agony of understanding, with the clarity of remembering.

Shadow priests danced around him, lifting, carrying, binding: tying him down as he thrashed, hatred and fear and pain escaping through sweat and spit and bile. Bitter and sweet liquids slid over his tongue. Brief periods of calm followed, enough to soothe his throat for another round of screaming when the panic returned.

The voices around him came more clearly now:

"We've lost him. He's broken."

"He might yet come out of it. Have some faith."

"He'll be the first."

"There always is a first time."

"Wish there was a *last* time."

Rueful laughter followed.

Kolan followed the laughter like a shaky lifeline: emerged with sunlight flooding the air around him and silence in the room. He lay still, breathing evenly, and blinked until vision focused: a simple wooden ceiling overhead, painted a soothing white. Nothing in the least interesting or notable about it.

He stared at that bland white through three dimmings of sunlight. Three days. His hand stayed wrapped around the marbles the whole time. Sometimes he clicked them together, or moved them to the other hand, just to remind himself they were there.

Mustn't drop the marbles. Someone could get hurt.

Even in the dark, he could see the sturdy beams of the ceiling, if he squinted a little now and again to keep it clear. The white turned grey and the black shadows between were like cracks back into the screaming; he watched them with care to be sure they didn't widen and come after him again.

On the third day of his quiet staring, he knew they wouldn't. Not while he watched them. It was safe to remember it all, to feel it all, to see it all.

"I remember," he said into the early morning stillness.

His voice moved through roughness, emerging as a barely intelligible croak: it didn't matter if anyone else understood him. He knew what he was saying. He needed to hear himself say it aloud. Nobody else mattered right now.

"I remember my name," he said. "I'm Kolan. I remember her name. Ellemoa. I remember all of it. Everything."

The tears came, then, silent and vast: as though Wae had chosen to flood Kolan's entire body with holy fluid, rinsing out the grey and the black and the red bits that were all stuck in ragged patches along his insides. With the tears came a light, and a clarity, and a sharpness; a touch from Payti, and Eki, and Wae, and Syrta, all at once, all around him: surrounding, comforting, explaining why it had all been the way it had been. Balancing the world again. Giving him a small, small patch of solid truth on which to stand.

At some point, the restraints loosened. At some point, the tears stopped.

A priest with short-cropped, sandy hair and sad brown eyes helped Kolan sit up. Fed him a light broth. Bathed him. Led him outside to sit in a chair near the honeysuckle and lilac.

People, both priests and–*others*–moved around a courtyard. There were some stone benches, and flowers, and other cottages. Kolan watched the priests. He didn't look at the *others*. He could feel their dazed hurt, too similar to his own. Seeing them, acknowledging them, risked opening those thin shadow lines into gaping hands that would drag him back into the times of screaming.

He'd always have to watch those cracks. That was one of the solid truths under his feet. The screams would never be more than a step away. The seeds of red and black and grey would remain in his soul, needing only a careless breath to bloom once more.

It was a balance. There was no true escape: not after going that far into the dark.

Balance brought his head up and his shoulders straight. Balance met the gazes of the watchful priests. Balance said, very quietly, "I'd like to go now, if you please. You've been very kind to me. I won't forget. But it's time for me to go home."

Kolan held out the marbles in his cupped palms.

"I'd like to keep one, if I may," he said. "To remind me of your kindness."

His first almost-lie under sunlight; they clustered around him, worried, anxious, skeptical. He kept his gaze clear and steady, his voice even, his tone calm.

Balance. Balance.

"I'm a priest myself," he said.

Their expressions tightened, their worry strained further.

"A priest of the Arason Church. I'm from Arason. I never served in Bright Bay."

Not above ground, at any rate, he added silently. They didn't really want to know the truth, these too-kind, so-sad men who thought they did the gods' work by keeping the *others* alive.

They thought they were redeeming themselves.

Kolan left them their illusions. It was the gods' place, not his, to explain the truth of things.

"I had nothing to do with the madness," he said, then gave them a very nearly outright lie: "I'm quite sane now. Quite safe."

I won't hurt anyone, at least. That much, I'm sure of.

They withdrew and talked about it for two days. He behaved with perfect courtesy, avoided the *others*, let himself be seen admiring flowers, ate what was put before him, handled his own needs without prompting.

At last they returned and quizzed him. He professed amnesia past a few basic points: from Arason. Priest. Not mad. Quite able to handle himself. Otherwise, all was blank.

Frustrated, they withdrew. He waited, infinitely patient.

They returned a day later with a pack of almost-new clothing; a few days worth of simple trail foods; enough coin for a carriage back to Arason.

He thanked them and walked out their gate without looking back.

Chapter Thirteen

The study had been dusty and silent last time Idisio saw it; in less than three days, servants had transformed it into what he could only call *Cafad Scratha's office*. From the predominance of black and white as colors to the squared-off lines of the furniture, the room matched the desert lord's angular personality perfectly.

Evkit's peculiar scent, a mixture of bitter almonds, sweat, and sour milk, was slow to fade from the room. Idisio moved a little farther away from the seat the diminutive teyanain lord had occupied, then decided to try the trick Deiq had mentioned during Conclave. Given that the only people left in the room were Cafad, Deiq, and Alyea, this seemed a safe enough time to dull his senses; none of them would hurt him.

He squinted at Deiq and Cafad, thinking that assumption over more carefully, then shrugged and closed his eyes. *Cotton in my nose,* he told himself. *A nice thick fluffy lining of—*

He choked, gagged, and spit. Panic flooded through him. He couldn't *breathe—*

Deiq's by-now familiar presence reached into his head and stripped out the muffled feeling, then, delicately, settled a lighter version along the insides of Idisio's nostrils before withdrawing again.

Idisio drew in a deep breath of relief and blinked watering eyes. Alyea was staring at him in alarmed bewilderment. Cafad and Deiq hadn't even looked up from their low-voiced discussion of trail supplies and map distances.

His sense of smell had faded almost to nothing. It was *wonderful*.

Thank you, he said, trying to focus on *quiet* and *Deiq*.

Deiq raised his head, pinned Idisio with a long, steady stare, then motioned Alyea's attention back to the discussion with Cafad.

Idisio grimaced and came back to stand beside Cafad's desk, feeling unnaturally large and clumbering–a street word for anyone too clumsy to walk without tripping over his own feet. Remembering the word brought a smile to Idisio's face and straightened his back a bit. He might be something of a clumbering idiot *here*, but put him in a crowded city and he'd–

This time Cafad *and* Deiq raised their heads and skewered him with ferocious glares.

Idisio made a faint *urk*ing sound and hurriedly dropped his gaze to the maps.

One of the men snorted dryly–he thought it was Cafad, but didn't dare look up to be sure. The papers before him seemed nothing more than a mass of incomprehensible lines and colors.

Desperate for a distraction, he blurted, "Uhm, so, where's Bright Bay?"

In the following silence, his ears began to burn. He could *feel* them staring at him.

"You've never seen a map before?" Cafad clicked his tongue, halfway between bemused and impatient. "No. Of course not."

"We'll leave you alone to explain, Lord Scratha," Deiq said. "We could use a walk to stretch our legs." *Say your goodbyes, Idisio,* he noted privately. *This is probably your last chance to be alone with him.*

Deiq steered Alyea out of the room without looking back.

Cafad watched them go, his expression pensive, then shook his head and looked down at the map. Pointing as he spoke, he said, "This one is an elevation map. The land is higher where the lines are thinner. This is water. This is land. This is the mark for forest, river, large city, fortress, small town, rocky land, true desert. Now you tell *me*–where is Bright Bay?"

Idisio squinted, considering, and finally put his finger on a small black dot with water to east and west and land to north and south; it was the only possible spot. Grinning, Cafad slapped Idisio on the shoulder.

"Good! See, it's not so hard. Distance is all that's left–look here–this line translates to fifty miles."

Idisio blinked, reassessing. From Bright Bay to Agyaer port made sense, but from the Wall to Scratha Fortress was twice that far, at a guess; and they'd stepped over it in moments. He shut his eyes for a moment, feeling vaguely ill, and hoped he'd *never* have to go through one of those weird portals again.

He looked up and found Cafad watching him with a peculiar expression.

"Idisio," the desert lord said, his tone shifting to a different flavor of seriousness. "It's been a long road since we met, and it didn't start out well at all. I'm sorry for how I treated you."

"Don't," Idisio said involuntarily. His eyes burned, not quite tearing, but hot and raw-feeling. "Just because you know I'm ha'ra'hain now–"

"No," Cafad said. He sat down behind his desk, regarding Idisio gravely. "I was sorry long before that. It took Riss to make me realize I'd been in the northlands too long. I wasn't raised to treat servants with violence or contempt. I disgraced my Family with my actions, and I can't erase that stain."

"Lord Scratha–"

"I pray," Cafad said, ignoring the half-protest, "that my blows were the last you'll ever receive, and my harsh words the last you'll ever hear directed your way."

Idisio bit his lip, not sure what to say.

"I'm not all that nice a person," Cafad said. His mouth quirked. "But at least I recognize my mistakes, and try to amend them. So to Idisio the street-thief, I say: you're honorary Scratha. It may come in handy, places where you don't want to be seen as ha'ra'hain but need some status to throw around."

Idisio's breath caught in his throat. "Thank you, Lord Scratha."

"You earned it," Cafad said. "As such, and as ha'ra'hain, you can come and go here as you please, and take whatever you like from the fortress stores, treasury, and kathain."

Idisio flinched. "They're not *chairs*," he said, surprised at his own vehemence. "You can't just give them away like that! What happened to not treating servants with contempt?"

Cafad's eyebrows arched, then settled into a frown. "I'm not offering you a traveling companion, nor a whore," he said. "I don't have that right. Kathain choose such things for themselves. I'm offering you your due courtesy while you're *here*."

Idisio looked away, his ears burning again.

"Idisio," Cafad began, then stopped and sighed. "You're still northern," he said at last. "Try not to let that influence your reports to the king too much." Paper skritched and shuffled. "Here—take this letter to Oruen. I've given you Scratha's formal backing, as I told you. Work with Deiq and Alyea on that accent of yours, by the way, before you step in front of him again. It's gotten better, but you still sound like a tradesman at best, not a respectable noble."

Idisio took the sealed packet; it had a definite heft. Cafad had written a half-dozen pages, at a guess.

"What's wrong with trades?" he said, a little sullenly.

"Nothing at all," Cafad said, "if you're a tradesman or a lesser. But you'll be among nobles. They won't respect you, ha'ra'hain or not, if you sound like a katha village reject."

Idisio shivered, words tangling together in his mind. *Kathain*. Anada. *Katha villages—*

Bile scorched his throat briefly. A grey haze covered his vision, then cleared to reveal a flash of bright red hair tangled with black. The ground swayed beneath him, as though he were back on that godsbedamned ship.

He shut his eyes and breathed deeply, shoving the vision aside, forcing his knees steady.

Opening his eyes, he found Cafad watching him with narrow-eyed consideration.

"Another vision." Cafad didn't bother making it a question.

"I haven't been having them as often," Idisio lied. "It's nothing."

"Have you spoken to Deiq about this yet?"

"I'm fine. I didn't sleep well last night, that's all. Need a nap."

Cafad pursed his lips and lifted a shoulder in a faint, irritable gesture that said without words: *You're a damn fool, but have it your own way.* Idisio grinned more from nerves than amusement.

"Lord Scratha, thank you," he said all in a rush. "I owe you–"

"Nothing at all."

"–*everything*," Idisio overrode him. "I would be dead by now if not for you. Anytime–if I can help. With anything. I will."

Cafad dipped his head in a slow nod, his fierce dark stare never leaving Idisio's face. "Gods walk with you and keep you safe, *ha'inn*," he said soberly.

Idisio couldn't resist. He tossed back, "May your hands always find gold and the guards look to the sky as you pass."

Cafad laughed, the weary strain lifting from his face. "Street thieves," he muttered. "Go get a nap. You've a long road tomorrow, traveling with the teyanain; and under an unchancy time of moon, at that. But I have a feeling *you'll* be fine, somehow."

Idisio offered a short bow, grinning with real amusement this time, and left.

Chapter Fourteen

In the northeastern caravan yard, the odors of horse dung, sour beer, sweaty humans, oil, metal, and dirt competed for dominance. Tank resisted the urge to wrap a piece of cloth around his face to block out the dust and smoke swirling through the air. The rainstorm had turned the dirt into quagmire, churned by boots and hooves alike; Tank slogged through the muck with immense care. Falling or losing a boot would be equally catastrophic at the moment.

He paused by the first caravan corral he came to. Inside was a contraption that had probably started life as a noble's in-town coach. It had been poorly modified into a long-haul carriage, with bags and boxes precariously strapped or bolted to every available outer surface, thicker wheels that didn't match the delicate frame, and a few crude attempts at reinforcing the light structure with metal and wooden bars.

A single overfed grey gelding was being strapped into harness by an equally fat, sweaty, irritable woman; it kept jerking its head up out of her reach as she tried to settle the carriage-bridle into place.

The woman looked up at the sky in exasperation, then caught sight of Tank. She glared at him and snapped, "Whatcher want, then? Lend a hand or stuff yer gawk up yer bootside."

He blinked, sorting out dialect; finally decided she'd said *backside* not *bootside*, and stepped forward.

"Glad to help, s'a," he said. "Mind telling me where I might find Venepe along the way?"

She straightened and considered him with a sour squint. "You think I know everyone in this godsforsaken yard?" she demanded. "Help or get clear. I've no time for gossiping with a redling."

He turned his back without comment and took two steps away from her.

"Tuh," she said. "C'm'ere, redling. What you want with that sheep-bagger escapes me. Get this leather over onto the bedamned trocker's head for me and I'll tell you. Husband usually does it, but the bagger's off swapping clods with his knits. Damn fool."

Tank resisted the urge to smile–or ask for a translation–and dutifully followed the woman's directions. The grey gelding rolled its eyes irritably but allowed Tank to settle the straps about its head.

The woman nudged Tank aside once the carriage-bridle was secure and began busily clipping lines together along the body harness and carriage rails.

"Venepe's up ahead," she said as she worked. "Go straight until you come to the yellow featherman's spot, then turn left. Venepe's up just past the black double-team. He's a sour little clod. You can't miss him."

I won't miss Dasin, at any rate, Tank thought, the double meaning of which killed any remaining impulse to smile at the woman's odd dialect slang and bizarre carriage.

"Thank you, *s'a*. Good journeys."

"Tuh," was all she said, shaking her head, and ignored him after that. He clumped on, trying to walk on the few non-mucky spots as much as possible.

The *featherman* turned out to be a man who sold birds: not live ones, but parts-pieces, from feathers to claws. His small, sturdily built carriage was a bright yellow, painted with colorful depictions of his wares. He himself dressed in vibrant blues and reds, with lace edging at the sleeves. His large black hat featured a single enormous firetail-bird feather, and tightly bound silvery-black braids draped over his shoulders.

As Tank passed, the featherman climbed up to the driver's seat of his carriage and set his team into motion, whistling cheerful and startlingly accurate imitation of several birds in rapid succession. His two bay mares, less enthusiastic, leaned into the harness, straining to drag the carriage through the sticky mud; as though by way of comment, one lifted her tail and added somewhat to the stench. The carriage lurched forward, sliding more than rolling. After a few lumbering steps, the wheels caught and the carriage jolted into true motion.

Tank turned to the left and went on.

The black double-team was easy to spot: two massive draft horses leaning sleepily against one another in the shade of a massive, ivy-draped pine tree. Beyond them stood a cart heavy enough to have pulled raw ore down from the northlands. Tank paused to study the beasts, noting the difference between their bulky build and the leaner riding horses he was–marginally–accustomed to. The hooves alone seemed larger than his head; he wondered if they were even *able* to break into a gallop. They'd probably leave craters in the road along the way, if they ever did.

He wondered what the cart would haul back north. It was likely to be a lighter load, unless the merchant involved had an arrangement with the Stone Islands marble quarries. Dasin had always been better at understanding trade matters, but Tank knew enough to figure by; and the coastal southlands didn't have anything heavy to offer the north. Possibly the lands south of the Horn might, but that trade wasn't easy for northerns to get and ran more expensive than an ore-cart hauler could likely afford.

He was delaying. *I can still turn around . . .* It was a tempting option. But Dasin being out of Aerthraim Fortress and attached to a local merchant meant that Tank would have to deal with him sooner or later.

Might as well be now. And he didn't *have* to take the contract. He was only going to find out what Dasin was doing here, nothing more. Say hello. Say goodbye.

He shrugged at the horses, who showed no interest in him whatsoever, and went on. A stone's throw past the black double team paddock, a sturdy, wide-bellied carriage with slanted vents along the top edges stood atop a series of wide planks, keeping the wheels out of the muck. Two bored-looking bay geldings stood at the far end of the small paddock, their long tails busy warding off flies. Closer to Tank, two men sat crossways on a rough wooden bench, facing one another, their heads bent together over a thick book turned sideways on the bench. One was older, with sweat-lank, thinning brown hair and a round figure; the other, his back to Tank, seemed barely wider than the bench he sat on, and his long, pale blond hair had been bound into an intricate series of braids, then tied back out of his face.

Tank paused at the rail of the paddock. The older man looked up immediately, scowling; then his eyes narrowed and he cut a sharp glare at the blond.

"This that redling you were telling me about, then?" he demanded.

The blond startled upright, turning before he was even clear of the bench; cursing, the merchant snatched the book up out of the way.

"Godsdamned–"

The rest of the epithet was lost as Dasin nearly tripped over the bench, hopped sideways on one foot to get clear, slid in the muck, and brought the other foot down hard in an effort to catch his balance. Mud sprayed and splattered. Tank ducked back reflexively. The merchant swore again, hunching over his book to shield it.

Tank grinned, straightening.

"You're graceful as ever," he commented. In the distance, the Palace Bells began to toll, marking off two hours past noon.

"Hopefully you're a better dancer than your friend here," the merchant said sourly, glaring at Dasin. "He *says* you're a fighter." His gaze tracked to the sword bound, southern-style, across Tank's back. "Didn't believe him when he said he knew a redling southerner. Your kind's all up by Stecatr, far as I know."

His tone made it clear he'd prefer them to stay there.

Tank set his teeth in his tongue, amusement fading. A glance at Dasin caught a frantic head-shake, warning Tank not to take issue; but *damn* he was getting tired of being called a redling. For all that he'd stood out in the southlands, he'd never been insulted over something as trivial as his hair color so routinely and casually.

Insults are what you make of them, he remembered Allonin telling him. *They have the power you give them, and nothing more.* That had seemed remarkably sensible, within the yellowed walls of Aerthraim Fortress; at the moment, it seemed remarkably foolish.

But when do you make a stand? he'd asked once. *When do you fight?* And Allonin had said, as though the answer ought to have been obvious: *When you have no other choice.*

"Merchant Venepe," Dasin said, shoulders hunching a little, head ducking to one side, "this is–"

"Tank," Tank interrupted, not wanting the other name to come out if it hadn't already been said.

Dasin squinted a little, the slant of his head more intrigued now than embarrassed.

"You have no grace and he has no manners," Venepe said. "Terrific." He stood, more carefully than Dasin had. "Let me go put the stock book somewhere *safe*." He glowered at Dasin again, then turned toward the wagon.

Dasin let out a long breath, rubbing a hand over his face, then came over to the fence, moving with exaggerated care. Face to face with Tank, he stood a handspan taller; his pale blue eyes searched Tank's face as though reading something new and unexpected there.

"Tank, huh?" he said. "Good thing I never gave Venepe a right name, apparently. I wondered, when that iron-assed captain at the Hall wouldn't allow to you being around."

Tank jerked his head in something between confirmation and gratitude. Dasin nodded back, his pale eyebrows scrunching into a frown.

"Are you here to sign, or to shake me off?" he demanded. "If you're not here to sign, then I've nothing to say."

"Now who's lacking manners? What's wrong with talking a bit?"

"You're not a talker, *Tank*. You want me clear of you, fine. I won't chew your tail."

Tank was saved from answering Dasin's unexpected hostility by Venepe's return.

"I carry cloth," the fat merchant said without preamble. "Run to Isata and back. Town to town contract; I don't like you anywhere along the way, I pay you and shake you. Dasin says you're Hall, so that pays half silver for the coast, three through the Forest and above. Don't expect to get through the Forest with me; I shake most of my southerner hires in Sandsplit. You lot are too much trouble in the northlands."

"I thought *my lot* was up near Stecatr," Tank said, unable to resist pushing back this time. *No other choice* felt nearer with every word.

Venepe's nostrils flared. "Don't get above yourself," he said. "I don't *need* another guard. I'm doing this as a favor to your friend, and you don't even look old enough to shave, so I'm doubting you're going to be any use at all. Take it or leave it."

That did it. Tank's back stiffened.

"Don't need favors," he said. "Hire me because I can do the job, regardless of *him*." He jerked his chin at Dasin. "You might have those as can swing a blade or scrap, but do you have those as can walk and think at the same time? And I can dance a lot better than Dasin, too," he added recklessly.

Dasin's expression went thin and strained; he cut a sharp sideways glance at Venepe. The portly merchant stood still, squinting at Tank with a newly sharp appraisal.

"I don't hire fools," Venepe said.

"If you don't hire fools," Tank said promptly, "then I'm a good match."

Why the hells am I doing this? he thought. *I'm jumping right in as though it's what I want to do.* But Dasin had thrown down a challenge, and Venepe had taken it right up, and the words came tumbling out of Tank's mouth as though of their own accord.

"And it's two full silver rounds a day along the Coast Road, five through the Forest," he said before Venepe could answer.

"One and four," Venepe said. "We supply the horse."

"Done." *Damnit,* he added to himself, abruptly wishing he could wipe clean the last few moments of conversation.

Venepe nodded. For a moment, he looked amused; then he soured back to business. "We leave tomorrow morning. Before sunrise. Dasin, take him over to the Bowse stables–*today.* Get his horse sorted out with our lot so we have time to see it's healthy before we go on the road. I don't trust that man far as I could heave one of his horses–so *don't* let Harpik palm off one of his edge-of-death trockers on us again. I don't have time to argue a bad pick; your friend will have to walk if the bagabins drops out from under two steps down."

Dasin's gaze wavered. Tank would have laid a gold round that Dasin hadn't the faintest idea how to judge a horse's health or quality, but all the blond said was: "Right."

Venepe flicked a thoughtful glance from Dasin to Tank, then nodded curtly and stumped away toward the wagon.

Dasin grabbed the top rail and ducked under it with ostentatious grace. Tank didn't move to offer him a steadying hand. The blond straightened; Tank took a long look at his smug expression, glanced over to be sure Venepe was out of sight, then hauled off and hit that smirk.

The blond went sideways and down, rolled, and came up plastered in mud and semi-liquid dung–and an oddly satisfied expression. It shifted to a furious glare so quickly that Tank wondered if he'd imagined that half-second smile.

"You *worked* me," Tank said. "You godsdamned weasel. Told him how to make me jump."

"Didn't," Dasin said, sullen. He wiped gobs of muck from his face, spitting to one side, then glared at Tank again. "Not my fault you jump at every chance to fight a flea." He looked down, lifting his ruined shirt away from his body. "Godsdamned loon. I'll find you a horse that'll bite your godsdamned ear off first chance."

"You'll be lucky to pick out a horse instead of a goat," Tank retorted. "I'd have a better chance of figuring out a good–oh, no you don't," he added as Dasin's smirk returned. "You're the one was told to take me to the stables and pick a horse out for me."

"But if you know so much," Dasin said, "and you're the one due to ride it, after all." He wiped more goop from his face and grinned brightly.

Tank spat on the ground near Dasin's feet, too frustrated to produce words. He'd forgotten how *good* Dasin was at getting what he wanted.

Dasin pointed with a muddy hand. "Stables are up that way and to the right," he said. "*I'm* going to the bathhouse down *this* way, and *you're* paying me back for the fee. *And* for them cleaning my clothes." He paused and offered a sly grin. "You could come along," he added.

"No," Tank said, very definitely. "And you pay your own fees and call it lucky I stopped with one, instead of burying you in the mud."

"Still got that temper," Dasin said. "Thought Allonin was supposed to train that out of you."

Dasin had no idea what their training had really been about, then; and Tank wasn't about to tell him. He held words back for a long breath, to be sure he had control of them, then said, pointedly, "I stopped. Want to see if I'll stop a second time?"

Violence is not always the answer, Teilo said in precarious memory, her milky-white eyes staring through him, flesh to bone to soul. *Are you going to fight everything you come across? Can you battle a nightmare, can you punch the ghosts of your past? You have to learn when to stop, Tanavin. You have to learn to think; you have to learn to lose once in a while, in order to win.*

Dasin's accusation echoed that: *jump at every chance to fight a flea.*

"Loon," Dasin said, smirking again, and turned away.

The hells with losing to win. Dasin would take a pebble and turn it into a mountain, given half a chance.

And Tank did have something to do while Dasin was cleaning up, something that would nag him unless he handled it before leaving Bright Bay again.

"Dasin," Tank said. The blond paused, looking back over his shoulder. "I'm not doing your job for you. Get yourself a bath and meet me at the stables." Tank glanced at the sky. "Second bells just went, so be there by fourth."

Dasin turned fully around, protesting, "That's not enough time—"

"Time enough for a *bath,*" Tank said, and stared him down.

The blond's narrow face creased into sullen lines. "Don't know why I wanted you along in the first place," he muttered.

"Neither do I," Tank said, "but you've got me. Stables. Fourth bell. Move."

Dasin spat on the ground and swaggered away, head high, back stiff.

Tank let out a long breath, watching him go; shook his head and turned to find Venepe standing by the cart, narrow-eyed and thoughtful. The merchant met Tank's glance, nodding slowly. Tank nodded back and turned away, picking his way through the mud, headed towards the southeastern part of town.

Chapter Fifteen

Idisio woke to find Riss sitting on the edge of his bed, looking down at him. Instinct brought him up and scooting back to put room between them. For a moment, her eyes seemed to carry a hazy overlay of greenish-gold; then that faded, and she smiled with something close to amusement.

"Time to wake up," she said.

She'd lit a green-oil lamp. The flickering light subtly darkened the planes of her face. Studying her with a new intensity, spooked by that flash of odd color in her eyes, Idisio noticed that she seemed to have lost weight in spite of her pregnancy. With her pale hair bound loosely back, dressed in ordinary drab, she reminded Idisio of the bedraggled stablehand she'd been when they'd first met.

A sudden ache wound through his chest, spreading throughout his body.

"Riss," he said, "you're beautiful." He couldn't remember if he'd ever said that to her before; certainly not with such sincerity.

Her gaze shifted aside a bit, her jaw tightening. She seemed about to say something, then glanced toward the door and shook her head a little.

"I'll be fine, Idisio," she said, and stood. "Get dressed. I already took care of your pack."

She studied his face for a moment, then turned away and left the room without looking back. Idisio watched her go, more than a little bewildered; had she been expecting him to say something? Was he supposed to call her back, or chase after her? Before he could decide, the door shut behind her. He felt her moving away, deeper into the fortress, away from the front gates.

So she had no intentions of saying a formal goodbye. He took in a deep draft of air and felt his chest loosen with relief as he let his breath out. No soppiness or last-minute tears; just *I'll be fine, get dressed.*

He reached for his clothes, his smile turning into a wide grin, and firmly dismissed that one unsettling flash of green-gold in her eyes as an illusion caused by waking too abruptly.

Alyea and Lord Evkit quietly sipped tea as the teyanain camp finished packing up. Deiq stood some distance away with his eyes closed, breathing evenly, apparently deep in some thought or memory. Idisio stood beside him, smiling like a newborn fool. He couldn't remember ever having been happier. For all that the travel arrangements clearly weren't to Deiq's liking, and Lord Evkit himself scared the breath out of Idisio with every glance, there was something irresistible about the notion of traveling again. He wanted to learn more, see more of a world that was turning out to be far more complex than he'd ever suspected possible; and he'd be doing it as someone with *status*, not a scrabbling, desperate street-thief.

He couldn't help wondering what teyanain kathain would be like. He cast a guilty glance back at the walls of Scratha Fortress, as though Riss could hear the thought; but he had a feeling that her curt farewell had been tacit admission that their relationship was, in essence, over. Deiq had been right: Riss had known all along it wouldn't last. She simply hadn't wanted to admit it.

Alyea and Lord Evkit stood and bowed to one another gravely. Servants took the tea cups, wiped them clean, and packed them away in a few swift movements. The teyanain began to assemble into a traveling formation around their guests; everyone stood still, although Idisio could hear the servants shifting about restlessly. Instinct told him dropping into an aqeyva trance was the right thing to do.

A faint pressure swirled around his body, and the three athain–Deiq had said the term meant *teyanin spirit-walker*–began to glow, as though lit from within. The glow dispersed into a cloud of green and silver speckles that flowed over their bodies and sparkled in their odd, triple-split braids for a few moments before dissolving. Idisio shut his eyes, submerging his unease; Deiq wasn't protesting, so this must all be normal.

A broad pressure settled all along his limbs, like vast hands closing gently around each of his arms and legs, but he could tell nobody had actually touched him. The pressure increased, tugging, as though urging him into motion; he allowed the direction, again, only because Deiq wasn't protesting. After a few shambling strides, he opened his eyes.

The land whipped by as though he were engaged in a full sprint, rather than an apparently casual amble. He blinked, moving only his eyes at first, and wondered why this didn't scare him. A few scant weeks ago it would have had him howling in terror and quite probably losing control of his bladder;

but now it was just one more strange thing on the stack.

More fascinating than strange, actually. He let his consciousness sink into the experience, weighing his physical stride against how quickly the world went by; discovering he could still see clearly, straight ahead, but the side views were slightly blurred. The pressure against his limbs never changed, and he could feel the scrape of sand and an occasional rock beneath his feet.

After what seemed a short time, the compulsion eased. They slowed, the land to either side coming into steadily clearer focus, then, finally stopped altogether. The land rearranged itself into solid stillness around him.

Deiq and Alyea dropped to their knees, panting as though they'd run the entire way without help. Idisio stared, bemused and a little worried; *he* felt fine. He glanced around at the teyanain, but they were already going about the tasks of setting up camp and didn't even look his way.

"I take care of them," Lord Evkit said with grave courtesy, and handed Idisio a waterskin. "Sit, rest, drink. I handle this."

Idisio sat down, finally feeling a dull ache lacing through his legs and back. He sipped surprisingly cool water while Evkit tended to Deiq and Alyea.

At last, Deiq climbed unsteadily to his feet, and Alyea allowed Lord Evkit to help her up. The difference in their heights made the moment strangely amusing. It was rather like watching a child trying help an adult to her feet.

Evkit turned his head and met Idisio's eyes, his expression flat and dangerous. Idisio bit his tongue and hastily looked away, making a tiny gesture of apology with one hand.

Deiq snorted softly and steered Alyea towards the center of the forming camp.

"He is tired," Evkit said, watching them go. "He is dangerous, tired." He slanted a sharp glance at Idisio. "Ha'ra'hain always dangerous when exhausted. You too, ha'inn. You rest. You sleep. Give him wide circle. Room. Yes?"

"Yes," Idisio said.

Evkit nodded, seeming satisfied, and followed Deiq and Alyea into the camp.

Give him room. Dangerous when exhausted. But Idisio had been worn out and exhausted any number of times over the years, and nothing had—

*Red hair tangled with black—the smoky fug of a dangerous tavern—*redling, *some-one said with a wagonload of contempt in their tone, and swampy mud splattered nearby—*

Idisio staggered sideways, dizzy; caught his balance and straightened, breathing hard.

"Just tired," he muttered to himself, and forced the panic quiet. "Just tired."

The rounded tents the teyanain called *shalls* were already popping up around the fire pit. He walked into the camp, a little stiff-legged to keep his knees from buckling. Evkit caught his eye and pointed him towards one of the *shalls.*

"Thanks," he muttered, barely aware of the frowning glance Deiq aimed his way. A shiver worked through his body; he dropped his pack to the ground beside the *shall* and crawled inside with only a vague wave of one hand to the elder ha'ra'ha.

A faint pressure passed across the back of his skull: Deiq checking on him.

It eased a moment later, and the elder ha'ra'ha said, indulgent, *Get some sleep. It was a long day.* He sounded smug about something. Almost inaudible under his words ran others: *I may be getting old, but I have better endurance than you yet.*

Idisio rolled his eyes, bewildered and indifferent all at once, then dropped into the darkening spiral of trance-sleep without even thinking about it.

Some time later, he emerged into awareness, feeling oddly restless. He lay still in the chill darkness, listening. Deiq and Alyea's voices murmured near at hand. Teyanain shuffled about, sorting themselves out for bed. The fire popped and hissed.

He could taste the lingering aroma of dinner: something sour and fermented and oily. He thought about digging through his pack for a piece of trail jerky, but he didn't want to move, and didn't feel particularly hungry, either.

"–still scare you," Deiq said, his voice clear as though he sat next to Idisio. Alyea said something blurred in response. Idisio's breath roared in his ears.

"*I'm* not what you ought to be scared of right now," Deiq said.

A long silence. Then Alyea said, "Of all the things that–"

His own pulse thundered through Idisio's ears, drowning out any other sounds. Heat flushed through him, banishing the chill. Now it felt like a comfortable summer night, not the freezing cold of the high desert.

A lizard ran over the sand half a mile away: *skitterskitterskitter*.

"*Damnit*," Idisio muttered, curling into a ball, and stuck his fingers in his ears. He tried to ease into an aqeyva trance, but for some reason couldn't focus properly.

Somewhere in the camp, two men grunted in rough and all-too-familiar rhythm. Idisio curled tighter, his eyes squeezed painfully shut.

"They couldn't wait until they got home?" he said aloud, uncurling, and flipped over to his other side. A desert owl's passage overhead came to his ears as a hissing, feathery mumble.

Deiq eased into Idisio's growing disorientation. *Think about your breathing,* he said. Idisio felt as though a large hand closed over one of his shoulders, steadying, reassuring, and all without any of Deiq's usual cynical amusement involved. *Breathe. One breath in, one out. One breath in, one out. Breathe.*

Noises faded into irrelevance. Deiq withdrew, and Idisio followed the thread of calm into a surprisingly peaceful sleep.

Chapter Sixteen

So many *people*, so many lives, so much light–Ellemoa couldn't endure it. She was forced to skulk in shadow, to flee from the daylight she'd craved so badly, until her eyes grew strong enough to handle more than weak moonlight. The noise, the smells — after an eternity of silence and unchanging rankness, they overwhelmed ears and nose alike, and sent her whimpering into hiding, over and over. Carriages and wagons rattled through the streets at all hours of day and night. Drunks and fools sang their unsteady way along the sidewalks, pissing in the gutters, fucking like dogs in the pale night.

A pretty young flower girl, basket filled with white roses, stood at a street corner. Ellemoa stood in shadow and watched men come by, exchange coin for a bloom, and leave again. After a time she realized every man who bought a bloom went into a nearby building; emerging, some time later, with a distinct stink drifting from their clothes.

Not sex, that smell, but something earthier and more subtle. A smoky smell, a sour perspiration: drugs. The sort of drugs Kolan and many other victims had been fed to keep them docile. She'd tasted it on their breath, as they writhed in her grip; licked it up with their sweat, their tears, their blood.

The drugs had names. She remembered a few of them: *Aesa. Esthit. Dasta.* The aesa had rendered victims slow of mind and prone to laughter. She'd liked that. The esthit had made it easier to reach inside their minds and take anything she wanted; Rosin had asked her to do that often. And the dasta . . . That had made them willing to do things they would never have considered, sober.

A moment's focus pulled the information from the girl's mind: the men were going into a *hopam*, which translated, more or less, to "dream-house";

which translated further, to these stupid humans, as a place to take illegal drugs.

She'd thought all those drugs Rosin had employed were only ever used as instruments of torture. But these humans were *paying* for the chance to haze their minds and distort their physical reactions. These ordinary, free, untouched humans thought it was *pleasant.*

They had no idea how vulnerable the drugs made them. Had no idea what was watching them from the shadows, and how easily they could die—or worse—this night.

Their stupidity was *sickening.*

Rage rose, out of control in a heartbeat.

The flower girl turned, too late, her eyes widening: flung up a hand in belated protest and whined at the pain of the first blow, like a pitiable child. She was young—so young! Barely older than Ellemoa's son would be—had the girl known him? Ellemoa knelt beside the nearly unconcious girl and reached without hesitation to sort through memory. The girl's whine turned into a bubbling shriek: Ellemoa crushed her vocal cords with an irritable gesture and kept searching.

The girl's mind was hazed with a lifetime of fear and pain and despair, her recall blunted by the many drugs she herself had taken over the years. If she had seen Ellemoa's son, it didn't stand out among the blurred and greyed threads of a useless life.

One memory came through: *My son. I lost my son.* She'd had a child herself, a son—and something had happened: a moment of carelessness, or unluck, or black fate. It didn't come clear whether the drug use had been part of the moment. It didn't matter. She was a mother. She'd lost her son.

Just like me.

But the girl was dying, bubbling breath by bubbling breath: Ellemoa couldn't reverse the damage done. Not, on consideration, that she particularly wanted to. Having a son didn't make one exempt from consequence: the girl had chosen to walk into a trade that caused irreparable stupidity among humankind. She'd chosen to use the drugs herself, to block out memory and absolve herself of responsibility for the death of her child.

Not like me at all. I won't ever forget, Ellemoa thought as she absently tucked the girl's body into a more compact bundle and covered it with a cloak to hide it from casual passerby. *I won't hide from the responsibility of taking care of my son. I won't make that mistake.*

As she stood to leave, she saw the basket of flowers, dropped and tilted on its side in the wake of her initial attack. Something about the innocent white of the blooms set her fury raging again: it was so wrong, to use such beauty for such evil. The dappling of red across the white only highlighted the wrongness. She grabbed the basket and smashed it to bits. Puffy white blossoms rolled and tumbled in a wide arc across the dirty cobblestones.

Someone shouted, a distance away; Ellemoa faded into shadow and night instantly, without waiting to see if the shout had been aimed at her.

I won't forget, she thought as she eased clear of the area. *I'll never forget. I have to save my son. He deserves so much better than this. He deserves real beauty, not the evil falsehoods humans pass off as truth. He will get what he deserves.*

I'll make sure of that.

Chapter Seventeen

Architecturally, Bright Bay could be divided into distinct sections: the southwestern buildings were heavy block, thick-walled and wide-windowed, inviting in the sea breezes swirling from the west and south. On the eastern side, especially the southeastern, buildings had thinner walls–often wood–and fewer windows, nearly always on the west face of the building in a hopeless effort to avoid the swamp-muck stench that permeated the far eastern edge of town. The streets tended more towards mud, sand, and shell fragments than the bricks and cobblestones of the western sections.

A thin, misty drizzle began as Tank crunched along the shellrock road into the southeastern market square. The booths stood empty for the most part, whether from the earlier drenching downpour or some local holiday he wasn't sure. A scattering of stubborn holdouts huddled under colorful cloth tents, their wares raised high on sturdy benches and tables, themselves seated on stools or standing on sandy piles of shellrock that barely crested the mud in some instances.

He paused, squinting through the drizzle, trying to remember the layout; glanced around at the surrounding buildings for reference points, and finally squish-gritted over to one of the occupied booths. A lean man with murky, lank brown hair watched Tank's approach with barely masked wariness.

"Bread today, s'e?" he inquired as Tank stopped in front of his table. His gaze flickered to the hilt of the sword over Tank's shoulder. "Fresh rolls, baked this morning." He drew back the corner of a thick cloth to show seven roughly circular lumps of bread beneath. "Best in the city." He didn't sound particularly convinced, himself.

Tank cleared his throat. "Was there . . . a woman, not long ago? Running this table? An older woman. A little on the stout side."

The man's face went cold as the drizzling rain. "My mother," he said. "Gone."

Tank didn't ask how; the vendor's expression said it all.

"I'm sorry," he said awkwardly. "I wanted to thank her. She was kind to me, once, and it meant a lot. I wanted to pay her back." He fumbled in his belt pouch and withdrew a half-silver piece, his hand shaking.

The vendor shook his head and waved the coin away. "That's what got her gone," he said, bitterness pervading his tone. "*Kindness.* She got gutted for helping some damn fool hide from the guards. Two days before Ninnic went out. Two *days.*"

Even though Tank knew it hadn't been his fault–she hadn't helped him hide, only given him a piece of bread–sour guilt over the timing raked through his stomach. *Two days.* Maybe scant hours after he'd seen her.

He wondered who she'd given her life to help: street thief or escaping nobleman.

"I'm sorry," he said again. "I'm sorry."

The vendor drew the cloth back over the bread and regarded Tank with a flat, unforgiving stare.

Tank laid the silver half-round down on the table and retreated. The man made no move to pick it up. His glare burned along the back of Tank's neck the whole way out of the market.

"Ssss," someone said as Tank cleared the perimeter of the market. He looked to his right and found the street-rat he'd met earlier in the day watching him. Her hair, slick with moisture, might have been a dark blonde or a light brown; the drizzle cut muddy trails through her skin.

"Ssss," he said back, a little wearily. "What now?"

She stared at him for another moment, then pointed back into the market. He followed the path of her finger and saw a form huddled beneath one of the tables, so still and grey that he'd walked past without a second glance. Not dead; the shoulders moved in restless sleep.

Tank looked back at the street-rat, frowning, puzzled; but she was gone. Of course. He hesitated, scanning the area for potential ambush, then shook his head and walked a few steps back towards the huddled figure.

Closer, a random branch beside the sleeper clarified into a heavy walking-stick. Tank's stomach sank in sudden suspicion, and he turned to glare back into the mist.

"Who the hells *are* you?" he said out loud, suspecting that she'd hear him, and received only silence by way of an answer.

The sound of his voice roused the figure from sleep. It rolled and shoved upright, very nearly catching its head against the underside of the table. The rough blanket fell away to reveal a face once broad and strong, now pinched and pale; the boy stared at Tank for a long moment without recognition.

Tank backed up a step. *Sorry* choked in his throat this time, for multiple reasons.

"You," the boy said at last. "*You.*" The word was a curse.

"Blackie. . . ." Tank drew a breath, trying to bring out more words; failed, turned, and fled.

He slowed to a walk after less than a block, breathing hard, but kept his pace rapid, his head bent, his shoulders hunched in a ferociously defensive posture. Nobody stopped him. People moved well clear of him, allowing him the straight-line path.

After another block he stopped, glaring at the ground. A splash of pale color caught his eye: a white rose, wilted and ragged, heavily flecked with brown, lay tucked up against a nearby building. He stared at it for a moment, oddly uneasy, then turned, examining the area with care. A few people hurried by, cloaks drawn tight and hoods up against the rain. Nobody spared him a second glance.

He found his gaze drawn to the building the rose lay against. A recessed doorway, three steps up from the street; shuttered windows; no sign or decoration announcing whether it was a home or a business. The hair rose on the back of his neck, and he looked around again, nostrils flaring as though scent might catch the source of his unease. Only the smell of damp, muddy stone came back to him. He glanced down, realizing for the first time that this particular street boasted actual cobblestones, not dirt and sand. That meant wealth, although every building he could see was starkly plain.

He found himself looking back at the rose, and a shiver ran down his spine.

Intuition said, as in the bar: *Get out of here.* He resisted this time, turning in place, and focused with more care on the various shades of grey and brown surrounding him. His attention snagged on a patch that wasn't–quite–right. Squinting a little, he made out a grey heap, much like the sleeper in the market square, tucked up under a stand of drooping featherleaf bushes at one corner of the shuttered building.

He swallowed back prescient nausea and edged forward. Squatting beside the bushes, he could see that the lumps beneath the brownish-grey cloak bore no resemblance to a sleeping human form.

Faint pink rivulets threaded through the puddle of water around the cloak. The tip of a black shoe protruded in one spot. The heel of another, or perhaps the end of a bone, tented the cloak at an impossible angle.

No intact human form, other than that of a child, could have fit beneath the cloak; and the visible shoe was too large for a child.

Tank stood and backed away without bothering to lift the blanket. He swallowed hard, looking around, every sense bristling at full alert: Nothing. Whatever had happened here was over. Whatever had done this was gone.

He yielded to the imperative prod of intuition, all the same, and got the hells out of there without further delay.

Chapter Eighteen

A fine drizzle muted the smells of the caravan yard, but failed to entirely wash them from the air. Kolan didn't mind. He'd smelled worse, over the years, and at least there was fresh air moving against his face, and rain from the sky, not the dank condensation of the catacombs.

He found the carriages-for-hire paddock and paused by the gate, watching men and horses swear at one another. After a while it occurred to him that he was hearing the men swear at the horses, which was unremarkable, but he was also hearing the horses curse back, which seemed a bit odd. And the men didn't seem to notice the barrage of irritable complaints: *Watch it, there,* said an elderly grey mare, turning her head and flicking long ears as a man tightened the straps of her harness. *That's tight enough, you hoofless gelding!*

The man paid no heed, yanking the strap another notch in with a grunt. The grey mare stepped back and sideways and kicked, all at once; straps broke and tangled into a hopeless mess. Then the mare stood still, placid once more, her tail twitching in what Kolan read as vivid amusement.

Fix that, you lice-ridden worm, she snorted.

"Stupid whorebag rackrib," the man swore, picking himself up, and swatted the mare on the rump. She turned her head and stared at him with large, mild eyes, to all appearances unmoved; but Kolan heard her laughing.

The mare lifted her head and looked directly at Kolan then, and her eyelids slid down in a slow blink. No–a horse wink.

This is the only outgoing carriage today, she said, one ear swiveling. *The others are already reserved or gone. You'll have to wait a bit, until they find a driver with sense. I'm too old to put up with fools.*

"I see," Kolan murmured. "Well, thank you." He bowed, prompting a strange look from a few people and a tail-twitch burst of laughter from the mare.

Perhaps he could get a ride with one of the caravans, instead. He wandered through the rows of paddocks for the rich merchants and the picket lines of the less-wealthy, looking for someone who felt honest, or at least reasonably reliable. He paused by one paddock, watching a skinny blond boy arguing with a plump merchant, then went on without calling out: the man radiated a slick green sourness, and the boy was laced with the black lines that led to the place of screaming. Neither one would be safe companions for him. He wondered, idly, how they'd get along on the road.

After an hour of wandering through the caravan yard, he sighed, accepting the inevitable, and asked directions to the northeastern gates of the city.

The marshes between Bright Bay and Kybeach emitted a rotting stench far too similar to that of the catacombs. Kybeach itself was little more than an arc of ill-built houses slouching in sullen heaps, their backs to the marshes as their inhabitants turned away from outsiders.

Kolan stood at the edge of the village, looking it over under the pale light of a dying moon–the Healer's Moon, he thought, accepting the knowledge as calmly as he had that of hearing a horse speak.

Stranger things were possible. He'd seen them. He'd done a few of them. *But never for Rosin. Never for that monster. I can be proud of that, at least. Ellemoa broke. I didn't. Can I be proud of that?*

He looked down at his hands, rubbed them together, then walked unhurriedly into the quiet village. The shadows seemed oddly sharp and dark for a waning moon.

"What's that? What's that?" someone croaked nearby. A hooded lantern clattered open; light spilled out, washing over Kolan like pale sunshine. An elderly man hobbled forward a step, squinting, sneering. "No time to come in daylight like an honest man, eh?" he demanded.

Kolan stared at him.

The elderly man stared back, uneasy now, then pushed forward a step. "Off with you, beggar," he snapped, "or I'll roust the town for a thief-hanging. On through, now, we don't want your kind here, day or night!"

"I'm not a beggar," Kolan said mildly. "I'm a priest."

The elderly man recoiled several steps, his face twisting. "The Northern Church is gone," he said. "Gone! All above the line of the Hackerwood, now, all but the swamp priests. You're coming from Bright Bay and expect me to believe you're a priest? No, no, there are no more priests coming from there. Not anymore."

Kolan blinked, surprised only that he wasn't surprised. "All the same," he said, "I'm a priest. Not a thief. Not a beggar."

"Ah, well, you'd say that," the old man said. He moved a step forward, thrusting the lantern ahead of him, studying Kolan's face with nearly manic intensity.

Something moved nearby; Kolan squinted, trying to see past the glare of the lantern.

"What's that?" The old man backed up and half-turned, peering at the motion, then made a disgusted sound.

The figure ambled closer, staggering a little every few steps: the sour, sweaty reek of too much hard liquor preceded it. The watchman made the disgusted sound again as a blond man stepped into the circle of lantern light. The drunk's face was as sallow and shadowed as one of the *others* at the beginning of a fit; Kolan stood very still, watching with care.

"Lashnar, be off to bed!" the watchman said sharply. "All respect, *s'e*, you're in no state. Go home to bed!"

The blond man stared at Kolan, ignoring the old watchman entirely.

"Who are you?" he demanded. "You can't have her. She's not here anymore. She's dead. Go away!"

"He's going," the watchman said. "He's *going*." He shot Kolan a fierce glare.

Kolan studied the blond man, assessing his temper, then said, "It's very late, *s'es*. I'd like to rest. Is there an inn here?"

"No rooms left," the old man said severely.

The blond man staggered a step sideways. "Outsiders," he said. "It's always the damned outsiders that bring the trouble. Well, I've nothing left, d'ya hear? Nothing at all! Not even my daughter! All because of you!"

He lunged forward. Kolan stood still; backing up would only make the man more aggressive.

"Lashnar!" the watchman said shrilly, retreating several steps. "Leave off!"

The blond man's hands closed around Kolan's neck, but loosely. Nearly nose to nose now, Kolan could read in the man's face that he'd expected Kolan to fight back and was uncertain how to handle the lack of response.

The touch sparked a wave of *other* memory; Kolan reflexively shifted the flow over to an outer loop and bled it off into the ground, unwilling to see anything this man had gone through. He couldn't remember: had Ellemoa taught him that trick, long ago in Arason, or had he picked it up during their captivity?

I wish I'd known I could do this sooner, he thought. *But then Rosin would have known, too, so it's just as well.*

The blond man staggered back, gagging. His skin went a pasty white, and his eyes seemed apt to go larger than his face as he stared at Kolan.

"You're a witch," he said. "A witch and a demon." His hands came up in the sign against evil: crossed at the wrists, fingers splayed out, thumbs curved forward.

Kolan blinked, surprised: had the light physical contact been enough to show the man his memories? Best he stay away from human company, if he was that open at the moment.

The watchman crowded between them, hissing at Kolan.

"You'd best be off," he snapped. "Merchant Lashnar needs his sleep. You get clear, you hear me, or I'll see you strung up as a thief and a witch before dawn."

Kolan shrugged and began walking.

"Not that way! Road runs east."

Kolan paused and pointed. "There's a road there." A silvery trail, little more than a footpath, really, ran ahead of him. It felt more interesting, more peaceful, than the prospect of walking the eastern road through the dark and hostile streets of Kybeach. "Where does that go?"

"Road runs east," the old man repeated stubbornly. "That way only goes to the witch's place. You've no business there, priest or thief; she'll take you apart no matter what you be."

Kolan looked at the slender path and smiled. "I doubt she's a witch, watchman," he said. "There's no such thing as witches."

There were only ha'ra'hain, and a female ha'ra'ha this close to Bright Bay– it *could* be Ellemoa. She *could* have escaped, and be trying to start over. He wanted that to be true. It was worth walking a little way to find out.

And if it wasn't Ellemoa, but another ha'ra'ha–well, it couldn't do anything to him that hadn't already been done. There was no reason to be afraid. More than likely it was merely a wise-woman who'd been unfairly persecuted by the ignorant villagers, and she'd be glad of some uncritical company, whether middle of the night or center of the day.

"Shows all you know," the old man snorted. "Witches all *around* us."

"*He's* a witch," the blond man said with idiot persistence.

Kolan turned and said, "If it takes me away from your village–"

"Town!" the old man interrupted, scowling ferociously.

"Village," the blond man muttered. "Stinking little pissass–"

The watchman elbowed him quiet.

"–what do you care which way I go?" Kolan went on. "I'll be gone, one path or another."

The watchman shook all over with what might have been fury or fear, but neither man had any answer to that; and Kolan, very quietly, very definitely, walked away down the path to the witch's house.

Chapter Nineteen

As the teyanain camp rose and readied themselves for the next leg of their trip across the desert, Deiq's mood turned sour. He barely glanced at anyone, and when Idisio risked a quiet "Thank you—for last night—for helping me sleep," he received only a brooding glare. He retreated hastily. The similarities between Deiq and Lord Scratha were uncanny at times, and while Scratha had been apt to knock Idisio into a wall when peeved over something, Deiq would probably do real damage.

A moment after retreating, Idisio found himself deeply irritated at that reaction. Deiq and Scratha were entirely different, and Idisio himself was no longer a street thief trying to avoid notice. He had status now. He had capabilities he'd never expected: popping open locks and hearing people's thoughts was apparently the least of it. *I need to stop backing down all the damn time. I can stand up—even to Deiq.* Fear shivered along his spine at the thought.

To distract and test himself, Idisio decided he would try to figure out how the teyanain managed the traveling-trick. A heartbeat later, Evkit turned his head and stared directly at him, eyes black as night and expression cold as midnight-chilled stone.

"You no do," Evkit said. He blinked once, lizardlike, then looked away again.

Idisio's breath caught in his chest. Deiq prodded him ungently in the shoulder and motioned him into the middle of the forming group.

Deiq said sharply, *You don't even* look *at the athain for too long, let alone try to figure out what they're doing or how.*

"How was I supposed to know that?" Idisio muttered.

"Because you're supposed to have some godsdamned *wits*," Deiq shot back in a low voice, and for all his plans to push back next time Deiq snapped at him, Idisio couldn't make himself answer that with anything but silence.

They blurred into that odd other-place before Idisio had fully let go of his annoyance with Deiq's irritability; but again, the intricacies of the moment caught him out of any other thoughts, and the day seemed to pass in mere breaths. As they slowed and stepped out of the haze, Idisio felt Deiq's sour mood, which had been a constant pinch against his mind the entire day, click over into something even darker and less controllable.

Ruins lay all around them, a grand city long since dead. Fantastic arches towered, worn but intact, with remnants of red and white stripes. Idisio could very nearly see what they'd looked like fresh–

"*Idisio.*" Deiq glared, blackly ominous. Idisio stopped gawking and tried to think about something else, not sure why Deiq was aggravated but understanding a clear danger sign when he heard it.

There was a *whispering* in the air . . . a dry, long-dead whisper that raised the hair on the back of Idisio's neck. By Deiq's expression, he heard it too. The elder ha'ra'ha directed another brief glare and bare head-shake at Idisio, as though warning him not to remark on the sound.

Idisio nodded, although he hadn't actually intended to say a word. A few moments later, Deiq stalked away from the group. Alyea stared after him, expression bewildered and a little hurt.

Keep her away from me, Deiq said bleakly. *Keep them all away from me.*

Alyea took a hesitant step. Idisio said hastily, "I'll go with him."

Her expression shifted to one of distinct relief. Idisio excused himself and followed Deiq around to the other side of a crumbled section of wall, out of direct line of sight from the campsite.

Deiq sat on a chunk of ancient rock and stared out across the ruins. "I don't want to talk to you, either," he said.

"So don't," Idisio shot back. Deiq shook his head and made no answer, which was as good as an apology, to Idisio's way of thinking.

He perched on another section of wall and looked around. The last wisps of brilliant orange and silver bands stained the lowest edges of the darkening western sky, limning a scattering of thin clouds. Around them stood the ruins of what must have once been a magnificent building. Some of the tall striped arches endured, as did jagged fragments of walls and floor.

Deiq leaned forward and picked up a hand-sized chunk of black stone, turning it over restlessly as he went back to staring at nothing in particular.

Idisio let the silence rest. He didn't really have anything to say. He reflected that given how adamant Deiq was about telling him not to brood, he did rather a lot of it himself.

Not looking up, Deiq said, tone grating, "That's because I know how to do it without shouting all over the godsdamn desert. You don't."

"So *teach* me."

Deiq shook his head slowly. "Not now," he said, tone muted. "Not . . . not here. Later. I can't . . . I can't concentrate right now." He raised his head and stared off across the darkening ruins, his expression pained and bleak.

"Then don't scold me for doing my best." Idisio stood, then squatted to pick up a smaller piece of the same black stone Deiq held. Sitting back down on the wall, he studied it curiously, rubbing a thumb over the smooth side.

Water, cast from the air, flowing over the stone; the harsh chanting of centuries: moondeath ceremonies, birthing rituals, full moon ceremonies, god rites, manhood ceremonies, all soaking into the very air, seeping into the stone, kept alive with water, water, water . . . .

Idisio blinked hard and dropped the stone, shuddering. He rubbed his hands together hard, trying to dispel the feeling of ancient memory slicking his fingers. Deiq glanced sideways at him, mouth twitching into a sour grimace, and said, "I'd advise against picking up any more rock."

But Deiq kept turning the piece in *his* hands over, apparently not in the least discomfited.

Idisio rubbed his hands against his pants legs, trying not to shudder; looked up at the sky, and found himself dreading the arrival of another moonless desert night.

"Moondeath," Deiq muttered, as though following Idisio's thoughts. "There would have been ceremonies . . . ." He fell silent again, staring at the black stone cradled in his palms.

"What ceremonies?"

"Depends on the moon. Right now is the Healer's Moon. Most of the old names carried over after the Split . . . The death of the Healer's Moon is a dangerous time. It's a time when injuries rot without hesitation, and minor ailments turn deadly in hours. It's a time to stay indoors and stay safe, a time to keep the fire lit all the night long and prayers going dawn to dawn to dawn to dawn . . . ." He sighed and set the piece of rock down slowly. "That's what they believed then, anyway. And many places in the south still honor that tradition and follow that belief."

"Is it true?" Idisio said, and set his jaw against Deiq's dry stare.

Deiq looked away, one shoulder lifting briefly. "That wounds rot faster? I doubt it, any more than they heal cleaner under the full Healer's Moon. But belief and willpower can accomplish strange things, even for tharr. I don't discount the stories out of hand."

He fell back into his brooding silence. After a while, he went on.

"Be careful what you touch. What you pay attention to. You're starting to hear and see the world beyond what humans perceive. A lot of it isn't pleasant. Stay away from people who get angry easily, like Cafad Scratha. Stay away from highly emotional people. They're dangerous. They'll overwhelm you. You're too young. You'll get swept up in their emotional storms and lose sight of yourself. If you're lucky." He paused, frowning at the rock in his hands, then, with a sigh, tossed it to the ground. "If you're unlucky," he added, "you'll lose your own temper and kill them before you know what you're doing."

Idisio gaped. The notion that he might raise a hand in violence, let alone kill someone, was beyond absurd. *I'm not like that. I couldn't hurt anyone! Deiq's different, he's older, he was raised differently—*

"We're not that different," Deiq said. "Not nearly, Idisio. You're ha'ra'hain. You'll start to see what that means soon enough. We have to talk—about a lot of things—but not with teyanain within earshot. And damn well not *here*." He stood and stretched. "Go back to camp. I have to go pull Alyea out of another of Evkit's damn games, and I don't need you shouting all over the sky, distracting me."

He stalked off into the gathering gloom.

Idisio sat still, annoyance rising fast. Shout all over the sky, did he? *I can be quiet. I'm good at being quiet. I bet I can follow Deiq and he'll never know. He's not so superior and all-powerful, and I don't have to be so afraid of him. What's the worst thing he can do? He's supposed to be my teacher. That means he can't really hurt me.*

He slipped from the wall and prowled off into the dark.

Chapter Twenty

Chich tasted like stale goat jerky mixed with the fieriest of the southern spices. Tank hated it, but the alternative was far worse. He chewed and spat, chewed and spat, until nothing was left but a stringy pulp, then spat that off to one side and swilled water round his mouth until the painful acidity dimmed to a muddy sourness.

The tremors gradually left his hands, and he leaned his head against the back wall of the stable, breathing deeply. The chill drizzle had eased again, sun squinting out from behind thinning clouds. Dasin squatted a few feet away, drawing careless patterns in the damp sandy ground.

"Still that bad," Dasin said without looking up. "Thought Teilo took care of that."

Tank shook his head, wishing Dasin hadn't been around to see the fit. At least it had been a mild one, and he'd caught it in time; it had only been the shakes and the fear.

"She said I'd never get rid of it totally," he said. "They started me too young." He shut his eyes, then rolled his head in a deep stretch and straightened away from the support of the wall. "Let's go get that horse."

"Think she was telling the truth?" Dasin said as he stood up.

"Wouldn't be her first lie," Tank said sourly.

"You think she knew how to get you totally clear of the addiction and didn't?"

Tank paused, studying Dasin with abrupt wariness. This was edging into areas he didn't want to talk about, with Dasin or anyone. Dasin met his gaze with guileless ease, pale eyes wide and innocent.

"She's just an old witch-healer," he said finally. "I don't think she knows more than mixing herb pastes and powders together. She probably didn't know the first thing about how to handle a dasta addiction."

Dasin's eyebrows went up, then slanted sharply down. "Tank—"

"Horse," Tank interrupted, and walked away without looking back.

Dasin swore and caught up in a few loping strides. "What set it off this time?" he asked as they rounded the corner of the stable. "You said once the fits are like echoes. What happened?"

Tank shook his head. "Horse," he said.

Dasin swatted his shoulder, hard. Tank cocked a fist; Dasin fell back a few paces, hands up defensively.

"Hammer to a flea, Tank," he said. "Come on."

Tank let his hand drop. "Leave it, then," he said. "Let's get the godsdamn horse and get back to the caravan yard before it gets dark."

Dasin shrugged and followed him into the stable without further comment.

The only choices, as it turned out, were a dapple-grey mare and a sway-backed black gelding. Tank looked them over carefully and decided the mare seemed to have more spirit and probably stamina, although he had a feeling she was older than the gelding by some years.

Harpik, a balding, lanky man with a sunburnt face and arms, nodded fervent approval of the choice.

"You oughter be able ter handle her," he said. "She's trained for carriage, but she'll hold for saddle fine. On'y come in a day or two ago an' already bit two of my boys. Damn near kicked my knee out once." He stared into the stall, brooding. "You tell Venepe I warned you. You tell him I ain't takin' this un back. I'll never get rid of her twice. Never oughter of traded for her in the first place, but I owed the carriage folk a favor, and they couldn't put up with a biting puller. They'd had enough, and by now, so've I. Naa, never mind. Go on—I'll even throw in a bridle and saddle, just to get her outa here." He pointed to the hook beside the stall, on which hung the former, and a saddle-tree underneath that, which held the latter.

"Tack ought to come with it," Dasin said sharply. "Venepe said—"

"Tack *is* coming with her," Harpik said. "That bridle, an' that saddle." He crossed his arms and glared, as though daring them to argue it further.

The grey mare stared at them, eyes drooping as though half-asleep.

Tank exchanged a glance with Dasin, who shrugged as though to say: *Your decision.*

"All right," Tank said.

"I'll wait out here," Dasin said, propping himself against a hay bale, "and watch you get chewed up."

Harpik leaned beside him, grinning dourly. "Oughter be a good show," he said, "an' now you took her, you got the problem of getting her outa my stables. I give you an hour, then I start charging you stabling fees." He spat to one side.

Tank lifted the worn bridle from the hook by the stall door, ran hands and gaze over it briefly, then shook his head. "There's a snarl on the bit," he said, turning. "Look–" He held out the bridle, pointing at the spot where something had scraped the metal to a raw, curvy point near the cheek. "Get a rasp and smooth it down, or get me another bridle. This one's shit anyway, damn near powder in spots."

He fielded Harpik's amused glare until the man shoved upright, snatched the bridle, and stalked away.

Dasin sighed noisily. "*Manners*, Tank," he said. "Couldn't you have put that a bit more nicely?"

"No," Tank said. "Not really." He examined the saddle, frowning, and decided it would do; worn, but serviceable, and the blanket beneath retained a fair bit of padding, although it would need to be replaced soon. For free, he couldn't ask for much more, and he didn't have but a handful of silver coins left between now and Venepe's first payoff.

Harpik returned with a newer bridle and handed it to Tank with exaggerated care, then leaned against the hay bales once more, grinning.

"Go on, then," he invited, waving at the stall door. "See how you do."

Tank didn't move. He looked over the bridle, felt across the bit, and glanced at the grey mare, frowning. For all that Allonin hadn't really explained much about horses other than how not to fall off of one, something felt wrong about the bridle in his hands. He ran his hands over the bit again, measured it with his fingers, looked at the mare's jaw.

"No," he said at last. "No, this isn't the right one for her. Get me something–something nicer." He didn't know the right terms, but there was something too harsh and sharp about the bit in his hand.

"*Nicer*? Boy, you're talking about a horse as *bites*. You want to be *nice* to her?" Harpik spat again. "And that's all I have in the value to give away, besides. Next one's a silver round."

Tank dug out a coin and flipped it and the bridle at Harpik without comment.

"Nicer," he said flatly. "And a lead-halter."

Harpik caught both bridle and coin, glared without any humor at all this time, and stalked off.

"Should have taken the black," Dasin muttered.

"Done is done," Tank said, not taking his gaze from the mare. She turned around, majestically slow, and lifted her tail. The hot, grassy stench of fresh manure filled the air.

Dasin coughed and put an arm across his mouth and nose, then sneezed violently. "Just take the next bridle and let's get out of here," he said. "*Please.*"

"Long as it's a good one," Tank said, crossing his arms.

It was, or at least felt more right than the last two, and the halter was nearly new. Tank handed the bridle to Dasin.

"No need for this right now," he said, ignoring Harpik's exasperated snort. "I'm not riding her back. This can wait."

"What are you going to do about the saddle?" Dasin demanded. "You don't think *I'm* carrying the damn thing, do you?"

Tank paused, considering, then said, "I'll put that on next."

"So why not the bridle too, and ride her?"

Tank shrugged, not sure how to answer. Holding the halter, he slipped into the stall, careful to latch it behind himself. The mare turned, ponderous and unhurried, and stared at him.

"Hey," he said, then paused, uncertain again. Allonin had made sure he understood the basics of tack, but it had been a while, and the horse hadn't been a biter.

The mare was awfully *tall,* this close. Tall, and broad-shouldered; Tank could well believe her strong enough to pull a fully loaded carriage.

Harpik snorted. "You're going to *talk* to her first? Gods. Try to bleed on the sawdust, not the boards."

Tank ignored him. Taking a deep breath, he put out a hand, moving slowly and watching the mare's eyes for warning signs; rested his palm against her warm, scratchy shoulder.

"Hey," he said again. "How about I get you out of here? You don't bite me, I don't bite you. How's that sound?"

Harpik laughed. Dasin let out a low, derisive snort.

Tank dropped his voice to a low murmur. "Let's make them out to be fools, hey?" he said. "Right, come on then."

He took his hand away and lifted the halter, fumbling a little as he eased it over her nose. After a moment, the mare dipped her head, allowing the crownpiece over her ears. He adjusted the fit, making sure it didn't pinch anywhere but wouldn't come off either, then looped the lead line through the jaw ring and tied it off.

She didn't bite him until he'd finished securing the saddle; and looked thoroughly surprised when, as promised, he hauled her ear down and bit her right back.

Chapter Twenty-One

Dawn flushed the sky to increasingly vibrant shades of blue and pink; Deiq's mood, by contrast, seemed not to have left the night behind just yet. His ostentatious refusal to meet Idisio's gaze spoke loudly of his continuing displeasure over being followed the night before. Idisio's satisfaction in having eavesdropped on the elder ha'ra'ha without being detected began to fade into a gnawing uneasiness: how long was Deiq going to sulk over it? Alyea was visibly unhappy over the tension, and just as visibly determined not to get in the middle.

He carefully *didn't* let himself think about that frozen moment when Deiq had seemed about to lose his temper completely . . . His assumption that Deiq wouldn't actually hurt him had been badly shaken in that instant, and he still wasn't entirely sure what he'd done to set Deiq off.

Evkit, on the other hand, seemed more cheerful than ever, as though pleased by the conflict between the ha'ra'hain. His grin widened every time he looked Idisio's way, and he strutted like a firetail bird as he declared, "Teyanain guard this city. This *ours*. We not like looters."

Idisio, looking at the ruined buildings around them, thought that the teyanain were doing a damn poor job of housekeeping. *Which is something Deiq might say*, he admitted to himself, and didn't like the recognition one bit.

Was Deiq's dark sarcasm aimed to cover the same sense of fear Idisio was feeling at the moment? Idisio had trouble believing that Deiq ever felt fear about anything.

Deiq shot him an odd, sideways stare; Idisio heard dark laughter swirl through his mind. *You're starting to understand*, Deiq said. *The face you present to the humans isn't the one you see when you close your eyes.*

"This was temple of city," Evkit said with a sweeping gesture. "The place for all to worship. Old gods, these. Before Three, before Four. Strong gods. Not nice gods." He smirked at Deiq. "Liked sacrifices."

A shiver ran down Idisio's back at that. *Sacrifices* . . . Yes, that felt right, somehow. And the victims hadn't all been animals . . . .

Idisio. Deiq's voice was nearly a slap. *Stop being so* aware *of everything. You're going to drive yourself crazy.*

Idisio grimaced and looked through the archway at the ruined floor; studied the holes in the ceiling and the empty spaces between the ribbed, arched stone walls. He saw no trace of an altar, or even an offering-ledge. The entire temple was one enormous, empty room.

He tried to imagine people moving around in this dead place: laughing, singing, playing, bringing their children to worship. He couldn't: even the visions were silent, here. The quiet was a heavy weight, squashing all coherent thought. Even the insidious, haunting whispering had stopped, but that only made the crawling anxiety worse, not better.

Why hadn't they stepped inside the temple? Everyone stood outside, staring in and talking. The hair on the back of his neck stood up. If he'd known anywhere safe to run to, he'd have been churning sand long since.

He drew a deep breath and quieted his roiling thoughts before Deiq could reprimand him again: more grateful than ever that Scratha had taught him aqeyva. Deiq nodded once, semi-approving, his mouth still tight and his attention on the temple.

The three athain knelt, each in a different archway, forming a perfect triangle. They spread their hands on the ground, bowing their heads, and as one murmured an identical chant in a language Idisio had never heard before.

So much to learn, Idisio thought, and abruptly wondered if learning a language was another ha'ra'hain trick, like lighting a lamp, that could just come in a moment's proper focus.

No, Deiq said. *Human languages are far too complicated for instant understanding. At most you'll be able to pick up a scattering of the most common words, but knowing "a", "the", "it", "he", and "she" doesn't really do you much good, does it? Never mind—they're ready.*

Before Idisio could ask "ready for what?", the athain stood, eyes shut. In perfect unison, right down to each step taken, they walked into the temple. Idisio watched, incredulous. The athain were headed right into each other,;they would collide in another step–

–and then they weren't there any longer.

Alyea yipped, startled. Idisio bit his tongue hard to stop himself from doing the same.

"I go now," Evkit said. "See, you safe. You come next, ha'ra'ha–" he nodded to Deiq. "Then you, younger, then the Lord Alyea."

Idisio didn't hear the rest of what the man said, too shaken by that order to hear anything else. *I have to do that, too? Oh, hells no. Not again!* The trip through the passage to Scratha Fortress had been unpleasant enough. He had no interest in repeating the experience.

Lord Evkit walked out into the center of the temple before Idisio could come up with a good reason to refuse, vanishing as abruptly as the athain.

You can't refuse, Deiq said. *They'll throw you through if you hesitate.*

So much for ha'ra'ha status being supreme, Idisio said sourly.

The teyanain are a special case. Come on —

Deiq squeezed Alyea's shoulder and walked into the invisible portal. Idisio glanced around at the teyanain and felt icy fear dribble down his spine at the restrained violence in their expressions. He went, praying the whole way that somehow this *thing* wouldn't work for him, and he could say, *Hey, sorry, guess I have to hoof it back—*

The floor fell out from under him. He tumbled through black cold. A spray of distorted color streaked across his vision; he saw—

—a dark, regal face, glaring with utter hatred at someone or something Idisio couldn't quite see—

—a fear of *madness*, of *un-control*, of a depthless anger and a bestiality that simmered, always simmered, just below the surface, and an irritable voice: *Why do you fight what you are? —*

—a hand lifting a jeweled dagger coated with some strange white powder, and slashing it into a hazy cloud of green and gold as though it had substance—

—a bottomless grief, a terrible, terrible fear—

—the cloud twisting, whirling, diminishing—

—*No! not again, not again, I don't want to do that again, don't want to be that again, not the madness, please, not the madness*—which sounded weirdly like a distorted cry from Deiq—

—a spray of blood that dwarfed anything Idisio had ever seen, and a *scream*—

Cold flared into dry heat. Solid ground slammed into his feet. He staggered one wide step, then felt Deiq catch his arm to keep him upright. His head still filled with the memory of that ear-wrenching scream and the distorted memories surrounding it, Idisio yanked free, afraid of conveying the bizarre images to the elder ha'ra'ha.

If Deiq saw anything, he didn't have time to comment on it. Alyea appeared, and Deiq grabbed her arm and pulled her close, as though to protect her from something.

Idisio barely had time to realize that Deiq was tensed in anticipation of an attack before a choking grit was flung directly into his face. The world turned the wrong color; sounds cut off into a thick buzz. His knees went out from under him, and everything dropped into black silence.

From black to nightmare: *Dirty walls, the smell of old sweat, rot, feces—flash of red, flash of black, flash of flash of flash of—white roses and blood—the laughter of a rich boy who thought hurting a poor boy would make him a man—laughter—laughter: You thought I wanted a whore? I could get better than you for that—and then pain—the simmering rage began to build—*

—*Only now I can do something about it, now I can kill them, now I can—but no, no, that's not right, I don't want to do that, to be that, to—not the madness, not the madness, please—*

Idisio rolled, tumbling through a mixture of memory his/not his, screaming without a sound. He smelled the tang of salt air, not the swampy touch of Bright Bay's eastern streets but a deeper, rock-laced brine—*coastal village,* someone said, and *northerns wouldn't know different anyway.*

Someone slapped him. Someone cursed.

Red hair and black–a skinny, trembling, wild-eyed fugitive, violence lacing his every twitch–and a not-his-own fear: *The voices, what are they? Why am I hearing the city whispering to me*–mixing with Idisio's fear: *Am I going mad? Have I always been mad? What do I do now? Where am I? How did I get here?*

Idisio rolled from haze into the sting of the slap and emerged into semi-awareness: a moment later, water poured into his eyes and nose, sending sparkling agony all through his body. He rolled again, pulling free, blinking vision clear, and found himself in a round stone cylinder of a room. The obvious solution for escape was to climb: but the wall defeated his attempts at purchase, and a thick grate blocked the opening far overhead.

Unprecedented claustrophobia sent him wildly searching for an exit. Deiq sat quietly, watching with bizarre calm, answering Idisio's frantic questions as though they were discussing nothing more important than a walk through town. Idisio scarcely heard the answers, but slowly the tone of Deiq's voice eased the panic.

The vision-memories of the red-haired boy faded from his mind. A moment later, a more familiar surety arose: *We won't die here. There's something else going on, something we ought to know, something Deiq ought to sense and doesn't for some reason. Just as Scratha couldn't tell when those people in Kybeach were lying to us, Deiq's missing something important–and I don't know enough to know what to look for, myself.*

The thought seemed as bizarre as his surety that Scratha wouldn't actually kill him, long ago in Bright Bay; but once more, Idisio went with it.

He drew a deep breath and sat down, leaning against the wall. He found the courage to cheek Deiq a bit by way of distracting himself, then fell into a fitful doze.

I am sorry, something said in the half-light of his almost-sleep. *I cannot help you. I cannot hold to the Law. You have to fight for yourself. You have to free yourself of this place. I am even more trapped than you are.*

Wishful dreaming, Idisio decided drowsily. Wouldn't it be nice if there was a friendly ha'rethe about, one that wanted to help? But it wasn't possible. Deiq would have known, and the ha'rethe certainly would have reached out to the elder first, not to a relatively insignificant youngster.

Significance is not the same from my perspective, the voice commented. *Your youth and your human upbringing allow you to hear me, where the elder is deaf. What he sees as your flaws are your critical strengths. Use those, honor those, respect those. Be careful of the trap of vanity and pride.*

Now, *that* all sounded like a soapy's lecture. Definitely a dream. Idisio let himself slide further into silence and calm, and the voice stopped talking. Some unknown time later, a spike of tension from Deiq brought Idisio scrambling upright before his eyes fully opened.

A previously hidden door opened, and Evkit stepped through. His bitter, sour-almond smell wafted into the room.

This time, Idisio welcomed it as the scent of freedom.

Chapter Twenty-Two

In the southeastern quarter of Bright Bay, the air hung thick with the smell of trash and rotten dead things. Still-living things moved in the darkness. El-lemoa stood still, listening, nostrils flaring: her son had been here. Had lived here. *Here*, in this filthy place–

One of the living things in the shadows came too close, knife in hand. She spun and hissed like an angry goose. The would-be mugger swore and backed away so fast he tripped over himself and fell.

She watched him crawl back to his feet, watched him sprint away, without feeling any real interest. He was insignificant.

This small, dank overhang, where an abandoned building had fallen in on itself: this mattered. She stooped and looked inside the various caves created by destroyed masonry until she found the lingering *presence* she sought.

He had slept here.

She went to her knees and crawled inside, into the darkness; turned to face the opening and sat in a huddled crouch, staring out as her son must have stared, night after night. It was a good place, a defensible place. But needing a defense meant one had enemies.

Her son had people who had tried to hurt him.

The rage came up again, and the dark place was now far too small, too confined. She could be trapped here, imprisoned by someone simply sliding a heavy rock over the entrance. This was a *stupid* den, a deathtrap.

She began to crawl out, and dislodged a small pile of stones. Under the stones lay a pair of battered sandals and a small bag. The bag held a few small coins: copper, one silver round, and one gold bit. She brought it all out into the moonlight to examine, noting that the gold bit was heavily nicked, as though scrapings had been taken off it at some point. The silver round bore similar markings.

One of the copper coins bore a strange feel; she turned it over in her hands for a few moments, frowning in concentration. It felt–*familiar*. As though some-one she knew had handled it, someone strong enough to leave an imprint on something as simple as a coin.

She let her eyes slide half-shut and gripped the coin in a fist, *listening*, and saw—

—red hair, skinny body sturdy frame, shivering, half-mad, hearing voices, whispers, calling him, calling him—

Ellemoa dropped the coin, panting a little with shock and anxiety. What was her son doing with a coin that *he* had touched? Could it be coincidence, in this large a city? She took another coin from the bag with a trembling hand and focused once more.

Thieving. Her son had become a thief; the coin resonated with a sense of wrongness. Her son had been forced to *steal* to survive, rather than taking what was due him, openly and fearlessly. *I must find him. I must save him. I can-not allow him to have such a life.*

She dropped that coin, too, and reached for another, an uncut silver, intent on every clue that might lead her to her son. The tracery of memory on this one was dim, ghostly, nearly evaporated with time; it had happened a long time ago, but been powerful enough to linger, all the same. She pushed harder, raking up every last fragment she could find, and saw—

Dirty wall in front, harsh panting behind, hands clenched, eyes shut, trying not to think about the pain—the smell of urine, harsh and sharp, and the laughter—

She screamed, high and shrill, and threw the coin and bag from her as hard as she could. *They dared to touch my son! They dared to use him so!*

She had to find her son. She had to take him away from the humans who had hurt him, twisted him so badly, turned him into something beyond ob-scene; had to return him to his proper place as ruler, not servant, before it was too late.

Before he began to see this horror as *normal.*

Hands trembling, she held the sandals up to her nose. *My son. These were my son's. Where is he now?*

After a moment's careful sniffing, she dropped the sandals. She had his scent now. She would find him. This den had been abandoned; he hadn't been here in days. That strange human man had taken him away somewhere, pos-sibly even out of the city.

But her son would return. She knew it. She could *feel* it, with the true-sight that every member of her line had always held. And when he did, she would find him and save him from the humans before they destroyed everything beautiful about her precious grey-eyed baby.

Chapter Twenty-Three

Rain pattered down, sliding through Kolan's hair, soaking through his clothes, chilling his flesh. He barely noticed the discomfort. Rain was a blessing, a cleansing, a beautiful dance of translucent droplets along a jagged green beech-tree leaf and a gentle song through the air. So what if his body shivered and stumbled a bit now and again? The weather felt like a gift from all the gods working in rare concert, welcoming him back into the world.

The path curved around a thick stand of trees and undergrowth. Impishly deciding to continue in a straight line, he left the muddy road and stepped in among the trees. Brambles and branches seemed to part around him; as he picked his way through the chaotic undergrowth, not a single thorn or broken branch snagged at his clothes or skin.

A doe raised her head, watching him with wary care, as he passed by. Snuggled up against her belly and back, two speckled fawns slept on.

The rain drifted into mist and back into rain, the soft staccato punctuated by frog *chirrks* and sleepy birdcalls. A squirrel hissed warning. Kolan looked up in time to see a fluffy brown-grey tail whisk away around the side of a tree, and smiled.

I won't hurt you, he thought; waited a moment, then shrugged at the silence.

Out of the slight wind, his body had begun to warm again, enough to stop the trembling. He examined his hands, intrigued by how quickly his chill had vanished into a perfectly normal temperature. Surely the forest air couldn't be so very much warmer than the open areas?

The squirrel reappeared on a higher branch, its tail still fluffed out in agitation. Kolan moved on to avoid causing the small creature unnecessary upset.

The stand of trees wasn't very wide, a matter of a half mile at most. No path existed, but somehow every step he took found a spot of clear ground and the only branches to either side were light and easily pushed aside.

He didn't think about that very hard, too entranced by the sound of the rain and the birds and his own footsteps. This miniature forest was a world all its own. He wanted to stay and explore every leaf, every branch, every insect and frog and bird, forever; but the squirrel had given clear warning. He didn't belong here.

When he stepped out from under the dripping green shelter, he paused and turned to look back, a pang of sadness thickening his chest for a moment. The squirrel–*a* squirrel, he corrected himself–perched on a low branch a stone's throw away, watching him intently, its tail fluffed out larger than seemed possible.

Kolan bowed gravely and said aloud, "Thank you, and may the gods bless your lives."

The squirrel didn't answer. Kolan turned away and plodded along the muddy path once more. Not far ahead lay a low-slung, tidy house. Kolan had expected something akin to a tiny cabin, but this was very nearly a noble estate.

Trees formed a dense belt all around the property. Within that ring stood another ring: a low stone wall, hardly hip-height, more symbolic than actual barrier. Within that wall lay the house, small stable, a well, and a garden–mostly raised beds, covered over with thick layers of straw and weighted oilcloth.

A large rosemary bush held up its proud-needled branches to the grey sky, rain dripping from it like liquid diamonds. A scattering of flat white petunias served as a border along the pebbly garden path. Weeds had begun to spring up through the pebbles.

Kolan stood outside the stone wall and looked at the garden for a while; waiting, patiently, for the thought stirring in the back of his mind to surface. At last, it came through: *Whoever lives here is gone, and expects to be gone for a long time.* Another connection, belatedly, formed. *The weather is wrong. It's only Suanth. It should be hot right now, not cold and damp. Something is very wrong.*

. . . fawns? In Suanth?

The thought faded away like the forest-lent warmth leaching from his skin. His hands began to tremble again. Reluctantly, he faced the fact that he needed to get under shelter.

He went around to the gap in the wall, where the road passed through to a large carriage-yard. He paused a stone's throw before the opening and squinted a little. Ha'ra'hain, present or not, could do extraordinarily nasty things to those who invaded their territory without permission.

Kolan shut his eyes and listened with every sense he had. The semi-silence writhed a little behind his eyelids, and cold air dug tiny barbs into his wet skin. He sensed nothing. No wards. No traps. No trace of *other*-ness; no sense of *presence*.

He sighed a little, disappointed, and took a step forward, eyes still closed; paused again, and cocked his head to one side. No wards, but he'd been hasty in assuming no traps. He opened his eyes and studied the path where it intersected the wall. A slight darkening of the wall, an irregularity in the dirt; he traced patterns with his eyes and began to work his way slowly sideways, step by step. At last he nodded, took a step forward, and vaulted lightly over the wall, immediately ducking low in case he'd missed something.

Nothing happened. He rose and moved towards the house, thinking about that trap. Surprisingly complex in its simplicity, it was probably a double line of hooked spikes meant to tangle and snap a set of wagon-wheels after the horses had passed. So the "witch" worried about trespassers stealing whole-sale from her home while she was away; that confirmed humanity. Ha'ra'hain wouldn't even think about thieves.

The path turned to muddy red brick not far inside the wall, widening into an impressively patterned carriage-yard. The stable and the house sat against each other in a wide "V", no doubt allowing passage directly from the house to the horses in bad weather.

Everywhere he looked, hungry weeds had begun to devour the tidy landscaping.

Kolan crossed the courtyard slowly, studying the house, avoiding two more traps along the way. It was built on a typical southern model, with wide, low windows taking up much of the front of the house. The windows were heav-ily shuttered. The neatly laid tiles of the roof had a steep slope; rain gurgled through wide guttering and down into chunky wooden rain barrels. Water rimmed their top edges, ready to spill over within the hour.

I should be more nervous, Kolan thought distantly. *I should be thinking of . . . ghosts, and demons, and all the creatures that lurk around abandoned places.*

But this place didn't feel haunted, or abandoned, or witched. It merely felt . . . quiet. Like a guest room neatly tidied and only waiting for a few touches to bring it back to life for the next visitor. Like a bell waiting for a hand on the rope.

Kolan put a hand to the front door, blinking rain out of his eyes. He ran his fingers over the damp wood, enjoying the delicate tickle of sensation. Sensing no traps on the door, he dropped his hand to the doorknob. It hitched, then turned freely.

He pulled his hand back, studying the knob thoughtfully. Had it been locked? It seemed unlikely that someone so careful about intruders would leave their front door open. He pushed the door open with care and stood just outside, staring in and waiting.

When nothing happened, he shrugged and went in—and realized, three steps later, that he'd made a very bad mistake.

Chapter Twenty-Four

Learn to lose.

Tank rubbed the dice between his palms, looking around at the dark stares of the others around the table, then tossed the bone cubes.

"Two and three," Rat said with satisfaction. Wisps of dark brown hair straggled along his broad face. He scooped the small pile of coin in the center of the table towards him. "Three silver bits for the next round." He glanced at Tank. "Had enough yet, boy?"

Tank sorted out three silver bits and pushed them to the center of the table without answering. Rat laughed and added three more. The other two men around the table put in their stake without comment.

Rat wiped the back of one hand along his stubbled chin, tilting his head.

"Tell you what," he said, "you go broke, I'll give you ways to earn some of it back. If you're *good*." He grinned, flicking a deliberately insolent glance down Tank's torso and back up.

"Aw, nah," a muscular, scraggle-toothed man named Breek said. "Venepe's a northern four-by, Rat, he'll go spare over that."

Beside him, Frenn, the final member of Venepe's crew, laughed. "Who says he has to know?" he said.

"He don't," Rat said. "Unless redling here wants to go licking his arse about it."

"Are you going to throw the dice anytime soon?" Tank said, never taking his gaze from Rat's. "Or are you more interested in your own wind? It's getting thick in here."

Rat's grin turned to a leering snarl. He tossed the dice; when they clattered to a stop, he said, "Five and six! Heh." Breek and Frenn groaned and muttered, and came up with nothing better themselves.

Tank picked up the dice and held them for a moment, debating; then rolled. Six and six.

Silence. Rat's eyes narrowed. Tank met his glare without flinching.

"Lucky bastard," one of the other men muttered, and made a shoving motion with both hands. "Get on with it already."

Rat's head dipped minutely. Tank ducked his own head in answer and scooped all but four silver bits towards him. The others tossed their coins down.

Tank glanced around the tavern, mainly to avoid Rat's still-hot gaze. The buxom, dark-haired barmaid drooped as she shambled from table to table. Kybeach locals sat in groups, staring into their murky ales and shooting hostile glares at the mercenaries. The room, ill-lit and musty, had sent a crawling unease up Tank's back from the moment he'd stepped inside; but in the company of Venepe's other three mercenaries there was no backing out.

He'd known as soon as he'd met Rat, Breek, and Frenn in the grey mist of a Bright Bay morning that *face* would be critical, and that his relative youth would make him a target for every trick and game they knew. The invitation to drink meant he'd held his own throughout the day; he couldn't afford to lose that edge now.

"Hate this damn town," Breek muttered, cutting a sideways glare to the equally sullen stares of the locals. "Feels like they're planning a knife in my back or a grab at my purse."

"You ain't got enough in your *purse* for even the slick to care about," Rat gibed.

Breek turned his attention to Rat. "You watch it," he said without emphasis. "You watch it, Rat. I'm not in a mood for your shit."

Rat blew a derisive raspberry. "Throw the damn dice," he said. "Play reverses, you're on."

The thick bone cubes rattled across the table. "Three and four."

Frenn scooped them up. "Two and three. Damnit."

Rat picked the dice up, threw, his stare never leaving Tank's face.

As the cubes rattled to a halt, Breek said, "Five and four."

The silence tautened as Tank weighed the dice in one hand, not exactly meeting Rat's glare but not avoiding it either. He threw without looking, as Rat had done. A moment later, Breek breathed out hard and said, "One and two."

Tension released; Rat scooped in his take.

Tank lost the next two rounds, then stood, lightly tossing the three remaining bits toward each of the other players. "I'm out," he said.

They nodded, barely glancing up at him as they sorted out their stakes.

He went outside and inhaled clean air, sharp with chill and his own vivid relief. Overhead, a vast spread of stars gleamed like shards of polished glass. A thin moon offered pale illumination. The ground was dense and soggy underfoot; the air hung thick with the reek of a swamp at low tide.

Tank made a face and wandered further from the tavern. Not far away, a stone-walled enclosure overlapped the marsh. Grunts and hisses came from behind the chest-high, slanted wall; curious, he went over to investigate.

Lizards. Huge ones, as large as asp-jacaus, and fat. They glared up at him, their tiny dark eyes studded with reflected starlight. Tank had never seen lizards this large; a single haunch would feed two people to bursting.

Something sharp, like a knife held by an uncertain hand, wobbled against his side. "What d'you think you're doing?" someone screeched in his ear.

Tank held still, more annoyed that he hadn't heard the man approaching than truly worried. He could smell the liquor on the other man's breath; hells, it was practically seeping from his skin.

"Looking at the lizards," he said. "That a problem, *s'e?*" Slowly, he turned his head.

For a disorienting moment, he thought Dasin stood beside him; but even under the dim light of a half-moon and stars, the man was too old, face too sallow, hair too lank. He stared at Tank with wild, hazed eyes. Tank had a feeling that the man had been drinking hard for days.

"Get away from my gerhoi!" the man snapped.

"Get your knife out of my ribs."

The man looked down as though startled, then stepped back, holding up a short stick. He cackled. "Tricked you," he said triumphantly.

Tank edged three cautious steps back.

"D'you like my gerhoi?" the man demanded. He dropped the stick.

"They're very large," Tank said. "How long have you been breeding them up?"

"Hah!" the merchant said, then repeated it: "Hah!" He stared at Tank for a moment. "You have no idea. *No* idea. They were bred up special, for a king. A king, mind you. I sold direct to the king's own kitchen." His shoulders drooped. "But Oruen doesn't like gerho. He . . . doesn't . . . *like* . . . gerho." His hands clenched into fists, and he spat to one side with a bitter passion. "Bloody kings," he muttered. "Bloody bastardy kings."

Tank edged back another two steps.

"I put a lot of work into these lizards," the man said, staring at the beasts. "I sold my soul, you might as well say. And now–it's gone. All gone. Even my daughter's gone."

Tank knew he ought to quietly ease away, but the raw pain in the man's voice held him still. "Where did she go?" he asked.

"She's dead," the man said, turning a ghastly grin towards Tank. "My fault. All my fault. I didn't listen to her, you see, and so some bastard dragged her out into the swamp and killed her. I should have listened." He sucked in a trembling breath. "Can't even bury her proper. No priests left to do the service. After all I've done. After all I've paid. They promised. And now there's a new king, and I'm left with nothing. A bumbling hymn from a man who can't read, a grave with all the other commons. A life's work, worth nothing." He looked at the lizards again. "She was supposed to be burying *me*, grandchildren by her side."

His speech had the odd clarity of the beyond-drunk. Tank couldn't think of anything to say; the silence began to drag out into tension.

One of the lizards hissed loudly. Another let out a distinct fart.

Tank bit his lip against a hoot of laughter.

The other man didn't seem to notice the sounds. "You came in with that merchant, didn't you?"

"Yes. Merchant Venepe."

"I've got to get rid of these damn beasts. They won't sell here. What the king won't eat, his nobles won't touch. D'you think–"

"He deals in cloth, *s'e,*" Tank said. "Not livestock." He hesitated, then added, with care, "South of the Horn, though, lizard's a very popular dish."

The gerho merchant rubbed a hand over his eyes, swaying slightly. "I don't know," he said. "Dealing with the barbarians . . . ." He peered at Tank, squinting. "What do you know about it?"

"I'm from the south, *s'e,*" Tank said, and waited for the sneer of disbelief.

"Oh," the merchant said. "How would I approach the barbarians on this matter, then?"

Tank opened his mouth, ready to say *We're not barbarians, you ignorant cretin;* took another look at the man's pale, miserable expression and let it go. "I can only speak to how to approach one Family," he said, deciding to risk a bit. "If you send a message to Aerthraim Family, you'd address it to–"

The man's stifled yelp cut him off. "*Aerthraim?* You're one of *them?*"

"No–" Tank said, his gut lurching. "No, no, I just know something about–"

The man's hands came up and crossed at the wrists, fingers splayed out, thumbs curved forward.

"I'm not a witch," Tank protested, indignant.

"Stay away from me," the man said. "Stay away from my gerhoi. I won't have it. I won't have it! I already lost Kera. I won't have it!"

Tank backed up a few more steps. "I'm not doing anything to you," he said, putting his own hands out, palms angled up. "I'm not a witch, *s'e.* I was trying to help. I'm only a simple mercenary, *s'e,* out for a walk before bedtime."

The gerho merchant stood still, shivering now. "Go away," he said. "It's too late. I can't do any more. I can't help you. Go away. Leave me alone."

Tank shook his head. The man had been drinking for a long time.

"Good night, *s'e,*" he said. "Gods hold you gently and–"

"Damn the gods! The gods got me into this," the man cried, then spat toward Tank's feet. "Go away!"

Caught between pity and disgust, Tank retreated, turning his steps to the inn. Walking through the village didn't seem so interesting any longer.

But it took him a long time to fall asleep, and his sleep was filled with the shifting gleam of gerho eyes and the despair of a man whose own dreams had failed.

Chapter Twenty-Five

The darkness pressed around Idisio, chill and thick; he kept his left hand on the wall and fiercely pretended that only open space lay to his right. His fingers slid across dozens of changes in texture: from dry roughness to slick damp to an oily, moldy sensation that almost made him pull his hand away. Only fear of a recoil accidentally sending him sideways into the other wall kept his arm steady.

Lord Evkit was a silent, stalking *presence* at his back, which made Idisio even less happy about the situation; but if the teyanain had intended harm, he and Deiq wouldn't be free now. Or relatively free. These tunnels were going on much longer than he'd expected, and their path had turned round on itself multiple times, by Idisio's uncertain reckoning.

He wondered if this was another of Evkit's odd games; if the offer of freedom in exchange for a promise not to return to the Horn had been a lie.

"No lie," Evkit said.

Nerves already too tight, Idisio startled forward and crashed into Deiq's back. The elder ha'ra'ha stopped, turning. Idisio could *feel* his glare, even in the inky darkness. Behind him, Evkit yipped his dry, teyanain chuckle.

Idisio swallowed hard and backed up a careful step: feeling for the wall, blinking hard. Flashes of grey came and went across his vision, bringing almost-clarity. Fear kept sliding sideways into a simmering, scalding anger: he pushed anger aside and went with fear, with projecting *weakness* and *non-threat*, as a much safer survival strategy at the moment.

"Stop *blinking*," Deiq said, his breath hot and sour, entirely too close to Idisio's face. "You can see fine. And stop letting that little shit intimidate you."

Evkit made a soft, thoughtful sound; hairs prickled all the way up Idisio's back.

"Stop–how do I stop *blinking*?" Idisio demanded, stifling anger once more. If being angry at Evkit felt unsafe, being angry at Deiq was ten times so.

"You don't need to," Deiq said, his tone impatient and irritated, but backed up a step as though sensing Idisio's annoyance. "It's a *human* reflex. Set your sight and don't blink until you're ready to switch back to human-normal."

Idisio blinked again, squinted a little, and found black clearing to a blurry grey vagueness; he tried again and managed a grainy, half-light vision, enough to see where he was going. Not blinking was more of a challenge. He held his eyes open until they began watering, muscles throughout his face insisting that he *had* to blink; kept them open, waiting for the strain to pass. Instead, it grew, doubled, and redoubled. He let out a faint whimper as the strain flared into a ripping agony and squeezed his eyes shut, tears streaming down his face, his whole body trembling.

Evkit hummed a few notes that echoed in the red-laced darkness behind Idisio's eyelids, then said mildly, "We go now, please."

"When he sorts himself out, godsdamnit," Deiq snapped. "You've pushed enough, Evkit. Even on your lands, you've gone beyond the bounds. You *wait*."

Idisio stood very still, frozen in abrupt panic. He'd thought being caught between Lord Scratha and King Oruen was bad, but that was a candle flame compared to the bonfire that scorched around him now.

Deiq slapped him on the shoulder. "Ignore him," he said. "Ignore all of these *ii-shaa ta-karne*. Open your eyes. Try again."

Evkit made that soft, thoughtful sound again. Idisio's knees wobbled a little. He forced himself to open his eyes and blinked a few times, paying attention to how his vision shifted with each blink. When he reached the clearest version, he held his eyes open and found much less strain rising in protest; more a memory of habit than a real need.

He could see features now: Deiq's, Evkit's, those of the two guides waiting in the tunnel ahead of Deiq. The rock wall to either side proved far too close, and the ceiling too low, as he'd feared; but being able to see it made the confined space marginally easier to bear. He glanced at Deiq and nodded.

"Good," Deiq said. He paused, then added, tone heavy with sarcasm, "Lord Evkit, thank you for your patience. *Teth-kavit*."

Evkit hummed again, then said, as bland as Deiq had been dark, "We go now, *please*."

They went on without speaking. Deiq walked with a slight stoop, putting up a hand to check the low ceiling every so often. His brooding, simmering anger made the space feel even more dangerous.

Every so often, Evkit whistled or hummed, as though thoroughly enjoying himself. Idisio, remembering the servants at Scratha Fortresses, suspected this was another code, and that any questions would be met with an even less helpful response.

To distract himself from thinking about that, he said, "Are all the passages this small?"

"No," Evkit said.

"Of course not," Deiq said at the same time. "We're being taken through *special* passages. Ones that don't connect to the main areas."

He clearly regarded that as yet another insult. Evkit hummed a seemingly random series of notes, then said, "We go, please."

Deiq's nostrils flared, his eyes narrowing; then he turned and resumed walking, his seething silence darker than ever. Idisio felt a fine sweat break out across his whole body. He was beginning to think these tunnels went on forever, and that Evkit was perversely trying to provoke Deiq into exploding with rage.

Idisio didn't want to be caught anywhere near Deiq losing his temper, and especially not in such crowded conditions.

Blood slicking the walls–he cut the memory of the vision in Scratha Fortress short, remembering Deiq's reaction last time, and thought instead about numbers and letters: *Two and two, that's . . . four. And four apples feed four people and leave nothing behind. Apple. A-p-p-l-e.*

Lord Evkit yipped teyanain laughter. "Apples good," he remarked. "Apples to apples make more apples." He yipped again.

"Stuff it up your rear and choke on it," Deiq muttered, then added, privately: *You're right. He is trying to get one or both of us to lose our tempers. Don't ask why, it's too long a story. Say the damn numbers out loud. It'll distract both of us. Godsdamned teyanain games . . . Two and two, go on from there. Hurry up.*

Idisio recited mathematics with grim determination, Deiq occasionally correcting him or posing a more complicated problem, until grey daylight showed ahead. Seemingly between one step and the next, they were emerging from the tunnel. Idisio's eyes stung, his vision whiting out. He blinked hard several times, his eyes watering.

The scene resolved: Alyea, her expression tense, standing beside a heavily-laden pack pony. She seemed unharmed, and Idisio found himself resenting that. Alyea had obviously been given a comfortable room to sleep in, and a good meal or two. If he'd been fully human, he'd have been sitting beside her, instead of suffering through insult, indignity, and fear.

He glanced at Deiq's sullen expression with a certain sympathy. But it wasn't Alyea's fault. She hadn't asked for the teyanain to isolate the ha'ra'hain. All the same, Deiq's glare laid blame squarely at her feet.

She returned the hard stare with surprising composure. In the background, the trail guide settled the two remaining packs into place on the pony.

"Go with the gods, Lord Alyea," Evkit said, bowing. Alyea broke her silent stare-down with Deiq long enough to return the farewell. Evkit glanced over at the two ha'ra'hain and added, "Ha'inn: teth-kavit."

Deiq's matching reply was blatantly insincere. The corners of Evkit's eyes tightened in a repressed smile–or maybe a scowl; Idisio wasn't sure. His nerves went taut at the sudden, thick tension in the air. Desperate to break the mood, he said, "Teth-kavit", deliberately mangling the pronunciation. It worked—everyone glanced at him, their expressions vaguely condescending.

The hair on the back of his neck settled, and he let out a quiet breath of relief. Then they were off, with no more ceremony than that, scrambling down a narrow path bordered by sheer cliff faces to either side. It was better than the black tunnels: there was sky high overhead, and daylight making everything steadily more visible.

Idisio hadn't minded promising never to return. He *hated* this place. The entire southlands was insane, as far as he could tell, and he devoutly hoped he'd never have to travel past the Horn again.

Deiq snorted at that, and said, sourly, *Be careful what you wish for, Idisio. When you get it, it's rarely what you thought it would be.*

Chapter Twenty-Six

The tavern was no more welcoming or sweet-scented under morning light. Tank paid a copper bit for a bowl of lumpy grey porridge and took it outside. He settled on a bench by the door, his pack between his feet.

Rat, Frenn, and Breek swaggered by, sneering. He kept his gaze on his bowl, and they went by without pause or comment.

A few moments later, Dasin came out of the tavern and sat on the bench beside Tank.

"Didn't see you in there," Tank said.

"Came in through the kitchens. Venepe wanted breakfast brought up to his room."

Tank tilted an eyebrow expressively.

"Yeah," Dasin said, catching the look. "He's one for *service.*" He snorted, hacking one bootheel into the ground, then eyed the bowl in Tank's hand. "You're actually eating that?"

"Better than hunger," Tank said, and forced down another spoonful.

"Better not tell you what the kitchen looks like, then."

"Probably best." He took another bite, then sighed, surrendering, and set the bowl aside. "You're not eating?"

"I'd rather trail jerky than that garbage," Dasin said, then: "Venepe's in a *mood.* I'm hoping the room service will sweeten him up. Some damn fool came banging on our door before dawn, wanting to talk business. Livestock trader, of all things, wanting Venepe to buy off his precious damn lizards. I thought Venepe was going to put him through a wall." He shook his head.

Tank grimaced. "I ran into him last night," he admitted. "Tried to tell him not to bother Venepe."

"Well, he didn't listen."

"Damn fool."

"Yes."

Tank leaned back against the wall of the tavern. The only word for the landscape forming around them in the dim dawn light was *dilapidated*. Even the straggly grass looked dejected. The small stable had several boards loose and a sagging spot in the roof; what white paint remained was streaked green and brown with mold. The inn was no better: bugs had skittered across Tank's arm four times in the night, and the floorboards had seemed to creak of themselves.

"Why did we even stop here?" he said aloud. "These people don't have the coin to buy decent cloth. The most I saw being sold yesterday was that piece as wide and long as my arm."

"And she paid with a fistful of copper bits," Dasin agreed. "I know. But Venepe says nobody else will stop here, and someday this place won't be so poor; he wants their goodwill for when things turn around."

"The only way things are going to turn here is into the ground," Tank said sourly.

Dasin shrugged, then squinted and pointed. "What's *that*?"

A low-slung reptilian form was waddling slowly toward them. "The hells," Tank said, standing. "It's one of the merchant's gerhoi."

"Are they dangerous?"

"No idea." Tank advanced cautiously. The lizard gave him a vague, unblinking stare and veered to pass by. Its lower jaw dripped with viscous red.

He stood still until it was past, his heart hammering against his ribs, then headed for the gerho pen. The gate stood wide open. Three of the lizards still stood in the pen, staring around incuriously. Thick, muddy tracks aimed into the nearby swamp showed where the others had gone.

Tank moved closer, peering into the enclosure.

"Oh, damn," he said, and put a hand to his mouth.

The blond man from the night before lay inside, long cuts on both arms from wrist to elbow. Blood still seeped out. The knife he'd slashed himself with lay near one hand.

As Tank watched, one of the lizards moved over to the body, sniffed with sleepy interest, and began to lap at the blood.

"Damn," Dasin said from behind him.

Tank turned to find a crowd gathering, all with varying expressions of shock and pity. Venepe, flanked by Breek and Rat, pushed through to look; after a moment's brooding glare at the scene, he shook his head.

"Let's get moving," he said. "Road isn't getting any shorter." He waved toward the stables.

"His daughter was killed," Tank said, not even sure what he was saying. "He told me last night."

"Are you the damn fool told him to come wake me early and whine over his reeking lizards?" Venepe demanded, glowering.

"No," Tank said. "I told him you wouldn't be interested."

"Weren't too convincing, apparently," Venepe snorted. With another black glare, he stomped away.

"Damn fool," Rat said in an undertone, then moved away.

Tank glanced after the dark-haired mercenary, wondering if he'd been talking about Tank, Venepe, the dead merchant, or something else altogether. It was hard to tell, with Rat.

"Don't waste your sympathy on that one," another voice said in his ear. Turning, he found the worn-out barmaid standing beside him. She stared at the body with an expression of intense loathing.

Tank glanced at the barn, weighing Venepe's impatience to get on the road against curiosity. "He killed himself, *s'a*," he said at last. "Means he was in a world of pain."

"Don't be too sure of that," she said cryptically, and went back into the inn. He shrugged and went into the barn.

Dasin stood outside his horse's stall, frowning at the beast with plain uncertainty.

"Tank," he said, looking up as Tank approached. "I had a hell of a time with this monster yesterday. D'ya think you could–?"

Tank cast a swift, assessing glance up the row; Rat, Breek, and Frenn were busy with their own horses.

"I'll talk you through it," he said. Dasin's expression went sullen, so he added, a little impatiently, "You don't want to look like you can't do it yourself. Quickly. What trouble are you having?"

Dasin stared at him, breathing hard, then said, "He *killed* himself, Tank!"

"Holy gods," Tank muttered. Louder, he said, "This isn't the *time*, Dasin. Just–forget about it. Get your damn horse sorted out, before I belt you back to sense."

Dasin's lip curled, his chin rising. "Go fuck a lizard," he said, and went into the stall without looking back.

Tank shook his head. His mare was in the next stall; he grabbed the bridle from the peg by the door and let himself in as Rat led his gelding by. The grey mare shook her head and seemed almost ready to go up on her hind legs. Tank slapped her near shoulder, hard, and said, "Stop that."

She shook her head again, but settled down with a heavy snort.

"Does talking to them actually *help*?" Dasin said through the bars.

"Beats me," Tank said. "Keeps me from getting pissed off, is about all I can tell for sure."

He slipped the bridle over the grey mare's nose. She eyed him warily but made no move to bite this time; her ears twitched in time with her tail. He heaved pad and saddle onto her back. She snuffled a little, almost like a sigh; stamped a back hoof once, then held still.

He cinched everything secure, checked, checked again, then turned to look through the bars. Frenn led his black gelding by, whistling under his breath, followed by Breek, who shot a mean grin at Tank as he went past.

Dasin stood staring at nothing, bridle limp in his hand. His bay gelding continued to doze, apparently uninterested in anything at all.

"Dasin," Tank said. "*Dasin*. Wake up."

The blond blinked and focused on Tank. "What? Oh." He looked down at the bridle and grimaced.

Tank slipped out of the stall, latching it behind him, and into Dasin's. He lifted the bridle out of Dasin's hand without comment.

"Get the saddle," he said.

"Thanks," Dasin said in a muted tone. "It shook me. All that blood. I don't–like blood."

"Yeah. I remember."

Dasin ran a trembling hand over his eyes. "Damnit," he whispered, and went to get the saddle.

Chapter Twenty-Seven

The day's travel went by in a blur of Alyea and Deiq bickering, the teyanain guide seeming intent on provoking Deiq into violence, a hazy heat that sent a steady trail of sweat down Idisio's back, and the constant awareness of being watched by hidden teyanain. Idisio had never thought he'd be glad to return to Bright Bay, but as they entered the alley of shops and inns that led up to the southern gates of the city, he very nearly broke into a run. A glance at Deiq's severe expression stopped him; the older ha'ra'ha's nerves were strung far too tight at the moment to indulge any foolishness, and he looked more than ready to take out his temper on the nearest safe target.

Don't be stupid, Deiq said sourly. *I'm not that much like Cafad Scratha, and you're kin. I won't lay a hand on you.*

Good to know, Idisio answered. *How about those gate guards? Or the nearest stray asp-jacau?*

Deiq shot a narrow-eyed, sideways glare at him and made no reply.

The southern gates were an odd amalgamation of regimes: originally nothing but a low brick wall, they had since been built up into a head-high structure tipped with ominous metal points. Idisio remembered hearing that at one point during the Purge, every spike bore the head of someone accused of conspiring with the south to undermine the kingdom. He squinted a little; some of the spikes did look stained and corroded.

The wall ran twenty feet to either side, then butted up against two massive guard towers, also built since the beginning of the Purge. Beyond that, the wall went on, interspersed now with the thick back walls of various warehouses, until it reached the sea to either side. Even given that this was the narrowest spot on the strip of land connecting Bright Bay to the Horn, it had taken a massive amount of brick and labor.

Prisoner labor, Deiq said, glancing along the wall himself. *A lot of bones and blood are in this wall. Can you sense it?*

Idisio took a closer look as they neared, squinting a little and *listening* with that odd other-hearing he'd been wrestling with of late. *No,* he said at last. *It's just a wall.*

I wish I saw it that way, Deiq said darkly. *I'd love to tear it down, but I don't know if I could stand to touch it. They waited far too long to kill Ninnic.*

The gate itself, wide enough to allow three oxcarts to pass side by side, had temporary barriers set up to funnel carts to one side and foot traffic to the other; at night, the barriers were removed and heavy metal gates slid across the opening. Few enough people were coming through at this late hour that the guards were in the process of removing the barriers. As Idisio and his companions approached, all four guards turned to form a line barring passage. Two of the guards bore predominantly southern features, two northern; one had red hair, the other three black.

A few steps closer, their faces clarified, and Idisio's heart sank. He knew all four of the guards; one had grabbed him during his initial encounter with Lord Scratha. The others he knew from rather earlier. He ducked his head and stared at his feet through sheer reflex.

He thought Deiq shot him a hard stare, but couldn't bring himself to look up. Didn't want to see if any of the guards recognized him; didn't want to remember, or even think about that time–

"I know that one!" one of the guards said, sounding startled and angry all at once.

Idisio stood very still, drawing in a long breath. A mixture of nausea and resignation surged through his stomach.

"Lord Scratha called justice-right on him. Said he was a pick-thief."

Idisio's breath let out in a nearly inaudible hiss, drowned out under the sound of Alyea's own shocked inhalation.

Oh, gods, nobody's told her anything *about my past?* He glanced at Deiq, who moved his head in the tiniest of negations. Frantically, Idisio sorted through possible responses: *Yes, I was, but I'm reformed now* had almost no chance of success. Neither did *You're mistaking me for someone else.*

Swallowing hard, he straightened. *I'm honorary Scratha. I'm ha'ra'hain. They can't hurt me.* "Lord Scratha decided to take me on as a servant," he said. "Would he have done that for a thief?"

Why wasn't Deiq speaking up? Surely he had a way out of this. The southern gates weren't all that stringent these days; the guards were probably grumpy at the end of a long day and looking to take out their temper on the last arrivals.

Alyea wants to be in the lead, Deiq said. *Let her damn well lead us through the gates into her precious city, then, and let her speak up for you.*

Idisio bit his tongue against his first, second, and third responses to that.

After a few more attempts to win the guards over, it was clear their bad moods were only worsening, and Deiq's eyes were taking on a dangerous glint. At last, desperate to get through the gates–he'd heard stories from other street thieves about the outside inns, and had no intention of spending a night in one–Idisio stepped forward, gathering all attention to himself with the movement.

Before he could think overmuch–or over*loud*–about what he was doing, he said, "*S'es*, we would appreciate your courtesy in letting us pass. Syrta bless your boots."

The guards all stared at him; three with dawning awareness, one with complete bafflement. The phrase hadn't been used in years, and only ever in one specific section of the city, to indicate that the speaker was seeking a young male prostitute.

One not picky about how he was handled.

Idisio set his teeth and tried to project utter serenity. *It's the past*, he thought, keeping as tight a rein on his thoughts as on his emotions this time. *It's over. Think about being tired. I'm tired. I want a bath. I just want to walk on by. I'm a different person now.*

"Ehh," the red-haired guard said, assessing. He exchanged glances with the others, their expressions rapidly fading to an unusual blankness.

When all three flicked uneasy glances at the fourth, who seemed to be the one in charge, Idisio let out a quiet breath, knowing he'd won. They understood the situation perfectly.

The change in kings had brought along with it a *sharp* change in common morality; King Oruen had laid down severe edicts about various street trades. Under current law, those three might well be headed for the hangman's noose if their past–and probably present, as men like these didn't change because of a law–became known to the right people.

Idisio knew the king had overreacted. Whoring was a profitable trade, far more so than thieving; and no matter what laws were laid down regarding ages and abuses, nothing would really change. But he wasn't likely to ever get the chance to say so, and the king was even less likely to listen.

"Go on already, then," the red-haired guard said, moving aside. As the still-bewildered leader opened his mouth to protest, an elbow accidentally landed in his ribs, and another guard trod heavily on his foot.

"We'll explain later," one of the others muttered. "Let 'em go, damnit."

Idisio kept his back straight and his gaze ahead as he went by. He could feel Deiq's temper beginning to simmer again as his own confusion cleared. "Syrta bless your *boots*?" Deiq muttered, his tone verging on a growl.

"Not something you want to know about," Idisio said, staring straight ahead. He didn't want to see Deiq's expression just at the moment. It was going to be hard enough to deflect the elder ha'ra'ha without the added strain of seeing that murderous glare in his eyes again—and the fear that his fury might turn on Idisio at any moment, for no known reason. It seemed entirely possible that Deiq would consider whoring such a despicable trade for a ha'ra'ha that he'd lay the blame to Idisio's shoulders and punish him for disgracing his heritage.

Thankfully, Deiq's reaction seemed to focus on the outrage perpetrated by the guards, which was a relief; but all the same, he wouldn't let it go. Wouldn't stop arguing it. Kept switching to mindspeech for his questions, which brought with it a harsh pressure against the edges of Idisio's mind, a silent demand that Idisio *talk* about something he truly wanted to forget. Alyea kept walking, drawing them farther and farther from the southern gates, away from the danger zone. Idisio knew perfectly well that Deiq could be back there in two bounds and a spit, but the increasing distance felt tremendously reassuring all the same.

Finally, Idisio just shut his mind, blocking out Deiq's persistent, nagging questions; not caring that it might incense his elder past all bearing. An open fight might be a relief, compared to the razor-edged suasion Deiq was employing.

Deiq snorted and moved up to walk beside Alyea. Idisio let out a low sigh of relief. He knew Deiq wouldn't ever be able to let the incident and the associated questions go entirely, and that was–that was all right, really. Now that the strain of fighting off Deiq's intense inquiry was gone, Idisio could relax and reflect that it had actually, been sort of nice to see Deiq get so angry. It had felt almost like having a real friend, real family. Someone who *cared*.

But if Idisio had been an ordinary human, Deiq wouldn't have given two bent bits on the matter. That realization took all of the charm from the moment.

I will never get that cold, Idisio promised himself. *Never.*

Chapter Twenty-Eight

The last rays of the sun melted across the edges and lines of tall buildings. Ellemoa stared at the light for as long as she could, then shut her watering eyes and retreated a few steps into the cool darkness of the nest she'd made. It was a better shelter than the one her poor son had built, and well hidden in an abandoned barn near the southeastern edge of the city. There were several exits, not one, and she'd warded them all. Only she could enter the barn. Strangers would find themselves turning away to other locations, muddle-minded; persisting would bring actual pain.

So far, nobody had tested her wards. A few drunks and fools had wandered by and gone on without questioning their decision to move away from the crumbling structure. The few surviving families of snakes, rats, and lizards had learned to steer clear, themselves; Ellemoa would have to range farther to find sustenance tonight.

Without *teyhataerth's* support, the need for physical food had returned; and hunting humans, while they were a far more satisfying prey than lizards, was too dangerous. It would draw attention, and her nightly forays in search of her son were already being noticed. There were humans with *sight* in the city—they called themselves *desert lords*—and they would soon begin hunting her, if they hadn't already. They could hurt her, if they caught her. They knew how to hurt ha'ra'hain. Some of the ones moving through the city now had been involved in killing *teyhataerth*.

She had to be careful. She had to avoid them. She had to find her son and get him out of the city before the desert lords found her.

How old is my son? How long was I in that prison? How long have I been free? It was so hard to track human time. So hard to remember that a *day* meant something to them. She walked through nightmare, never quite sure if what she saw was real-now or vision-then, or some muddling of everything at once.

She might have hurt some of the humans during the worst of the walking nightmares. She wasn't entirely certain.

Humans are to be left alone, the Elders had said. *They are not our prey. We have an Agreement with them. We do not harm these humans. We protect these humans.*

But Rosin had said that the Elders' restriction only applied to humans in Arason; in Bright Bay, *teyhataerth* was the sole Elder. *Teyhataerth* held the authority over who to protect and who to harm.

And Rosin told *teyhataerth* what to do . . . had told . . . They were both dead now, and she was alone without guidance in a strange place, trying to find her son.

She wiped her eyes clear and went back to the doorway of the barn. The sun had nearly set; the streets hung in streamers of deepening grey. She could endure what stripes of light remained. She had to keep pushing herself until sunlight was once more pleasant to stand in. It was time to begin her nightly search for some hint of her son, and hunt food for another night.

Perhaps she'd find another stray asp-jacau. That would be far preferable to lizards. She hated their swampy, muddy taste and how little real meat lay on their skinny bodies. The bones had a distressing tendency to catch in the gaps between her remaining teeth.

Her son had probably eaten lizards to survive. As she ghosted through the streets, easily turning aside the attention of any humans she encountered, she wondered if he liked them.

I must remember that question. Questions like that are important. Her son had been raised as a human, and humans always needed to talk about trivial matters; once she won his trust with small questions, she could teach him about proper ha'ra'hain behavior.

The wind shifted, bringing in scents from the west: a late blooming of white daffodils and a lush fennel plant somewhere nearby. Ellemoa raised her head, sniffing the air, and moved towards that intoxicating combination. She'd always loved fennel. The smell brought back memories of good things: mainly that of her mother's cooking on *visiting* nights.

The elders had come to visit regularly. Never affectionate, by human standards, but present. They never took so much as a sip of tea or a nibble of bread, but seemed to appreciate the rich aromas lacing the cottage. They had spoken, quietly, of local events; asked after Ellemoa and her mother's well-being; protected them from the harassment of the human community.

After Ellemoa's mother died, the visits had continued with the same grave courtesy, even though Ellemoa's cooking efforts fell far short of the standard her mother had set. They'd been polite enough not to be critical in any way–about anything–right up until she began spending time with Kolan. They hadn't liked her spending time with Kolan. Not one bit.

I should have known they were right about him, she thought vaguely. *He didn't like fennel.*

Evening stretched grey fingers across the world around her, and the night-crickets began their strutting arguments as she walked slowly towards that strong scent. Drawing shadow round her was a simple trick. Humans scurried past without a glance, too preoccupied with their own small lives to notice the bewitching aromas around them.

Cloud gathered nearby, and moisture hung heavy and dank in the air: there would be rain soon. She liked that idea. She might stand outside in the rain, let water untouched by human hands rinse her clean of all pain and fear for a little while. She'd loved standing out in the rain as a child.

Did her son like the rain? *I'll find out one day,* she thought. *That will be one of the questions I will remember to ask him.* She had so many questions to ask him, and so much to tell him; so many years of absence to make up for.

Does he even know how to feed? Have the humans taught him anything useful or true, or only a pile of lies? More probably the latter. But she could fix that. She would fix that.

My son is alive. Nothing else really mattered.

The smell of fennel edged into her thoughts again, distracting her back to the moment's truth. It was close now, but the darkening air made it impossible to make out more than faint outlines. She paused and moved to stand up near a building, out of the way of careless passerby; not that there were many here, nor torches to light the streets. She liked this section of town. It was *quiet,* but in a good way, a healthy way, with a sense that people were nearby, living their small, meaningless human lives with no notion of her presence.

She liked being the invisible one, ghosting past them. She liked sensing the still-ragged edges of their fear, the scars they hadn't quite healed yet. They'd learned about what real evil was. They would understand her, if she ever stepped out of hiding. They would help her, if she asked, because they would understand.

Nobody will ever understand you, Ellemoa, Rosin's voice echoed in her memory. *I'm the only one who understands you. Everyone else will run from you . . . Everyone else will hate you. I'm the only one who cares enough to help you . . . .*

The people of Arason hadn't helped. They hadn't raised a hand to save her from Captain Kullag. They hadn't stopped him. They hadn't stopped Solian, either, although they had to know he was a threat. The elders had *warned* the humans, after the first time Solian came by her cottage.

Arason had some lessons to learn about the nature and consequences of evil. Her son had suffered as much as she herself; she'd let him deliver part of the lesson. Once she found him. It wouldn't be long now. She could almost taste his scent in the air. It wouldn't be long at all.

A small cottage blocked her sight: the fennel was planted on the far side of it. She moved forward, vaguely impatient now, and stepped over a low-hanging metal chain without really noticing it. A few steps later, she stopped, catching a new, disturbing smell in the air, and looked around more carefully.

A great slab of stone lay ahead and to her left. Smaller ones were spaced further away. Great piles of wood and baskets with conical metal lids stood near each slab. The air here smelled of ash and carbon, of burnt flesh and a strange, bitter unguent.

Burning slabs. This was a graveyard.

Who plants fennel in a graveyard? she thought, deeply offended. Such a beautiful smell didn't belong around death. It verged on obscenity.

She edged away from the slabs, towards the small cottage which lay ahead and to her right. That must be where the gravekeeper lived. Another obscenity, that humans assigned a person to live a life performing such a horrible duty: handling the dead bodies of their own kind, burning them, sweeping up the ashes.

She shuddered, revolted at the concept, then circled around the back of the cottage and found the fennel plant at last. The rich aroma filled her senses. She reached out and gently stroked one of the feathery leaves, releasing a new cloud of intoxicating scent. Glancing down, she saw the daffodils, all in shades of amber and pale grey, rather than the vibrant white and yellow she'd so often dreamed of seeing again.

I will have to come back in the daytime, she thought. *As soon as my eyes can tolerate the light. I will come back here and look at the daffodils.* And once she was able to tolerate full daylight, she'd never again willingly hide away while the sun shone outside. She would live in the light from now on, and be a person her son would be proud to call *Mother.*

Kolan would be proud of me, she thought with a distant sense of grief, and wished he was still alive. He would have enjoyed meeting her son. *Did I kill him?* She couldn't remember, and that troubled her for a moment. Then she went back to stroking the fennel plant, inhaling the licorice aroma contentedly.

The front door of the cottage opened.

Ellemoa wrapped shadow tighter round, anxious to avoid discovery; she wasn't quite ready to deal directly with humans yet.

A plump woman in a long, shapeless dress walked slowly around the corner of the cottage. She stopped a few paces from where Ellemoa stood, cocked her head to one side, and sniffed the air thoughtfully.

"Hello," she said, very calmly. "Would you like to come inside and have a cup of tea?"

Chapter Twenty-Nine

"You still haven't said," Tank said, keeping his voice low, "how you came to be in Bright Bay, signed with Venepe."

Midafternoon heat glared down from a sparsely clouded sky. The *thuck*ing of hooves and creaking of the wagon blended into the oppressively humid air.

A few horse-lengths ahead, Rat glared up at the sky and said, "Ta-neka of a storm building." His deep voice carried effortlessly.

"Freak heat's telling me that," Frenn answered. "From all pissy and cold yesterday? This ain't right." Tank didn't think either one of them knew how to talk quietly; they were accustomed to shouting over the sounds of a crowded caravan yard or other similarly noisy obstacles.

"You didn't ask," Dasin said, from much closer to hand. Tank tore his attention from the mercenaries ahead and looked to his right. Dasin's face was pale and strained, dark smudges marking the fair skin under his eyes. He didn't look at Tank, his gaze fixed somewhere vague.

"So I'm asking," Tank said.

"Storm ought to bring the temperature crashing back down," Frenn said. "Gonna be ugly."

"Hope it waits until we're in Sandsplit," Rat said.

Just visible ahead of the wagon, Breek rode point, his back straight and his attention sweeping the area. By contrast, Rat and Frenn almost slouched in their saddles, reins held casually across their laps, and seemed more inclined to talk than watch their surroundings.

Frenn said something Tank couldn't quite make out, and Rat laughed. They both glanced over their shoulders at Tank and Dasin, grinning, then looked at one another and laughed again.

Tank bit his tongue and told himself to mind his temper. *You fight when you have to.* Allonin and Captain Ash had both warned him to expect a certain amount of hazing when he joined any mercenary group. They'd stop soon enough.

"I learned as much as I could without going on the road myself," Dasin said. Tank blinked and looked at him, bewildered for a moment. He'd almost forgotten having asked a question. Dasin, still staring ahead with an abstracted expression, went on without pause. "I asked to start out of Bright Bay. I look too northern to be any use in the southlands, and I'd heard you'd decided to base out of Bright Bay as a mercenary; I hoped we'd cross paths again." He shot a sideways, frowning glance at Tank. "You might have sent word, you know. That you weren't coming back. Might have been nice, not hearing that from gossip."

Tank tucked his chin against his chest and frowned at his horse's ears for a few moments. "Didn't think it would matter to you that much," he said at last.

Dasin snorted. "You didn't think at all," he said, sounding remarkably like Allonin.

Tank checked to be sure Rat and Frenn weren't listening. They were discussing something to do with their horses. He dropped his voice even lower and said, "Didn't Allonin tell you?"

"He barely stopped before he was off again," Dasin said. His tone took on a petulant edge, and he made no effort to speak quietly. "He didn't look to talk to *me*. Once he decided he was done training me, he had no more interest."

Dasin hadn't exactly wanted to train with Allonin, and certainly hadn't made the process easy on the man; but Tank didn't bother pointing that out. No point raking up old sores, especially in current company. So far, Rat and Frenn hadn't paused their own discussion to listen, but if Dasin started to get mad, they'd focus back in a heartbeat.

Dasin flicked a glance at the mercenaries, as though tracking along the same line of thought, then shrugged and lowered his voice a little. "Gossip says he went up along the coast. You know anything about *that*?"

Tank kept his expression mild with an effort. "Not likely," he said. "Allonin isn't much for confiding his plans." His stomach fizzed with sudden excitement. The coast. The katha villages. Was Allonin really going to hold to his parting promise?

Dasin glared, clearly not believing the demurral, and shrugged angrily. "You and Allonin," he muttered. "Two of a kind."

Tank swallowed twice to set his voice to calm, then asked, "Gossip say anything else?"

"What am I, the village crier? You weren't there to hear it yourself, so the hells with you," Dasin said, then retreated into sullen silence.

"You finally land that slick?" Rat said.

"Nah. Her sister."

Their voices rose a bit, enough for Tank to be sure they intended him to overhear. He sighed a little and readied himself for another gibe.

"Ugly ones are always friendlier," Rat observed. "I wouldn't mind being stuck in Obein during a storm, myself. Got a few interesting ones I been working on there." He shot a meaningful glare over his shoulder at Tank and added, "I'll point 'em out to you, when we get there–so's you can avoid 'em. I won't have some wet ta-neka cutting in on me."

Frenn glanced back, grinning widely, to check Tank's reaction. Tank kept his eyes on the space ahead of Taggy's ears and ignored the feminine implication of the insult.

"Don't worry," he said, "I'm not interested in cutting in on your amusements."

"What, you take the other road?" Frenn snorted. "Damn well not sharing a room with *me* tonight, then."

Tank felt hot color flood his face. "No, damnit," he said before he could catch himself, then set his teeth in his tongue and shook his head mutely. Beside him, Dasin straightened in the saddle a little, his own expression going dangerously blank.

"Aw, we ought to aim that skinny weaver his way, when we reach Obein," Rat said.

"What, the one with that great black mark upside her face?"

"Yeah. She seems his type."

"What, too damn dumb to know what goes where?"

"Too damn dumb to charge, anyway," Rat said. He and Frenn laughed, loud and coarse.

Tank chewed his tongue and prayed Dasin wouldn't react. He didn't dare even cast a glance to his right to check or to give a warning; he kept his chin tucked to his chest and his stare on his horse's ears.

He could feel all three of them staring at him.

"Ta-neka," Rat said, as though testing, and laughed once more.

"Ehh," Frenn said, the sound dismissive. The mercenaries drifted into silence interspersed with lazy conversation about the weather, apparently content with the results of their gibes for the moment. Tank hastily signaled Dasin to drop back a little. When the mercenaries were far enough ahead that low-voiced conversation wouldn't be overheard, he let out a long sigh.

"I ought to be riding beside the wagon," Dasin said, staring straight ahead. "With Venepe."

"Only words," Tank said. "Forget it."

Dasin shot him a pale-eyed glare. "I don't need them to accept me as an equal," he said. "After Venepe, I'm in *charge*. They need to see me as–"

"Oh, the hells you're in charge," Tank said before thought could stop him.

Dasin's face tightened with scalding rage. "I'm in charge of *you*," he snapped.

"Try it," Tank invited, grinning. "You just try that." He pointed at the mercenaries ahead. "While you're at it, you try telling them you're the one giving orders, when Venepe's not around. See how far that goes."

"I say a *word* and Venepe lets you go," Dasin said. "You're only on this job because I spoke for you."

"So say the word," Tank said, unimpressed. "I sure as shit didn't *ask* for you to get me hired on, Dasin. You came to me, remember? You cornered me into this situation. I'll hop off and walk back in a heartbeat, so you go right ahead and say the word."

Dasin's glare could have curdled goat milk. Without another word, he kneed his horse into a trot, veering sharply around Rat and Frenn; seemed about to keep going to the horizon, but yanked his gelding into line beside the wagon at the last moment.

Rat and Frenn glanced back at Tank, their faces creasing in newly malicious smiles. He sighed, knowing another round of hazing was about to begin. He could see it forming behind their eyes: *Had a spat with the boyfriend, did you?* would be the start of it.

"Damnit, Dasin," he muttered, urging his mare forward to catch up with the other mercenaries; and suspected that in the coming weeks on the road, he'd be saying that quite a lot.

Chapter Thirty

Idisio walked through an unknown city. His days as a street thief had been spent on the east side of Bright Bay, between the Coastal Plains Road gate and the docks. He'd always avoided the southwestern side: the thieves here were a tightly knit group, and territorial beyond all reason.

Walking these streets, even in noble company, even with his new status, pushed him back into old patterns with irresistible force. He found himself startling at small noises, and sharp chills kept working up his back. Deiq didn't seem to notice. He was easing his temper by teasing Alyea over small matters: her family estate backing up against the infamously poor and derelict Red Gate district, her request that he *mind his manners*, and anything else that might get a reaction out of her.

The buildings close to the southern gate were squat and sturdy, with wood-shuttered windows painted in cheerful blues and greens. Wide-trunked, towering southern pines, limbs draped with various vining plants, nestled amid stands of sawtoothed palm and pepperwood shrubs. The air was thick with clouds of evening midges and mosquitoes. A faint breeze brought the smell of hot metal and soured milk to Idisio's nose, along with the sound of clanging metal on metal and a baby crying.

As they walked farther north and west, the cheer disappeared. Many buildings had been dismantled down to the foundations, and those that survived looked grim and defensive, with shutters hanging askew and paint nearly obscured beneath coatings of ash and dirt.

Deiq stopped trying to provoke Alyea into arguing with him and fell silent, looking around with a brooding expression. Alyea, apparently intent on getting to the Seventeen Gates as quickly as possible, and probably more irritated with Deiq than she'd been letting on, stared straight ahead and kept a rapid pace.

An owl hooted behind them. Idisio turned around fast, searching the gathering dusk for the source of that not-avian sound. A nightsinger warbled ahead; he spun to face front again, his heart pounding, and realized Alyea and Deiq hadn't stopped walking. He bounded to catch up, earning a dark stare from Deiq and a vaguely questioning flicker of a glance from Alyea.

"Birds," Idisio muttered.

The owl call had been a question, and the nightbird was cautioning *wait*. He ached to respond with the traditional warning, but there was no way to screech like a gull without making Alyea, at least, think he'd lost his mind–or worse, suspect that the guards had been right about his true origins.

Deiq's eyes narrowed. He cut a sharp glance around, then shook his head. "Don't worry about it," he said, the words scarcely audible. "They won't bother us."

Not reassured in the least, Idisio kept a wary eye to the shadows and rooftops. After they had walked another block, he heard a shrill cackling sound from behind them: a horribly bad imitation of a squirrel, as best he could tell.

Open targets, that meant. *Go for it, take them for everything they have.*

"Damnit," he muttered. Deiq shot him an inquiring glance.

"I'll catch up," he said without explaining. "Slow her down a bit, if you could."

Deiq gave him a steady, thoughtful stare for a few steps, then nodded and moved to walk on the other side of the mule. He put a hand on the beast's headstall, apparently a casual gesture; but the mule and Alyea both slowed to half their former pace.

Idisio let out a long breath and stopped walking. He stood still in the gloom, his chin tucked to his chest, arms crossed and hands tucked up into his armpits. A breath later, a seagull grackled loudly, then another. Idisio remained still. Alyea and Deiq would be left alone now, but that was only half of the matter.

He could sense the circle forming around him. They made no sound as they ghosted out of the shadows, until the leader said, from a step beyond arm's reach straight ahead, "So who are you to call protection on those two, then?"

Idisio lifted his head and straightened his spine, but kept his arms crossed, hoping the signals were the same here as on the east side of town; a misunderstanding here would get him killed.

No. It won't. They can't hurt me. Remember that: they can't hurt me.

He said, "They're dangerous targets. The one will rip your hand off for trying and the other will turn your brain inside out. Maybe the other way around, come to it; can't say for sure. Thought you'd prefer a warning."

"And who are *you* to know anything at all?" The leader was an angular line of gathering shadows within which pale hair and ragged clothes were barely visible.

"You don't want to believe me, fine," Idisio said. "Go ahead and take your chances."

Silence gathered around him like a line of smoldering embers waiting for a breath to flare into catastrophic life.

"Give us a name," the leader said, "or none of you make another ten steps."

"I'm Scratha," he said.

That provoked a hiss from in front of him, and a more thoughtful quality to the silence around him.

"*You're* claiming Scratha?" the leader said at last.

"Affiliation, not birth," Idisio said. The silence still hung too thick and dangerous, so he added, "And if that doesn't matter to you, consider another name I'm claiming affiliation with: Deiq of Stass."

Another hiss; he could feel the circle melting away around him, taking to the shadows. More seagulls cried out, sounding agitated this time.

"Marked," the leader said curtly, then faded with the rest.

Idisio swallowed hard to settle the nervous bile in the back of his throat, then uncrossed his arms and sprinted to catch up with Deiq and Alyea. He couldn't help feeling a little bit resentful that Cafad's name held so little power, while a scant mention of Deiq sent everyone scattering.

As Idisio eased into position behind Alyea, Deiq said, *This area is heavily influenced by F'Heing and Darden Families. Scratha means almost nothing here. I've gone out of my way to have my name known in a variety of places and aspects. This side of town connects my name with some—unpleasant episodes.* He glanced at Idisio, and his teeth showed, pale in the murky dusk. It might have been a smile, or something less friendly; Idisio had a feeling the latter was more accurate.

It would have been entertaining, Deiq said thoughtfully, *to rip off a hand at the wrist. I haven't done that in a long time. It is a bit more difficult than it sounds, by the way. It's easier to pull an arm off at the shoulder than a hand at the wrist. Has to do with relative leverage and bone strength. The hand tends to become pulp long before it's actually torn off.*

Idisio set his gaze straight ahead and tried not to think about anything at all. Most of all, he tried to stifle how nauseated Deiq's matter-of-fact delivery of such gruesome facts made him feel.

Thank you, Deiq said, more seriously. *You handled it well. You're better at keeping your temper, in such instances, than I am.*

Idisio felt his spine straighten a bit more with the praise. "Yeah, well," he muttered. "Some things don't require violence."

He could feel Deiq's attention sharpen. *To a lesser form of life,* he said. *Yes. The ha'reye are quite fond of saying that. It's a pity they don't follow their own advice more closely, and more often.*

Abruptly, he closed up into a bitter silence, as though he'd said too much; and Idisio was more than happy to let the quiet settle in for a long stay.

Chapter Thirty-One

Kolan pushed the door shut behind him and took three steps into the silence; and ducked. A thick wooden pole whistled past. He promptly dropped full-length on the floor, face down, arms splayed out to either side.

"No harm," he said, voice muffled by the floorboards, into the resounding lack of sound that followed. "No harm, s'a. No harm."

One end of the pole thumped lightly against the floor; he guessed she was leaning on it, studying him, thinking the situation over.

"I'm only seeking shelter," he said, turning his head to allow the words to come out clear, but kept his eyes shut. "Nothing more, s'a."

"You'd seek shelter in a witch's house?" she demanded. Her voice was a light alto, and wobbled slightly.

"You're not a witch, s'a," he said. "And neither is the owner of this home."

The end of the pole landed firmly in the middle of his back, right on the spine. He winced but made no protest.

"How do you know I'm not the owner?" she demanded. "How do you know I'm not a witch?"

"There are no such things as witches," he said. "There are mechanical traps laid out at the gate, not spells; the place is shut down as though the owner went away. Are you here by invitation, s'a?"

The pole pressed a little harder, then lifted away. "Yes," she said. "I am. But you aren't. Back out into the rain with you, thief. Find your shelter elsewhere."

He stayed still, splayed out on the floor. "I'm not a thief," he said.

"You avoided the gate traps and came through a locked door," she said. "That speaks of thievery to me. On your knees and crawl back out the door.

I'm not taking any chances on you."

"I'm wet through, tired, and hungry," he said. "Have some grace, s'a. I'll sleep here by the door if you'll allow me; it's better shelter than I'll find elsewhere tonight. I give you my word, under the grace of the Four, I won't move a step without your permission."

"The Four," she said bitterly. The pole prodded him in the side. "A thief taking an oath on the Four. How appropriate."

The depth of her anger told him not to admit he was a priest; that would make matters much worse. "I'm sorry for your pain, s'a," he said. "I can't change the world. But I'm not a thief, and I mean no harm."

"What are you then, if not a thief?" she demanded.

"A simple traveler," he said. "I hail from Arason, originally. I'm trying to get home. I went through Kybeach, but the watchman there rousted me out before I could ask for a room. This road seemed as good as any other."

"He *would*," she muttered. "Nasty old bastard."

"You're from Kybeach, then, s'a?"

"I didn't say so!" Her voice sounded panicked now. The pole caught him on the hip this time. "No, you're nothing but trouble. You won't find shelter here. Out you go!"

He sighed and labored to his knees, taking his first look at her. Tall and slender, with long blond hair bound tightly back into a severe tail, she was dressed in shabby servant-clothing of grey and dun. Her feet were bare, and her hands showed no rings; he put her age at somewhere above thirty and under fifty.

Her grey eyes held a familiar shadow, the mark of old and poorly healed pain. She watched him without fear, holding the heavy wooden pole ready. He set his hands on his thighs and tilted his head to look up at her.

"Out," she said, but made no move to open the door.

"Throwing me out won't change what I know," he said. "You're hiding from someone in Kybeach. A husband, I'm guessing, who beat you until you ran. Yes?"

She stared at him, the color draining from her face.

"Did he *send* you?" she said in a near-whisper.

"No. I told you, I was rousted out before I could so much as get a room. And I won't go shouting back to Kybeach about you. I'm not holding that as a threat over you, s'a. Don't think that." He rubbed a hand over his face, trying to think. His mind felt vague and clouded with exhaustion all of a sudden. The room lurched around him. His palms scraped against the floor, his forehead touching the boards; he stayed still, breathing hard, and tried to catch his balance.

Dizziness threw him back into vivid memories of pain and darkness: Ellemoa's voice hissing and whispering as he hung upside down, flame tracing delicate patterns over his skin as her hands moved, and the abrupt flip upright as he was about to lose consciousness . . . .

He moaned and shuddered, curling tightly into himself, knowing that wouldn't save him. They wouldn't let him go into the dark, not yet, he hadn't screamed nearly enough for that–but there were no voices, no flames; his hands rested on wood, not stone. And the darkness, to Kolan's intense relief, flowed across him without impediment.

He woke to warm dry air, soft cushions beneath him, a thick blanket over him, and the smell of rosemary and apples. Out of long habit, he lay still, eyes shut, while he sorted out where he was and what was going to happen next.

Someone was moving around; a woman. Memory seeped back: he'd fainted. She'd apparently taken mercy on him and dragged him in here–by herself? She must be stronger than he'd thought. Then again, he'd heard the priests remark that he weighed remarkably little for his size.

She made little noise as she padded around the room. He could hear her only because he was listening carefully. After a few moments, her soft tread faded as though she'd gone into another room.

He turned his head to examine the room. Nearby, a cook-stove radiated warmth and good aromas. A pie–probably apple–sat on a wide stone shelf beside the stove, cooling. Other shelves, further from the stove, held small glass jars of what looked to be jams, chutneys, and pickles.

He propped himself up on his elbows, wincing at the accumulated aches that announced themselves with movement. The kitchen turned out to be a long room, with two wide benches set near the cook-stove, one of which he was occupying. Three tall, glazed earthenware vases stood empty and somehow forlorn along one side of the room.

His clothes hung on a drying-rack beside the stove. *All* of his clothes.

"So you're awake," the woman said, coming back in through a curtained entrance at the far end of the room. "Good. Are you clear-headed enough to answer some questions?"

Her tone held no more sympathy than it had before, for all that she'd brought him close to the fire and undressed him. Kolan pondered for a moment, then pushed the blanket aside and sat up, swinging his legs over the side of the bench to put his bare feet flat on the floor.

She regarded him without any reaction at all, so he said, with matching bluntness, "What do you want to know?"

"Who are you?"

"Kolan. From Arason."

Her gaze moved to the scars webbed across his body, and her mouth tightened. "I can see you were hurt," she said. "Is anyone after you?"

"No."

"Why are you here? Why did you come all the way out to this place, instead of following the proper road east to Arason? The truth, this time."

He hesitated a moment, then said, with care, "I had hoped to find–an old friend here. But I was wrong."

"Who's this old friend?" The woman pointed at his chest. "The one who did *that* to you?"

He put a hand to the ropy scar that ran from his left shoulder across his chest to his lower right hip, tracing it absently. "Not this one," he said. "But some of the others. Yes."

"So you're looking to kill her?"

"No," Kolan said, and smiled at her evident surprise. "No, there's no point to that. I'm hoping she's alive, but that's probably foolish."

"What's this old friend's name?" the woman demanded, still emanating prickly suspicion.

He checked intuition to be sure it was safe, then answered honestly. "Ellemoa."

Some of the tension left the woman's slender frame. "Ellemoa," she repeated. "And you truly don't know whose house this is?"

"Just that it belongs to a supposed witch," he said.

"So your Ellemoa is a witch, then?"

"She's been called that," he admitted. "But she's no more a witch than . . . than I am." He looked down at his hands and frowned a little. "She's not a witch," he added, not looking up.

"Why don't you want to kill her?" The question held a barbed anger. "After those scars—why don't you want to kill her? Never mind. Not my concern. Don't answer that." She shook her head and hurried past him to check on the stove.

A cloud of damp, rosemary-laden air rushed out as she opened the oven and withdrew a large clay casserole pan. Setting it on top of the cook-stove, she put the heavy potholders aside, closed the oven door, then glanced over her shoulder at Kolan. "Are you hungry?"

"Yes."

"Good."

He stood, went to the drying-rack, and checked his clothes: warm and dry. He dressed without haste, then sat back down on the bench he'd woken upon and watched her fill bowls with a vegetable-noodle mixture of some sort.

"Arason noodles," she said as she handed him a bowl. "Ought to be a nice taste of—"

He sat still, his eyes abruptly flooding with tears.

"—Kolan?"

He sucked in a shuddering breath, rubbing a sleeve across his eyes, and offered her a wan smile. "Sorry," he said. "It's been a while since I've—been home. Eaten food from home. I miss it."

She sat beside him, her own bowl cradled carelessly in one hand, and tried for a little smile herself. "Sometimes I miss home as well, horrible as I know Kybeach must seem to an outsider," she said. "I had to leave my daughter behind. She thinks I ran off with a southerner, or that I'm dead, or some such. But if I'd taken her, my husband never would have stopped hunting, and he would have killed me when he caught us. She meant far more to him than I ever did. This was the only safe place I could think of, close enough to watch—"

She stopped and looked down at her bowl, prodding her spoon through it, then shrugged and began eating.

He followed suit, content with the silence and her slowly thawing temper.

"It's none of your concern," she said at last. "No more than your woman is of mine."

He looked at her sidelong, considering; then said, "What's *your* name?"

"Rodira," she said. Then, a little defiantly: "Rodira Lashnar."

"Rodira," Kolan repeated slowly. "Lashnar." He lowered his bowl to his lap and frowned down at it. "I think I met your husband when I passed through Kybeach."

She started up, her face shaded with fresh alarm, and retreated three long steps before he had a chance to say anything else.

"He sent you!" she said, a bit shrilly. "I knew it!"

Kolan shook his head and stayed seated. "No," he said. "He was very drunk. He came along while the night watchman was trying to herd me out of town."

She frowned, her head tilting forward a little. "Drunk? He doesn't drink that much. I don't think that was my husband."

"The watchman called him Lashnar," Kolan said. "Are there others in Kybeach?"

"No." Rodira hesitated, then came to sit beside Kolan again. "Only the one. He was blond? About as tall as me?"

"Yes. He was . . . ." Kolan paused, thinking back, then said, very softly, "Oh. Oh, no."

"What?"

"He was saying . . . something about his daughter being dead."

She went very still, staring at him with eyes that suddenly resembled chips of ice. "No," she said. "No, Kera was here—not long ago. Not long. I'm sure of that. She didn't see me, of course, I was hiding, I can't let her know I'm this close, but I saw her, she was bringing in supplies for Lady—" She stopped, her lips thinning. "She's not dead. She's *not*."

Kolan didn't say anything.

"Did he say what happened?" Rodira demanded. She moved as though to grab one of Kolan's arms. Remembering her husband's reaction to physical contact, Kolan hastily rose and skipped backwards a few steps, his bowl crashing to the floor. Noodles spilled, slick with oil and butter, across the polished wooden floor.

"No," Kolan said a little breathlessly. "He didn't say. He said it was all his fault because he didn't listen to her. That's all I know."

She stared at him incredulously. "My daughter is *not dead*," she said. "I won't believe a raving lunatic like you! It's a trap to get me to go back to Kybeach. He'll catch me when I go back, I'm not protected if I leave this house. You've been lying all along. This is all a *lie*."

Kolan shook his head, not sure what to say, and backed up some more as she stood, glowering at him.

"Get out," she said, pointing toward the curtained doorway she'd come in through. "Get *out*. Take your pack—" she pointed again, and he realized it had been laying alongside the bench the whole time— "and *get out*. Right now."

This time, Kolan didn't argue.

Chapter Thirty-Two

Obein sprawled over considerably more ground than Kybeach's arc of dilapidated buildings covered, and with much more cheer. The buildings here were mainly painted in shades of white and yellow; a few boasted doors of a bright orange, green, or blue. Businesses had flower- and herb-boxes laid out in precise patterns around their shops; homes had front-yard gardens laden with herbs, trellised beans, late-season peas, and squash.

Tank had never seen anything like it. After the muddled chaos of Bright Bay and the depressing stink of Kybeach, Obein came as a shock and a relief all at once.

"Hey," he said to Rat, riding to his left; the first word of conversation he'd offered since Frenn had moved up to join Breek in front of the wagon some time ago. "How long we staying here?"

"One day," Rat said, glancing over. Dirt and sweat accented the weary lines of his face. "Today being Earthday, that puts us as leaving on Fireday morning."

At least those day names were the same, north to south. Tank hesitated, measuring the older man's temper, then decided against commenting on that. Instead, he ventured, "Nice place here."

Rat nodded and went back to watching the road ahead. After a few moments, he said, "One of the better along the way. I always like this stop." He tilted his head a little, glancing at Tank again. "Don't go thinking of staying," he added. "It's nice to pass through these places, but you stop and you'll find out real fast, they're all the same underneath."

Tank blinked, surprised; he'd never heard Rat say so much at one time, and certainly not without swearing profusely.

"I *do* know how to talk straight," Rat said, catching Tank's expression. "When there's a point to doing so."

Tank looked at the mare's ears, feeling the tips of his own heating.

"Lost a few hires in the past that way," Rat went on. "Especially the ones as come from bad backgrounds. They see this and think it's heaven. By the time they find out they're wrong, half of 'em wind up dead and most of the rest have lost the taste for fighting." He spat to his right, away from Tank. "You're not half bad, for all that you've got an attitude needs broke down. Be a waste for you to stay here, is all I'm sayin'."

"Thanks," Tank said, his chest loosening with sudden relief. He'd won Rat's semi-approval, at least; and given that Rat was more or less the leader of the mercenaries, that would make life significantly easier down the road.

"Mind that attitude," Rat said. "You come off all Hall-hot and moral-the-most, you'll get yourself thrashed good one of these nights."

Before Tank could say anything else, Dasin turned in his saddle and waved them forward. "Venepe wants a word," he called.

"'Course he does," Rat muttered. "Man's famous for telling his hires how to piss—and getting it wrong half the damn time, at that."

Tank laughed; Rat's mouth creaked into a reluctant smile.

"Come on, then," Rat said, urging his horse forward. "Let's see which hand we're supposed to use this time."

Venepe pulled the wagon to a halt as the mercenaries gathered around the driver's seat.

"Black-moon market starts tonight," he said. "We'll be here one day of it, then move on. I don't like dealing during the dark of a moon—everyone's expected to lower their prices, for some fool reason—but that's how the schedule falls this time around. The market's over there—"

He pointed to a wide, grassy field not far away; a dozen people were moving about in it, setting up sturdy wooden tables and tents, laying out ropes to mark paths, and performing various other preparatory tasks.

"Riding horses go to the main stable; wagon and cart horses go to the merchant's stable, other side of town. You three—" He pointed at Rat, Breek, and Frenn. "You go take care of your horses and lodging, have your evening of fun, and sort out your schedule for the morning. I'll be setting up at dawn; don't be late. Tank, you stay with me."

Dasin, apparently, didn't need instructions. He stayed beside the wagon as they rumbled on through town. Tank pulled his horse around to the other side and slightly ahead, watching for trouble at first; then Venepe snorted and said, "Don't worry. Nobody will bother us here."

Tank dropped back level with the driver's seat and shot Venepe a puzzled glance. "Then—pardon, *s'e*, but why have me follow along to the merchant stables?"

The plump merchant looked over to Dasin, then back to Tank.

"Appearances," he said, "in part. And mainly—" He glanced at the blond again. Dasin's back had gone rigid, his jaw tight; he stared straight ahead. "He didn't tell you, then?"

"Tell me what?" Tank said through his teeth.

"You weren't hired to guard me, you damned fool," Venepe said curtly.

"You were hired to guard *him*." He jerked a thumb at Dasin.

Sometime later, his hands wrapped around a mug of hot wind wine–as predicted, the temperature had begun to drop sharply over the course of the day's ride–Tank glared across a wobbly wooden table at Dasin and said one word: "*Explain.*"

"I tried to tell you," Dasin said.

Tank bit his tongue against *The hells you did.*

"I'm listening now," he said instead, "so *talk.*"

Dasin turned his own mug round and round, not looking at Tank. "I'm the only Aerthraim merchant north of the Horn. That's not such a small thing, Tank. Something happens to me, Venepe gets the blame. He's twitchy over it."

"So why'd he take you on, then, if he's so piss-scared?"

Dasin slanted a sardonic glare at Tank. "Come on!" he said. "Alliance with the Aerthraim? He's not *stupid*. I figure he almost wet himself with excitement." He paused. "Then he saw me . . . and got less happy."

"Thought you'd be older?"

Dasin nodded and sipped at his wine without enthusiasm. "Gah. Yeah. And I don't look southern, or . . . well, particularly impressive." He grimaced. "Venepe was expecting someone like Allonin and Stai all rolled into one, I suppose."

"A handsome barbarian warrior-merchant," Tank said, and snorted laughter.

Dasin grinned ruefully. "Something like that, I think. So I made a suggestion, and went looking for you, and got lucky. He waited an extra two days to see if I could find you; otherwise, he would've had to pull one of his mercs over to the job, and we both knew *that* would be a bad idea for all sorts of reasons."

"So having you traveling along means he has an alliance with Aerthraim Family? Nice deal for–" Tank watched the small changes in Dasin's expression and stopped smiling. "*Dasin.*"

Dasin went back to looking at his mug.

"It's not my fault," he said, reverting to a sullen tone. "Stai wrote the letter. He misunderstood a couple lines."

"And you didn't correct him." Tank leaned back; then, remembering he was on a bench, not a chair, leaned forward again, planting his elbows on the table. "*Damnit*, Dasin."

"It's not a *lie*," Dasin said. "Just not . . . entirely accurate."

"So what *is* the truth?"

Dasin glanced up and around the small room, as though checking for listeners; a bit late, in Tank's opinion, but the dingy alehouse was as empty as it had been when they entered. "He's allowed to carry a few trade items, if I ask for them specific, long as I'm traveling along. He wants to try a route south of the Horn, I can go along and ease the path with my own status. And, well, I *am* the only Aerthraim trader past Bright Bay. There's the *chance* they'll offer him favored trade status, if he impresses me into recommending him." Dasin paused and took a sip of wine. "So far . . . he hasn't, particularly." He shrugged and sipped more wine.

Tank said, "Don't you think you ought to *tell* him he's supposed to be kissing your ass?"

Dasin shook his head slowly, his smile resurfacing.

"No," he said. "Not really."

Chapter Thirty-Three

The sky had nearly darkened to true night, the barest wisp of a beginning moon tilting against the horizon, as Idisio, Alyea, and Deiq entered the Seventeen Gates. The guards here, at least, offered no real challenge once they saw Alyea's face, and she called two of them by name.

Alyea led them east and south past several estates, each ringed by its own heavy fence. She paused at the first set of open, unguarded gates, looking across the courtyard to the stately mansion beyond. Idisio noticed that the fencing, while expensive metal, showed heavy rust and obviously hadn't been as well maintained as the other gates they'd passed.

Inside the courtyard, ordinary torches in long-stemmed holders burned in wide-set rows leading to the door, and chunky stone planters offered weary-looking bushes whose leaves seemed desperate to drop to the ground. The simple colors and geometric pattern of the courtyard bricks was reflected in the austere lines of the mansion beyond, and a single pair of guards flanked the large double doors of the front entrance.

Alyea stood still for a moment, staring at the mansion. At last she let out a deep sigh and muttered something under her breath. It might have been a prayer.

"Keep your tempers," she said then, at a more normal volume. She started forward, leading the pony as though she'd forgotten it even existed.

"Alyea." Deiq eased his hand under hers, taking the lead-rein. "Let us go handle the stabling and unloading packs, while you go tell your mother you've returned. We'll meet you inside."

She loosed her grip without protest.

"Yes," she said. "Yes, I'll–don't be long. There's a stable-side entrance–over that way–"

Her voice trailed off. She walked away without looking back.

"Oh, I can't *wait* to meet her family, if they get her this rattled," Idisio muttered.

Deiq shook his head, grinning, and motioned Idisio to follow him around the side of the house to the stables.

Some time later, pony and packs settled in adjoining stalls and a servant set to guard both, Deiq steered Idisio into the main house through the rear door. After meandering through a few back hallways, they emerged into a large room. There was probably some formal term for it, but Idisio hadn't the faintest idea about words like that. The front doors were visible at one end, and arched entrances led off in all directions. Massive, thick stained-glass windows to either side of the front doors depicted herons standing regal and stilted on one leg, their glittering eyes aimed at anyone approaching the doors from inside.

Idisio shivered. He didn't much like herons. They had a nasty smell, like the mud-dwelling lizards and frogs they fed upon, and their harsh, croaking cry always gave him a headache—like the one fast forming. He worked his jaw in a vain attempt to relieve the building pressure.

"Deiq," Alyea said, turning and beckoning them forward. "Idisio." She hesitated a moment, biting her lip, then shook her head a little and said, "Lady Peysimun, allow me to present Deiq of Stass and Idisio of Bright Bay, my traveling companions."

Beside her, a plump woman with sallow northern features and limp brown hair glared with no pretense of welcome; quite possibly infuriated by Alyea's near-slip of introducing *her* to *them*. Idisio had a feeling that two ha'ra'hain outranked a minor northern noblewoman, but also suspected that particular etiquette explanation would set the woman into a frothing sulk on the spot. Out of the corner of his eye, he caught Deiq's slight nod, as though the elder were agreeing with that reasoning.

Lady Peysimun wore a ridiculously conservative dress: the hem reached to the floor, the sleeves covered her wrists, and a light ruff concealed her neck. A king's ransom of jewelry glittered and clicked at every available spot.

Idisio stared back, bemused. Who dressed this formally in their own home as a matter of course? But perhaps they'd interrupted an important meeting or dinner.

No, Deiq said, sounding amused. *I believe this is her normal manner.*

He bowed gravely over Lady Peysimun's hand. She allowed it for the briefest moment, then turned her glare to Idisio. He swallowed and instinctively tried to look harmless if not entirely witless.

Normally I'd tell you to stand up straight, Deiq said, *but in this case, allowing her misconception to stand is the best course to gaining a reasonable night's sleep. Just don't overdo it, please. Watching you shrink like that turns my stomach.*

Lady Peysimun's lip curled. She looked back to Alyea without bothering to offer Idisio any greeting, as though she'd decided he simply wasn't worth the effort. Alyea's eyebrows drew sharply down.

"Deiq and Idisio are my *guests*," she said, voice icy enough to stop a blazing fire. "And will be staying for a time."

Lady Peysimun stiffened, first impulse visibly outrage that her daughter had dared correct her in front of outsiders. She turned her ire on a nearby maid instead. "Make a room ready for *s'e* Deiq and his servant," she snapped.

Alyea glanced at Idisio. He shrugged, too tired to fight over silly matters of status. After all, being a guest in a noble house was more than he understood . . . deserved . . . What was he doing here? A haze of dizziness swept over him, and he blinked hard, fighting not to sway like a tanked fool. Lady Peysimun was saying something; the words blurred into nonsense drawls.

You need some rest, Deiq observed, setting a hand on Idisio's shoulder. The world steadied at the touch, words clearing:

" A tray for our visitors, please. Bring it to their room. I'm sure they'd prefer to retire for the evening. And do bring them a bathing tub and water."

Lady Peysimun's acerbic tone and stare made it clear that she found their road-grimed, sweaty appearances less than pleasing. Well, Idisio didn't much care for his own stink at the moment. He'd take a bath, with thanks, and never mind her attitude.

He found himself dimly regretful that Peysimun Family wasn't likely to offer kathain.

I'm sure one of the servants would be willing to share your bath, Deiq said dryly.

It wouldn't be the same, Idisio said, vaguely surprised at his own lack of embarrassment.

No. I suppose not.

"Breakfast is an hour past dawn, *s'e*," Lady Peysimun said, sounding as though it pained her to admit as much. "If you'd grace us with your presence."

"I would be honored," Deiq said with a deep bow.

Taking the cue, a servant stepped forward, motioning for them to follow. Deiq nodded to Idisio, and they left Alyea to deal with her mother on her own.

They dropped their packs in the assigned room and went to the kitchens in search of food, both unwilling to wait for a servant to assemble a tray and return. Idisio found himself stealing surreptitious glances at the furnishings and decorations as they walked, assessing resale value.

A ceramic vase had real silver edging, but the one beside it was worth more: unflawed glass, colored a rich purple with white swirls throughout, and a distinctive Sessin Family stamp visible along the bottom edge. A hanging tapestry caught his eye: he'd seen the pattern before, but the threads weren't fine enough for it to be a real Stone Islands weave. It was a fake, intended to impress the ignorant.

The Palace bells struck the hour; the resonant sound, far closer to hand and considerably louder than he was accustomed to, startled him out of his appraisal and into a flush of shame. What was he *thinking*? He was here as a guest, not a thief. If he wasn't careful, he'd find his pockets filled with small valuables like that tiny glass dove on a low shelf over there—he stuck his hands firmly under his armpits as they passed it by—there would be all hells to pay if someone caught him doing *that*.

He glanced up to find Deiq watching him with a dark amusement. "We're not in the southlands anymore," the elder ha'ra'ha said quietly. "These people would raise a fuss over us taking the least stick of wood, and explaining our right would only make matters worse."

"Our *right*?" Idisio said, startled.

"Doesn't change based on where we are," Deiq said. "But the northlands have forgotten, over the years; and now there's so much superstition and fear woven through what they do remember that it's more dangerous than it's worth to tell the truth."

His eyebrows dipped into a faint frown, and he stopped walking.

"For example, I shouldn't know my way around so well," he murmured, holding out a hand to stop a passing servant, a young man with buck teeth and a scattering of acne dotting his face. "Excuse me. Where are the kitchens? We're hungry."

The servant pointed back the way he'd come. "Second right," he said, "and on to the end to the door straight ahead."

"Thank you." Deiq smiled at the servant, who flushed a bright red. Astonished, Idisio watched the young man's grin turn foolish and adoring in a heartbeat. He half expected the boy to bend over on the spot.

Idisio's breath turned sour in his throat.

Deiq blinked. A grey chill settled over his features. The servant shivered as though struck with a bucket of ice water, stared at both ha'ra'hain with dawning horror, then practically bolted.

Idisio couldn't believe what he'd just seen. Deiq had been *showing off*; demonstrating how malleable humans were for ha'ra'hain. He regarded the older ha'ra'ha with a thick feeling of disgust churning in his gut.

Deiq sighed. "I hate the north," he muttered.

"Because he didn't drop them for you?" Idisio said, knowing it for a petty comment even as he spoke; but that adoring glaze in the servant's eyes had stirred uncomfortable memories that weren't at all safe to think about just now.

"No. I didn't want that. But I hate that he felt ashamed for wanting to."

Unable to think of anything else to say, Idisio settled for: "You have an opinion of yourself, don't you?"

Deiq shook his head, face going blank, as though repressing his own memories. "Not really," he said. "Right now I'm of the opinion that I'm hungry, nothing more."

Idisio opened his mouth to say something; Deiq's abruptly far-from-blank expression stopped him. Once again his resemblance to Scratha in a dangerous mood came to mind and never mind his protestations that Idisio was *kin* and thus, apparently, untouchable. That moment of near-violence in the desert ruins had put a hollow ring to that declaration, as did moments like this.

He dropped his gaze to one side, shrugged, and followed Deiq to the kitchens in a mutually sour silence.

Chapter Thirty-Four

Ellemoa breathed in the scent of fennel, calming herself, then stepped out of concealing shadow and said, "How did you know I was here?"

"Living in a graveyard, one picks up a few tricks." The gravekeeper's voice was amused, but kindly. "Come on in, then, s'a, in your own time. Door's open." She retreated around the corner.

Ellemoa stroked the fennel, thinking it over. This woman seemed completely unafraid of a stranger lurking round the back of her cottage. That was . . . interesting. And how had the woman known Ellemoa was there?

Curiosity drew her to the front door. Beyond, a merry fire gave heat and light to the small living room. Several comfortable chairs crowded each other, with little space to slip between or around. Ellemoa sidled a step inside the door, then paused.

The gravekeeper, sitting in one of the chairs across the room, rose and smiled at her. "Sorry about the mess. It's just been a meeting day. Let me make some space—"

She tugged two of the chairs through a flower-curtained doorway with rapid efficiency, then began rearranging the remaining chairs. Ellemoa eased another step into the room and said, "Meeting?"

"Yes. Once a month, people come here and talk about the loved ones they've lost and the pain they've been through. It's been such a rough time of late, you know; people are still recovering from the shock of it all."

"I'm surprised anyone would want to come to a graveyard to talk about death," Ellemoa observed.

"Oh, folks have stronger stomachs than that. And Lord Eredion's the sponsor of the group, as well; he's got a way, that one, of charming folks into doing what they never expected. He attends most of the meetings. Missed this time, but then, he's a busy man these days."

"Lord Eredion?" The name put an uneasy chill down her back. Why did it seem so familiar?

"Yes, that's right. He's from Sessin Family. Proper nice, for a southerner. Not nearly the arrogance most of 'em carry about." The woman straightened, wiping strands of fine brown hair from her face. "How about that tea, now? And then you can tell me what's on your mind."

"No tea," Ellemoa said. She sat down, very cautiously, in one of the chairs.

"All right," the woman said, unruffled, and sat down across from Ellemoa. "So, what brings you to my cottage?"

"The fennel," Ellemoa said. "I could smell it. I've always loved fennel."

"That's a new answer," the gravekeeper murmured. Then, more loudly: "Would you like some clippings, or perhaps seedlings?"

"No," Ellemoa said, slightly puzzled. "I like the smell."

The silence grew and thickened; Ellemoa realized the gravekeeper was waiting for her to speak first. That annoyed her. She didn't want to say anything. She stood up and turned for the door. It had been a very bad idea to come inside; the door remained open, allowing in a draft of cool night air, but the cottage still felt like a trap. If that door shut—

She hurried outside, panting a little, and stood well clear of the cottage. *Not again. I won't be shut away from the light ever again.*

"*S'a,*" the gravekeeper said from the doorway of the cottage, "I've seen that reflex before. You've been hurt, and badly. Who was it? Rosin himself, or one of his thugs?"

Ellemoa took a restless step forward, then sideways. *Rosin.* She wished the woman hadn't said that name. The fennel had made it better for a little while, but now the memories were flooding back. All because the stupid human woman didn't know when to shut up. She had to keep talking: typical human. Always talking.

Rosin had talked, endlessly.

"I'm guessing Rosin Weatherweaver," the human woman said. "I'm sorry, *s'a.* Please, tell me about it. Let me listen. I'll send for Lord Eredion himself, if you like; he's proven better than I at handling Rosin's direct victims."

Ellemoa wanted to rage at the woman: *Stop saying his name!* Memories seemed to thicken her breath and darken her vision every time she heard it.

"Come inside and have some tea," the woman coaxed. "Let me hear your troubles."

Nobody will ever appreciate you the way I do, Rosin's voice ghosted out of memory. *You're so precious to me, darling, and all those petty little humans would turn and run from you if you told them the truth.*

Ellemoa shook her head and turned in slow, hesitant arcs, back and forth, back and forth. *No,* she thought. *No—the humans who went through the pain he brought, they'll understand. They'll see that I didn't have a choice. They'll help me.*

Rosin's laughter echoed in her mind. *Try it,* he suggested. *Tell her what you are, and see what she does. Go ahead, sweet, let's see who's right.*

She took two steps forward, focusing her vision to see the woman's face clearly. "I don't think you truly want to help me," she said bluntly. "I'm not like you. I'm not human. I'm ha'ra'ha. You don't really want to help me–do you?"

The last words came out far more plaintive than she had intended.

The gravekeeper stood very still for a few breaths. "Ha'ra'ha," she said at last. "Like that–that creature who caused all the–the problems? Ninnic's child? You're–one of them?"

Ellemoa could smell the rank stench of fear drifting in the air. "Yes," she said. "I lived in the darkness with *teyhataerth* for a long time."

The woman's face went bone-white and her voice shook as she said, "I've heard stories of a–a woman, from the survivors. I thought they were only seeing an aspect of Ninnic's child. Lord Eredion was sure of it–but–was that *you*?"

"Yes."

The woman stepped back, then back again, nearly tripping over the doorsill. "I can't help you," she said. "I can't. You're–no. What they've said you — no. That's too much. Please–go away. Do one kind thing and leave me in peace. Please."

The door slammed behind her a moment later.

Rosin's laughter built, cascaded, overflowed. *And what are you going to do now?* he taunted. *Confirm her decision that you're a monster by ripping her apart? I can tell you want to, sweet. Go on, it's what you were born to do, isn't it? It's what you love to do . . . .*

Rage built, choked — faded into a bleak, aching sorrow.

My son. Has he ever killed anyone? Will he see me as a monster? Will he understand?

She stared at the door for a long time, hoping it would open, hoping the woman would offer to try to understand. It stayed resolutely shut.

Rage began to simmer again, rising to tint the corners of her eyes. *I didn't have a choice. I was trying to survive. It's not my fault.*

She started forward a step, her hands forming into tight fists.

I'll make her understand. I won't kill her, but I'll make her understand, I'll make her apologize for being so disrespectful to one of her betters–these humans have to learn —

Another stream of wind swirled past her nose. She froze, focusing on an elusive taint in the air.

My son. He's here. He's here!

She turned and melted away into the darkness, following the meandering wind's backtrail; lost it once, twice, three times to a cloud of guttering torch-smoke: finally broke through to a clear area and circled, humming anxiously under her breath, until she found it again.

The West Gate clicked shut as she stepped out of shadow. A stone's throw beyond the metal bars, she could see the retreating backs of three travelers and a pony. A woman, a man, and a slender young boy.

My son. My son. That has to be my son!

She threw herself forward, keening. The guards outside the Gate raised their pikes; the guards inside straightened to alertness. She stopped, backed up, and turned away, each step dragging as though heavy weights had suddenly attached to her feet.

Three streets away, she stopped, bewildered. Why had she left? The guards couldn't have stopped her. *My son. My son! I have to go to him . . . .*

But tearing through the guards would draw attention. The desert lords in the area would be alerted to her presence. No. She had to move secretly. She had to avoid notice. The wall—that was it. She would climb over the giant wall and find her son, save him, escape with him.

She slipped through shadow to a part of the wall out of sight of the Gate and set her hands to the flat surface; jerked them back with a low hiss of agony as the stone seared into her palms.

What—?

Moving a few steps sideways, she tried again, with a tentatively placed fingertip. Her finger slid aside before touching the wall as though she'd encountered a curved sheet of glass.

Anger rose again. *Wards.* Someone had warded this area against her. *Her,* specifically; a general protection wouldn't have caused her such pain. This was set to stop her from passing into the Seventeen Gates area.

She began feeling her way along the high wall, searching for any weakness, any gap, any spot where she might slip past the barrier. But the protection was solid and carefully built; by the time she'd gone ten feet she knew the crafter wouldn't have left any gaps. She could go around the entire perimeter of the Gates and not find a hole to creep through.

She tried reaching through the wards to find her son, to coax him to her side; once, twice, she felt a dim response, but it faded away before she could be sure he'd heard her. She might have reached him, she might have prompted him into coming to her side—or she might not. She had no way to know. The wards simmered constant distraction along the edges of her mental vision, fracturing her increasingly desperate attempts to find her son. This wasn't going to work either. She had to find another way.

Frustration shivered through her muscles. To be so *close . . . .*

Who would do this to me? Who knows I'm alive? Who knows I escaped? Who knows me well enough to use my imprint in a ward—

In a burst of seeming irrelevance, the gravekeeper's cottage came to mind: *It's just been a meeting day . . . Lord Eredion is the sponsor of the group.*

Sledgehammer in darkness. An agonized scream—

Connections snapped into place. She *knew* Eredion. He'd been the one to set her free. And his presence was the one woven all through these wards. More connections formed in a rapid cascade: she'd felt him skulking by, easing into prison cells day after day, year after year, to heal the wounds of those with a chance left of survival. Rosin had known, of course. Rosin had laughed about it, and promptly brought the refreshed victims to Ellemoa.

Most of them never left. Some few, on Rosin's orders, had been carried out, whining like scalded kittens.

Eredion had to have known something like that would happen. After the first few times, he'd definitely known. Yet he'd continued to interfere, dooming the prisoners to a much worse fate than dying in their cells.

She remembered now. If he hadn't hated himself for sending so many to become piles of stripped bones, Ellemoa wouldn't be walking above ground. She'd allowed him to live because of that alone. She remembered, and that memory dragged her sideways into another: the walls of her prison wavering around her, dank and oppressive.

Darkness spread across her vision. Clouds filled the sky overhead, and thick droplets of water splattered around her.

I should have killed him. I will kill him. He's keeping me from my son. I will kill Eredion. Where is he? She sniffed the air, focusing all her attention on the question: *Not inside the Gates,* came the answer. Eredion had passed into the city proper. He was within her territory, within her grasp.

She slid between the coalescing raindrops and began to hunt.

Chapter Thirty-Five

The Obein market seemed to have twice as many women as men, both as vendors and as customers. Most were dressed in ordinary working clothes: long split-skirts, peasant blouses, modest caps, and sturdy boots. Some few had proper dresses on, mostly with low-cut bodices; Rat, back in full *rough-mannered mercenary* behavior, whistled softly at those women as they passed, chuckling when they shot him icy glares.

"Prancing around on wet muddy grass in little slippered feet," he observed at one point. "Damn stupid, you ask me. One of 'em will be ass over sometime this morning, you watch. The ones with the boots got some sense, at least." He studied a gaggle of approaching bodices, then whistled more loudly than usual. He laughed outright at their collective glares. "These ones are more fun to watch, though. 'Specially when they fall down."

Tank didn't say anything. Rat glanced sideways at him and laughed again. "You ought to see your face," he said. "Told you about that attitude, re-member? Shake it loose. Half of these ain't so fine once they settle down out of public eyes. More'n half, I'd guess."

Tank lifted a shoulder in a sullen shrug and kept his attention on Dasin, who was currently cutting up lengths of cloth and packaging them for the steady trickle of customers around Venepe's booth. Guarding Dasin rankled far more than anything Rat might be doing or saying at the moment; but it did make sense, from Venepe's misinformed point of view.

If—or, more probably, *when* Venepe found out about the misunderstanding, the arrangement was likely to go sour very quickly. Tank had a growing, un-easy suspicion that he really should have listened to Captain Ash and steered clear of this contract.

Too late now. He'd have to make the best of it as he went along.

A slender, pale-haired young lady in an exceedingly low-cut gown bent over the corner of the table, examining a length of fine Stone Islands silk-weave. Dasin's eyes followed a predictable path, his hands stilling on the bundle he was currently wrapping. Tank himself couldn't help studying the curves presented from the opposite angle.

"Oh, hells," Rat breathed, then headed for Venepe's booth at a rapid trot. Dasin, catching the sudden movement, looked up, eyebrows rising. The young woman glanced up at Dasin's face, then looked over her shoulder. Seeing the fast-approaching mercenary, she blanched and gathered up her skirts to flee.

Three fast steps away from the booth, her feet skidded on wet, muddy grass; she went down in a squalling heap of flounced cloth. Rat was on her a moment later, hauling her upright with one big hand wrapped around each of her upper arms. The front of her dress had pulled sideways, clearly displaying one bare breast.

Rat grinned, glancing down, and said something Tank didn't catch. The woman, face even whiter than before, shrieked and kicked uselessly at Rat's shins. Activity ceased as heads turned throughout the market.

Tank found himself pushing between, breaking Rat's grip on the woman, before he even knew he'd started moving.

"What the hells are you doing?" he demanded.

The woman retreated a few steps, glaring. Mud was splattered over her face and splotched across her dress in great, grassy smears. "I'll have you up on charges of attempted rape," she snapped, yanking her dress back into place. "Assault and rape!"

Rat laughed, baring small, discolored teeth. He said, "I told you before, stay away from Venepe's booth. You think that changed?"

The woman sneered at him and retreated further, then turned and hurried away–with considerably more care this time.

Rat turned slowly and leveled a bleak stare at Tank, all amusement gone from his expression.

"You ever get in my way again," he said, "I'll have you *hurting*, boy. You understand me? She's a thief. Hits the booth most every time we come through here. That low cut dress ain't but a game, and you and the other wet ta-neka fell right into it. I'd've had her this time, if you two hadn't messed it all up."

Tank could feel his face heating. "I thought . . . ."

"Thought I was after her ass? Thought I'd take her right there in public, in front of my employer and half of Obein?" Rat shook his head and spat to one side. "You got some bad thinking to unlearn, boy. There's play-time and work-time, an' this is *work*. I may not be Hall-hot like you, but *I* earn my pay."

Tank glanced over at the booth; Venepe seemed to be delivering a similar harangue, more quietly, to a red-faced Dasin.

"Sorry," he muttered.

Rat, with a final ferocious glare, returned to stand across from Venepe's table. After a few moments, Tank slunk back into place beside him, ears still burning.

It took a long time for his embarrassment to fade enough to risk a question. "What did you mean, you're not Hall like me?"

Rat slanted a brief sideways glare, plainly still irritated. "I'm unsworn, you dense little fuck," he said curtly. "We all are but you. Di'n't your pretty boy tell you that yet?"

Tank's jaw dropped open; answer enough. Rat rolled his eyes and went back to watching Venepe's booth with a steady glower.

"You're gettin' paid more," Rat said after a while, unexpectedly. "You ain't got a pebble of the experience and you ain't old enough to shave and you ain't got the godsdamned *sense* of a dead goose, but you're gettin' paid more and respected more, 'cause of a stupid godsdamned wooden coin. So do us all a favor–shut down the attitude before you get a noseful of dirt."

Tank bit his lip, feeling his face flaring again.

"Sorry," he muttered again. "I didn't–I didn't know."

"Now you do," Rat said, not looking at him.

Dasin, looking both sullen and cowed, was back to cutting cloth. Tank noticed that when women approached the booth, Dasin's gaze stayed carefully above the neck, whatever the provocation. He grinned ruefully; then he remembered that once again, Dasin hadn't given over a critically important piece of information. Without meaning to speak aloud, he muttered, "*Damnit, Dasin.*"

Rat snorted. "Poor pick as a lover," he commented. "You'd've been safer with the thief."

"We're not," Tank said through his teeth, his irritation with Dasin suddenly sidetracking to focus on Rat.

"Tuh," Rat said. "If you say so."

Tank's breath strangled in his throat for a moment. "I say so."

"Mind the attitude," Rat said. "*Mind* the attitude, boy."

Tank inhaled through his nose and held it, counting, until his fury subsided to something like sense again. He let out the held breath noisily.

"Better," Rat said, glancing at him appraisingly, then nodded at an approaching trio of middle-aged women in sensible clothing, baskets already laden with flowers and produce. "Look. Watch. These'll bicker and bother for a good while before settling on a length of the ugliest, cheapest godsdamned thing Venepe carries. Then they'll try to get your pretty boy's attention, and if they manage, he'll be asked to *personally* carry it to their home tonight." He tilted his head back and laughed up at the cloudy sky, a rough bark of amusement. "Figure they'll wear him out fair solid. We call 'em the Horny Vultures."

Tank, surveying the three women, couldn't help snorting laughter himself. "You're joking."

"Not a bit of it. Like I said–place like this ain't as pretty on the underside as it looks. They've been after Venepe a while now, but he ain't stupid enough to smile at them–look. There your boy goes, grinning. They've got him."

"Oh, gods," Tank said, his amusement fading. "I ought to warn him–"

"Ehh, let him unwind," Rat said. "Do him good. Get the stick out of his ass. You too, since you're on nursemaid duty. Walk him over tonight, have some fun. Better you than me, mind you, all the way around." He laughed.

"No thanks," Tank muttered. He remembered very clearly how Dasin liked to play; he'd never liked seeing women handled that way, willing or not, and he certainly wasn't inclined to join in. Rat wouldn't understand that, though, so he settled for: "That's not my idea of fun."

"So? Maybe it's his. Kick your heels on the step or in a bed, the one's more comfortable than the other," Rat said, and winked, grinning.

"I'll take the step," Tank said.

"Suit yourself."

Chapter Thirty-Six

It proved to be a mistake to sit down to dinner together. Deiq seemed as tired and out of sorts as Idisio felt.

"You don't see the half of what's happening around you, whatever you might think," Deiq said, "and you misunderstand what you do see more often than not. I'm beginning to lose patience with you, Idisio."

"And you don't *tell* me the half of what's going on," Idisio retorted, "so how am I supposed to understand it? Aren't you supposed to be explaining all this to me?"

"Try asking instead of insulting and challenging me," Deiq said severely. "Try listening instead of judging. Maybe you'll hear some of what I've been trying to tell you."

They sat quietly for a while. Finally Idisio said aloud what he couldn't get out of his thoughts. "Fine. I'll ask, then. That servant, in the hallway." He stirred his soup, not looking up at Deiq. "Would you have?"

"Would I have *what*?" Deiq's tone was edged with dark frustration and exhaustion.

"You know." He couldn't help remembering Riss's accusation: *Word has it he'll fuck anything that moves.* It was hard to see Deiq as all that different from the gate guards, at the moment.

"Taken him to bed? Not in the middle of the hallway, no. And certainly not against his will, whatever ideas you might have formed."

Idisio prodded his soup, took a few bites, then stirred it some more. "I thought you liked women."

Deiq said nothing for a long moment, then: "I have no preference. That's one of the human biases I don't happen to share. Do you?"

Idisio felt his face color. "I don't care for that side of the road."

"Well, you were raised human," Deiq said, tone tinged with condescension. "Perhaps you'll grow out of that in time."

"I doubt it," Idisio said, his voice thin and tight. "I really doubt it."

Deiq looked up quickly, his dark eyes narrowing. His jaw set, and his whole face went taut for a moment. "Those guards–"

"*Leave it alone.*"

Deiq's stare felt like burning coals burrowing under his skin, seeking out the tender bits. "Very well," he said at last, and returned his attention to the soup.

They didn't speak again until Alyea came in. Idisio left soon after she arrived, intending to go turn in and get some sleep. His headache had only worsened; the thundering rain overhead felt like millions of tiny hammers against his skull. His eyes felt as though they were ready to burst into flame, and his jaw ached as though he'd been gritting his teeth for hours.

A few steps past the kitchen doorway, the hall went from ordinary to bizarre. Rich tapestries, perfectly fitted, *clean* stone floors, vases of tall red-sage and gods-glory flowers: this wasn't his world. This wasn't where he belonged.

What the hells am I doing here?

He looked down at his feet, astounded to realize he was wearing *boots*. Clothes without holes. A belt, for the love of the gods, and a belt knife. Only a light rime of dirt showed under his nails, and he'd recently eaten–the warm, taut feeling in his stomach was unmistakable.

What the hells–?

As quickly, the disorientation passed. He stood blinking like a newborn idiot in the middle of an ordinary servant's hallway. *Ordinary.* He looked down at himself again and almost laughed. A year ago he wouldn't have believed such an outfit even worth wearing. Far more useful to sell it; the coin for the shirt alone would have meant food for a week.

But this was his world now. This was his life. He'd succeeded. He'd left the sewers behind forever. He never had to go back to that scrabbling, dangerous lifestyle. He grinned and took a step, his confidence returning.

A man turned the corner ahead and came toward him: almost as tall as Deiq, broad and loose-limbed, with sloppy dark hair and a mean smirk on his face. Idisio sucked in a breath as though gut-punched—he remembered that smirk, that hair—rather shorter, years ago, and the boy had put on a few pounds since then, but—

Silver coin flipping through the air, the sound of Church bells drifting on a humid breeze, and laughter—

He'd never heard names, didn't know what to call this arrogant young man striding toward him; and the youth stared at Idisio without recognition or any attempt at courtesy.

"You one of the southerners come back with my cousin?" he demanded, his dark glare raking Idisio from head to foot.

Idisio couldn't help returning the glare. *You think all I wanted was a whore? There's better than you for that–*

"You staring at something, southerner?" The dark-haired youth swaggered forward another step.

"Nothing important," Idisio said acerbically, and delivered a contemptuous survey of his own. "*Nothing* important."

A heavy flush rose to the young man's face. "You watch yourself," he growled. "Little thing like you, I'll take you apart pretty fast." He pushed forward another step.

A sudden, black anger rose in Idisio. "Give me a half chance, I'll be *glad* to settle with *you*," he said without meaning to voice it aloud. He heard the old street-thief accent coarsening his words; that, as much as the unexpected aggression, seemed to give the young man pause.

"'Settle'?" the youth said, and squinted. "We met before?"

Idisio drew a deep breath, a little frightened, a little intoxicated by the depth of his rage; but starting a fight here would reveal his background to Alyea—and Alyea's mother. Welcome would be thin and short after that, no matter his current status.

He could almost *feel* the silver coin between his fingers, though.

"No," he said, careful with his accent this time. "Alyea's in the kitchen, if you're looking for her. Now get out of my way."

The youth stared, taken aback. Idisio waited a moment, then started forward. The youth gave ground, moving up against the wall, and stayed plastered flat until Idisio had passed. Then he muttered, "Southerner ta-neka."

Idisio turned, fast enough to startle the youth sideways another crabbing step, and said, "You want that fight after all?"

The youth glared, bewildered and sullen, then swung away from the wall and headed for the kitchen without looking back, his shoulders stiff with outrage.

Idisio swallowed hard and headed for his room, praying the boy wouldn't change his mind and come after him. Once round the corner, he managed to slow his pace. He found himself panting, his heart hammering in erratic bursts.

What the hells am I so afraid of? he thought, bewildered. *I'm not a street thief any longer. He can't hurt me!*

He hesitated. Fear urged him to flee to his room; rage demanded he pursue that fight.

Whoring, while distasteful, was one thing. Even what the guards had done was insignificant, compared to what that boy had done a few years back, to prove himself to his leering companions.

Idisio had been grateful, if a little puzzled, that the scars had disappeared in a matter of weeks.

Trapped and shrieking, bleeding, torn—soaked in urine, covered in raucous laughter and contempt—Now you're a man, someone said, patting the black-haired youth on the shoulder. Now you've proven yourself . . . No, no need to kill this one, this was enough for today . . . .

The clatter of a single silver coin landing on the ground beside his head, and their voices slowly receding . . . He'd never been able to make himself spend that coin. Touching it made him feel filthy all over again. He'd brought it out to look at any time he thought about going back to that way of making money, as a reminder of why he'd started thieving instead.

Idisio shook his head, pushing the memories away, and went on, more slowly, to his rooms. He needed more time to think this through. That had been Alyea's cousin. He'd always known the boy came from somewhere inside the Seventeen Gates, just from the accent and posture. But–Alyea's *cousin*?

He couldn't go after his long-dreamed of revenge. Not without drawing Alyea into the fight, and Deiq. He didn't want them involved, because . . . .

A faint haze crossed his vision, an almost-dizziness. He put a hand out to the wall, steadying himself.

What was he thinking? Revenge? Against a noble? Absurd. He didn't have the right. He was . . . just . . . a . . . street thief.

He looked down at his sweat- and dirt-stained shirt and leggings and felt a dreadful disorientation. He didn't *belong* here. No wonder Lady Peysimun had looked at him with contempt, and that boy had seconded the appraisal. He was filthy. He'd always been filthy unless it rained. No—no, he'd bathed recently. These clothes had been reasonably clean, at a recent point. He didn't live on the streets any longer—but the intervening days, abruptly, lay as blank as a new moon in the sky. How in the world had he gone from a ragged street-thief to—wherever and whatever *this* was?

Memory rose and tumbled like randomly tossed pebbles: that silver coin, turning over and over in his hands; wiping away tears with the back of one hand . . . *Hand*–a strong hand, clamping over his wrist, a desert-eagle glare bearing down on him. Lord Scratha. Black-hilted throwing knives. Rosemary, roses . . . flowers . . . *daffodils*, someone said wistfully, and sighed with longing.

Idisio gagged and staggered sideways and forward, feeling for the wall, grasping after tangible reminder of reality.

I should have stayed on the streets . . . I should have left you there . . . Swaying, seasick, vomiting; There is a lake, a ghosty lake . . . In the town, they said . . . said. Red. Red was looking for his son . . . .

My son, someone said, in the tones a starving man might have used to say *my steak.*

Idisio patted at the wall frantically, trying to force himself out of memory. He found himself implacably dragged through flashes of the long, weary walk up the Wall, through half-lit tunnels, and into the moment they stepped in front of the Scratha ha'rethe to cement Lord Scratha's binding. Memory focused on a vivid glimpse of the vision he'd been trying to forget ever since:

"Demon-spawn!" a male voice shouted, heavy with anger. "Burn it! Drown it!"
. . . a horrible wrenching sensation, an echoing scream–

A burst of pain shook him from the waking nightmare. He'd fallen, shoulder first, scraping along the wall. The arm of his light shirt was shredded, and his arm burned, invisible fire connecting the scraped-raw spots in a blazing net of pain.

Hauling himself to his feet, he looked around to see if anyone had been there to see. The hallway stood empty at the moment. Praying he wouldn't meet anyone else unexpected, he broke into a dead run.

As soon as the door to his room shut behind him, the disorientation returned. He fought it, staggering to the washbasin, roughly sponging off his scraped skin, using pain to keep focused on the moment. Scant moments after he managed to change out his ruined shirt for a relatively clean one, the strangeness roared in, unstoppable as the tide: he felt a strong need for a cleansing walk through the torrential downpour outside. The fresh–the clean– the safe–he shook his head, blinking, then accepted the simplicity of it. He was a street thief. He didn't live indoors. He lived *outside*. He *needed* room to walk, to wander. The walls here were too close, the air too warm and stifling and dead.

Dead . . . .

The word sent a shudder down his spine.

I should yell for Deiq, he thought. A heartbeat later, even that dim alarm lofted away in a scramble to get back outside to the streets, where he belonged.

Chapter Thirty-Seven

Kolan had grown up with the Hackerwood on his doorstep—or so he'd thought. As he wandered east through the rough farmlands far from the Coast Road, he came to realize that the looming mass of trees always to his left was a far darker thing than the softly wooded hills of Arason had ever dreamed of being.

He'd always felt safe walking among the outer belt of the Arason Hackerwood. The trees had been spaced apart, thick with leaf-litter, cheerful with squirrels and birds. Sunlight shone through in wide swatches, bringing a dappled peace to every step.

These trees huddled close together, thick with thorny bushes and broadleafed southern ivies fighting for space; sunlight wouldn't reach past the upper branches at best, and the only sounds Kolan heard were the small, slithery noises of snakes and rats.

He didn't try to enter the woods, which turned out to be a wise instinct. He spent a day here and an evening there, helping farmers and housewives with some small task in exchange for a meal and a dry corner of shed or barn to curl up in for as long as it took to finish the work they had to offer. It served as a reminder of how to live as a human; he watched the people around him, mindful never to get caught at it, as he picked late-season produce, stripped bark from logs being readied for winter, tilled fields under for their end-of-season rest, cleaned out chicken coops, or performed a dozen other tasks found for him.

Nobody asked him prying questions or troubled him with the weight of over-kindness; he did the work and took a bit of food for the road by way of payment, and moved on. Sometimes he left without payment: in the middle of the night, if it suited him. Darkness had been familiar for so long that it was . . . comforting, in a strange way. As good as sunlight felt, he felt an atavistic craving for darkness at times.

Until he heard the voices: until his walk on the night the Healer's Moon first died to full dark.

Beautiful . . . look . . . look . . . Look over here, over here, over here . . . .

Kolan stood still, very still, and drew in one breath after another, thinking only of the air moving through his nose and throat and lungs.

You know us. You found us. You love us. Come, come, over here, over here . . . .

Kolan kept his eyes shut and counted his fingers and his toes six times over.

We love you. We need you. We cherish you. Let us help you, here, here, over here . . . .

"One and one is two," Kolan said aloud. "Two and three is five. Four and three is seven. Eight minus two is six. Eight minus one is seven. Seven plus six is thirteen."

A sense of perplexity drowned the voices into silence. Kolan kept reciting random simple mathematics until utter silence returned to the night.

He sighed in deep relief and stopped counting. That had been one of the few tricks to work on *teyhataerth*, on the rare occasions when Kolan was clear-headed enough to use it; the ha'ra'ha had always tried to find a pattern in the numbers, and had gotten distracted into a series of its own esoteric calculations very quickly.

That had granted Kolan and Ellemoa precious *days* of peace, as *teyhataerth* ignored everything until it came to the conclusion of whatever puzzle it had posed itself.

The temporary loss of his ally's attention and support enraged Rosin, who inevitably arrived in short order to inflict a punishment himself . . . But a human-directed torture was simple to endure, compared to what *teyhataerth* could do.

By the slickness in those voices, these ha'ra'hain were very nearly as twisted as *teyhataerth*. Not quite as dangerous, though: if they'd had *teyhataerth*'s strength, they would have pulled him in, instead of calling and coaxing.

He blinked, then blinked again, and looked at the line of the Forest more closely. A series of faint, squarish shimmers ran along the edge of the wood. He wasn't inclined to go closer to find out more; it was enough to know that someone or something had laid a line of protection along the Hackerwood. Those dangerous voices could only coax. They couldn't emerge into the fields and villages of the coastal southlands to take their victims directly.

That line of warding also meant that Kolan couldn't cut through the Forest to reach Arason. If he tried the Forest Road, some distance away, he would be trusting that it was as well protected; and if that protection turned out broken at any point along the way–No. It was too high a risk.

For all his bravery in approaching the witch's house, for all his willingness to confront Ellemoa, he couldn't make himself walk into the agony-laced darkness these twisted creatures would surely deliver. He couldn't go through that again.

I won't let anyone hurt me again. Not again. Never again.

He would have to travel farther east, through the swamps and hills. That wasn't such a bad idea, really; it meant he could stop and see his brethren in the holy salt mines, a pilgrimage many priests in Arason longed to make. Perhaps the gods would speak to him again there.

He turned his steps south, away from the looming darkness.

"You always walk around counting out loud to yourself?" someone said from his left.

Kolan stopped, squinting a little, and saw only shadows among shadows. "When it amuses me," he said warily. "Who are you?"

"Odd way to amuse yourself." The voice drew nearer. Kolan's vision cleared as though a full moon had dawned overhead: movement sorted out into a short, slender form. "Then again, this is an odd area to pass through in the middle of the night, all by yourself, so perhaps that suits the moment."

"You're alone," Kolan pointed out.

"Am I?"

Kolan stood still and shut his eyes, listening intently. After a moment he said, "Yes. You are." He opened his eyes. The short figure stood two steps out of arm's reach now; a boy–no, Kolan decided, studying the barely visible line of stubbly beard and thinning hair: an adult man.

"Interesting that you say that so quickly," the stranger said. "Are you a witch?"

"No," Kolan said. "Not really. I just have good hearing."

"Extraordinary hearing," the stranger commented. "You can call me Fen."

"Kolan. Of Arason. And you have good sight."

"Yes. Ah. You're far from home." Fen stepped a little closer, tilting his head to look up at Kolan. "And out late, far from the path to either Bright Bay or home, at that. What are you doing out here, besides counting to yourself?"

"Just . . . walking," Kolan said. "Just walking. I didn't want to be around people, so I took to the fields." He glanced around. "Is this your land?"

Fen laughed. "My land? No. I don't own any land. I barely own the clothes on my back. I'm a wandering thief and a beggar, my friend, and a brigand when fortune turns to my favor. What do you have by way of money?"

"Very little," Kolan said.

"Give it over," Fen said pleasantly. A knife glinted in his hand.

"No," Kolan said, surprised at himself. "Not for a threat, not for a thief." The shadows thickened around him. A faint whining began in the back of his mind.

Fen advanced another step. "You're probably not worth the trouble," he said, "but it's never safe to assume, is it? Come on. Hand over the coins and I'll leave you your clothes. It's a cold night."

Kolan walked straight toward him; Fen, his own vision apparently as sharp as Kolan's own, held his ground for a heartbeat, then yielded, scrambling sideways and back.

"Are you mad?" he demanded. "I've a *knife*, you damn fool!"

Kolan kept advancing, not saying a word.

"You keep on," Fen panted, trying to turn their path to a giant circle. Kolan aimed a little to one side or the other, forcing the thief to retreat in more or less a straight line. "I'll cut you!"

"Go ahead," Kolan said, and lunged.

Before the startled thief could do more than yelp, Kolan had knocked Fen's knife hand aside. He reached out and closed his hand firmly around the thief's throat.

"If you want to threaten me, tell me you can do something worse than this," he said, bringing his face close to Fen's, and let the screaming roll to the front of his mind. It sank into Fen's awareness like water filling a sponge; Kolan blinked, a little surprised at his sense of instant recognition: *He has some of the blood himself. Just a touch. He probably has no idea—*

Fen made a thick, gagging sound. A moment later, his thoughts slid into Kolan's mind: *Oh gods, I should have run, I knew I should have run, I'm a fool, I can't even use the damn knife, thing doesn't even have an edge, what was I thinking?* His eyes rolled, showing white in the pale moonlight. Raw horror shrieked through his mind as Kolan's memories hit him full force. He sagged, knees folding under him. Kolan let go. Fen sprawled on the ground. The rank stench of urine thickened the air.

Kolan drew a deep breath, struggling against rage, his vision hazing. The knife lay on the ground beside the thief. He could so easily pick it up . . . so easily turn it point down, so easily draw lines, swirls, patterns. . . and if Fen had enough ha'ra'hain or desert lord heritage to see clearly at night and absorb shared memories so readily, he might have that precious ability to heal. Which meant that the pain could be drawn out . . . for a long time . . . and perhaps leave Kolan completely free. It was possible—or seemed so, in that intoxicating, seductive moment.

Kolan's fingers brushed the hilt of the knife. Moonlight disappeared from around him, and the world went dark, so dark, *so dark . . . .*

Harm none, a voice out of memory said, stern and disapproving, laced with the echo of prayers, hymns, and recitations gone by. *Harm none.*

Kolan sucked in a noisy breath and stumbled a few steps away, then sank to his knees, shivering all over. The feel of the worn-slick leather wrapped around the hilt lingered on his fingers, burning like Payti's own kiss.

It would be so easy . . . He could still take a step and pick up the knife, infect someone else with the screaming, maybe pass a portion of the burden on to another, lessening his own pain in the process.

Is this what it was like for Ellemoa? Is this that first step into being lost?

Would it even work? Would it be worth the price?

His fingers sank into the cold ground, fisting up handfuls of grassy, sandy dirt. He dry-heaved, spitting a thin trail of drool. His stomach wrenched as though trying to turn itself inside out.

I have the right—I had to defend myself—and if he gets up he'll attack me again—

But Fen's thoughts had been clear: he was a coward at heart, only good at bluffing. His knife wasn't even sharp. Kolan couldn't use it to cut butter, let alone inflict pain on the hapless thief.

Gods, what will I do if someone actually attacks me? And I heard his thoughts— what's happening to me?

Kolan wrapped his arms around himself and shuddered, breathing hard, fighting the red-laced hatred that flared through his entire body: inviting, inciting violence. Finally, his vision clearing, he staggered to his feet. A moment's rummaging through his belt pouch produced a single marble, a lumpy blue globe swirled with strands of green. It had been the most flawed, the only one not quite perfectly round.

He clenched it tightly, rolled it between his palms; focused on the bumpy, pitted texture until the last of the red faded from his mind.

I need to stay away from people. I'm not nearly as sane as I thought. He wondered if he should go back to Bright Bay and submit himself to the care of the priests once more. But that would put him into the company of the others: the ones who, like Ellemoa, had chosen to walk the paths outlined by the screaming. Surrounded by that pressure, he would lose his already tenuous hold completely.

Water. The cure for fire: water. I'll douse Payti's hatred in Wae's love until I see truth clearly again.

He replaced the blue marble in his belt pouch with a quick murmur of gratitude to the Four for their cooperation in producing such a marvel; then staggered to his feet, cast a last glance at the unconscious would-be thief, and hurried away into the strangely not-dark night.

Chapter Thirty-Eight

As Venepe's caravan left Obein, Rat and Frenn moved to the point position, Breek falling in beside Tank at the rear. Dasin rode beside the caravan, his shoulders stiff, ostentatiously not looking back.

Tank sighed a little and rubbed a hand over his face.

"I hear the Vultures decided they liked the taste of redling better than baby merchant," Breek said, grinning.

"They went hungry," Tank said shortly.

Breek laughed, loud enough to jerk Dasin's head around for a ferocious glare. Tank tried not to visibly wince. He knew Dasin would never believe Tank hadn't started in with salacious jokes at his expense.

"Ah, he's jealous," Breek observed as Dasin turned his back on them again. "Always tricky, having it on with merchants. They're sensitive types." He laughed again, the sound carrying forward clearly in the still air.

Tank watched Dasin's shoulders go taut and sighed; then, belatedly, thought about what Breek had said.

"I'm not sleeping with him, godsdamnit," he said.

Breek grinned, displaying gapped and chipped teeth. "Right," he said. "And my mother's a black goose with crabs. Heh."

"Wouldn't be surprised," Tank shot back. "Crabs and worse, I'd guess, and passed it all on to you."

Breek's grin disappeared. "Don't you start with me, boy," he said. "I don't take that kind of shit from Rat, let alone a wet little ta-neka like you."

"I hand out what I'm given," Tank said.

Breek snorted. "You're barely old enough to piss without help, boy. Don't try going up against *me*."

"I'm smart enough not to hit my shoes," Tank returned. "Yours look a little damp to me."

"Gods *damn*, boy, you looking for a burial, you keep on with that mouth," Breek nearly growled. "I'll take you to pieces and leave it to your lover to put 'em back together."

"I doubt it," Tank said, unable to stop the words from emerging even as sense shrieked at him to back down. To his horror, his mouth kept on moving: "If you were good enough for that, *you'd* have a Hall coin in your pocket."

Breek glowered. "That's *enough*. I'll settle you tonight," he promised. "I ain't slowing Venepe down. But once we finish for the night–you're done, boy. You're *done*."

They rode on in sullen silence.

The grey mare snuffled into Tank's hair as he checked her hooves. He took his time brushing her down and combing snarls from her tail; she stood patiently, as though she could tell his mood was as foul as the clouds brewing outside.

"You've been a good horse," he muttered, leaning against her warm side for a moment. "Hope I haven't been too hard on you, myself."

She shifted her weight sideways, taking herself neatly out from underneath him. He laughed, slung his saddlebags over one shoulder and his pack over the other, and left the stall. He paused two doors down to watch Dasin grooming his bay.

"Not bad," he said over the open half-door, "for someone who didn't know how to use a currycomb right way round a few days ago."

Dasin looked up, face streaked with dirt and weariness. "Thanks," he said, a little sourly, then straightened. "You being nice because you're expecting to get taken apart?"

Tank frowned at the bay and didn't answer that. "He's favoring the back left," he said. "Check for a stone."

Dasin bent and hauled the bay's hoof up.

"Damnit," he said, "I hate dealing with this. The hoof's all over shit." He shot Tank a hopeful glance. "Since you're being so nice?"

"Not a chance," Tank said, grinning. "Do it yourself." *Take your time*, he added silently. Although he wasn't entirely sure why, he really didn't want Dasin seeing the fight waiting outside the stable doors.

He turned his back on Dasin's cursing and left the stables. As he crossed the threshold, Breek straightened from the tree he'd been leaning against, his face grim.

"Time for your lesson, boy," he said.

Tank slung his saddlebags and pack to a dry spot of ground. Breek's sword harness and dagger belt were looped over a low-hanging branch, so Tank unbuckled his weapons as well, balancing them carefully over the saddlebags.

He took a quick glance around as he straightened: nobody around. This would stay between him and Breek, then; that was a relief. He turned to face Breek and moved forward a few steps, studying the big man's stance with a detached, critical assessment.

"I'm gonna give you some rules, so's I don't kill you and upset Venepe," Breek began, rocking to stand with his feet splayed and his hands on his hips. "No knives, no–"

When you have to fight, Allonin's advice had been, *don't let the other person set the rules.*

Tank leapt in close, drove his foot in a hard, scraping kick down the larger man's shin, and tumbled out of the way as Breek howled in pain.

"You little ta-neka!" Breek shouted, turning to follow.

From a braced spot on the ground, Tank kicked out again in a sweeping movement, catching the back of the man's knees. Breek crashed down. Tank rolled away and to his feet, sank into a balanced crouch, and waited. His entire torso felt strained and pebbly grit covered his arms, hands, and back; but the move should have been impressive to a man used to fistfights. It might be enough.

Breek, breathing hard, staggered to his feet and stared at Tank for a few moments without moving. He seemed to be favoring the shin-kicked leg and showed definite stiffness in his left shoulder, probably from landing on it badly during the fall.

"So you know something about how to fight," Breek said at last, grudgingly.

"Yes."

Breek flicked a quick glance around. Dasin stood in the stable doorway, openmouthed. The big mercenary's face hardened.

Tank swore under his breath. If nobody had been watching, Breek would probably have let the fight end there. Now, with Dasin of all people as a witness, he had to prove himself better.

"You got lucky," the big mercenary growled, and started forward again. "Won't happen again, boy."

No other choice . . . .

Tank set aside awareness of anything but Breek, moving, circling, drawing back for a swing–

–turned sideways to the blow, grabbed Breek's arm just below the elbow, and twisted, turning again–

Breek stumbled in a half circle, yelping in a mixture of outrage and pain as his shoulder wrenched, arm hoisted high behind his back.

"Hold still," Tank said, "or I'll dislocate your arm."

Breek let out a bellow and yanked sideways, his thickly muscled arm sliding out of Tank's grip, and spun with astonishing speed. Tank ducked an off-hand blow; Breek could fight with either hand, then. Good to know.

Past Breek's shoulder, he saw Rat, arms crossed and frowning. Not far away, Frenn grinned, bouncing on his toes, clearly expecting Breek to finish the job momentarily.

A movement brought Tank's attention back to Breek in time to avoid being pulled into a grappling hold. He twisted aside and retreated a few steps.

"You *finish* this, redling," Breek panted. "Don't you run away from me."

"Not running," Tank said. "Giving you a chance to quit."

Breek snorted and charged.

Tank stepped sideways, dropped into a braced squat, and kicked out, low and hard. Breek crashed over him and into a sideways sprawl. Bone snapped; Breek howled and rolled over to his back, clutching at his left shoulder.

Finish it—

Breek began to rise, his eyes red-rimmed with murderous fury now, whimpering a little. "Take you apart, redling—"

Tank stepped in and kicked Breek's left shoulder.

Breek howled and collapsed, nearly frothing curses as he writhed on the ground.

A heavy hand landed on Tank's shoulder and spun him around. A moment later, a fist drove into his stomach. "Nasty little redling southerner," Frenn snarled.

Tank dropped to the ground, fighting for breath. Frenn drew a booted foot back. Tank rolled clear, not quite far enough. The kick caught the side of his shoulder hard enough to make him yelp. He scrambled to his feet and spun to face Frenn.

"My fight was with Breek," he panted. Agony spidered down his arm into his fingers, and his stomach felt as though it had been driven straight through his spine; he clenched and unclenched his hand, trying to shake that pain out, at least. "What are you doing in the middle of it?"

"You need taken down a touch," Frenn said, advancing. "You'll be good and down by the time *I'm* done with you."

Tank backed and circled, risking a quick glance at Rat. The dark-haired mercenary stood still, arms crossed and frowning, clearly unwilling to interfere. Tank hoped that extended to not getting in line for the "lesson" Breek had begun.

Frenn swung, with more precision than Breek had shown. Tank stepped inside the punch, pushing it aside with one hand; turned his wrist, grabbing Frenn's, and twisted, turning sideways and heaving.

Frenn went sprawling with a concussive *thump*.

Dasin yelped surprise from somewhere far away, then: "Aw, look *out—*"

Breek, rolling, grabbed Tank's ankle and yanked. Tank hit the ground in a bruising, graceless sprawl; a moment later, Frenn was looming over him, grinning wide and mean.

If Frenn sat on him, the fight would be *over*.

Tank kicked free of Breek's grip and frantically rolled up into a crouch as Frenn aimed another kick at his head; grabbed Frenn's ankle and foot and twisted, shoving with everything he had. Frenn went down again, face first this time. When he rose, blood streamed from his now-misshapen nose and he wore the same murderous glare Breek had displayed.

"You're *dead*," he said, and took a step forward.

"Like *hells*," Dasin said from behind him, and swung a heavy branch. It connected with the back of Frenn's head with a sickening thunk, and the big mercenary went over like a felled tree. Dasin hefted the branch and glared down at Breek, who'd wobbled to his knees. "Try it," he threatened. "*Try* it."

Breek stared, puffy-eyed, bleeding, and sullen; then staggered to his feet and over to Frenn.

Breathing hard, Tank locked his knees to keep them from folding under him. He looked at Rat. The dark-haired mercenary hadn't moved. He met Tank's gaze levelly for a long moment, then said, "I *warned* you about that attitude. Hope you don't plan on sleeping anytime soon, boy."

"Call 'em off," Tank panted. "Damnit, Rat, I didn't start this!"

"Your mouth did," Rat said, unyielding. "And I got no say over them. Got any sense, you'll sleep with your boy tonight." He cast a scathing glare at Dasin, then shook his head and walked over to join Frenn and Breek.

Dasin dropped the branch. "Godsdamnit, Tank," he said. "*Godsdamnit.*"

Tank took a long look at Dasin's white face and set expression, then said, "Let's go find a drink. Or ten."

Dasin exhaled noisily and nodded.

Tank shrugged sword harness and knife belt on, scooped up pack and saddlebags, then led the way.

Chapter Thirty-Nine

Ellemoa worked her way through damp, uneven streets, the rain humming in her ears. No sound but that drone and no thought but *find Eredion* existed. Emotion dissolved like suka taffy in the persistent rain; absently, instinctively, she shaped mist and pulled rain around her as a shield, her only conscious thoughts focused on finding the desert lord who'd stopped her from reaching her son.

Some things do not require violence to a lesser form of life, a stern voice said across the years of memory and madness. Ellemoa shook her head, batting that aside, but an uneasiness ran along her spine all the same, a relentless sense of *not rightness*.

Harm none, Kolan pleaded with her in a far darker memory. *Don't let yourself become this thing they want you to be! Ellemoa—don't do it—*

Kolan had refused to do what Rosin wanted. No matter that Rosin punished Ellemoa for Kolan's disobedience, no matter that Rosin would punish *him* if Ellemoa refused.

She hadn't refused, after the first few such lessons. He had never yielded. Not once. No matter how much pain it brought her . . . .

She snarled under her breath with remembered frustration and took a single bounding leap, high up into the embrace of a sprawling, ancient stone-pine tree. Catching at a branch, she swung herself up to a secure perch and scanned the city, stretching her vision to its utmost. She could scarcely see a full mile, and the edges of that were painful to bring into focus. It would take time to see properly once more.

She put *if* out of her mind. Ha'ra'hain could recover from anything. She'd have her full sight back soon enough. Meanwhile, she could still hear, could taste, could *smell*—and she had *other*-vision to work with.

It was easy to find Eredion, with the sight. Easier than she had expected. He stood out, apparently too arrogant to even think of hiding from ha'ra'hain vision—or perhaps, and more likely, ignorant of the need.

Brine coated her nose. Bitter, earthy hops ran across her tongue. A rough song echoed along her inner ear, then faded before the words came clear.

"Time to get moving," someone said. "Nearly dark."

"Has it stopped pissing down rain yet?"

"No."

"Damn. Graveyard's going to be all over muck—"

Trivial, useless conversation. She steadied herself, gasping a little. Like physical sight, this was proving harder than it should be. Gathering determination, she reached out again: met a stolid, stony blankness.

He heard me eavesdropping. He knows I'm hunting him.

She chewed on her knuckles reflectively. Would he scurry back to the safety of the Seventeen Gates? She thought not. He had an unflinching nature, this Sessin lord: he'd face a confrontation without running away.

Her eyes narrowed with her wide smile. She did like the ones who didn't run. *Now, where do I find him?*

Graveyard.

People come here to talk . . . Lord Eredion's the sponsor of the group.

Ellemoa's grin widened. It wasn't even all that far away. She could take her time arriving; she would let them get settled down with that insolent gravekeeper—all *trapped*, in one tiny building, the building with but one exit.

She settled back to enjoy the rain for a while. She even dozed a bit, confident in her plan, in her safety, in her balance: the stone pine felt warm, and solid, and *real* around her. Humans went by, huddled against the weather, not looking up, not thinking of danger: arguing, loving, sulking, laughing. Insignificant beetles, each and every one of them.

Abruptly, a vision flickered across her inner sight:

Grey eyes, swimming with fear and rain—

She sat up sharply, catching at a nearby branch to steady herself.

A voice, a thought, filled with confusion and panic: *What am I doing out here? I should be indoors. What was I thinking?*

She held her breath, hardly daring to hope.

I couldn't lift a purse in this weather if someone paid me to do it. Wait—what? I'm not a thief. Not any longer. I'm . . . I'm . . .

My son, Ellemoa called out, wild, ecstatic. *My son—here, I'm here*—

The chattering thoughts abruptly slid behind a wall of silence as opaque as Lord Eredion's.

Of course. He doesn't know me. I'm just a strange voice in the darkness—oh, my poor son—She dropped to the ground, landing in a crouch, and sniffed the air hungrily. Found a skittering, ghostly pull toward a fixed point: the graveyard. Somehow, some way, she would find what she wanted at the graveyard. Her son must be headed there.

He mustn't fall into the grasp of the desert lords. They were dangerous. They would hurt her son. Kill him. Humans all wanted the ha'ra'hain dead or enslaved. Rosin had told the truth about that. She knew truth when she heard it, and he'd told her so many things about the secret plans of the humans.

We should kill them all, before they can put us in cages.

She shook her head. *Focus. My son. Must find my son. Get out of here. Get away from this place.*

Laughter coiled through memory as she launched herself toward the grave-yard: impatient now, angry, batting aside anything in her path.

Close. Close now. She gathered calm, wrenched control, abruptly recalling that a forewarned desert lord was a very dangerous creature. Allowing anger to drive her risked failure, risked capture, risked losing any chance at taking her son home.

She took another bounding leap, landing silently atop a nearby rooftop. Clay tiles and wooden ridgelines scraped, cold and wet, knobbly and sharp, against her bare feet as she ran.

On the corner of a roof in clear sight of the graveyard, she paused, crouched; tilted her head, eyes nearly shut, and *listened*. Rain dribbled through her hair, slicked her clothes, curled around her inner elbow and thighs, pooled between her toes.

Water and wind carried messages, but she'd never been good at reading them. Rosin hadn't known the trick, and *teyhataerth* had only dimly grasped the language. It had been easier in Arason, with her lover's guidance.

I'll be back there soon. Soon. With my son.

The cottage held only one human life, no desert lords. Eredion and his com-panion either hadn't arrived, or—

She blinked without opening her eyes and studied the area with awaken-ing wariness. *Yes. There.* Eredion and his companion—two—no, three. *Four* in total.

No: *five*. There was a *presence*, so tightly closed in on itself that she'd al-most missed it. The four stood around the fifth. Ellemoa opened her eyes and squinted through the rain, straining to see; the rain she had called in blurred even her vision. She reluctantly began redirecting the storm, angling wind and water aside to get a clearer view of that small group of humans.

Hearing cleared, as always, before sight: "—Forgive me if we take the time to check on that story of yours," someone said.

"Do that," that *presence* shot back. "And while you're at it, be sure to ask for Deiq of Stass. He's staying at Peysimun Mansion. I'm sure he'll be happy to explain."

"What the hells is he doing back in town?" the first voice exclaimed, dis-tinctly unhappy: a desert lord, carefully shielded, but she could tell he didn't like or trust this *Deiq*—another familiar name she couldn't quite place at the moment.

"He's lying," another voice said. "He's just a street thief, lying to get out of trouble."

"I wouldn't lie to desert lords. I know better."

Ellemoa lost the next few sentences as she struggled with an unexpectedly difficult current of rain, and a blast of wind that almost tumbled her from the roof. At last she had the immediately local weather under control—a moder-ately hazy rain, enough to keep their attention on the ground—and focused on the conversation below.

" —is that supposed to *help* your case?"

"That depends on whether you respect ha'ra'hain. Because I'm one too, you know."

Ellemoa screamed, batting aside the last of the mist and rain, and leapt. *My son. My son!*

She reached the group in two long bounds, her attention only on her son, on his wide grey eyes and pale skin, on the shocked expression on his face as he staggered back, away from her—*No, no, I won't hurt you, I'm rescuing you,* she tried to call to him: found his mind shut, reflecting back images of *white, screaming, whirling motion*—herself, through his eyes.

A moment later a foulness coated her, acidic grit seeking every tender spot in eyes and mouth and nose. Her legs began to buckle from the pain and *wrongness* of it. She screamed again, reflex driving her back and away: barely aware of leaping to the safety of the rooftops, of calling more rain and wind to shield her retreat.

Instinct threw her head back, water rinsing the stinging from her eyes and nose; she spat, gulped rainwater, spat again. At last vision and sense cleared, but the area was long since empty, the trail cold and washed out in the storm. Logic said they'd taken her son back within the protection of the Seventeen Gates: taken him *prisoner.*

Leaving her alone and helpless, while they tortured her only son to bend to their will. That foulness had weakened her: even now, she could feel the poison working through her body, sapping her strength, slowing her movements. *It's dragging me down to being human. Being vulnerable.*

I need to feed. That will drive this poison from my body. A combination of cunning and fury brought her to earth again, streaking across the wet ground: Eredion would rue this night's work, by the time she finished.

Softly, softly, sweet, Rosin cautioned. *Don't ruin it by going too quickly. You've earned this, don't you think? Take your time and do it right. And if she's Eredion's ally, she might have some of that foulness to hand, for her own protection against you.*

Yes. Yes, of course . . . You're very wise, Rosin. Thank you.

She slowed, padding forward with feline grace; raised a hand and knocked, very gently, like a timid, grieving human, on the door of the gravekeeper's cottage.

Chapter Forty

"You realize we're done working with Venepe," Dasin said. He sipped his hot spiced wine and delivered a severe stare. "Because you can't mind your manners."

Tank glared back, sullen, and said, "*You're* the one whacked Frenn with a damn great branch. Up to that point I had it handled." He risked a sip of wine; it stayed down, and didn't hurt as much as the last one had.

"You were about to get your ass handed to you, is what you had handled," Dasin said. He shook his head. "I'll admit it was impressive watching you throw someone twice your bulk like he was made of feathers, but you were *losing,* Tank. They never intended to let you win."

"I *know* that, you godsdamned idiot," Tank said. "If you hadn't walked out of the stables to gawp, I could have settled it a lot easier. Breek would have come after me again some other time, I'd have let him lay me out, everything would have been done with. You staring like that turned everything serious. And you godsdamned well shouldn't have gotten into it yourself. That's what tore it." He took a larger mouthful of wine. The crippling agony in his stomach and ribs was easing, little by little.

Dasin shook his head and sipped wine.

"I don't pretend to understand your world, Tank," he said finally. "I don't think I want to. I'd rather handle percentages and politics than what you're into."

"Just a different kind of politics," Tank said. He touched his face gingerly, feeling across the assorted bumps and cuts. "But you're right on one thing–you've never been any good at it."

"That's *not* what I said," Dasin said, aggrieved.

Tank grinned, then winced at what the movement did to the sore spots on his face. "Well, I don't mind admitting that I'm no good with numbers and lengths of cloth," he said. "And you know Venepe better than I do. So how do we get this sorted out?"

Dasin didn't answer right away. He frowned down at his mug, apparently deep in thought. Tank let him be, watching the room while he waited.

A dice game rattled at a corner table. At another, six men crouched round a card game, eyeing each other suspiciously and holding their cards close to their chests to shield them from view. A series of wall-mounted lanterns, each one securely bolted up against a metal plate-covered section of support beams, provided more light than most taverns offered. The air, while noticeably tinged with sweat, dirt, and spilled ale, seemed less foul than Tank had expected; certainly less noisome than Kybeach's dingy tavern had been.

Then again, the inside of a dungpile would smell better than anything in Kybeach.

The only women here were serving girls. Tank watched them move among the tables: smiling, evading the occasional half- or wholly-drunken grab. When an auburn-haired serving woman old enough to be Tank's grandmother glanced his way, he raised his mug slightly and nodded at Dasin. She nodded, came over, collected their by-now nearly empty mugs, and returned them brimming with steaming liquid a short time later.

Dasin picked up his mug without seeming to notice it had ever been gone and took a sip; spluttered and set the mug down sharply enough to slosh hot wine onto his hand, glaring at Tank accusingly.

Tank laughed. Dasin wiped his hand on his pants leg, grimacing, and said, "I don't know that I want to sort out things with Venepe."

Tank stopped laughing. "What?" he said. "Why the hells not?"

"Venepe's an ass," Dasin said. "I know more than he does, and I'm not even half his age. He spends his evening with servant girls instead of with the rich people in town; he puts his attention on currying favor in places like Kybeach; he hires a bunch of thugs to guard his wagons and doesn't have the sense to ask hard questions about a letter from a foreign political entity who has a reputation for being manipulative. I'd lay good bits that Stai *intended* him to misunderstand that letter. She's not stupid, herself. Hell, Venepe probably doesn't even know what he's dealing with. He knows it's a name with power, and a name that makes expensive damn trinkets that are going to be in demand now that the Church is out of the way, and he goes jumping the moon without looking for a ladder."

Dasin took a cautious sip of his wine.

"I could double his business if he'd listen to me," he added. "All he sees is my age. Damn fool."

Remembering the attractive young lady-thief in Obein, Tank couldn't help wondering if Dasin had underestimated Venepe the way he himself had underestimated Rat. Venepe might not be making piles of coin, but he had a solidly established customer base and enough money coming in to hire four mercenaries, however low unsworn status might weight the pay.

He knew better than to say any of that aloud. Dasin would take it into a loud argument, and Tank already had a thundering headache that the wind wine was doing little to ease.

"Dasin, I have a contract with Venepe," he said instead. "A Freewarrior Hall contract. I can't walk out on that."

"You have a contract with *me*," Dasin corrected. "Venepe's only involved because my pay's based on *his* profits."

"He's the one paying me, he's the one I'm contracted to."

Dasin shook his head, looking disgusted. "This is *my* kind of politics, Tank. Trust me. Your contract's with me, whatever your Hall log might say."

"Fine," Tank said. "I quit."

Dasin laughed, loud and sharp. Heads turned around the room. Tank put a hand over his face, cringing; he *hated* that laugh. It always signaled trouble.

"Not so fast. There's a merchant in town," Dasin said, "name of Yoo-eyr." He pronounced the name with exaggerated care. "Venepe's shit-scared of him for some reason. He's not even staying a full day in the morning; he's planning to be on the road again by noon. He's told me flat out he hates this town. He's skipping through here as fast as decency and pride allows."

The hair rose on the back of Tank's neck.

"Oh, gods, no," he said, not at all sure why. "No, Dasin. Don't–"

"The way *I* figure," Dasin interrupted, ignoring Tank's inarticulate protest, "this Yuer's someone who's got a double handful more smarts and power than Venepe. Which means he'll pay better, for one." He sipped at his wind wine, looking smug. "And merchants with that sort of influence always need reliable help that won't steal the silverware out from under. Me having status of my own–all right, *both* of us having status–"

"Not me," Tank said adamantly.

"You've got the same as me," Dasin said. "You're as much entitled to throw around the name *Aerthraim* as I am."

"Keep your voice down," Tank said, casting a quick, anxious glance around the room. "That's not a name I'd wave around north of the Horn, whatever Venepe might think." He paused. "You didn't tell Venepe I'm–?"

"No," Dasin said. "I know you like to keep yourself to yourself. And when I saw that hall captain's reaction, I figured I'd better leave it at *this red-headed scrapper I met along the way who's signed with the Freewarrior Hall here in town.*" He paused, and seemed about to ask a question, then shook his head and took another sip of wind wine instead. His expression settled into its familiar sullen lines. "I'm going to have a talk with this Yuer, see if he needs a hand on one of his wagons. Come on with me, I'll get you a spot alongside."

Tank shook his head, unable to put a name to his sense of dread. "This is a bad idea, Dasin," he said. "A really *bad* idea."

He put a hand to his stomach, wincing a little, as a cramp stitched briefly up the left side.

"You're scared," Dasin said flatly. He gulped down the rest of his wine and laughed. "If I hadn't just seen you thrash two men each twice your weight and age, I wouldn't've believed it. You're running scared over a social visit to a merchant. You know, Tank, you're the hells' own mouse sometimes."

The flush in Dasin's face came from more than the heat in the room. Tank glanced down at his own, nearly full mug and grimaced.

"Dasin," he said. "You're halfway to drunk. This isn't a good time for you to–"

"*Mouse*," Dasin said, standing. He steadied himself with a hand against the table and grinned. "Are you coming or not?"

"Sit down, you damned fool," Tank hissed as heads turned once more. "You're in no damn state to negotiate a piss, let alone a contract."

Dasin made a few soft squeaking sounds. "Come on," he said. "Walk with me or go crawling back to kiss–"

"All *right*," Tank said before Dasin could finish that sentence in his now *far* too loud voice. He scooped up his pack and saddlebags, then added, in a low voice, "*Damn* you, Dasin."

Dasin grinned and strutted out the door.

Chapter Forty-One

Dawn was turning black to pink when Idisio faced the king for the third time in his life. The meeting wasn't in a small casual room this time, but in the vast magnificence of a ballroom converted to a temporary audience hall. Floor-to-ceiling murals covered the walls, and the gilded sconces hanging from the ceiling had so many candles that each one had large catch-basins hanging below to collect the meltings. They weren't lit at the moment; instead, the shutters of the wide windows were thrown open. A thin pre-morning breeze sifted through the room, dispersing the smoky haze of a dozen squat table-lamps.

Idisio tugged uncomfortably at his borrowed shirt. It smelled of harsh soap, and the mended patches on the shoulders, sides, and back were of a coarse material that scratched against his skin. The pants were marginally better; they hung loose enough on Idisio's skinny legs to avoid rubbing him raw.

Everything seemed to be bothering him at the moment. The smoke from the oil lamps irritated his nose, the light hurt his eyes, the servant-loose cut of the clothes made him feel clumsy and ugly. The distrustful wariness of the desert lords aggravated his pride, and King Oruen's severe stare prickled that further.

Or was that *Lord* Oruen, given Idisio's new status? He decided that sticking with *king* was probably safer for the moment.

"I thought you went east with Scratha," the king said. "Did he turn back for some reason?" His expression boded ill for any answer besides *no*.

"He claims to be in town with Alyea and Deiq, of all people," the stocky man beside Idisio said.

The king's eyebrows lowered further. "If that's true," he said, "*one* of them went *far* off the course they'd been set!"

Idisio endured the king's fierce glare as blankly as he could.

"I *see*," the king said ominously.

The desert lord cleared his throat. "I've sent messengers to inquire, and they are in town–arrived last night. They should be here soon. Ah–" He turned as the main doors at the far end of the hall opened just enough to admit two people. "Here they are."

There was a moment of silence as Alyea and Deiq entered the room. Everyone stared at Deiq with various degrees of horrified fascination. He didn't walk in: he *strode* in, as though he owned the room and everyone in it. The vivid green of his silk shirt, the gold chain around his neck, the rings on his hands, even the finger-thin braid pulled apart from the rest and draped down his chest all combined to mark Deiq out as the single most powerful person present.

Beside him, Alyea was practically invisible.

Oruen's startled stare quickly hardened into a glare. Deiq met it without apparent concern, smiling a little.

Idisio, he said. *Has anyone hurt you or been rude?*

I'm fine.

That isn't what I asked.

Alyea, as though she were the only person of worth in the room, strode to stand in front of the throne. "Lord Sessin," she said, chin high. "Lord Oruen. Idisio."

Gazes shifted from Deiq to Alyea, gaining more than a slight tinge of amusement.

She doesn't quite understand yet, does she? someone said.

No, Deiq answered. *I'm working on it.*

Might want to hurry on that a bit.

Alyea was staring directly at Idisio now, as though waiting for an answer, and Deiq's black stare was fixed on him as well.

"Lord Alyea," Idisio muttered. "Deiq. Glad you're here."

You didn't answer my question, Deiq said, his stare hardening.

Pahenna, Idisio retorted, not entirely sure where he drew the word from, or even what it meant, but somehow knowing it to be the appropriate language. *I can handle myself, thank you!*

Which is why you're standing in front of a king and multiple desert lords, all of whom are looking at you like you've stolen the king's drawers? Deiq inquired tartly.

"May I present my escort, Deiq of Stass," Alyea said. Idisio heard a stifled snort from one of the other desert lords. Alyea appeared oblivious to the amusement her attitude was causing. "You've already met Idisio, I see. He's . . . under the protection of Peysimun Family."

"And mine," Deiq said promptly, which drained the half-smiles from the faces around them. *Answer the question, Idisio*, he added. *It's important. Did they hurt you? Were they rude?*

Nobody hurt me, Idisio said. *I handled the rudeness. Leave it alone.*

No. Not this time. You need their respect.

Let me earn it myself, then!

You don't know how. And don't *try telling me to teach you right* now!

"Welcome to my court once again, s'e," King Oruen said, blatantly insincere. Idisio felt Deiq's volatile temper darken even further.

Lord Sessin cleared his throat. *Deiq,* he said, his mental tone considerably calmer than the elder ha'ra'ha's, *let me handle this. Please.* Aloud, he said, "I think, as we're reasonably alone here, it's time to drop the nonsense, Lord Oruen. You know who–and what–Deiq is."

You're being too damn nice, Eredion, Deiq said.

I'm doing my job.

Then make sure Idisio gets the respect he deserves.

Lord Sessin flicked a fast, startled glance at Idisio, then looked back to Deiq. *He really is a ha'ra'ha?*

Yes. He really is.

Ah, damnit. Eredion met Idisio's gaze squarely, and his next words were aimed at Idisio alone. *My apologies for earlier, ha'inn. It's been a confused time of late. I'll make it up to you–*

"Yes. You're right," the king said grudgingly. "My apologies, *ha'inn.*" He flicked a glance at Alyea, as though checking to see if she knew the word; she stared back, blank-faced, giving nothing away.

"'Honored One'," Deiq said. "I do like the sound of that."

Idisio couldn't tell if he had translated the word for Alyea's benefit or to irritate the king by emphasizing his superior status. Whatever the intent, neither the king nor Alyea looked particularly happy.

"Enjoy it while it lasts," Lord Sessin said dryly. *Stop poking the hornet's nest, Deiq,* he added silently. "And I believe you owe Idisio the same courtesy, actually."

"Are you telling me a *ha'ra'ha* tried to pick Lord Scratha's pocket?" Oruen exclaimed.

Alyea turned to stare at Idisio, her expression a mix of outrage and astonishment, then shot a deeply suspicious glare at Deiq, as though sharply reassessing her trust in him. Deiq returned the glare in kind; she blanched, then flushed and dropped her gaze as though in mute apology.

Don't let her push you around, either, Deiq told Idisio. *Especially not in front of this crowd. You stand your ground, you hear me? I'll make Scratha look like a playmate if you embarrass yourself here.*

How come you never took him to task over the way he treated me in the beginning? Idisio demanded, glowering.

Just because you don't see something doesn't mean it doesn't exist, Deiq retorted. *I had a talk with him, believe me. Now pay attention. There are too many desert lords in the room for us to indulge in an extended private conversation.*

Aloud, Deiq said, "So what is important enough to bring four full lords and two trainees all the way into Bright Bay?"

Idisio withdrew into himself, feeling more than a little sullen. Deiq seemed to expect Idisio to stand up for himself while at the same time treating him as barely above incompetent. It was getting irritating.

Stand up straight, Deiq said, the words very nearly a mental slap. *You're acting like a scolded child. Stand up!*

"How much does she know about what really happened with Ninnic?" Lord Sessin asked, glancing uneasily at Alyea. Idisio had the feeling that he'd really have preferred to ask the question privately.

He should have, Deiq snapped. *But I was busy talking to you, and keeping everyone* else *from hearing you, so he couldn't.* Aloud, he said, "I have no idea. Ask her."

"You mean the mad ha'ra'ha who was controlling Ninnic," Alyea said. "Yes, Lord Evkit told me about that."

Oh, gods, Idisio thought, horrified. *That's where the voices came from. That's what was driving people crazy all over town.* He'd really thought it came from something dumped in the wells by Rosin's sadistic followers. *But then why didn't I ever hear the voices?*

That's one of the questions I'd very much like answered once we get to Arason, Deiq said. *At a guess, someone put a protection round you: ha'rethe or ha'ra'ha, more than likely—and it must have been one of your parents, for it to take so well and last so long.*

Lord Sessin said, "Did Evkit tell you we had to kill it?"

Idisio felt as though every drop of his blood drained to his feet. *We had to kill it? We?* He was standing in the presence of men who knew how to *kill* ha'ra'hain?

That's why you don't flinch around them, Deiq snapped. *So stop looking like you're about to piss yourself!*

"He didn't say *who* was involved," Alyea said, glancing at Idisio with a worried expression. "I believe you had good reason, though."

"Idisio, you're in no danger from us," Lord Sessin said hastily. "This was an extremely exceptional situation."

"And you're not going mad," Deiq added, more likely to reassure the king and Alyea than for Idisio's sake. "Believe me, Idisio, I would know. Probably long before you did."

So ha'ra'hain go mad often? Idisio demanded, shivering. *This is something you're good at spotting?* If he'd been speaking aloud, his voice would have scaled up to a squeak by the last word.

Deiq shook his head, delivered another severe glare, and pointedly turned his attention back to the audible conversation. Idisio tried to pay attention; noticed that the king seemed unable to take his gaze from Alyea for any length of time, and rapidly assessed the man's fascination as more politically than emotionally based. Alyea, for her part, seemed intent on proving herself the equal of any man in the room, much to everyone's poorly hidden amusement.

Lord Filin kept a calculating eye on Alyea as well, and *his* words were aimed at making himself look stronger and smarter than the other men in the room: *Mating behavior,* Idisio thought vaguely, not entirely sure why Alyea's presence seemed to be polarizing the room.

She's a new desert lord, Eredion said mildly. *That generally brings on . . . certain changes.* He cleared his throat and went back to the vocal discussion without further explanation; Idisio, taking another look at the way the men were all covertly watching Alyea, discovered he didn't really need clarification after all.

As I'm hearing it, Riss said in memory, *it's not going to be a matter of choice.*

Idisio blinked and looked at his toes, ferociously blocking his mind to utter blankness; he did *not* want Alyea knowing what he was thinking at the moment, let alone Deiq.

"I found something unexpected when I started cleaning the underground areas," Eredion said, his voice tightening; Idisio seized on that as a cue to put his full attention on the conversation. Eredion seemed . . . embarrassed by something, and more than a little frightened. "Some*one*, actually—"

"Oh, how tactful," Lord Filin snorted, crossing his arms.

"I'll admit the term might be a bit shaky at the moment," Eredion said, and his mind went blank with the same abrupt finality that Idisio had used to fend Deiq off, dropping a hollow flatness into his voice as he went on. "But it serves the moment. The child had kept someone alive down there in its lair. I still don't know how, or why, or who; the moment I opened the door it—she—attacked me. I wasn't expecting it." He scratched his cheek and avoided their gazes; even with his mind blocked off, the next words clearly embarrassed him tremendously: "I went down. Blacked out. And when I got up, she was gone."

Now *Deiq's* mind went opaque, so firmly that if Idisio shut his eyes, he couldn't tell Deiq even stood there. A chill ran down his back: on a dark night, he'd never sense Deiq coming.

Could the desert lords around them do the same trick? Was that how they—

Not as well, Eredion said, his jaw tight. *But you're being a bit loud, I'm afraid.*

Idisio hurriedly hauled himself under control and directed his attention to the voices around him again.

"She seems drawn to the graveyard at the edge of town," Eredion was saying aloud, "which is where we set a trap last night—and caught *him*." He jerked his chin at Idisio.

"There was a certain amount of confusion over his identity," Filin said with a pompous deliberation, as though trying to sound more refined in contrast to Eredion's plainer speech. "While we were standing around arguing, the creature—"

"Woman," Eredion murmured, which set Idisio into another round of internal questioning: if the *creature* they described was ha'ra'ha, which increasingly seemed likely, then Filin's insistence on using *it* rather than *she* opened up a new pit in front of Idisio.

What if I'm only male because . . . I've never thought of myself any other way? Suddenly, Deiq's comment that Idisio would grow out of his heterosexual preference took on a new, and dreadful, implication.

No, Deiq said. *You're male. I'll explain all that another time. Pay attention!*

Idisio chewed his bottom lip and made himself concentrate on the conversation, listening to the spats and the maneuverings and the half-truths being traded. His guess that the creature—the woman—who'd attacked last night had been a ha'ra'ha proved out, which did nothing to set his mind at ease. Neither did Eredion's awkwardness as he said, "It's not hurting anyone, it's not feeding—anymore . . . ."

Deiq's glower could have melted iron. Eredion faltered into silence; a moment later, just as Alyea began asking questions about that term, Idisio felt a thundering pressure *whomp* through his hindbrain, leaving him dizzy and breathless for a moment.

Not now, Deiq said from somewhere infinitely far away. The pressure dissipated as fast as it had built, and Idisio shook his head, blinking hard and disoriented.

"Well, never mind," Eredion said, looking oddly green about the ears. "Right now, the woman is searching for something."

Idisio lost the next words under another, softer haze of dizziness; muddled in and out of coherency, and finally pulled his vision and hearing straight in time to hear Deiq say, "Idisio, why were you out in the middle of the night? In the middle of a rainstorm, no less?"

"I just . . . I had to get some air," Idisio said, wishing he could get out of this room and do that now. "I felt so hot, and restless, and I wanted to walk the streets alone, the way I used to." *The way I'd like to do right now.* "I don't know. I felt . . . called. Drawn. Like something wanted me to come out of the house."

"You shouldn't have felt our bait-call," Eredion said. "Not that far away. What did it feel like?"

Bait-call? They'd been trying to trap him? No, wait—they'd been after something else. They'd been after . . . that woman in white, and there was something Idisio wanted to think about regarding her, but a sudden pressure sent him back into the moment's reality and away from thinking anything through.

"Like someone was riffling through my mind," he said. "My memories. I couldn't seem to stop it."

"That definitely wasn't us," Eredion said, looking alarmed.

"No," Deiq said. "That was the ha'ra'ha woman you're after. She seems to have taken an interest in you, Idisio. I wonder why."

Idisio shut his eyes and wondered, for his part, why that statement rang completely false in his ears. Deiq *knew* something, and wasn't telling—which didn't surprise Idisio in the least; but all the evasions were getting *aggravating.*

In a back corner of his mind, he heard Deiq's sour laughter.

Get used to it, the elder ha'ra'ha said. *It's all in the way of things, Idisio: telling the truth will only get you killed, nine times out of ten, around the humans . . . and you generally don't want them to tell you any real truth, either. You'll learn.*

And don't ha'ra'hain ever tell the truth to one another? Idisio shot back.

Oh, especially not that, Deiq answered, no laughter in his tone now. *That's the quickest way to get yourself killed that I can think of.*

Chapter Forty-Two

Tank had hoped that a walk in the rapidly cooling evening air would shake Dasin back to some version of sense and sobriety. As Dasin paused, looking at the brick path to the stately brick cottage beyond, Tank bit his lip and silently *prayed*.

"Mind your manners," Dasin said at last, curtly. "Remember, *I'm* in charge."

Tank abandoned both patience and hope. "Dasin, this is a *bad idea*. Venepe probably has a damn good *reason*—"

Dasin lifted his chin and started forward. Tank swore under his breath, viciously, and followed.

The brick path, wide enough for a carriage where it left the main road, curved around to the back of the house in a slow, majestic sweep; a narrower path branched off toward the front door. To either side of the door, flanked in turn by torches in holders as tall as themselves, stood burly men in dark shirts and darker pants. Stone Islanders or southerners, Tank guessed, and felt his nibbling unease strengthen to a gnaw.

Another few steps, and the features of the two guards came clear: definitely southern. Too olive to be northern, too sharp to be islanders. The guards watched Dasin and Tank approach without any visible reaction, and the gnawing grew more like savage bites with every step Tank took toward their black, dead eyes.

He knew that look. He'd seen it, far too often, and far too close at hand.

Dasin whimpered a little in the back of his throat, and his step faltered for a moment. Tank tensed, waiting–*hoping*–for the overriding flinch that would send Dasin bolting for safety and sanity.

Anyone who hired guards like this was a man Tank did *not* want to meet, now or ever. It took a grim effort to keep his hands away from the hilts of sword and knife alike.

Dasin finished his step and kept going as though his legs simply refused to move in any other direction.

They stopped a few steps shy of arm's reach to the door, far too close for Tank's liking. The guards stared, ominously silent. Tank suddenly felt several inches shorter and pounds lighter, and had to fight against cringing.

"We're here to see trader Yuer," Dasin said, his voice nearly warbling.

The guards focused on him, their mouths widening into identical slow smiles: predator's grins.

"You got an appointment?" the one on the right asked.

Dasin opened his mouth, shut it again. A fine tremor ran through his thin frame.

A different tremor ran through Tank's muscles: an old, black rage beginning to simmer. He drew in a sharp breath and bared his teeth at the guards with no attempt to make it look like a smile. Their attention moved to him immediately, their smiles fading as quickly.

Nobody spoke for a long, razor-edged moment. Then Tank said, flat and fierce, "We don't *need* an appointment. He'll want to hear what we have to say."

The guards exchanged a dark, thoughtful glance that sent renewed chills up Tank's back; then the one on the left shrugged and the one on the right jerked his thumb at the door and said, "Go on, then."

Tank set a hand on Dasin's shoulder blade, digging his fingers into the soft spot by the spine. The blond jerked away, and the motion flowed into a stride forward, two, three–Tank glared at the door, refusing to acknowledge the guards, who were well within reach to either side now–Dasin fumbled at the handle with trembling fingers. A bitter, oily musk hung in the air, steel and leather and dirt mingling in Tank's nose.

Dasin's hand closed around the doorknob, twisted, shoved; they lurched forward and through. Tank knocked Dasin's hand away from the edge of the door in time to stop him from slamming it behind them, then shut it, gently, himself.

The first thing Tank noticed was how hot the room was; an enormous fireplace at one end of the room sent out smothering waves of heat. Then he focused on the occupants of the room: an exhausted-looking young woman with long dark hair and a bizarre little old man with more wrinkles on his face than Tank had ever seen on a human being. In spite of the thick heat in the air, the man had a blanket pulled over his legs as though chilled.

Four comfortable chairs sat arranged evenly around a low, round table. On the table sat a white, unadorned teapot and two tiny white cups shaped nearly like half of an egg. Both cups were empty.

"Greetings," the old man said in a strong baritone voice fifty years younger than his body. "Please sit."

He waved a hand at the empty chairs on either side of him. The young woman, sitting in the chair directly opposite the old man, dropped her gaze to her hands. Her face was heavily shadowed with fading bruises; Tank felt his temper begin to rise again. To distract himself, he glanced around the room.

A red and gold carpet covered most of the stone-flag floor. A sideboard with thick glass decanters and silver-ribbed glass goblets took up a large portion of one wall. A series of framed architectural sketches hung over the sideboard. There were three exits: the front door, a door on the left wall, a door on the right wall. No–five exits, counting the two windows. The glass was fine enough to smash out easily. He glanced up at the ceiling, in which support beams had been left exposed like sturdy dark bones. Remembering the outside of the house, he guessed at least three good-sized rooms above and five down.

Given the size of the fireplace, there was an enormous pile of wood out back. Given the way the driveway had curved around behind the house, there was likely a stable around back as well.

Whatever this merchant might be, he had *significant* wealth. Dasin had that much right, at least; but after seeing the guards outside, Tank found that more reason than ever to run away while they still could.

Dasin put his shoulders back and his chin up. He said, voice quite steady now, "Trader Yuer? I'm Dasin of Aerthraim Family–"

"I know who you are," the old man said, and pointed once more to the chairs. "Sit."

The word contained more command than offer. Tank waited, watching Dasin's faint twitch; after a taut moment, the blond dropped into a chair and motioned for Tank to take the last empty seat. Tank sighed and began unbuckling his sword harness, wondering if switching to a northern waist-belt style would be better suited to northern chairs.

"I've been waiting for you to show up," Yuer said, a smile barely visible under the drooping folds of skin around his mouth. "Dasin and Tanavin of Aerthraim Family."

Dasin made a slightly strangled sound, staring as though he'd forgotten how to speak altogether. Tank eased sword harness, pack, and saddlebags to the floor at his feet, where he could grab them up easily, and kept his own mouth shut.

Yuer's smile widened a little.

"Would you like some tea?" he inquired, gesturing to the small ceramic teapot and two empty cups.

"How did you know–" Dasin started, then cut himself off almost mid-word. "Yes, please. Tea sounds perfect."

"Excellent," Yuer said. "Wian. If you would be so kind."

The young woman slipped from her chair to kneel beside the table. She poured a double mouthful of rich amber-brown liquid into each cup, replaced the teapot on the table, then slid each cup to just shy of the edges of the table nearest Tank and Dasin. A rich, earthy aroma tinged with jasmine filled the room.

"Thank you," Yuer said.

Wian returned to her chair and sat staring at her hands again, her expression utterly blank.

"This is true Stone Island red tea," Yuer said.

Dasin leaned forward and took up the teacup. "I'm impressed, trader Yuer."

And honored." He took a small sip. "This is excellent."

"I keep an extra case or two on hand," Yuer said. He looked at Tank, at the untouched cup on the table, back to Dasin. "I hear the bards of the Red Tower in Arason are developing a taste for it, thanks in part to the head of the Arason Church."

Dasin sipped his tea without saying anything aloud, but his expression would have suited a hunting asp-jacau. Tank watched the dark-haired young lady, who seemed intent on studying her folded hands to the exclusion of all else.

"This young lady's name is Wian," Yuer said. "She's from Bright Bay. And will be returning there soon."

Wian shivered and hunched into herself as if expecting an attack.

Tank bit his tongue against an impulse to say, *Leave her alone!* The old man hadn't actually said or done anything threatening.

"Do try the tea," Yuer said, his dark stare fixed on Tank. "It's quite exceptional."

Tank picked up the small cup and held it loosely in one hand, openly frowning at the trader. "I'm not much for tea."

"*Tank*," Dasin said in a nearly inaudible whisper. Tank ignored him.

"I'm afraid it's all I have to hand at the moment," Yuer said as if Tank's tone had been polite. "If coffee is more to your taste, I believe I'm due a shipment of Ridge Mountain coffee beans sometime in the next tenday. I'll hold some aside against your next visit."

Dasin sat up a little straighter. "*F'Heing* Ridge Mountain coffee?"

"Several ranking members of the Isata News-Riders Guild are quite fond of it," Yuer said calmly. "I deal in profitable wares, *s'e* Dasin. Small, relatively lightweight, quickly portable, not particularly fragile as long as you keep them very dry, extremely *profitable* wares."

He shifted his gaze to Wian. She sat still as stone, apparently indifferent to everything around her; Yuer's mouth moved into a slow smile too similar to the guard's predatory leers for Tank's liking.

The old man looked at Dasin, still smiling. "Spices, coffees, and teas are *reliable*," Yuer said. "They never lose their appeal, north to south to west to east. Housewives need them for cooking. Priests need them for ceremonies. Healers need them for salves and poultices. It's an endless market."

Something smoldered in Dasin's stare now: *ambition*. Dangerously close to *greed*. Tank cleared his throat, hoping to draw Dasin's attention, to shake him loose of the dangerous fascination this wrinkled old man seemed to hold for him.

"I'm able to pay my assistants very well," Yuer said softly. "On the order of forty percent of profits, as a starting number." He closed his eyes briefly, then splayed a thin-fingered hand over his stomach and looked at Dasin once more. "Unfortunately, I'm not able to travel. I've been afflicted with a . . . delicate . . . digestion in my old age."

His gaze moved to Wian again, and this time she shivered a little. Tank clenched the hand not holding the cup, his short nails digging painfully into his palm.

Yuer went on, "Business is quite good, but I'm in need of an extra hand, as it happens. Someone to take a route from Bright Bay to Sandlaen and back. Would you happen to know of any responsible young merchants looking to take over a very profitable trade route?"

The silence hung for a moment. Dasin opened his mouth.

Too easy, Tank thought. *He knew what Dasin wanted. He knew our names. This isn't just a bad idea; it's a flat-out trap.*

"We're signed with Venepe through Isata," Tank said loudly, and ignored Dasin's furious hiss.

"Ah," Yuer said, squinting at him thoughtfully. "I didn't realize you were a trader, *s'e* Tanavin. I'd been told you trained as a mercenary." He pronounced *mercenary* in tones another might have used for *diseased rat*.

"Yeah," Tank said, deliberately lapsing into a coarser accent. "But Dasin's signed with Venepe too."

Dasin glared at him.

"But all I asked," Yuer said, smiling, "was whether you knew of anyone interested, *s'e* Tanavin. I'll take that as a *no*." He nodded to Wian; she rose, collected the teapot, and left the room without once looking at Tank or Dasin directly. "So nice to meet you both."

Tank set down his untasted cup, a foul taste in his mouth. "How did you know our names?" he asked bluntly.

Yuer's smile became even more predatory. "Good day, *s'es*."

Before Tank quite realized he was moving, he found himself standing outside with Dasin, hands filled with a clumsy tangle of pack, saddlebags, and sword harness. The blond shot him a hard, hostile glare and stalked away. Behind him, the guards coughed sniggers of laughter; Tank hunched his shoulders and followed Dasin without looking back.

As he walked, the wind rummaged through his hair, as though trying to get his attention. A voice without a throat whispered: *Forest. No go. Elder woman say, no go Forest. Stay on Road.* It didn't–quite–have the slick, greasy feel of one of *those* voices; instead, it carried a fragmented, fractured feeling to it. Where the voice in the darkness under Bright Bay hadn't *cared* about knowing human speech, this voice once had understood it very well indeed–but couldn't quite recall how to produce it any longer.

Gods, Tank thought, panic turning his skin icy for a moment. *Now I have ghosts following me around . . . Either that, or I finally am losing my mind completely.*

He tried to shift everything to one hand, to allow himself to bat at the air by his head, stupid as he knew that would look. Straps slid and weight shifted; he went down on one knee, grappling at the cascading weight of his belongings.

The low, mean laughter of the guards came to his ears clearly, and the breeze stilled for a moment. Then, abruptly, it whiffled through his hair with renewed force, whispering: *Elder woman. Tee. Low. Say no go, no go, no go inside Forest. . . .* The voice faded away along with the wind and stayed silent.

Tee Low? "Oh, hells," he said aloud. "*Teilo?*"

Dasin had very nearly disappeared in the murky darkness ahead. Cursing under his breath, Tank stood, hoisted everything into an awkward armful, and hurried after him; wishing he could outrun the shivers that were settling into his very bones.

Chapter Forty-Three

The Palace lay inside a wide belt of connected gardens: Idisio cut through each one, following the often meandering paths without really seeing his surroundings. The conversation with Deiq cycled and recycled through his mind: *I should have stayed on the streets*; and Deiq's prompt, unsympathetic response: *You'd be dead by now.*

Idisio had assumed that the trip south with Scratha had somehow triggered his heritage, but Deiq seemed certain that Idisio had been about to start changing anyway.

Like Alyea's going to change soon. He tore his mind away from the implications of how all the desert lords had been covertly watching her — as though they expected her to throw herself at them any moment. Idisio didn't see himself ever being that overcome by baser impulses. Not after what he'd been through. Not unless he went completely mad.

But Deiq had been positive in his response to that fear: *You're not going mad. All the changes you're going through, however strange they may feel, are normal.* Thin reassurance, but better than the gut-wrenching fear that he couldn't trust his own mind or body in the coming days.

At least he didn't have to worry about dying. *It's very hard to kill an adult ha'ra'ha,* Deiq had said. Apparently it had taken a considerable effort, and more than a little treachery, to even damage the one beneath Bright Bay. Several desert lords, some of whom had died or gone mad in the effort . . . and Tank.

Now *there* was a name Idisio hadn't ever expected to encounter again, for all that he'd been having visions about the redheaded boy for weeks now. He'd assumed those visions had been prompted by wondering whether there could be a connection between the big, funny sailor Red and the skinny, mad-eyed redhead he'd found huddled in a trash-filled alley years before. It still seemed an insane coincidence, even with Deiq's careless comment that ha'ra'hain were apt to draw such connections to themselves; and Deiq's explanation of Tank's true purpose had left a hard, uncomfortable feeling in Idisio's stomach ever since.

He'd been a distraction. A sacrifice. *Bait.*

And now they're using me the same way: as bait to catch another mad ha'ra'ha. Just like they used Tank. And he's dead because of it. They killed him.

Idisio wasn't sure why that upset him so much. He'd barely known Tank; the redhead had stayed for a matter of days before the incident with Blackie— and other matters—had driven him out of Idisio's life. *So why am I having visions about him all the damn time?*

They didn't tell Tank the whole story, and they're not telling me the whole story. Once more, so much for the vaunted status of being ha'ra'hain. I can't even trust Deiq, apparently—he's perfectly willing to put me out on the hook.

Idisio slowed, looking around, and found himself in an herb garden. To his left, a long, raised bed of fennel served as a feathery screen considerably taller than himself. To his right, a lower, circular raised bed overflowed with a ruddy-tinted, small-leafed sprawling plant. A stubby-legged wooden stool sat at one corner of the fennel bed. Idisio sighed and sat down on the stool. Walking wasn't helping to sort out his thoughts.

A breeze wandered by, stroking a cloud of licorice aroma into the air; Idisio half-turned on the stool, watching the thread-thin fennel branchlets shiver and sway. There was something hypnotic about the movement, and the smell seemed to collect at the base of his spine, spreading a thick warmth along his entire back.

He inhaled deeply, smiling, his anxiety easing. *When I get home, I'll plant some fennel,* he thought. *Lots and lots of fennel.*

What an odd thought that was! Home? What was *home*?

It hit him like a blow to the head: *I don't have a home any longer.* Granted, a corner up out of wind and rain where he could bury his small cache, a small patch of territory he called *his*—that didn't make for much of a home. But since Scratha had lifted him out of the muck into this new, strange life, he didn't have even that much certainty of a place to stay at the end of the day. He was entirely dependent on the respect and kindness of the people around him for a bed and a bath and a meal.

He didn't like that notion at all.

He shook his head, standing, and turned back the way he'd come. A young woman in a light blue dress was standing a hefty stone's throw away, apparently examining a gigantic rosemary bush. She shot a quick glance at Idisio, ruining the pretense completely.

He walked toward her, not sure whether to be annoyed or amused; she ducked her head, her light skin flushing to a bright pink, as he neared.

"You're following me," he said.

"Yes, my lord." She smoothed her hands across her stomach, as though to ease wrinkles from her dress, and nodded without meeting his eyes. "Lord Eredion said you oughtn't to be left wandering about alone." She flashed him a quick, impish smile. "So did the king."

A surge of aggression brought sharp words out: "So you're one of the spies around here?"

Her smile faded. "No, my lord," she said. "I'm not one of the Hidden. I'm a servant, sent to keep an honored guest company."

Idisio opened his mouth to retort that he didn't *want* company—especially since, whatever the girl said, her purpose was mainly to supervise his wanderings. Then he paused, thinking about the situation more carefully. "Lord Eredion sent you after me?"

"Yes."

The king might well have sent the girl after Idisio as a thinly disguised spy, but Eredion was a desert lord. Anada's face and voice surfaced in Idisio's memory. Did this girl count as kathain, in Eredion's eyes? Would it be offensive to Eredion if Idisio sent this girl away?

Don't flinch, Deiq had said, and: *You need their respect.*

He studied the girl more closely. She had rich chestnut hair curled into soft ringlets around her narrow, aristocratic face. Her dress, while it covered all the requisite skin for modesty, fitted closely enough across chest and hip to leave no doubt about the curves beneath.

She stood still under his inspection for a few moments, eyes politely downcast, then lifted her chin and met his gaze directly. He smiled, aggression fading: she reminded him of, well, himself. *No point in cowering*, her demeanor said clearly. *Might as well stare him in the eye; he won't respect anything else.*

It amused him that she was right. "I'm Idisio," he said. "What's your name?"

"Taci, my lord."

"Idisio."

She hesitated, then said, "No, my lord. Lord Eredion was quite firm about that. He said if you insisted, to say that it was a matter of northern culture and to stop arguing."

"What else did he say?"

"That as long as I stayed honest I had nothing to fear from you," she said promptly. "He said that you would consider treating me kindly as a sacred obligation."

Idisio let out a long breath. *Sacred.* That came too close to the phrasing Anada had used. So this girl was, for all intents and purposes, kathain: well, so, Idisio wasn't inclined to argue. He didn't mind a bit of distraction from his sour thoughts just at the moment.

Remembering the reaction Deiq had provoked from the Peysimun servant, Idisio smiled at Taci brightly. Color flooded her neck and face as her eyes widened. His breath thickened as he took a step toward her; and in the back of his mind, so faint that he almost dismissed it as an illusion, came the sound of Deiq's sardonic laughter.

"Lord," Taci breathed, blinking hard as though against tears, "please, not— not here, not so—brazen. Don't treat me as a whore."

He stopped, his whole body suddenly icy.

She wiped a hand across her eyes, her color fading into a mottled embarrassment. "I'm sorry, lord," she said. "I'm not refusing you, just asking for—"

"Dignity," Idisio said. "Yes. I understand." He swallowed hard, thinking:

I don't deserve any special status. I'm no better than those gate guards. I would have used the bench, right out in the open—

So what? Deiq said, cold and precise. *If being seen troubles you, I'll set wards to avoid interference.*

Idisio met that suggestion with a ferocious *No.* Aloud, he said, "Let's just— walk, then, Taci. And you can tell me—about the gardens. Or whatever interests you."

She smiled at that, relief returning her skin to its normal pale color.

"Thank you, lord," she said, and took his arm in a carefully proper manner. "As it happens, I do know a bit about these gardens . . . ."

So you care about the feelings of the humans around you, Deiq observed. *Lovely. I care about the economic and political stability of the humans around me, as it happens; and the tath-shinn threatens all of that. I'd put myself out on the hook if I thought it would work, Idisio; but the tath-shinn is interested in* you, *not me. So get your nose out of the air, take the girl on the damn bench, and clear your mind for the night's work ahead. It's not going to be pleasant, however it turns out.*

Idisio set his teeth together and said aloud, "What's that flower there called, Taci?"

Deiq snorted and withdrew; as Taci began to chatter cheerfully about plants, Idisio drew a thick block across his mind, a refusal to hear anything else Deiq might have to say.

Chapter Forty-Four

The inn where Venepe and his mercenaries had booked their rooms was quite probably the cheapest in town: a wooden building, its walls and floors gapped and warped with age and humidity. The doors were as crooked as the rest of the place, so light–and shouting–came through clearly.

Tank leaned against the wall to the right of Venepe's door, arms crossed, and stared bleakly into the light-striped darkness of the hallway around him. Dasin had been right to order him to stay outside, galling as the submission had been; Tank would have long since planted a fist in the fat merchant's face for a few of the more lurid comments that had drifted out through the cracks.

The shouting was mostly on Venepe's part, so far, but Dasin's voice was rising steadily.

Something moved in the darkness. Tank straightened, one hand going to his belt knife; too crowded here for a sword to be of any use at all. One foot brushed against his pack and saddlebags. He moved a step away from the trip hazard, squinting at the approaching figure.

"Rat?" he guessed.

"Yes." The big mercenary stopped a pace out of arm's reach. "Heard the shouting. Dasin?"

"Yes." Tank hesitated, then said, awkwardly, "Breek and Frenn?"

"Mad as hell, but they'll live. Don't turn your back on them anytime this side of the Black Gates." Rat paused, then said, "Be best if you didn't continue on with us, though. Same with Dasin."

"I know," Tank said, and resisted the impulse to apologize. It would only make things worse. "Dasin's trying to get me to sign with Yuer."

Rat said nothing for a long moment. In the pauses between the moments of shouting, Tank could hear his breath whistling between his teeth. At last, he said, "Bad notion to draw his attention. I'd stay out of that yard."

"Dasin's already dragged me over there," Tank said. "We're just back from talking with him, in fact."

"He made you a offer?"

"Not in so many words, but yes."

"Then you're in it," Rat said. "Your boy's a damn fool, and you're stuck." He paused, apparently listening to the argument going on inside Venepe's room. "Good and friendly gods. Is that little ta-neka actually trying to convince Venepe that he's worth keeping around because he's *smarter* than Venepe?"

"Yes."

"What a fucking idiot."

"Yes."

Rat shook his head, the motion barely visible in the dim light. "You might as well sign with Yuer," he said, "because Venepe won't have you back, and he's not going to keep Dasin around either, at this point. And at least under Yuer's hand, you won't have Breek and Frenn coming after you."

A heavy feeling settled in the pit of Tank's stomach. "Why not?"

"*Nobody* touches Yuer's people," Rat said. "He *owns* this town, damn near. Most of the Coast Road, too, at the end of the day." He paused, as though listening to the much quieter conversation for a moment, then added, "We may not carry that pretty little wooden coin, but we're not *stupid*."

Tank winced. "I'm sorry," he said before he could stop himself. "I really didn't mean to say that to Breek. I really didn't."

"But you did," Rat said without any sympathy. "Keep in mind, you mouth off to Yuer–*he* don't scrap or posture. He kills you." He paused and seemed to be regarding Tank thoughtfully. "Doubt you'll make it a full tenday under his hand."

"That ought to make Breek happy," Tank said sourly. "I'm sure you'll all lay wagers on–"

The door jerked open and Dasin stormed out, nearly crashing into Tank.

"Let's go," he snapped. His pack was looped carelessly over one shoulder. "I've got your pay."

Rat melted away into the darkness, silent as a shadow; but Tank could feel the big man's grin boring into his back as he followed Dasin out of the inn.

"This tea," Yuer said, "is a lovely white rose hip from the edge of the Ugly Swamp. I find it helps my digestion and eases stress." The wrinkles around his mouth moved as though he were smiling.

"Merchant Venepe has–" Dasin began; Yuer raised a withered hand, shaking his head.

"No business yet," he said mildly. "Tea first. One cup each." He lifted his own cup and took an ostentatious sip, his gaze steady on Tank's face.

Tank leaned forward and collected the small cup of nearly colorless liquid. All three sipped without speaking for a few moments. The dark-haired girl sat mute and motionless, staring at nothing in particular. Tank didn't need any warning that he had to ignore her for the moment.

He won't scrap. He'll kill you.

Tank sipped tea and kept hands and shoulders relaxed. The tea held a delicate perfume that seemed to rise from the back of his throat into his nose, reminding him of sunny days and lush flowers. Dasin's breathing steadied and lengthened, his nerves visibly settling.

Yuer watched them from under drooping eyelids. While the ruin of his face generally made expression hard to read, Tank suspected the old man was tremendously amused by the situation.

He knew. Somehow, he knew we'd be forced into his service.

Wian slipped from her chair, collecting and refilling empty cups one by one. When everyone had a fresh cup of tea in their hands, Yuer took a ceremonial sip, then said, "Now. What brings you back to my door, barely an hour after I asked you to leave?"

While his tone remained polite, the underlying danger put a razor edge on the words. Dasin shot a quick sideways glance at Tank, then dipped his chin toward his chest and said, "We talked it over, and we'd like to sign with you after all. I've ended my contract with Venepe."

Yuer took another sip, seemingly unimpressed. "What makes you think I'm interested in signing you on as a merchant? You're barely old enough to shave, the both of you. Why would I trust you with my reputation and my goods?"

Dasin opened his mouth, looking indignant; then shut it and drew a long breath through his nose.

"Never mind my age, s'e," he said steadily. "I can do the job. I've been personally trained by the merchant-master of the Aerthraim, and I'm her top student. I wouldn't have been sent out on my own otherwise, would I?"

Yuer laughed, a grating chuckle without much humor to it. "The Aerthraim lie like a fish breathes water," he said. "Even to their own people. I don't find that connection much by way of recommendation, I'm afraid."

His gaze moved to Tank's face and stayed there for a long, thoughtful moment, then returned to Dasin.

"I might be inclined to give you a trial run, if you do me a small service first," Yuer said. "As it happens, this young lady is from Bright Bay. She needs to return to her home, and I'm short of escort staff at the moment." His mouth twitched.

The dark-haired girl's shoulders moved a little, and her chin dipped to her chest. She shut her eyes.

"She doesn't look like she *wants* to go home," Tank said bluntly, ignoring Dasin's warning hiss. "Do you, s'a?"

She made no answer.

"She has nowhere else to go," Yuer said in a way Tank *really* didn't like. "And it's really not your concern what she wants, either, Tanavin."

"Tank," he said absently, still studying the girl.

"Excuse me?"

"He's calling himself Tank now," Dasin said when Tank didn't answer.

"I see. That's certainly interesting." Yuer's tone indicated he found it any-thing but. "Regardless of the current moniker, Wian's *wants* are still none of your concern. She will be returning to Bright Bay, and staying there; you can either accompany her to ensure she comes to no harm along the road–"

Tank looked again at the fading bruises on the girl's face and set his teeth together hard.

"–or I'll have to send one of my friendly doormen along."

The cup cracked in Tank's hand. A splash of warm liquid ran down his wrist and onto his trouser leg.

"*No*, you *won't*," he said though his teeth, and barely stopped himself there: reined in more by the memory of Rat's earlier warning than any sense of his own. *He doesn't scrap. He kills you.*

Dasin sat still, white-faced and stiff, staring somewhere past Yuer's left ear. The girl hadn't moved nor opened her eyes.

Tank drew in a shaky breath and jerked his head in mute apology, then focused on setting the remains of the cup down on the table and picking small ceramic splinters from his palm.

The girl rose, wordless; collected the cup and left the room. She returned with a thick hand-towel and a small knife, then knelt beside Tank's chair and motioned for him to give her his hand. He glanced at Dasin, then at Yuer; both seemed to be staring off into space, ostentatiously ignoring him.

She tucked the towel under Tank's hand and began delicately scraping the sharp fragments from his skin onto the cloth. He held still with an effort, not at all comfortable with someone holding a knife that close to his wrist.

Nobody spoke while the girl worked to clean Tank's hand. He glanced at Yuer and Dasin uneasily, feeling more and more like a lumbering fool with every passing breath. It seemed like hours before Wian tugged the cloth free, bundling it up around the knife, and retreated from the room again.

This time she returned with a replacement cup. She set it on the table and glanced at Yuer; he offered the faintest ghost of a nod. She filled it, set the cup on the table in front of Tank, then returned to her seat, sitting as mute and withdrawn as before.

Tank picked up his cup with a trembling hand and took a sip he really didn't want.

Dasin breathed out in a near-sigh and said, "My apologies, trader Yuer. You were saying?"

"Take Wian to Bright Bay," Yuer said, his gaze on the girl now. "Her fam-ily will give you a reward of sorts: a package for me. Bring me that package, unopened, undisturbed in any way, and we'll discuss whether you're able to handle an actual trade route without a caretaker."

Tank bit his tongue. He dearly wanted to ask: *And what if we decide we don't want to work with you?* Rat's dire prediction that he was stuck rankled almost as much as taking orders from Dasin.

"That's a long trip on no coin to prove ourselves," Dasin said.

"True." Yuer smiled. "Wian will have coin for you to spend."

Dasin shot a quick glance at the girl, then at Tank. Tank jerked his head at a slant, not quite a yes or no: *Don't argue it*, that meant, in the code Allonin had drilled into both of them. Dasin exhaled hard once more, then said, "Very well."

"You may leave in the morning," Yuer said. His gaze moved to the packs at their feet. "I have no guest rooms available here, unfortunately, but if you give my name at the Traveler's Rest, they'll find a room for the two of you. It's a street over, on the corner of Sand and Copper."

"Thank you," Dasin said, his tone muted.

"Wian will be returning to the Fool's Rest Tavern in Bright Bay. She knows the way. I will provide horses and trail supplies. It should go without saying, but I'll say it regardless, that I'll be severely disappointed if the horses return in poor shape, or not at all."

"We'll take good care of them, trader Yuer," Dasin said, not looking at Tank.

"Indeed. Good night, then. Be here at dawn."

Dasin set his nearly empty tea cup on the table and rose. Tank set his nearly full cup on the table and followed suit.

"Good night, trader Yuer," Dasin said; then, as if testing, he added: "Teth-kavit."

Yuer said nothing, gave no visible reaction: his gaze as compassionate as that of a hungry lizard watching the fluttering of a nearby insect.

Chapter Forty-Five

Rain poured down from a thunderously black sky. Wind howled past the edges of buildings and beat bushes sideways. Ellemoa smiled as she eased through the downpour. If the situation hadn't been so serious, she would have been running and laughing, as she had in childhood whenever the Elders called in storms to ease the seasonal droughts in Arason.

Mustn't get caught. Mustn't let them know I'm still alive.

Eredion *was* an enemy. He'd known Ellemoa would come for him. He'd set up the trap. He'd been *calling* her: her decision to hunt him hadn't entirely been her own. It had come from him. He'd *allowed* her to eavesdrop for that critical few moments. He'd *dared* manipulate a ha'ra'ha!

Eredion will find his victory over me hollow when he finds his gravekeeper friend, she thought savagely. *He walked away without a second thought as to what I'd do after he drove me away from my son. He could have come after me and stopped me. Risked his life to protect his vulnerable human gravekeeper friend, not a hundred feet away. But he didn't think of her at all. Humans. They keep no faith with one another.*

And now he's using my son as bait. He thinks he's clever. As though my son hasn't been through enough! They see me as a dangerous monster, and they're using him to draw me out. Me! I'm no monster. They're the ones using an innocent child as bait.

I just want my son back.

She stood against the side of a building, invisible, cloaked by the rain, and sorted through the presences around her. Her son–*Idisio*–a strange name he'd taken, or more likely been given by the humans. She wondered if it meant anything. Humans tended to assign names with meanings, which seemed, to her, very odd: a name was a *person*. How could it be more than a single identity? That only confused matters.

She dragged her thoughts back to the moment. Her son stood, huddled and miserable, under the minimal shelter of a tree-shaped statue–another example of human thinking, that: building a statue, duplicating something that already existed; using *rock* to craft a *tree*–the very concept was insane.

Her attention went back to her son. Her baby. He was wet, and cold, and *scared*–all because of the humans, because of these *desert lords*–they would *suffer* for doing this to her son . . . .

Focus, she told herself, and reluctantly tore her gaze away.

There were three . . . no, four . . . She paused, eyes closed, *listening.* Four desert lords: Lord Eredion and three others. Lord Eredion was remarkably good at hiding himself; she had almost missed him. He wasn't far from where she herself stood, but all four had a line of sight on each other and were on full alert. She wouldn't be able to get to Eredion without being attacked by the other three.

But they didn't know she was the one controlling this weather. They had no skill at redirecting the torrential downpour, or they would have done so already; which gave her a distinct advantage.

She shaped wind and drove rain sideways into alcove after overhang until, cursing audibly, each one emerged from his secure spot and sloshed noisily into a new hiding place. Eredion emerged last; she aimed the wind to drive him steadily in her direction. True to human weakness, he followed the easiest path and put the wind at his back.

She smiled and began to raise her hands, ready to pull him in, pull him apart–

For a handful of heartbeats, as she focused on him, Eredion's grumbling thoughts pierced the rain as though he'd spoken aloud: *Wish I could raise my body temperature the way Deiq does–he's probably sitting in cozy comfort over there– dry, even, damn him–*

Ellemoa paused, her eyes narrowing. The *over there* in Eredion's thoughts had been to her right, in an area she hadn't sensed anyone occupying. She withdrew into complete stillness and let Eredion pass by as she searched the rain-shrouded darkness to find the presence she'd missed–it had to be there–

It was. A deeper, darker, very solid presence; she'd taken it for another pointless statue, in fact, until Eredion's grumbling had made her look at it more closely. She focused on the motionless form, listening closely, avoiding any pressure that might alert him to her inspection. A scattering of thoughts floated by: *there's a chance, just a chance . . . hate this rain and cold . . . have to try. Have to try. Damned rain. Wish I dared try redirecting it, but the storm's settled in too solidly . . . It's kin. Whatever it's done, it's kin. I have to try . . . have to reach it, have to take the chance.*

Ellemoa began to relax a little. Another ha'ra'ha. She was safe. Like the Elders, he was here to protect her, to serve as intermediary with the humans, to keep them from misunderstanding–

And if this thing does attack Idisio, I can let loose and kill it before anyone gets hurt trying to stop it themselves . . . .

Her blood went as cold as the rain thundering down around her. *This thing. Kill it. Kill me? He sees me as a* thing. *As an* it. *He's willing to kill me to avoid harm to the humans. He thinks I'd attack my own son!*

Ice turned to fire as rage narrowed her vision.

He's willing to break the oldest Law and kill his own kind. He was no child, himself; the solid mass of his presence told her that. He was old, and as strong as *teyhataerth.* He could kill her; and unlike *teyhataerth,* who, even under Rosin's twisted direction, had never dared cross that line–this one, this *Deiq,* would.

For the sake of the *humans.*

She put a hand to the wall behind her and funneled rage through her fingers. Her hand sank into the granite with a soft crackling sound. She wouldn't break the Law. She wouldn't kill him. But he was a threat–more of one than Eredion, who had walked past her with no notion of her presence. Deiq needed dealing with, and then she would take her son and get out of this horrible place. Vengeance wasn't as important as her son's safety.

She'd go home. She would take her beloved son home, and they'd live in peace at the edge of the Lake, where nobody would dare hurt either of them ever, ever, again.

Withdrawing her hand, she balanced a fist-sized chunk of rock on her palm for a moment, then smiled and started forward.

Chapter Forty-Six

A rainy night, and a windy one, would have been bad enough without having to stand in the vicinity of a graveyard. Idisio leaned against a statue that offered minimal shelter and watched bits of debris fly by, feeling thoroughly sour.

"Couldn't we have put this off for a night with better damn weather?" he muttered to himself. "Only something insane would even come *out* in this rain, and what does that say about me?"

Nobody stood close enough to hear him, even with the sharp hearing of a desert lord. The screaming wind and incessant rain drowned any sound beyond a shout. And what would it be doing to the stibik-laced catch-ropes? Nothing good.

"We should try this again in better weather," he muttered. The rain had put him into a foul mood filled with recollection of slogging through flooded back streets in search of shelter. Even in this deluge, he could see at least three better spots to wait out the storm: but Eredion had been firm, if apologetic about it. Idisio needed to be visible. He tugged his hood down to shield his face and turned a bit more sideways to the gusts. His feet were already soaked and his skin clammy all over. Deiq had tried to teach him how to keep his body warm by willpower alone, but for some reason it hadn't stuck, or maybe the weather was simply too extreme for that discipline to hold.

Would the desert lords even notice if Idisio simply snuck off to sit in a warm, dry place for a while? Peering through the curtains of rain flooding the streets, Idisio thought, glumly, that they probably would. And then they'd be ferociously annoyed with him for ruining their grand plan. *Just like a street-*

thief, they'd say, and would shake their heads. They wouldn't take him back into their company, and he'd be out on the street scrabbling for copper bits again—

He shivered under a wave of disorientation. What the hells was he doing out here? *I'm a ha'ra'ha, not a street thief. I can do whatever I want.* But Deiq seemed to see this as a necessary exercise, and wasn't calling it humiliating: so Idisio took the cue that *he* had no right to complain over it. This was—this was—a duty. A responsibility. A worthy reason to be standing out in the cold and wet like a damn idiot, wishing himself anywhere else, tucked up into a nice dry spot and waiting for the rain to break and the marks to come back out on the street, careless in the steamy damp, purses heavy—

"My poor baby," someone said in his ear.

Idisio yelped, spinning to face the speaker: a person cloaked and hooded against the rain, hunched like an old woman.

"You're all over cold and wet, baby," the woman went on, reaching toward him with a bone-thin hand. "Let's get you in out of the rain."

Idisio backed away a step, fear shivering along his skin, turning him even colder than the icy weather had managed.

"Uhm, I'm fine," he said, unable to think of anything else. He shot a quick glance around: where were the desert lords? They weren't paying much attention, if the tath-shinn could walk up to him like this–and he had no doubt that was what stood before him.

Old women didn't randomly wander around in tearing thunderstorms and act all motherly to anyone they encountered.

The woman stayed still, swaying in place a little.

"They've poisoned you," she said. Her soft voice, implausibly, cut through the howling wind to reach Idisio's ears without any distortion. "They've made you fear me. I won't harm you. Come with me, love–Come on, come on, I'll explain as we go. We have to get out of here. Those men who hurt you are coming back. They'll find you. They'll hurt you again. I'll protect you, but you have to come with me. Come on . . . Come with me, come, come, with me, this way . . . ."

Her hands moved, beckoning, pulling, *drawing* at him. The rain around them faded into a vague haze of disorientation. *I should yell for help,* Idisio thought, a shiver racking up his back, and opened his mouth even as his feet began to move.

"Shhh, love, shhh, the bad men will hear you," the woman said. She tucked her hand into the crook of his arm; at the contact, he forgot why he'd had his mouth open in the first place. "You're safe now, love, you're safe. I won't let them hurt you. This way, this way . . . ."

A blissful, warm sense of complete security descended upon him, as though he were a baby being rocked in his mother's arms. He sighed in relief, nodded, and let her steer him away through the rain.

"My pack," he said after a while. "I don't have my pack." He put a hand to his belt, relieved to find the long Scratha dagger and his belt pouch, at least. But why didn't he have his pack? And when had it stopped raining–or had it? It seemed as though a misty haze surrounded them; he couldn't properly focus more than arm's-reach in any direction.

"That doesn't matter," she said, tugging him on without pause. "I'll provide anything you need, love. There's nothing in that pack of yours that's as important as getting away right now. Getting out of this place. Going *home*."

"Oh," Idisio said. "That's to the south of us. South and east. This way." He started to turn down a side street; she gripped his arm fiercely and shoved him back on a northeasterly path.

"That's not your home," she said. "Your home is *Arason*."

Arason. The word sparked a slow-forming connection in his mind. Arason. What did he know about—

There is a lake, a ghosty lake . . . .

"Red," he said aloud. "He sang about Arason."

"What?" Her step faltered. She peered at him from under her hood. "Who?"

"A sailor. On the trip to Scratha Fortress. He sang . . . ." Idisio tried to remember enough of the tune and words to sing it himself. It wouldn't come clear. "I don't know. It wasn't a nice song. The one about Dusty Rose was funnier."

"*Who?*" Her tone held only bewildered impatience.

"You know, that king who dressed up like a woman and renamed himself after his favorite prostitute—"

"And that's *funny* to you? The diseased maunderings of *humans* are *funny* to you?"

"Uh . . . ." He squinted at her, his vague acceptance of everything around him fading. He looked around, drawing on a lifetime of walking through Bright Bay in every kind of weather. His vision clarified. They stood in a pouring rain, one of the worst winter storms he'd seen in a while; a vicious wind was whipping around what street trash hadn't been soaked immobile by the rain. What they were doing walking in this mess, Idisio couldn't understand. Perhaps they were on their way to hire a coach.

He said, hopefully, "Are we going to the caravan yards?"

"No." The woman tugged at his arm, but Idisio set his heels and refused to move. "We're going home."

"This *is* home," he said, and backed up a step, clarity seeping into his mind. "Who the hells are you? How did I get—"

"You're in *danger* here," she said sharply, lunging to sink her fingers into his forearm.

He dodged, jerking away, and backed up several more hasty steps. Instinct turned a step back sideways and into a full-scale sprint. Buildings blurred by with unprecedented speed; a half-dozen heartbeats later, he went sprawling and tumbling across wet ground.

The tath-shinn loomed over him, hissing like an enraged goose. Idisio bounded to his feet, ignoring aches and scrapes, and launched into another run—

—his muscles froze. Off-balance, he stood on the edge of toppling for a stretched moment of terror. Then the tath-shinn stood beside him, steadying him; she patted his arm gently.

"Time to go home, love. Come, Idisio. Come with me. This way. That's right . . . Good boy."

He shuffled into motion again, his mind turning to a blank grey fog, content in the secure and absolute knowledge that she would take care of everything.

Chapter Forty-Seven

"She ought to ride in front," Dasin said, squinting at their horses as though he knew what he was looking at. They were big, black beasts, with fine lines; Tank would have wagered with gold that they had once lived in a nobleman's stables. "She won't be able to hop off and run that—"

"She's not going to run, you godsdamned ta-neka idiot," Tank snapped.

Dasin turned a ferocious glare on him. "Don't you talk to me like that!"

Tank grinned unpleasantly.

"Get on your horse, Dasin," he said. "Then tell me, if she sits in front, who's controlling the situation?"

Dasin glanced at the looming bulk of the horses, studying the lay of stirrup and saddle horn. "All right," he said, "fine. You didn't need to be rude about it."

"So fire me," Tank said, and turned to Wian, ignoring Dasin's simmering irritation. "S'a, the saddles look to be big, but you'll still have a tight fit. Best you sit with Dasin; he's skinnier."

She glanced at Dasin, then shook her head, moving three steps closer to Tank.

Tank sighed, not surprised at all.

After some scrambling, she sat pressed close behind him, which wouldn't have been entirely unpleasant except for her occasional faint hisses of pain.

"Sounds like you shouldn't even be riding," Tank said over his shoulder. She tucked her forehead against his back and shook her head, then pushed the palm of one hand lightly against his lower back. He understood the signals: *No, I shouldn't, but let's get moving anyway.*

It was too much like the subtle sign language he'd grown up with for comfort, and he almost balked right then and there, unwilling to have anything to do with this increasingly distasteful matter. But Dasin scrambled into his own saddle and said, "Well, if she's hurting, that makes her less likely to run, doesn't it?"

"She's not going to run," Tank said.

"Why not? You're the one said she doesn't want to go back."

Tank shook his head and nudged his horse into motion. As they clattered out onto the main road leading west, he said, "Why didn't *you* ever run, Dasin? Why didn't I?"

Dasin's glare could have melted glass. "*Tank.*"

Wian stirred against his back, but didn't say anything.

"You saw those guards same as I did, Dasin," Tank said, staring straight ahead. "What kind of *home* do you think she's going back to?"

"Shut it," Dasin said sharply. "*Shut it,* Tank."

Tank turned his head a little and spoke over his shoulder. "Are you going to run? I'll look the other way if you do."

He could feel her sigh. She laid her head down against his shoulder without replying.

"She won't run," Tank said, flicking a glare of his own at Dasin. "We could toss her off the horse and kick her to get away from us, and she'd walk right on back to Bright Bay on her own."

Dasin, white-faced and taut as a drawn bow, was the one to stare straight ahead this time. "Loon," he said. "Fucking *loon.* Shut up already. *Shut up.*"

Tank felt an agreeing prod to his left shoulder. He shrugged and let the silence settle in for a time.

The rising sun did little to take the chill from the air. Even though her cloak was a thick felted fabric, Wian shivered almost continually, her hands tucked up into her armpits, and leaned hard against Tank's back.

He glared ahead and resisted with all his might the impulse to dismount, tuck his own cloak around Wian, and stroke her hair reassuringly. He couldn't afford to do that. He couldn't afford to care. His treacherous thoughts ran with that idea and looked backwards: had any of the handlers in the katha village ever wanted to offer comfort to their–? No.

Think on that too much and he'd cross the border into madness in short order.

It's the past, he told himself. *And she could say a word, one single word, and I'd–what? Run away with her, kill Yuer, kill the family waiting for her in Bright Bay?* He had no better options at the moment than to keep moving forward along this road. Captain Ash might be able to find a way out of the mess Dasin had put them into, but Tank already knew without asking that Dasin wouldn't leave Yuer's service.

I ought to quit, take Wian off somewhere, try to convince her it's stupid to go back– but she wouldn't listen.

He'd seen that look in too many eyes while growing up: the certain, blank knowledge that there was nothing else, no other road, no other option. He'd probably worn that stare himself, before his removal to Aerthraim Fortress. No. She wouldn't listen.

"You ought to run," he muttered over his shoulder, unable to stop himself. "I'd *help*, damnit."

Her head moved in slow negation against his back.

"Can't change the world," she murmured, so softly he barely heard her.

"You can change *your* world," he retorted.

She shook her head again and made no other reply.

They rode into Obein as dusk made the path hard to see, and booked one room at Cida's Haven for all three of them. The innkeeper, a stocky woman, squinted at them thoughtfully.

"Didn't I see you just pass through, the other way, with Venepe?" she asked.

Her attention lingered on Wian. A frown deepened the lines on her face.

"We took another contract," Tank said. He resisted the urge to tell the innkeeper that he and Dasin hadn't been the ones to put the fading bruises on Wian's face.

The woman nodded and handed over a room key. Tank felt her hard stare on the back of his neck for some time afterwards, even when they'd turned past her line of sight.

"You hungry?" Dasin asked as they tucked their packs and saddlebags under the two narrow beds.

Tank shook his head and sat on the edge of a bed, suddenly too exhausted to even speak clearly. "You g'n," he managed. "You go."

"Huh," Dasin said, and glanced at Wian. After a moment, he added, with clear reluctance, "You hungry?"

She shook her head and sat on the edge of the other bed.

"Give me the money for a meal, then," Dasin said, his face settling into sullen lines.

She lifted a blank, exhausted stare to him, apparently bewildered; then, shaking her head a little, dug in her belt pouch and tossed him a single silver coin. Dasin caught it, scowling.

"More'n that," he said.

"That's enough for a meal, Dasin," Tank said wearily, rousing from his half-sleep.

"Not unless I want rat shit in the soup! This is *Obein*, not Kybeach, Tank. A decent meal costs more, and after all day on the road I want a *meal*."

Wian motioned listlessly at Tank with one hand, as though to say: *It's not important, never mind.* She reached into her belt pouch and tossed Dasin another silver round.

"*Thank* you," Dasin said heavily, and stalked out the door without looking back.

Tank kicked off his boots, peeled off stockings, and flopped back on the bed. As his eyes slid shut, he thought he heard the girl say something.

His muscles twitched in a futile effort to sit up and look at her. He couldn't move past the crashing weariness. His whole body hurt, especially thighs, shoulders, and calves. The notion of getting back on the horse in the morning made overtaxed muscles twitch in protest. Behind closed lids, his eyes rolled uncontrollably for a moment. He hadn't been this tired since Allonin's intense training sessions.

Whatever she wanted, it would have to wait.

Sometime later, a faint whimpering noise woke him. He pushed up onto one elbow and squinted into the darkness, listening: grunts, heavy breathing, the shifting of mattress and blankets. And the occasional, stifled whimper or yelp from Wian.

"*You fucking ta-neka*," he said, already moving. His bare feet hit the cold floor; he lurched two steps, reached, grabbed what felt like a shoulder, and shoved.

Blankets thrashed. Tank sensed Dasin rising up, swinging blind and hard. He threw up his own hand, turned the blow aside, grabbed Dasin's forearm and yanked hard. Dasin thudded onto the floor, cursing. Pillows and blankets scattered.

The smell of wine hung heavy in the air: Dasin had spent the extra coin on drink, not food.

Tank leapt backwards, misjudged the amount of room and tripped over his own bed. He managed to turn the fall into a graceless sideways roll that put the bed between them.

Only the sound of Dasin's angry panting broke the silence. Nobody moved. Tank crouched behind the shielding bed, listening, straining his eyes to see through the dark.

"What's the *matter* with you?" Dasin said at last, hoarsely. "You want some for yourself, you could have asked."

Tank's hands clenched. "Dasin," he said, "I know you like to run rough, but with *her*? How *could* you?"

"She asked for it," Dasin snapped. "Crawled under the covers and grabbed. She's a whore, Tank." His tone shifted to a sour amusement. "She's a pretty good one, too."

Tank held a number of responses silent. "Wian," he said, trying for a level tone and almost managing. "Come here. Please."

A faint shifting sound, a curse from Dasin: "Go on, then, damnit!"; and Tank could *smell* her approaching, moving tentatively through the dark room. She smelled like roses and dirt and arousal. He bit his tongue and gave silent thanks for the darkness.

"Get in the bed, Wian," Tank said, not moving. "I'll take the floor."

He barely managed not to say the thoughts thundering through his mind.

Dasin muttered something, then blankets *shsshed* as he dragged them back over himself. Wian sighed as she settled into the warmth Tank had left behind. He let out a long breath and knelt beside his pack to dig out his rain-cloak; at least it might shield him somewhat from the chill of the floor.

"I was stupid," she said in a near-whisper.

He stopped and stared at the barely darker spot where the bed stood. "What?"

"It's why I'm in this mess," she said. "I was stupid. I trusted someone I shouldn't have. And then it all got . . . out of hand. What Dasin did–wasn't anything. Not to me. Not . . . not really."

"See?" Dasin said. "Whore."

"Shut it," Tank said, biting the words off.

"I . . . I knew what he would do," Wian went on. "And I don't . . . I don't mind so much."

"*I* mind," Tank said frostily.

"That's because you're too scared of women to really let loose and–" Dasin began.

"*Dasin.*" Tank glared through the darkness. Dasin fell silent.

"Thank you for caring," Wian said, nearly whispering the words. "Please– don't sleep on the floor because of me. It's too cold for that. Please–"

Dasin snorted and said loudly, "Yeah, right. That's what she told me. 'I'm so cold, the floor is so cold.' Then she grabbed my crotch and offered to help keep me warm if I let her stay. Go ahead, Tank, climb in bed with her. I'll be listening to you riding her next!"

"Dasin," Tank said, keeping his tone mild only because letting the anger into his voice would end with him charging across the room, "if you don't shut up, you won't walk, let alone fuck, for six months. I *promise.*"

Dasin made a disgusted noise and jerked blankets closer around him.

Tank stood quietly for a moment, considering the chill of the floor under his feet, thinking about how damn *warm* the bed had been.

"I'll take the floor," he said at last.

Nobody argued this time, although Wian gave what might have been a disappointed sigh.

Chapter Forty-Eight

The damp brought out insects: they flittered past on multicolored wings, settled in Ellemoa's hair, crawled along her son's shirt. She brushed away anything that could sting and let the rest be unless they crossed her face.

I have my son back. And they were clear of Bright Bay, clear of the madness that infested those streets. She could breathe properly, it seemed, for the first time since her precipitious departure from Arason.

A land bird with a fat body and skinny legs erupted from the brush to her right and ran recklessly in front of them. She watched it go, smiling; *swasson,* her son said drowsily.

She turned a startled glance on him. His eyes remained hazed and his gait remained under her control: still, it was worrying that he'd been able to perceive the bird, let alone remark on it. She thickened and tightened the layers of compulsion. He sighed a little, subsiding, a vague frown crossing his face.

Ellemoa bit her lip and glanced west: a light carriage rumbled toward them at a steady, early-morning pace. Beyond the carriage, dense black clouds obscured the towers and turrets of Bright Bay; she'd pitched the storm to stay over the central area of the city until she was well clear. It would take days for the torrential downpour to ease. To the east, empty road bent around a tall mass of trees and vanished from sight.

Kybeach, her son said: faint, fuzzy, but nonetheless alarming.

"I'm weaker than I thought," she muttered aloud, and drew her son to the side of the road, watching the carriage approach with a sharp calculation. One driver on the bench, and—she focused vision and *sight* alike—one passenger, dozing within the carriage itself. Not a merchant's vehicle, but a private, headed for a visit somewhere along the Coast Road.

The horse, a splotchy black and grey beast, began to balk as the carriage drew near. The driver swore and shook the reins, tapped with the whip; the beast planted its feet and refused to continue, tilting and tossing its head to keep a wary eye on Ellemoa.

"Clear out, then, you!" the driver called out, motioning Ellemoa aside. "The beast don't like your smell, maybe. Whatever, you move yourself aside, I've no quarrel with you. Get aside, get aside!"

Two humans would be more than enough to restore her strength, and the horse would suit for riding—her son knew how to ride. He could teach her.

She set her son aside, commanding him without words to *stay put*, and took a single step forward.

His hands locked around her upper arms from behind. *No*, he said, very definitely. *No*.

She spun, badly frightened now, and searched his face for any trace of awareness: but the blank stare and clouded mind remained undisturbed. That protest had come from *deep* within him, from a consciousness that knew very well what she'd been about to do—and rejected it utterly.

Her breath caught and shuddered in her chest. She remembered, with abrupt clarity, the refusal of her lover to harm the humans to save her; remembered that he'd chosen to save the child rather than save her; remembered that her son had been among the humans his entire conscious life.

"Move aside, move aside!" the driver howled, shaking his whip at her in clear threat. Too rattled and anxious to take issue with the disrespect, she pulled her son clear of the road, deep into a thin spot of brush, and allowed the carriage to pass undisturbed. The horse broke into a gallop and charged by without pause, eyes white and nostrils flared; the driver shot a brief, dark glare into the brush where she'd withdrawn.

When the road lay empty once more under the rapidly blushing morning light, she steered her son back to an eastward path.

"So you don't want me to hurt the humans," she murmured as they walked, considering, and stole rapid glances at his slack face. "That's going to complicate matters, son. It's a very long journey to Arason, I think, even for us." She mulled it over for a time, then sighed deeply and said, "For you, son—for you. I'll try. To make you happy, I'll restrain myself until you're ready to understand. For you."

"Kybeach," he said aloud, the word so slurred as to be almost unrecognizable.

"What about Kybeach, son? Oh—you want to stop there?" She glanced back at the dark clouds obscuring Bright Bay on the western horizon. "Well—it should be safe enough. Yes, son, we'll stop in Kybeach. I'll allow you a human meal and a human rest, to set your mind at ease, and then we'll go on."

"Send word. Send. Send word."

"Send word to who? Oh—those men I rescued you from? No, son, no, there's no good can come of letting them know where we are. No, you don't want to contact them. *You don't want to contact them.*"

"Send. Send. Send. Word. Word. Send."

She stopped walking and studied his taut face, frowning. "No, son," she said. "No. *Bad idea*, son. No."

"Send. Send. Send." His throat worked as he fought to produce the words, his head bobbing and tilting back with the force of his insistence.

She worried at her lip for a time, glancing anxiously along the road in each direction. "Very well," she said. "I'll allow you to send word, son. Let's go to Kybeach, then, and find a meal and a scribe."

His hands rose, twitching, then dropped to his sides again. She stepped back a pace, alarmed: he repeated the gesture once more, then said, "Send. Send."

"You can write?" she said rather breathlessly. "All right, son, all right, I'll allow you to write the letter. Please, son, come along, come along—Let's get to Kybeach, not stand here on the road all day."

He shambled into motion without further protest, and she let him take the lead: thoroughly unwilling, at this point, to have him anywhere *behind* her.

Chapter Forty-Nine

The floor *was* cold, and a constant current of chill air flowed into the room from the space under the door. Tank curled into a ball, head resting on his pack, and shivered his way into a light, restless doze, wandering in and out of odd dreams. In one, Dasin curled up on the floor beside him, offering his own body warmth; in another, Allonin made him get up and run in place to warm up. Lifty pushed him away, snarling: *I don't walk that road, damn you, hands off!*

Tank twitched uneasily, half-rousing. Chill attacked the back of his neck and his arms. He tucked down into a marginally warmer huddle and drifted back into dream. The heat of sunbaked rock radiating up into his body mixed with Allonin's voice and the scraping shiver of steel as he learned the proper way to sharpen a blade. *Good, Tanavin, you're getting it; good.*

Tanavin.

A name he'd left behind for good reason: he never should have chosen it in the first place.

It wasn't an homage, as he'd thought it would be. It was a cruel joke, dragging the dead into the world of the living. They deserved to be left in peace. Tank didn't *want* to remember them any longer. Didn't want to think about how Tan and Avin had died, while he had lived . . . didn't want to think about Allonin's sideways admission as to why the Aerthraim had rescued him and not them.

Ice was warmer than that calculation had been.

He sighed and stretched a little. Warmth pressed close, too solid to be a dream. He opened his eyes, blurred and slow, and said, "Dasin?"

"Shh," Wian said. "Don't wake him."

Dasin's snores rumbled through the room.

"Not likely," Tank muttered. "After that much wine, he sleeps like a rock." He pushed himself up on one elbow, blinking, trying to focus.

"Please," Wian said, voice low. "It really is too cold. You're shivering. Please, take the bed."

He grunted, memory slow to fill in the details of why his first instinct was to say *No*.

"Trade off," she said. "I've been warm half the night. You take a turn. I'll take the floor."

He rubbed a hand over his eyes and squinted at the barely darker outline of her form kneeling beside him. Exhaustion thickened his thoughts into a slurry of *Gods this floor is cold* and *If she wants to suffer that's her own business* and *Gods I want to be warm for a while.*

"Thanks," he muttered; shoved himself to his knees, lurched forward, and tucked under the covers of the bed in what felt like one swift stumbling movement.

Darkness descended like a hammer between the eyes. He moaned once and went out.

He woke an unmeasurable time later to a very close warmth and a hand tracing down his stomach.

"Damnit, Dasin," he mumbled, "not now—lemme sleep—"

The warmth stirred, presenting curves that didn't belong on Dasin's skinny body. He grunted and came the rest of the way awake, reaching to capture Wian's hand.

"No," he said. "*No*. Not you."

Her breath hissed out between her teeth. "I'm clean," she said. "No diseases. And I'm not doing this for coin. I want—"

"No," he said again, cutting her off. "Just no." He tilted his head, listening to Dasin's snores, and sighed a little in relief.

She stirred against him, warm and undeniably naked. "You want him, don't you?" she said, a bare breath of sound in his ear.

"What? No," he said, frowning at her outline.

"You called for him," she said. "Twice."

Tank shook his head, thoughts muddled. At last he said, "Either get back on the floor or I will."

She said nothing for a long moment, then: "Let me stay. I promise, I won't—I won't touch you. I just—The floor really *is* cold. And I can't stand you suffering on my account. Please."

Tank sighed, weariness dragging at his eyes again. Dasin would have a fit, but somehow that didn't matter. And if he refused again, he had no doubt she'd be crawling in beside Dasin next.

"You promise," he said, voice blurring again.

"On my mother's grave," she said, her voice hitching a little. "And I don't break that sort of promise."

"Hhhh." Tank's eyelids drooped all the way shut, and the blackness returned.

Screams filtered through the door; torchlight flickered, the smell of smoke and blood and metal mingling in her nose. The wardrobe was large, and dark, and solid, and safe around her: even if her parents hadn't ordered her to stay there and be quiet as a ghost, she wouldn't have stirred from hiding.

Not after the screams began.

Her father's enraged bellow had shrunk to a broken whimpering some time ago; her mother's fury shattered to the occasional sickly moan. She could still hear the men—the ones who'd said they were the King's Guards—grunting . . . laughing . . . joking.

She couldn't hear her sister Delli at all. That was good. That meant Delli was still in hiding herself, and they might not be discovered.

Tears ran down her face unchecked. She breathed shallowly through her mouth, into a blanket clutched close to her face, and forced herself to breathe evenly. No sniffling. No choking. No sobbing. They would hear her.

At last the grunting and jokes stopped. The men moved around the main room of the cottage for a time; from the comments, she knew they were collecting the valuable books her mother had been so proud of.

"Heretic trash," one of the guardsmen said. "We'll bring them in to the burn pile."

Her mother said nothing in protest, not even a whimper.

Crockery broke; glass shattered; wood splintered.

"That's enough," one of the guardsmen said. "That's enough. We have other trash to take care of tonight."

"We ought to search the place," someone else said. "There might be more of these books."

"No," the first guardsman said. "If there are, they'll burn. We just needed a few to show we'd done our job. Toss a torch around the room as we go; that'll take care of the rest."

The front door opened and closed. Moments later, a hissing crackle invaded the air.

She shoved out of her hiding space, panic swelling through her at last, and stumbled out into the main room of the cottage—

Tank thrashed his way out of dream and into consciousness. Wian shivered in his arms, her whole body jerking with stifled sobs. Dasin's snores echoed through the chill air.

"Godsdamnit," Tank said, his mind not quite clear, and shook Wian roughly. "Stop that!"

She gulped air and half sat up, whining a little, then made a sleep-thick inquiring noise.

"What? What's going on?" Her breath hitched mid-word; she reached up to brush the tears from her face.

"You had a nightmare," Tank said, his own breath still rough in his throat. "Damn near kicked me into a eunuch."

"I'm sorry," she breathed. A heavy shiver worked through her body. "I must have been dreaming–there's a nightmare I have sometimes; I can't help it."

Tank drew in a breath through his teeth and squeezed his eyes shut, unwilling to tell her that he'd seen her nightmare in vivid, horrifying detail. Instinct told him to get the hells away from her. Something rooted in his own grim darkness took over and said, "Tell me about the nightmare. Best way to get back to sleep."

She went still in his arms, breathing hard. At last she said, "You–really? You want to hear–*my* nightmare?"

"Just tell it," he muttered, one ear on Dasin's breathing. Was he waking? "Hurry up."

She drew in a breath and said, "It's–about what happened to my parents. When I was–about eight, I think. They were both scholars. Teachers. Educated. Intelligent. And they had books. Collections of folktales. Myths. Legends. Stories from the southlands. C-c-children's . . . b-b-books . . . ." She stopped, swallowing hard, then went on. "The king's guards came to our door and demanded all of the books. Said they were heretic trash that undermined belief in the Four and they were under king's orders to take them all. My parents said no."

Tank gritted his teeth and kept silent.

"The g-g-guards . . . ." Wian paused again, breathing uneven, then said, "My parents made me and my sister hide before they opened the door. They told the guards that we were visiting our aunt. The guards raped both my parents. Tortured them. B-b-b . . . ."

"Branded them," Tank said through his teeth, remembering the end of the nightmare all too clearly. "Go *on*."

"They took some of the books and set the house on fire as they left." Wian's voice turned chill and emotionless. "I came out of hiding. I found my–what was left of my–my parents. I found my sister and tied a cloth over her eyes so she wouldn't see–what had happened. I got her out of the house. There was no time to grab anything else, we were in our nightshirts, the house was burning . . . ."

She drew in a deep breath, another. Tank stayed silent, suspecting what was coming.

Wian said, very steadily, "The men were waiting outside. They'd known we were there the whole time. My sister . . . didn't live past what they did to her. I did."

A heavy silence hung in the room.

"I've never told anyone that story before," Wian whispered. "I never–felt safe–Nobody cared."

Tank sighed, sorting through possible words. Nothing useful came to mind. Finally, deciding it was as good as anything else at the moment, he said, "Feel like you can sleep now?"

"Yes," she murmured, tucking her head down into the crook of his shoulder and neck. "Thank you."

Her breathing was warm on his neck and chest, and went into deep rhythm surprisingly quickly. Tank lay still, listening to her sleep, listening to the silence. At last he moved his head a little to aim his voice away from Wian's ear and said, "You heard that, did you?"

Dasin stirred, the bed creaking protest: answer enough. He didn't speak.

"Go back to sleep yourself," Tank said. "No point in anything else. Go back to sleep."

It sounded as though Dasin rolled over. Tank blinked, laid his own head down on the pillow, and let the darkness roll in again.

Chapter Fifty

Idisio's hair tickled as though bug-tossed; he put up a hand reflexively, scrubbing fingers against his scalp. The itch dealt with, he rubbed his eyes and looked around, bewildered and vaguely dizzy.

The small, sun-washed room around him gave little information. A man's bedroom, by the look of it: pale walls streaked with the beginnings of mold and furniture that had been handed down through generations of abuse. The most solid piece evident was a writing desk in one corner, inkwell and writing supplies neatly laid out on the surface.

"Son," a voice said from behind him.

Idisio yelped and spun, memory cascading on the instant. The tath-shinn started back a step, her grey eyes widening, then caught herself and folded her hands before her.

"I'm not going to hurt you," she said very softly. "You're my son. I won't hurt you."

He backed up a step, another, then stopped: remembering how fast Deiq could move, how fast he'd already seen *her* move. He wouldn't get three steps.

"I won't hurt you," she repeated. "Look—you wanted to send word to your human friends, that you're safe and they needn't worry over you. See—I put the supplies out for you. Write your message, son. I won't hurt you."

He blinked, one word catching and spinning in his mind: *Son.*

She angled around him, moving with ostentatious care, and began rummaging through a large, battered armoire at the other end of the room.

"Son?" he said aloud.

She didn't turn. "Yes," she said. "Write your message, son."

"I don't—That's not—" He shut up and rubbed his hands over his face. "No," he said after a few moments. "I'm not believing any of this." He took two steps toward the door.

"Believe it, don't believe it," she said, tone indifferent. "It's the truth. Are you really going to walk away without knowing the full story?"

He turned and stared at her back. Pale streaks in her brown hair caught and glittered in the sunlight.

"You're not my mother," he said.

She lifted a pile of heavy winter sweaters aside and hummed a little; reached forward and pulled a folded parchment from the recesses of the armoire. "Here we go," she said. "You've been wondering about this, I believe."

She laid the parchment down on the writing desk and retreated across the room to stand by one of the two small windows. Bathed in sunlight, smiling as serenely as a s'iope in one of their religious paintings, she seemed nothing more than a thin, tired middle-aged woman.

Idisio looked at the door, looked at the desk, looked at her; took another step toward the door.

"The letter on the desk," she said, not moving, "was written by a merchant named Asti Lashnar some days ago, as a confession of his sins. He'd intended to send it to—someone important, it doesn't matter who—but his courage failed, and he put it in the back of the clothes chest instead."

Idisio's breath caught in his chest. "Lashnar?" he said. "We're in Kybeach?"

She motioned to the desk, still smiling.

"Read the letter, son," she said, "then write your own, and we'll be on our way to Arason."

"*Arason?*"

"That's where you were headed, isn't it?" she said mildly.

"With Deiq and Alyea!"

"They aren't able to take you," she said. Her pale eyes darkened, then washed out again. "I'm your guide now."

He gaped at her, unable to believe she'd said that with every appearance of reason. "*You*—you're—you—*what?*"

"Read the letter, son," she said yet again. "Then write your letter, and we'll be on our way."

He took another step toward the door, which put him beside it; set his hand on the knob, watching her for reaction. She regarded him without apparent concern.

"I will explain everything," she said, "but not if you turn that knob. It will all make sense, when I explain; you've been fed a lot of lies, son. A dreadful lot of lies. I'm going to tell you the truth, but only if you stay."

"You're *not* my mother!" he shouted at her, abrupt rage frothing out into words.

"Because I'm not pretty?" she asked. "Because I'm not—admirable? Let go of the childish dreams, son. Look at me. *Look* at me. Do you really doubt?"

He looked at light brown hair and wide grey eyes, a face so like what he witnessed in mirrors and a build that, while thin and malnourished, mimicked his own well enough.

"No," he said, one last desperate protest; then bowed his head and shut his eyes, accepting the truth.

"You belong with me, son," she said softly. "You know you do. Those desert lords you were with didn't understand that. We need to make sure they understand that. We need to write that letter, and let them know that you're safe, and we're going to Arason, and they needn't worry about you any longer. You asked me to stop here so that you could send word, and here I am. So write the letter, son: write the letter."

Her words dragged at him, velvet suasion; he shook his head, certainty fading, and crossed to sit at the writing desk. He'd asked her to stop? That implied that he'd agreed, at some point, to follow her willingly—which didn't match up at all to his memories. But memory, at the moment, seemed a dim and unreliable thing, and she wasn't presenting as the least bit dangerous.

He put the folded bit of parchment in his belt pouch without looking at it, considering that to be a matter for later: writing his letter seemed more important than reading someone else's. He was only vaguely aware of her standing at his shoulder as he began to write; was only vaguely aware of writing; was only vaguely aware of what was being set down on the page.

"There you go, son," she said as he folded and sealed the letter. "There, now, I've let you do what you wanted. Let's get back on the road."

"Needs to be given to a News-Rider," he said, looking toward the window. "To be delivered."

"I'll make sure it gets delivered, son," she said. "I *promise* it will be delivered."

He hesitated, uncertainty creeping in, and stood up. What had he just written? He couldn't remember, and that bothered him. He looked down at the folded parchment in his hand, frowning; the writing on the outside seemed oddly blurred, as though his eyes just couldn't focus on the words.

"It will get to the right person," his mother said. "I promise. Leave it be, son, I'll make sure it gets delivered to the right person."

"Let's just drop it off at the tavern," he said. "They'll hand it off to the next News-Rider."

She stared at him, seeming both irritated and surprised.

"Very well," she said at last.

His stomach grumbled.

"And a meal," he said, flattening his hand against his stomach. "I'm starving."

Her eyebrows quirked, her mouth drawing aside.

"Oh, I doubt that, son," she said. "But very well. A meal, and this letter, and then we go. Agreed?"

He nodded, uneasy again for no good reason, and looked around the sunlit room. Worn, but reasonably clean: and empty in an oddly final manner.

"Where's Lashnar?" he said. "This is his house, right? Where is he?"

"Not home," his mother said, and steered Idisio outside.

The tavern was no more pleasant than it had been on Idisio's last visit. The drooping barmaid gave him a look of unabashed loathing when he stepped through the doorway, which moderated only slightly when she noticed Ellemoa.

The tables stood empty, the air somehow the more rank for the absence of other people.

"Take your pick of seats," Seshya said, throwing her hand out in a wide gesture. "We're having a fine night, as you can tell." She glanced over her shoulder, as though searching for someone, then looked back to Idisio. "We're short on food, too. Biscuits and greens, potato soup, that's all we're offering tonight. Take it or leave it!"

"That's no way to speak to us," Ellemoa said sharply.

"Why?" Seshya demanded. She pointed at Idisio. "Last time he was here, the only decent person in this town wound up with a knife stuck through her."

"It wasn't me!" Idisio said, anger sparking instantly.

"Well, you have an uncanny knack of turning up around death. Lashnar slashed his arms open. No saying why. And then his witch-apprentice wife shows up and takes everything of value that Lashnar could claim ownership over, from stable and home and town: rather a lot, that was, and left Kybeach with the dregs of what wasn't much to begin with. So do you want the damned biscuits or not?"

"Take them for your supper," Ellemoa said unexpectedly. "We'll leave you in peace. Idisio, give her the letter and we'll be on our way."

He took three reluctant steps and held out the letter. "For the next News-Rider traveling to Bright Bay," he said.

She took it, her mouth twisted into a sardonic grimace. "I'll be sure to send it along," she said, then hesitated, glancing between Ellemoa and Idisio. "Let me get you a biscuit for the road, at least."

"That would be a kindness, thank you," Idisio said quickly, before his mother could disagree.

"It's been a rough time of late," Seshya said, shaking her head, then turned and went into the kitchen.

"Why not sit for a meal?" Idisio demanded in a whisper as soon as the barmaid disappeared.

"There's only enough in that kitchen for our meal or hers," Ellemoa said as quietly, her eyes a peculiar, glittering color. "Let her have it, son, we can get more."

"How can they not have any food? It's a *tavern!*"

His mother just shook her head and motioned him silent. Seshya emerged a moment later with a wrapped bundle. "It's not much," she said a bit awkwardly, "but—well. Thank you."

The warmth of the biscuits seeped through the cloth, heating Idisio's palms. "Thank you, s'a Seshya," he said, then, in a rush: "Are you—will you be—why don't you have any food?"

She shrugged and folded her arms before her, slumping into a sullen posture again. "More travelers than stock," she said. "Less money than need. Lashnar was half-owner; he handled the orders and the finances. The other owner's in some town down the way, never seen him in my life; but Lashnar killed hisself without leaving provision as to who's in charge—and then his wife came and scooped up whatever she could carry—which included a large part of the kitchen stores. The cook's more drunk than sober these days, and *I* avoid him when I can."

"I'm sorry," Idisio said helplessly.

"It'll sort itself out," she said, then looked pointedly at the door.

"Good day," Ellemoa said, then tugged Idisio outside again.

"You shouldn't have asked," she scolded in a low voice. "That was rude, son, to make her tell her shame like that."

"How is it *her* shame?" he demanded. "None of it's her doing!"

She clicked her tongue impatiently. "Never mind," she said. "I'll explain to you one day. For now, we have a long way to travel, son—let's get started on it."

He took a step, another; balked, looking back to the west. A heavy dark cloud hung over Bright Bay, which seemed wildly improbable against the crisply clear morning they were walking through: Bright Bay wasn't *that* far away.

"Let's *go*, son," his mother said, more sharply.

He wavered, doubtful, another moment: but the letter had been written, and would be delivered, and there was really nothing more to be done. He was going to Arason with his mother, and—

"What happened to Deiq and Alyea?" he said. "Deiq was—he was watching, when you—found me in the rain, he was supposed to—to stop you from—" He paused, frowning, and looked at his mother. Her dark grey stare caught and held his, ferociously intent.

"You're going to Arason, *with me*," she said. A thick layer of cotton began to wrap around his mind, blurring his thoughts into incoherence. "You're coming home to Arason," she said from an increasing distance. "You're coming home to Arason, with me, with your mother . . . ."

Sound and sight faded into a grey, muffled haze.

Chapter Fifty-One

Dasin shook Tank awake as night turned to a deep grey.

"Get up, loverboy," he snarled, and stomped across the room. "Time to go. I want to get to Bright Bay today."

Tank sat up, bemused and still sleep-hazed. For an unfocused moment, Dasin's hostility puzzled him; then he looked down at the girl curled against him.

Wian stirred, opened her eyes, and smiled up at him. It was such an unguarded, peaceful expression that his breath caught in his throat for a moment.

"Thank you," she said.

"For what?" he said, reflexively twisting upright and away.

His bare feet hit the cold floor, shocking him more towards wakefulness, as she said, "You don't remember? It was *wonderful*."

Dasin turned and glared. Tank aimed a severe stare over his shoulder at Wian, mainly to avoid seeing Dasin's outraged expression.

With a sour grin, she said, "Don't worry, Dasin, you didn't miss anything *you'd* consider exciting. I fell asleep and didn't have to wake up to service anyone along the way, that's all."

"*Whore*," Dasin spat.

Tank jerked back around. Before he could take the first step towards breaking every bone in Dasin's skinny body, Wian stood and came swiftly around the end of the bed.

"No more than I've had to be," she snapped back. Dasin's eyes widened; then he averted his eyes, a wave of color flushing into his pale face. Wian gave a hissing, contemptuous sound. "So, you won't look at me the next morning to see what you enjoyed in the dark? *Coward.*"

Dasin's head jerked up. He glared at her; then his gaze drifted across her body again, as though helplessly compelled. He dropped his gaze to the floor, the color fading from his face.

"I didn't realize," he muttered.

Wian spat on the floor near his feet, then turned to Tank, her eyes fever-bright. "What about you?" she demanded.

Tank blinked slowly, his gaze on the web of scars that criss-crossed her entire body; the purple-black bruises, the yellowing ones, the cuts . . . the old brands. He looked back at her face and said, "What about me? I've got my own set of scars. So what?"

She stared at him, breathing hard, then abruptly turned away and grabbed up her clothes.

Dasin sat on the edge of his bed, back to them, and said nothing.

As Wian yanked her clothes on, she said, "I grew up in Bright Bay under Ninnic, serving the rich and powerful. I don't have family, nor friends; only these damned scars to keep me company, and whoever I'm told to entertain each day. At least *you* two have each other."

"Some of those cuts are less than six months old," Tank said, keeping his voice flat.

"Changing the king doesn't change the world overnight," she said. "The ways for a female servant to survive inside the Seventeen Gates don't change all that much when a different rump is on the throne."

He watched her wriggling into her loose shirt, careful to keep his face still and expressionless.

"If you don't have any family left there," he said, "why go back?"

She didn't answer right away, her attention apparently on arranging the folds of her shirt properly.

"And go where?" she said at last. "I can't stay anywhere along the Coast Road if I betray my promise to Yuer; and south of the Horn or north of the Hackerwood, he'd find me sooner or later." She paused, studying Tank. "And he'll kill the two of you if I don't arrive at the Fool's Rest in reasonable time. You may not be family, but I don't want your blood on my conscience. So let's get moving."

"You don't have to go back," Tank said quietly. "We can handle ourselves."

She laughed a little, without humor. "You don't know what you're dealing with."

"Yes, we do," Dasin said unexpectedly. He stood, turning to look at her. "We know." He glanced at Tank, ducking his head a little, then back to Wian. "He's right. You can–we'll be all right. If you go."

She shook her head. "No. I've done what I've done," she said. "I've earned these bruises and whippings ten times over. Don't feel sorry for me. Don't try to help me. It'll get you killed, and that's the first truth I've handed out for free in years. I'll meet you at the stables."

She walked out without looking back.

"Damn," Dasin said after the door had closed behind her. "Tank . . . ."

"Yeah, I know," he said, rubbing at his mouth, wishing he could wipe away the bitter taste in the back of his throat; then bent to pull on stockings and boots, glad that he hadn't actually gotten around to undressing the night before. He'd never allowed Dasin to see his own childhood memorabilia, and didn't intend to start now; especially considering the inevitable comparison Dasin would make, with *that* sight fresh in his mind. Tank needed every ounce of respect he could wring out of Dasin's cynical mindset.

"We *can't* . . . ." Dasin made a helpless gesture.

"We have to."

Dasin shook his head, looking as miserable as a kicked asp-jacau. "It isn't *right*."

"*Right* is for priests and children," Tank said. He grabbed up his gear and left the room without waiting for Dasin's reply.

In spite of Dasin's best intentions of reaching Bright Bay before dusk, the sky was already black by the time they reached Kybeach, and Wian was sagging sideways against Tank's back.

"We'll have to stop," Tank said. Dasin growled a string of southern obscenities but reluctantly agreed.

"Stick to trail food," Dasin said.

"Intended to." Tank nudged Wian awake; she offered the same overall opinion of the choice as Dasin, if more wearily.

They booked a single room, with one bed for all; whether that was honestly the only room left, or the only option the sour-faced innkeep was willing to offer, Tank saw no point in arguing. A quick, shared glance agreed: none of them wanted the service to get any worse, if that was even possible.

Tank slept in the middle of the worn and lumpy mattress without a word needing to be said. Dasin kept his back stiffly turned and as far to the edge as he could. Tank pushed Wian away twice during the night; although to be fair, he could tell that she was asleep and seeking nothing more complicated than contact each time.

Dasin and Tank both rolled out of bed equally surly; Wian, quiet and moody. None of them spoke much on the way to Bright Bay.

Tank had never ridden into Bright Bay before. It was a nice discovery that the nods from the gate guards turned respectful as he went by. People moved out of the way, hardly looking up at him, and children stared with open envy and admiration—just because he was on a big horse. It was all surprisingly exciting, and he grinned like a newborn fool as he and Dasin went through the eastern streets.

"Loon," Dasin muttered, glancing over. "She got her hand in your pants or something?"

"If I did have," Wian retorted before Tank could answer, "I've a feeling it would be a better handful than *you* were."

Dasin bared his teeth at her. "Try again with some spirit next time, you'll see a difference."

"That's enough," Tank said, irritated. "Gods, have *some* taste!" Then he tilted his head back, accepting their shared eruption of laughter, and shrugged at his own poor choice of words. At least they were bantering; even crude humor was an improvement over the sullen, icy silence that had hung over most of the day's ride.

At least the weather had warmed; while a thick line of scattered dark clouds promised more rain that night, the air hung warm and relatively dry for the moment. Tank put his attention to enjoying that while it lasted, and ignored the shots Dasin and Wian took at one another from time to time.

When they reached the easternmost of the Seventeen Gates, the burly, bristle-haired captain of the day squinted with visible suspicion.

"Your business?" he asked, his tone clearly implying they couldn't have anything legitimate to do in noble territory and that they'd likely stolen their horses.

"Fool's Rest Tavern," Tank said.

Wian leaned around him and said, "Captain!" in a tone filled with warm honey. "How have you been?"

He stepped forward and squinted at her. Tank realized the man was likely near-sighted.

"I know that voice," he said, a smile moving the bristles on his face into sow's jowls. "I wondered where you'd gone, sweet. And the Fool's Rest? That's a step up, I'd say, and well deserved."

"Thank you. I took a short trip with some friends," Wian said. "It's good to be home."

The man's squinting gaze moved to Tank and Dasin, clearly assessing whether they were the *friends* in question.

"These two *ka-s'es* are my escort," Wian added. "They made sure of my safety along the way."

The man's scowl cleared instantly. "Will I be able to see you tonight?"

Tank's hands tightened on the reins; Wian's hand tightened on his shoulder. "I'd really like to have some rest for tonight, and settle in to the new place," she said easily. "It's been a terribly long road. Perhaps the day after tomorrow?"

"Fair enough," the captain said expansively. "I'll be looking for you in two days, then. Don't you go hiding on me, sweet!"

"I wouldn't dream of it," she answered.

The captain's gaze moved to Tank. "You'll need to bind that," he said, pointing at the sword slung across Tank's back. He dug into a large belt pouch and handed up a length of slender red cord with knotted ends.

"I'll do it," Wian said, taking the cord, and secured the blade with a few swift looping movements.

"Good enough," the captain said, and waved them through. "Two days, sweet, don't forget."

"Not a chance, Captain," she crooned. "I'll be watching for you."

"They won't fuss over me, will they?" the captain said, raising his hand to stop them once more and suddenly looking a bit anxious. "Being not a noble-born, that is. They won't deny me entrance for that?"

"I'll be sure to tell them to let you through," Wian said. She nudged Tank in the back as the guards stepped aside. "Go, Tank," she murmured in his ear. He ground his teeth and nudged his horse forward, pointedly not looking at the captain as he passed.

On his way through the gate, Dasin's gelding went abruptly sideways, almost crowding the captain into the wall; he tugged the horse clear at the last possible moment amid a volley of curses.

"Sorry," he called back, waving. "Stupid damn beast . . . ."

Wian laid her forehead against Tank's shoulder, shaking with suppressed laughter.

When the gate lay safely behind them, Dasin said, "I thought you were *returning* to the Fool's Rest, not going there for the first time."

"No," Wian said. "I'm in Yuer's service now, like yourselves. I was working for–someone else, before this. And in–other places. I think the Fool's Rest will probably be a good bit nicer, at least, than some of the places I've been." She sighed. "And if the gods are in *any* way good," she added, so softly that Tank barely heard her, "the Fool's Rest *won't* let that pig-fucker in."

Chapter Fifty-Two

He should at least know his father tried . . . .

What difference would it really make? Would it erase the years he spent in dark places? . . . Think about it . . . What would hurt more; not knowing that his father tried – or knowing that his father never tried?

Idisio rolled through the grey haze of memory, mulling over a new question: if Red and his son actually met, would they even *like* one another? Perhaps, sometimes, being an orphan was better after all . . . .

"I'm going to be a good mother," someone murmured. "The very best. I will take care of you, son. You can trust me. I won't let anything harm you, ever again. You can like me. You can love me."

Idisio blinked, the grey dissipating, and discovered sandy, edge-of-road soil slipping by under his feet. He worked his mouth, discovered it dry, and summoned up saliva with an effort.

"Your father will teach you," the woman beside him said, not looking at him. Her grey stare seemed fixed on some unknowable point in the far distance, and her hand held a steady grip on his upper arm. "He'll show you the way, as a father ought. He said to return when it was safe. It's safe now. That evil man is gone. We're going home, and I'll raise you as I should have been allowed to do from the beginning."

Idisio stumbled to a halt, resisting the pressure of the woman's tugging.

"Where am I?" he said, looking around. The sun was setting at their backs, sending vast streamers of color across still-pale sections of sky. "Who are you? What's happening?"

Still gripping his arm, she turned with him to look at the sunset.

"I'm your mother," she said with fond patience. "You've had a nasty knock to the head, son, and you keep forgetting things; but I'm your mother, and I'm taking you home. Come, now, we've a ways to go yet."

Something didn't feel quite right about that explanation. His intuition felt muddy and stifled for the first time in his life, but he knew that quivery chill across his lower back all too well: *danger.*

"My mother?" he said. "I don't have a mother. Or a father. I grew up— alone." Memory cleared as he spoke, certainty solidifying as to his own background.

"You grew up alone," she agreed. "But you're not alone any longer. I'm here, and I'm taking you to your father."

She pulled at his arm. He set his feet and refused to move; her eyes narrowed in disapproving startlement when she couldn't budge him.

"Wait," he said. "Wait. This isn't right. Who are you?"

"I'm your mother," she said. "Don't you remember? We already spoke about this."

He rubbed at his eyes, frantically searching memory; came up with a fragmentary recall of her standing against the backdrop of a sunlit window, looking tired and old. *No,* he'd said, despairing, accepting.

"Yes," he said slowly now. "I suppose—I do. But—"

"We're going to Arason, as you wanted," she said. "I'm taking you to Arason, where you wanted to go. It's your home, you know—that's where you were born, and where your father is, and where all the answers you're looking for can be found. But we need to keep moving to get there, son. We need to *go.*"

His muscles rippled with the force of that command. He held still and glared at her defiantly.

"No," he said. *Don't flinch,* someone had said recently. He let determination fill his body, refusing to show fear.

You don't get to order me around, he said, as he would have to Deiq; the words fell flat against a pervasive grey haze. Switching to speech, he said it aloud instead.

She squinted at him, lips thin; then she smiled. It was a horrible rictus of a grin, the expression of someone who had forgotten what good humor was really about. She said, "Are you hungry, son? If there's a clean place to eat nearby, you can rest and recover your wits a bit, and we can talk."

His stomach rumbled immediate agreement. Idisio hesitated: he didn't trust this woman, mother or not, but *gods* he was hungry all of a sudden.

"Yes," he said. "Let's go get something to eat. And you can explain what's going on."

"Of course," she said, and steered him into motion again. "But only if we can find decent food and clean rooms. Kybeach was so—so *sad.*"

"We already went through Kybeach?" He looked around, bewildered, nearly dizzy with the need to fix his location to at least some degree. A massive pine tree stood not far ahead, on the left side of the path; its drooping lower branches had been trimmed sharply back from the road, presumably to allow travelers to pass without facefuls of needles.

He remembered that tree. Remembered his horse veering, inexplicably, *into* the tree. Remembered Cafad Scratha laughing fit to fall off his horse as Idisio struggled to bring his recalcitrant beast under control.

Obein. They were approaching Obein. His whole body relaxed.

"Obein is a good place," he said. "They'll have good food and clean rooms."

"I'll judge that, son," she said sharply. "You don't know good from bad, at your age."

He blinked, startled at the sudden change in her demeanor.

"I'm not that young!" he said, then hesitated, frowning. "How old *am* I?" His mother, certainly, ought to know the answer to that.

She stared at him for a long moment, her brow creasing. "Too young for proper sense," she said at last, her confusion clearing into brisk command. "Come along. We'll find you some food and a nice rest. And we'll talk. I'll explain. And you're so hungry, I can hear your stomach."

As if on cue, his stomach rumbled again, and the haze of hunger and weariness increased. Questioning or arguing with her simply didn't seem useful. He shrugged away a pointless surge of anger and trotted after his mother, hoping that whatever Obein tavern they settled into would have warm biscuits—and not at all sure where that thought had come from.

Chapter Fifty-Three

The Fool's Rest Tavern sat, tidy and compact, on a small corner of land just inside the westernmost of the Gates. From the outside, it looked like a sleepy, conservative place to get a good drink in a clean mug or glass. Neatly trimmed hedge-bushes flanked the single door, and the bright blue paint on the wooden walls was fresh and crisp.

Tank stepped ahead as they approached the tavern and opened the door, holding it for Wian and Dasin to pass through; Wian expressionless, Dasin sullen.

"Now you show manners?" Dasin muttered as he passed.

"I think she deserves it, don't you?" Tank retorted in as low a voice. Dasin didn't answer.

They stepped into a large, wood-floored room. Sunlight flooded down from narrow glass windows high overhead and wide ones set lower to the ground. The amount of fine glass alone indicated the massive amount of wealth passing through this seemingly simple building; more than a whorehouse would reasonably bring in, if that were the only trade in question.

A sour taste began building in the back of Tank's mouth.

Several round tables stood in a ring around the center, which had been left clear; for dancing, Tank guessed. From that perimeter to the edges of the room were rectangular bench seats, their length set parallel to the walls. The back wall boasted a well-filled wine rack and a series of sturdy shelves on which more potent liquors lined up in variously colored bottles and jugs. No rough mugs here: the drinkware was all cast from fine silver or glass.

A desultory dice game rattled at one of the tables, the four players heavy-eyed and quiet. The dice were a fine blackwood marked out with divots of a paler wood, and had probably cost more than Tank would have spent on a week's lodging.

From his spot behind a long, polished table by the shelves and racks of drink, the thin, narrow-faced barkeep squinted at them sourly.

"Welcome back," he said without enthusiasm, then pointed to a curtained-off doorway past the end of the bar. "Seavorn's waiting on you."

Wian froze, staring at the barkeep; her breath hitched. "Geil?" she said. "*Seavorn?*"

The barkeep–presumably Geil–grinned.

"Dincha know, sweet?" he said. "Owner of this place didn't make it through the Purge, an' he was kind enough to sign it over to his *dear* friend Kippin just afore he was marked out. A few others did the same, by pure chance." He tilted his head, his grin widening. "Did you actually think you was *clear* of us? Not in this city, sweet. Not nowheres in this city. Not now, for sure."

"But he *said*–" She stopped and shut her eyes.

"You thought Yuer was sendin' you to allies as could stand up against us? Aw, now, that's a shame. Dreadful, innit, when men lie to pretty girls like you?"

Wian let out a low whine, as though her throat had suddenly grown too tight for breath.

"*Wian*," Tank said under his breath. She shook her head without looking at him, lifted her chin, and walked to the curtained doorway without apparent hesitation; but he noticed her hands were clenched into tight fists.

"You two wait a bit," Geil said, and pointed to a bench near the curtain. "Sit. Seavorn will call you in when he's ready to talk to you."

The gamblers hadn't looked up from their game even once.

As he and Dasin sat down, Tank found himself very aware of how close Dasin had chosen to settle; close enough for the scent of the rough soap Dasin used, not to mention the sweat and dirt of a day's riding, to fill Tank's nose. Wian's comment of the night before rolled treacherously through his mind. *You want him . . . You called for him twice.*

He edged sideways a little, trying to make it a casual movement. Dasin's instant glare said he'd failed.

"You stink too, you know," Dasin snapped.

Geil glanced toward them with a distinct smirk of amusement. Tank looked away, his gaze roving around the tavern for a few moments, then settled on staring at his hands.

It seemed like an endless stretch of time before the curtain drew aside and Wian beckoned to them, her face dead white and her hands trembling more than a little. Walking past her without comment took a tremendous effort of will.

The long, narrow room behind the curtain was obviously intended as a storeroom. Barrels and jugs, racks of spare goblets and bottles, cleaning sup-plies, and all the miscellanea of a busy tavern lined the walls, leaving little room for the small rectangular table tucked into the back corner. Behind the table sat a short, dark-haired man wearing finely tailored clothes and a smug smirk. He managed to lounge in his simple chair, and made no attempt to rise as Dasin and Tank came to a halt in front of the table.

"You've offered her freedom," he said without preamble, nodding past them.

Dasin made a faintly strangled sound. Tank reflexively glanced over his shoulder and found Wian standing, her back to them, near the curtained entrance to the main room.

"Oh, she didn't tell me. I can tell by the way you looked at her as you came in. I'm a fair judge of character." His eyes narrowed, his gaze switching between them. "Obviously she refused, and that's wise; she knew what she was dealing with. You don't. I don't want you to have any more contact with her after today. Is that clear? Not a word, not a touch, not a glance. And if she disappears on me of a sudden, I'll be calling for the two of you to answer for it."

Dasin stared straight ahead, jaw rigid, and said nothing. Tank studied the ceiling and said without inflection, "Yuer said you have a package of rare spices for us to bring back to him. Is it ready?"

"Spices," the man repeated, and laughed a little. "Rare spices? Yes. I have the package ready." He chuckled again.

Tank lowered his stare to the man's face. The man's amusement faded, his expression chilling to a harsher cast.

"Don't tangle with me, boy," the man said softly. "Name's Seavorn. Remember it. Ask around what happens to those as cross me. I'm Yuer's ally, for the moment; that doesn't mean I won't kill you soon as see you if you annoy me. Giving me Wian was a goodwill gesture on his part; sending the *spices* is a goodwill gesture on mine. They don't need to be carried by *you*, and believe me when I say Yuer won't miss either of you a bit."

Tank blinked and dropped his gaze to the floor. Dasin cleared his throat, then said, "I'm not inclined to get into a tangle of politics at the moment, *s'e* Seavorn. I'm aiming to handle a trade route for trader Yuer, nothing more, with Tank here as my guard. Your arrangements with Yuer are your own business; but if you have any complaint against Tank, now or future, that needs to go through *me*. I'm the one holds his contract, and he's sworn out through the Freewarrior's Guild here in town as well, so there's Captain Askhis to deal with."

Tank shut his eyes briefly, grateful that Dasin had at least been careful to pronounce the name with the proper inflection. He'd always found it safer to say *Captain Ash*, himself; a decision the dour captain encouraged among his hires.

"He doesn't worry me," Seavorn said. "And neither do you." He stood and offered them a bright, unpleasant smile. "I'll give you the box only because it's Yuer you answer to if anything goes wrong; I'm clear of responsibility for the mistakes of his own messengers. If I sent my own man, I'd be liable if he went off course. You two aren't my problem."

He reached to the back of a shelf near his right hand and pulled out an ornate box slightly larger than Tank's fist. Setting it on the table, he looked at Dasin and Tank, the mean smirk reappearing.

"This box is sealed," he said, pointing to a band of braided leather strips wrapped around the center of the box and a thick coating of wax along the rim and hinges. "Don't open it. Don't let it get wet. Don't crush it. And don't turn it over to any guards or allow it to be stolen. Yuer probably mentioned all of that, but no harm repeating his instructions. The value of this box is rather higher than I think either of you would like to repay."

"What's inside?" Dasin said, still staring straight ahead. "Need to know what I'm transporting, *s'e*. For the gate tax."

"Spices," Seavorn said, "what else? And you're an ass and a fool for even thinking of declaring that." He cocked his head to the side, studying their faces, then shrugged and added, "If you're that intent on putting your neck in a noose, declare it as salt."

"Salt," Dasin said flatly. "How is that a dangerous thing to declare?"

"You've a lot to learn," Seavorn said. "That there is a damn fine batch of Horn salt–with no southern gate tax mark. That might cause the eastern gate some concern, but that'll be on your neck, not mine."

"You're asking me to carry smuggled goods?"

"It slipped someone's mind to declare it," Seavorn said, grinning unpleasantly. "Understandable mistake, really. But if that makes you wet yourself–as I said–you don't have to be the ones carrying it."

That hung in the air for a few moments. Then Dasin said, still not looking directly at Seavorn, "Thank you for explaining, *s'e* Seavorn. We'd best be going. It's a long trip back to Sandsplit, and we'll be wanting an early start in the morning."

Seavorn snorted. "Take it," he said, pushing the box forward, "and you cease to be my problem for a good few days, and hopefully longer."

Dasin stood rock-still for a long, taut breath, staring at the wall past Seavorn's head; then, in a graceful movement, scooped up the box and tucked it into his belt pouch.

"Gods hold you gently, *s'e*," he said.

Seavorn rolled his eyes. "Save the blessing for those as believe," he said. "My view, either they don't exist or they're nothing I'd be willing to pay service to, given the job they've done handling matters so far."

"What parting words do you use, then?" Dasin said distantly.

"I generally find that a kick upside the arse suffices for anyone horsey enough to expect *parting words*," Seavorn said.

Dasin turned sharply and strode from the room without further comment. Tank followed on his heels, and kept his gaze straight ahead as he passed Wian's rigidly still form.

Chapter Fifty-Four

Wide, low-silled windows, shutters closed against the evening chill, stood above raised beds filled with herbs and flowers, many withering down as the growing season drew to an end. A large rosemary bush stood as proud welcome near the front door of the inn; beside the rosemary, a brightly painted sign read "Cida's Haven."

Idisio stared at the sign, trying to figure out why it looked so familiar.

"I've been here before. I think. Why can't I remember anything?"

"That's the knock on the head again, love," his mother said, looking a little anxious for some reason. "You're all muddled, you poor thing."

The front door opened and a plump woman came out, a lit longmatch in hand. Idisio's mother startled back a step, hissing a little; the woman cast her an odd glance, then set the match to the lantern hanging ready by the door. As it flared into warm light, the plump woman shook out the longmatch and secured the cover. Then she turned her attention to them, a frown creasing her face.

"Now, you look familiar," she said, nodding at Idisio. "Didn't you come through this way with that great looming noble lord of yours? And took Riss with you when you went. I'm not liable to forget that kindness! She's a good girl. Is she well?"

Idisio's grey bewilderment cleared instantly. *Riss.* Sweaty stablehand in the moonlight, a stubborn jaw and a black sense of humor—

"Yes," he said. "She's doing very well. She's going to be an ambassador to a noble southern Family."

"Ah, well, that'll keep her occupied until you get back to her, then," the woman nodded. She beamed at Idisio's mother. "And who's this, now? Another noble you're escorting along the way to somewhere?"

Idisio's mother went very still, eyes widening. "A noble?" she whispered, scarcely audible. One hand crept to the base of her throat. "Me?"

"Ah, well, you have that look, you know," the innkeeper said. "You'll want a room for the night? You look exhausted. Been walking all day, I imagine? I've one single-bed room to the west and one two-bed to the east, if you want private; two four-beds on the west with a spot open in each. More for the private rooms, of course, but I'll cut the price from this one's kindness to Riss. She deserved more care than her own family gave her, to be sure—"

"Private room," Idisio's mother said, firmly cutting off the woman's friendly babbling.

The innkeeper nodded, apparently not in the least offended. "Well, then—dawn in your face, or do you sleep in?"

"Sunlight," Idisio's mother said. "Sunlight." She hesitated; with care, as though the word were unfamiliar to her, added, *"Please."*

"Well, of course," the innkeeper said. "Right this way." She ushered them inside, humming to herself contentedly. "Dinner's about ready next door, I should think. We've hired on a new cook; I ought to have gone with someone less skilled . . . ." She patted her stomach, chuckling, then stepped behind a narrow desk standing inside the front door. A heavy lantern on a hook beside the desk cast a wide arc of light across the wooden surface. "Just a moment there, let me sort out the right—here we go." She set a key on the desk. "Four silver bits, if you would."

Idisio's mother made a vague, helpless motion with one hand, then looked at Idisio. "Son?" she said.

"Oh, this is your mother?" the innkeeper said delightedly. "Well, that's not half sweet! I can see the resemblance, now you say so. Was that your father, then, before, not your lord?"

"His father lives in *Arason*," Idisio's mother said with sudden acidity. "And my son bows to no lord."

"Ah, well," the woman said, but her eyes narrowed and stayed that way. "The silver bits, if you would."

Idisio dug into his belt pouch, not at all sure what he'd find. His fingers sorted through oddly shaped small objects—was one a metal deer? and was that a rose? What in the world was he doing with *that* in his belt pouch?

Clarity sparked once more: *I stole from Alyea. Oh dear gods, what am I doing?* He looked sideways at his mother—*my mother! Oh dear gods, my mother?*

Her flat stare, as much as the narrow-eyed gaze of the innkeep, warned him not to reveal his distress. Whatever he'd stepped into, he had to play it out before he could grasp control of the moment again.

He nudged the strange objects aside and scooped up a handful of metal bits with no idea what he was bringing out.

In the smoky light, color glinted: silver—and gold. He closed his hand up swiftly, drawing it closer to his chest, and hoped his shock didn't show on his face. Had he stolen *gold* from Alyea? *They're going to hang me for sure.*

He drew a long breath, straightening his back, then opened his hand and picked out four silver bits. He avoided the innkeeper's stare as he placed the coins on the desk.

"That'll do," she said, whisking the coins up in a swift movement. He could hear the new chill in her voice, could read the abrupt distrust: *And just what did happen to that master of his, I'm wondering,* came a thought. *Best I watch the both of these, looks to be.*

Idisio fumbled the handful of coins back into his belt pouch and picked up the key, wishing he could think clearly enough to say something that might ease the moment.

"Room's down that way," she said, pointing. "May the gods send you kind dreams."

Idisio noticed that she hadn't specified *which* gods; then wondered what he was thinking about. What other gods were there, besides the Four?

His head hurt. He felt distinctly sullen and didn't know why. He didn't know where he was or what he was doing here—*Food,* he thought. *I was supposed to be getting food. Why are we checking into a room instead of getting a meal?*

"You need to rest, Idisio," his mother said in a low voice. "That's more important right now. You're very tired and need to rest."

"Yes," he said, abruptly yawning. "I am really tired." The innkeeper stared at him as though he'd lost his mind; he avoided her gaze and followed the hallway to the room that fit the key in his hand.

"Your face was bruised," his mother said as he opened the door.

"What?"

"I'd forgotten–sorry, *s'ieas.* A light for your room," the innkeep said from behind them. He turned in some surprise; between one breath and the next vision flickered and dimmed to darkness, lit only by the wavering yellow of a candle in the carry-saucer she held in one hand.

"Thanks," he said.

"You have a good memory," the innkeeper said, not moving as he took the candle from her. "To remember the layout of this place, in the dark no less. I've people who come by once a tenday for three years now and still need told where their room is in broad daylight."

"Thank you," Idisio said, more sharply this time.

"Your face," his mother said, as though the innkeeper didn't even exist. "Bruised. She saw you with a bruised face. I don't like that, son."

The innkeeper backed up a step, becoming a shape among shadow. A blink clarified vision: the innkeeper was staring at Idisio's mother with hard suspicion.

"You let me know," the innkeeper said, backing up another step. "You let me know if you need anything."

She turned and left without waiting for a reply.

"She's worried that you hurt that man," his mother said, eerily soft. "She worries that you'll hurt her. Or that I will. Or that I'd put more bruises on you. What a stupid woman. But you were bruised. Who did that to you? Who was that man you traveled with before, son, who dared lay a hand on you?"

Idisio lifted the candle saucer a little, noticing that her attention instantly went to tracking the tiny flame. He backed through the open door into their room. She followed, watching the candle with an almost hypnotized interest.

My mother. He needed to get away from her. He needed . . . He needed a meal. He was so *hungry*. His hand wavered, and he nearly dropped the candle. *Focus. Focus. Get a meal first. Get a meal. Then . . . then think about what to do next.*

"I think you should rest, mother," he said, so low as to be scarcely sound at all. "I need to get something to eat, and I think you should rest while I do that. You look tired. You should rest."

He felt beside him with one hand until he found the table-lamp; risked looking away from his mother and hastily lit the triple wick of the lamp. Her gaze fastened on that, hungrily; she sank down to sit on one of the beds and said, vaguely, "Light . . . ."

Idisio set the carry-candle down on the stand beside the lamp, pinched it out, and backed toward the door, moving with intense caution, like a deer evading a hunter. As he began searching behind him with one hand for the latch, she turned and looked full at him. He froze, his heart hammering in his ears.

"I'm sorry, son," she said. "I haven't been kind to you, have I? I haven't taken any time to explain at all. You must think me completely mad."

He stood still, unable to think of anything safe to say to that.

"It's been so horribly, horribly long, you see," she said. "Since I walked with the sun in my face and the wind on my skin. I've been through so much pain . . . so much pain." She paused, her eyes swimming with sudden tears. "I haven't wanted to tell you about any of that, because you're so young and you shouldn't have to know these things about your mother. But a mother shouldn't know that her son's been so badly hurt, either, so perhaps we ought to talk about the things that have happened to us, after all. About those bruises the innkeeper saw on your face. About . . . about other things."

Idisio opened his mouth, shut it, then let out a slightly strangled squeak. He cleared his throat and tried again. His stomach grumbled loudly.

"I need to eat," he said. "Let me go get something solid in my stomach, and I promise I'll come back here and we'll talk about . . . whatever you want. You're right. You haven't explained anything at all. I want to know. I want to understand. I really do. Please, let me eat first."

I'll get a meal and get my thoughts sorted out, and then I'll get the hells out of here, is what I'll do, he told himself privately. *She might be my mother, but she's the tath-shinn, too, and she's a bloody raving lunatic. I don't know how the hells she dragged me this far, but it's time for me to head back west as fast as a clee-trance could carry me.*

Her mouth stretched into an odd smile. "I will trust you, son," she said. "I will trust that you're old enough to understand the weight of a promise. I will trust you not to abandon me. I will sit here and wait for you. That's how one builds trust: keeping small promises. You keep yours to come back. I will keep mine to explain. Yes?"

"Yes," he said, "definitely." He found the latch with his hand and backed out of the room with frantically cautious haste.

"Son," she said before he managed to swing the door shut between them. "Yes?"

"This girl the innkeeper mentioned. Riss. How did you meet her?"

"She was a stablehand here," he said. "She asked to travel alongside me on my way south, and I agreed." It seemed best not to mention Scratha.

"The innkeeper seemed to think you were her . . . her . . . ." His mother made a vague gesture with one hand. "Are you married to her?"

"No," he said. "We're friends."

"Friends," she repeated, skepticism inflecting her voice. "But you're going back to her? The innkeeper thought you were . . . going back to her. Going south. One day."

"I don't know," he said.

"Do you love her?"

His mouth twisted; he straightened it out in a hurry and said, "I don't know."

She sat silently for what seemed like a long time. At last she said, her voice distant, "Go get your meal, son, then come back and we will talk of the matters that need to be discussed."

He nodded, shut the door the rest of the way, and headed toward food as though he hadn't eaten in a tenday.

Chapter Fifty-Five

Clouds drifted by overhead in bands of near-black and streamers of gold-edged white. After two days of torrential rain, Tank was relieved to see that clear a sky. The cheap inn they'd booked–for a brief overnight, as they'd thought–had been nearly unendurable under that long an enforced wait, and the stable fees had come dangerously close to eating up the remainder of Yuer's coin. Tank gave silent thanks that Wian had at least been bright enough to hand over the bag of money before their arrival at the Fool's Rest; she'd clearly seen it as a gesture of goodwill, confident in anticipation of her new and improved position.

He and Dasin hadn't–carefully hadn't–talked about Wian during their two days of enforced companionship. In fact, they had spent their time avoiding each other and conversation alike: either drinking wind wine that could have been boiled in a boot in the shabby commons room, or in their own room, mending and sharpening various items until they ran out of that small chore, or sleeping.

Tank had done a lot of dozing. Dasin had done a lot of drinking.

"Are we going to get on the road *today*?" Dasin demanded.

"Almost done," Tank said. He tore his gaze from the clouds and returned it to the paper before him. Smooth rocks the size of his fist held it in place, but the corners flittered in the erratic breeze. He moved one of the weights to give his hand room to scratch out the last few words.

He handed the quill back to the patiently waiting scribe, then took a moment to read over what he'd written:

Captain Ash–

I was dismissed from merchant Venepe's employ while in Sandsplit. I am currently working with trader Dasin as a primary employer, and he in turn is working with trader Yuer of Sandsplit. I was surprised to find that Yuer keeps an impressive number of bluebirds close to hand. Some are very large and hard to avoid, and Yuer has found homes for more than a few in Bright Bay itself.

I will stop by the Hall on my next return to Bright Bay.

–T

No time, under Dasin's impatient prodding, to go for a visit in person; and the rain over the last days had made seeking out a scribe worse than useless. This would do. He nodded to the scribe. The tall young woman neatly blotted the page, which had almost completely dried under the breeze–Tank had never been fast at writing–then rolled it up.

"Sealed or tied?" she inquired.

"Seal," Tank said, and dug his Freewarrior Hall coin from his pocket. She lifted a lit candle from its holder on the ground, dribbled a neatly placed blob of wax onto the roll, then traded candle for letter and held the rolled letter steady while Tank pressed the feather-side of his Hall coin into the warm wax.

"Feathers," Dasin said, interested. "Is that on all the Hall markers?"

"No," Tank said. "It's what I asked for as my signature. Each one's different."

"What happens if you lose the coin?"

Tank handed the roll off to the scribe, paid her, and tucked the Hall coin safely back into the bottom of his belt pouch before answering.

"I don't lose the coin," he said. Then, to the scribe: "This goes to Captain Ash of the Bright Bay Freewarrior Hall. Today."

"Runner goes that way in an hour," she said. "*Tvit, s'e.*"

Tank swung a hard glare at her. "*What* did you just–"

Dasin waved a hand to divert Tank's attention, and said, "It's a derivation, Tank. *S'a*–you're from the Stone Islands, I'm guessing?"

"My parents brought me here as a child," she said. "I grew up with their ways of speaking." She looked at Tank. "Good winds and gods'-blessing, is what we mean by it. Don't know about his *derivation*." She flashed a quick, bright smile, then turned her attention to an elderly woman's slow approach. "*S'a* Bele–another letter for your son, then?"

As Tank and Dasin untethered their patiently waiting horses, Dasin said, "*Tvit* comes from *teth-kavit: gods hold you and blessing to your strength.* It's a version peculiar to the Stone Islands."

"Damn close to *tvith*," Tank said. He swung up on his horse.

Dasin laughed and followed suit. "I made the same comment," he said. "Stai said the islanders don't believe in *tvith*. They don't even have a word for circumcision."

Tank shook his head. "Good thing you were there to explain, then."

Dasin slanted an amused glance at him and said nothing as they turned their horses toward the eastern exit that led to the Coast Road.

Tank wondered, as they went, if he would ever lose the crawling sensation that skittered over his skin every time he passed through Bright Bay, or the pervasive distaste that soured the back of his mouth, or the flash of startlement when seeing half-remembered landmarks. There–that building, hadn't he run past it when–? No, this was too far north and east. He'd always been farther south and west–hadn't he?

The worst of it was not being able to remember clearly.

Tendrils of green and gold flickered, acidic, at the edges of his vision; he couldn't tell if it came from memory or reality. He jerked round to look behind him. His mount snorted and went sideways. Dasin swore, pulling his own horse out of the way. A fat woman, herself forced to dodge, showered them both with invective.

"Sorry–" Tank said, wrestling his now-skittish gelding back under control. "Sorry. I thought I saw–never mind." Unease ran like cold fire across the back of his neck and up his arms.

Dasin snapped, "If you're done *dancing* with your horse, let's get out of this pox-infested place already!"

That comment drew a number of unfriendly glares from passing residents. Dasin glared back, his thin nostrils flared as though daring them to start a fight.

"Now what about manners?" Tank said, not quietly enough.

Dasin shot him a hard stare.

"I don't like this city much," he said. "I can tell you don't, either. Why?"

Tank didn't answer.

They started their horses moving again, side by side, at a slow walk, then drew to a halt again as the crowd around them thickened. Ahead, an open wagon filled with what looked like bins of still-green tomatoes and peppers trundled through the narrow gate opening toward them. Outbound, a News-Rider mounted on a leggy bay gelding fretted behind a sturdy ore-cart waiting its turn. The cart was loaded with something heavy–not raw ore: that would be the return trip. A waterproof cover hid the contents, and three alert guards flanked the cart to sides and back.

"What d'you think he's carrying?" Tank asked, nodding to the cart.

Dasin squinted a little, studying it, then said, "Tools. There's a master-smith in Bright Bay who turns out the best mining and farming tools in the kingdom; he's got a trick with turning the wood, I think, that makes it easier to grip, or sets the balance just right–I don't know. But he won't go north for any amount of money, nor train anyone in his methods. I think there's a cousin involved, along the way, who's convinced the local lords to send this job south. In any case, the ore and wood gets shipped all the way down here, and he makes the tools, and they trundle back on up through the Hackerwood."

He paused, as if thinking, then dropped his voice and leaned over a little to put his next words into Tank's ear.

"I'd lay a few rounds of any color you name that there's a bit more than mining tools in that cart. Weapons carry a heavy export tax–that's another law that hasn't been repealed yet. A dozen good swords can bring in a nice profit if they get past the gates without a tax stamp."

Tank shook his head and repressed the urge to ask if Dasin intended to declare the box. They were far too close to the gate to risk that question being overheard. He already knew the answer, anyway. Dasin had wrapped the box in multiple layers of oilcloth, swaddled it with more care than an infant, then tucked it securely into the very bottom of a saddlebag.

Tank let the conversation drop and studied the gate instead. Calling it a gate was generous. It was little more than a section of low stone wall blocking off either side of the road, allowing only one wagon through at a time. Walking travelers filed past the checkpoint without challenge, but riders had to pass through the gate; and wagons, apparently, had precedence over riders.

Most riders, anyway. As soon as the produce wagon cleared the gate, the impatient News-Rider spurred his horse, clattered around the ore-cart, through the gap, and was gone in a flurry of curses from those on both sides who had been patiently waiting their turn.

The guards made no protest to the precipitous departure. The line backed up further with more arguments over who'd been first before the Rider had sent everyone diving out of the way. The guards went through their checkpoint routines stolidly, not in the least impressed by the rising volume of protests.

"Oy, s'e," someone said to Tank's right. He glanced down into pale eyes and a familiar, dirt-smudged face. She'd collected a few bruises since he'd seen her last, and her lower lip was puffed and split, but she stared up at him with grim determination.

"Finally come out of hiding, then?" he said, keeping a close watch on her hands. "What do you want?"

"You're looking for Lifty," she said. It wasn't a question.

"I'm curious," he said. "Won't say *looking*."

"Take me out of here and I'll tell you where he is. I seen him." Her head tilted back, almost perpendicular to her skinny shoulders, and both her thin hands wrapped around Tank's booted foot. "Promise you get me out of here," she said. "Now, right now, today. Drop me the next village over, I don't care."

"She'll cut our throats and run away with the money," Dasin observed.

"Will you?" Tank said, watching the lines of her face shift through animal cunning for a moment; grinned at her, not allowing it to be a friendly expression. "You will."

Her fingers tightened around his boot. "*Please*," she said, and there was true desperation in it this time. "Get me *out* of this place! I'll make my own luck from there, but give me a *ride* at the least! I want well away from here *now*."

"Why?"

"Because–" She hesitated and cast a furtive glance around, then looked back up at him. "You saw," she said. "Just out of the market. By the hopam building."

A thick chill ran across Tank's skin.

"Drug house?" Dasin said, frowning. "Tank, when were you at a–"

"You saw the rose-carrier," the girl pressed, ignoring the interruption. "That's not the only one like that out there. And it's getting worse. Whatever the night-demon is after, it's getting angrier about not finding it. And I've got the *sight*. I'm *already* a target for demons. I been hiding for *days*. Get me out!"

The line began to trundle forward at a steady pace. The girl dragged at Tank's boot.

"Come on, s'e!" she shouted up at him, her face less pleading and more a snarl now. "Damn you high-born *ta-nekas*!"

"Huh," Tank said, his grin honestly amused now, and held out a hand. She locked skinny fingers around his wrist; he curled his hand around both her wrists and lifted. Barely the weight of a sack of feathers, she swung dirty feet up and twisted to stand on the horse's rump for a moment, forcing Tank to release his grip as his arm twisted behind him painfully.

The horse snorted and sidestepped, not at all pleased with her acrobatics; once more, Dasin swore and circled his mount out of the way, glaring. Skinny hands pressed on Tank's shoulders, and she slid to sit close up behind him, taking up far less room on the wide saddle than Wian had done.

But *gods*, she stank. Tank breathed through his mouth and said, "Lifty?"

"Yah," she said, comfortable and assured now. "He went south with his desert lord, way I hear it."

"*Hear* it?" Tank said, aiming a severe stare over his shoulder at her. "You said you *saw* him."

"Told you," Dasin muttered as they drew to a halt once more. A fully loaded ore-cart, incoming this time, blocked much of the road, and the guards were holding all outbound traffic, even walkers, until the ore and its bevy of guards cleared the gate.

The girl stared back at Tank, unafraid. "I did," she said. "Just not in person." Her sharp chin tilted. "He'll be back in Bright Bay. Might already be here. Latest, he'll be here in another day or two at most."

Tank had no interest in staying "another day or two" to find out if she was right. He didn't have the time, as Yuer was waiting, and didn't trust that it wasn't part of some elaborate trap.

Night-demons. Getting worse.

He found himself suddenly very glad they were leaving Bright Bay.

The ore cart cleared. The gate guards waved them forward.

"Anything to declare?" one asked. "Carrying anything to sell along the way, any items that require an outgoing tax or pass?"

"Nothing," Dasin said. Just then, his horse decided to turn irritable: threw its head up, then hunched and twisted, scattering guards and onlookers from its path.

Dasin, white-faced and cursing, hung on with everything he had. Three hops later, the horse as abruptly settled and turned itself round to stand, perfectly placid, beside Tank's horse once more.

Tank couldn't help a bellow of laughter as Dasin scrambled to regain stirrups and reins without falling off altogether; the blond shot him a vicious glare that promised retribution at the first opportunity.

The guards regathered, eying Dasin's mount more cautiously than before; as tempers settled, the leader's attention went from Dasin to the girl riding behind Tank, and his eyebrows rose. Before he could say anything, the girl called out, "Seen Anani lately, Nafa? She's *missing* you."

The guard's face went a dull crimson color. "Don't know what you mean," he snapped. "You watch your mouth, or I'll have you off and arrested for whoring and these two for child pandering."

"It ain' whoring afore they pay me," she shot back, and this time Tank felt his face heat rapidly at the assessing look the guard raked across him and Dasin alike.

"Godsdamnit," he said over his shoulder, "*shut it.*"

She yipped irreverent laughter and stuck out her tongue at the guard.

"*S'e,* we've no intent to–" Tank began, intending an apology to smooth the moment over; the guard shook his head and waved them through.

"At least she won't be troubling my city if you get her out of here," he said. "We're better off without her. But mind you don't both sleep around her, she'll have your throats cut and your purses bare before the first snore."

"If that were true," the girl shot back, "you'd be rolled into the swamp a dozen times over, wouldn't you?"

"*Shut. It,*" Tank growled, and kneed his horse forward before either the girl or the guard could say anything more. Dasin clattered along behind him.

"Just what we need," Dasin groused as they rode through the eastern gate. "A mouthy whore-witch child."

"Tuh," the girl said, contemptuous. "I'm not a whore nor a witch, no more than you're a noble-born or a hawk, merchant. I have the *sight*, and I live on the street. Now an' again there's a price for those things. Don't make me a witch nor whore."

"Tell that to the Church," Dasin said, and that silenced her for a while. He shot a glance at Tank in the ensuing quiet, one eyebrow lifted, and mouthed: *Hopam?* Tank jerked his head at a slant and motioned with one hand: *Later.* Dasin shook his head, frowning, but let it rest.

"Drop me off in Kybeach," the street rat said at last, more subdued. "I'll find a place there."

"They're in need of a hand at the local inn, I think," Tank said. "And if you put back the money you took out of my belt pouch, I'll leave you with enough to get by on for a bit. Otherwise I'll take that thieving little hand off at the wrist."

"Tuh," she said, sounding surprised this time. "Loon."

"Yes."

"You wouldn't."

He twisted, grabbed her hair, and had her hauled out of the saddle and laid over in front of him before she could do more than screech. If she'd been any heavier he couldn't have managed; as it was, his horse snorted and turned in a complete circle by way of protest.

"*Bastard!*" she screamed, twisting to glare at him. Fresh blood seeped from her puffed lip. "*Ta-karne!*"

"Stay still," he advised, mildly surprised that he'd been able to bring the horse back under control so quickly. That probably had more to do with how well the horse was trained than any special skill on Tank's part. Not for the first time, he hoped he wasn't riding a horse stolen from some noble's stable. He wouldn't put anything past Yuer at the moment. "You wriggle around, you're liable to go ass over, and the horse will trample your skull like a melon."

"The fucking saddle ridge is in my stomach!"

"Stop swearing."

She lay still, panting, and went limp in apparent defeat.

"Sight or not," Tank said, "you're stupid." He hooked both hands into her skinny armpits and heaved her upright. "All you had to do was play straight." He lowered her roughly over the side of his horse, dropping her the last few handspans: her feet went out from under her, and she sprawled in the hot, sandy dirt, glaring up at him. "Your having the sight don't impress me into wanting to help you. Get to Kybeach on your own."

"*Fine*," she spat, scrambling to her feet, and dug ferociously into hidden pockets, producing four silver rounds and one gold. She held them up, her hand shaking.

He leaned down, reaching for the coins. She yanked her hand away before his fingers closed. "Take me the rest of the way," she said. "I ain't walkin' that far."

He bared his teeth at her and said, "Coins first."

They stared at each other. Dasin muttered something under his breath.

At last, she held out the coins again. This time he captured them; sorted out one of the silver rounds, and tossed it to her. She caught it reflexively, then scowled at him, understanding the gesture perfectly. "You *lied*!"

"Yes." He straightened in the saddle and kneed the horse into motion. "*Tvit*," he added over his shoulder, but doubted she heard him through her cursing.

"She took more than the one gold," Dasin said once her shrill voice had faded behind them. He wore a curiously satisfied expression.

"I know," Tank said.

"Don't want to get it back?'

"No."

Dasin shot him a sideways grin. "Soft hearted, aren't you?"

"What would you have done?"

"Besides not picking her up in the first place?" Dasin laughed, then sobered. "Same thing."

They rode on in easy silence.

Chapter Fifty-Six

Last time through, the tavern had been filled with quiet, genteel patrons and the air had been laden with exotic scents. Tonight, ginger and clove had been replaced with the well-oiled aroma of roast chicken, underlaid with a sharper smell, one Idisio wasn't entirely certain of; but it made his mouth water just the same.

The patrons were no less well-dressed, but considerably fewer this time, and no dice or card games were in evidence. Instead, the two occupied tables each seemed intent on separate, low-voiced but intense discussion. They glanced up with clear suspicion as Idisio entered from the inn-side door.

Idisio averted his gaze, unwilling to invite trouble, and moved to a table across the room. After a few moments, they relaxed and went back to their talk.

The serving girl came over, smiling, and lit the triple-wick lamp on his table. The strong scent of fish oil warmed the air.

"Roast chicken just came out," she said. "Potatoes, greens, ear of spring corn, half a silver round. Lemon-nut pie, another two silver bits."

She still smelled of sweetened ginger. Idisio smiled at her with considerably more confidence than he'd possessed last time they'd met.

"You look familiar," she said, swaying to put one hand on an outthrust hip. "Didn't you come through here a while back with that great handsome nobleman? Both of you ate near your weight, if I recall right."

Idisio shrugged, half-embarrassed, and dug out a silver half-round's worth of bits. She took it, winked in a way that brought a burst of heat to his ears, and went off to the kitchen. Idisio sat back in the chair, looking around, thinking about Scratha; thinking about how much had changed since he'd come through here before.

Riss. His mother's question about how he felt brought it all back: the way her face had looked in moonlight, the way she'd laughed and tucked into a meal with a man's appetite on the road; the way she'd writhed when—

He bit his lip and thought about how good the food would taste instead. How hungry he was. How pretty the serving girl was, and whether *she* might—*Oh, hells,* he thought, exasperated with himself. He'd never been the sort to chase after every girl in sight. What was the matter with him? *You're still developing,* someone said in memory. Who had that been? He squinted at the table as he tried to force memory to clear. Instead, he found his fingers sliding over the rough wood, every slight rill and worn spot crisply evident. A brief shock of heat raced through him; he shook clear of that and tried to sort out his swirling, muddled thoughts.

The serving girl returned with a well-loaded platter: half a chicken, a fist-sized pile of greens, as much crisp-roasted potatoes, and a roll.

"Roll's normally extra," she said as she set the platter down, "but I like you." She winked again.

This time Idisio winked back, and she was the one to blush and look away.

"Thank you, *s'a*," he said. "You're very kind."

She ducked her head, seeming embarrassed, and retreated to the kitchen.

He grinned and dug into his meal with enthusiasm. When he'd slowed down to picking over the nearly-stripped bones and burping contentedly, she returned.

"Room for pie?" she asked. Her fingers played over the edge of the platter, and she didn't quite meet his eye.

A wild, brazen mood overtook him. "It's a slow night in here," he said, "and a nice one outside. Care to take a walk with me?"

She glanced swiftly at the two other occupied tables, over to the barkeep, then back to Idisio. Scooping up the platter, she murmured, "A walk sounds lovely. I'll meet you around back."

He smiled with a wholly unprecedented satisfaction: they *definitely* weren't laughing at him any longer. He dismissed a pang of unease: he needed to get out of here . . . head back to Bright Bay as fast as he could run . . . soon. Soon. He had time. Thinking of Riss had made him recall how . . . lonely he was. Lonely. Companionship. Just a short walk, and then he'd start out for Bright Bay.

He spared a moment to hope that Riss was flirting with someone even now. She deserved someone more faithful than he'd turned out to be.

Some time later, his hands and mouth busy, her breath coming in stifled gasps, his mind on nothing but the moment, a voice said, "*Idisio*" in tones of blackest disapproval.

His hands tightened. The girl yelped right next to his ear. Idisio jerked his head back reflexively, wincing; then, finally, registered the other voice that had spoken. All the blood seemed to drain instantly to his feet.

"Oh, *shit*," he said aloud, turning his head to look, and found only empty, chill darkness and the hum of night-bugs surrounding them.

"You said you'd come back to talk," his mother said from somewhere to his left. The crickets never paused in their chirring.

"I was–"

The serving girl wriggled free and yanked her dress back into place. "I'll have bruises come morning," she said accusingly. "You try explaining that to my father! Gods, don't you know your own strength?"

He stared at her, bewildered. "What are you talking–"

"You said all you wanted was a meal," his mother said from somewhere behind him.

"This isn't–" Idisio began, twisting his head to search the shadows.

"A bit of fun is one thing," the serving girl said, "but I don't like being roughed up, thank you! Go find your fun somewhere else." She raked her hands through her hair and began to turn away.

At the same time: "You don't want anything to do with that girl," his mother said, her voice an eerie underlay to the girl's outrage. "She's a slut. You'll find plenty of nice girls in Arason."

"Wait," he said to both voices, "wait, I didn't mean to–"

"I've heard that one before," the girl snapped, and stalked off.

"I trusted you," his mother said. "You said you'd come right back to talk. And here I find you pawing some slut instead. That's not being true to your word, son."

Shame swamped through him. *I lied. I lied.* A newfound sense of being lesser, a sense of being wrong, placed her in the right; gave her an absolute superiority over him. *She trusted me. I let her down. I have to make it up to her.*

Don't flinch. Don't flinch.

He tried to explain, as a bridge between the two demands. "I was coming back," he said, watching the servant girl's receding back.

"Really," she said, flat and mistrustful. "Say that twice."

I lied. I lied. I broke her trust. He shook his head hard, pushing away the disorientation. *Don't flinch.* Giving up on eyesight as an aid, he shut his eyes and listened to the small sounds around him.

"You never intended to come back to me," she said.

He opened his mouth to protest his innocence: remembered, in a burst of sudden embarrassment, his initial intention to run like all the hells were after him as soon as he'd eaten and settled his thoughts. How had he become distracted with the servant girl? That had been stupid. He'd allowed thoughts of Riss to distract him from something important.

"You see," his mother said, icily severe. "You lied to me. So there's no talking to be done right now. You've eaten; your stomach is full. I won't allow you to fill that—*that* need. Not yet. Not until we reach Arason, where you'll have suitable girls to approach. Right now it's time for you to sleep. You like to sleep. You've slept every day of your life and you still think you need to—so, now you trot back to the inn and go to sleep."

Idisio yawned. He was terribly, terribly tired—but something she said didn't make any sense. He had to ask her about it. After a moment, he managed words: "I *think* I need to sleep?"

"You'll understand when you're older, son," she said. "Time for bed now. Let's go."

He nodded and obediently trudged back toward the inn.

"I'll be in a bit later," her voice whispered in his ear as he went. "I'm finding that I'm a bit hungry myself now. Since you broke your promise . . . Never mind. You go sleep. Sleep. Sleep . . . ."

She woke him shortly before dawn. He sat up, blinking; his vision shifted over to bring a grey clarity to the dark room.

"Time to go," she told him, her voice light and cheery. "Here–I found you some clean clothes. Put them on and let's go."

Half-asleep, he pulled on the clothes without looking at them closely and followed her obediently, knuckling his eyes as he went. She'd found new clothes as well: a dress that fit her better than the last but still hung loose on her skinny frame. He dimly wondered who she'd bought the clothes from in the middle of the night, and with what coin. Then she smiled at him, and the half-clarity faded away completely.

"What a lovely place that was," she said as they started out of town. "I hope the next one is as nice."

Chapter Fifty-Seven

By mutual agreement, moving faster now without Wian's weight slowing them down, Dasin and Tank went through Kybeach without stopping. No loss, in Tank's opinion. Just the sight of the arc of worn buildings, their many flaws highlighted by the merciless southern sun, depressed him.

"Wonder if we'll ever find out," Dasin said as they passed the last of Kybeach's scraggly cornfields, now little more than withered and rotting stalks.

"Huh? About what?" Tank stared at the fields, thinking about what it would be like to have to farm here. It looked like poor land to begin with, and he had a feeling it had been mismanaged. Kybeach had the air of a place that had been struggling on the edge of survival for a long time.

"That gerho merchant."

Tank glanced at Dasin, surprised.

"Why do you care?" he said without thinking, then felt a flush cross his face at Dasin's cynical squint. "It's not like either of us knew him."

"No," Dasin said, "but it matters, because the story behind it affects how the village is going to react. If it makes them more hostile to outsiders–if that's even possible–it's going to make traveling through Kybeach a chancy business; and we'll be going through Kybeach a *lot*, if we do this back and forth along the coast for Yuer."

"If," Tank said, picking on that word with a sudden surge of hope. "You don't want to do this?"

Dasin shook his head. "Oh, I want to," he said. "Never mind that he says he could ruin us; I can handle myself, and so can you. That doesn't scare me. But you don't see what he's offering. We're going to be rich, Tank; we're going to see giving gold rounds to a street thief as nothing much. And we'll be *known*."

"I don't *want* to be 'known'," Tank said. "And don't forget the *salt* in your bag."

Dasin's cheer faded. "I haven't," he said, more quietly. "But I don't feel as strongly about that as you do, Tank. I wasn't fed dasta, remember? And there's nothing saying we're running that, anyway. It could be something as harmless as . . . as dreamweed."

Tank blinked and looked away, watching a hawk spiral against the clouds now scudding across the sky.

"It's not dreamweed," he said at last, "because aesa is always put in leather or cloth pouches, not ornate boxes. At best, it's esthit; more likely, it's dasta. And I *won't*–" His throat closed. He dropped his chin to his chest and stared fiercely at his horse's ears.

"But it could be esthit," Dasin pointed out. "It might even be something totally innocent, to test our integrity. To see if we'd break the seal. It's the kind of game Yuer would like, isn't it?"

"I don't trust him."

"No. Neither do I. But what he's offering–it would take *years* to build up to this, Tank. I'm being offered lead spot on a caravan, with some heavy backing; he has *nobles* buying from him! I'd normally have to serve as junior merchant to a pack of fools for years before being offered something like this, until I was the 'right age'." He spat to the side away from Tank, bitterness edging his voice.

Tank shook his head. "That doesn't impress me," he said. "My job's the same regardless of who's in charge or what the load contains, and money isn't all that important to me."

"It matters to *me*," Dasin said. His voice climbed over the next words: "Money means *power*. Means *freedom*. Means never again having to say *yes* to–" He stopped and bit his lip, staring straight ahead, then drew in a sharp breath and shook his head. In a more level voice, he added, "Will you stay with it–for my sake, if not for money? I'd like to have one familiar face around."

Tank shrugged, deeply uncomfortable with that glimpse into Dasin's own background pain. *Over, over, over, past and gone,* wound through his mind like a living shield against the echoes of memory raised by that half-said sentence.

"We'll see what Yuer says when we get to Sandsplit," he said roughly. "Maybe he'll have decided I'm too rude and he doesn't want me around after all."

"If he offers you the job, will you take it?"

There was a small child's terror lurking behind the question; just a whiff, but Tank heard it clearly.

"Maybe," he said. "I'll think about it. That's the best I can give, Dasin. I'll think on it."

Dasin let out a breath, his expression deeply relieved.

"Good," he said. "That's–good. Thank you."

"Not doing it for you," Tank said; but the echo of his own words, in his mind, sounded false.

Dasin shot him a sideways grin, arrogance resurfacing, and said nothing.

The blue-shuttered house on the eastern edge of Obein proved to be, on first inspection, tidy and quiet, much like the Fool's Rest Tavern in Bright Bay. Closer, Tank saw men sitting at outside tables. During the day the tables would have been within a shady spot. Now, with evening rapidly drawing down, the men sitting there were little more than bulky shapes against the greying light.

Closer yet, their expressions were visible: they watched Dasin and Tank's approach with the same cool amusement as Yuer's guards had displayed.

Dasin dropped back a pace, allowing Tank the lead. Tank took it and strode toward the front door, ignoring the tables, as though intending to walk straight into the house. Not surprisingly, two of the men were on their feet and blocking his path before he came anywhere near the doorway. He stopped well out of arm's-reach, met their flat stares directly, and said, "Seavorn sent us. We're to stay the night here. We're carrying a package for Yuer."

The men studied him, in no hurry to make a decision. At last, the shorter of the two, a muscular man with heavy pox scars, missing teeth, and thinning brown hair, said, "Haven't seen you before. You replacing Baylor, then?"

"Don't know who that is," Tank said, not giving any ground. "Just know what Seavorn told me to say. Do we go somewhere else for a meal and a bed, or do you let us in?"

The man snorted, seemingly amused. "You don't go anywhere after prancing up with that sort of talk," he said. The wavering light of the single torch by the front door did his pitted, scarred face no favors. "Ever hear of manners, boy? *Hello* and *please* go a long way, you know."

"I wasn't under the impression you were the type cared much for formalities," Tank said. He could feel Dasin's fear shivering along his back, and hoped Dasin wasn't letting it show on his face.

The man stared at him, breath hissing between his teeth, then said, "Boy, you got some nerve. If Seavorn hadn't sent word to watch for you and let you through, I'd be wiping you through the dust right now."

Wisdom said *Apologize and let it go*; as usual, temper won.

"Go ahead," Tank said, stepping back and spreading his hands. "Give that a try."

Dasin made a vague, agonized sound. The men at the door looked past Tank and laughed.

"Your boy there's about pissing himself over that," the taller one observed. "Doesn't like the notion of you getting scratched, I'm guessing. Nah, let it go, Ger. He ain't worth aggravating ourselves over. He won't last, not with that attitude."

"Tank," Dasin hissed, barely audible, *"don't,* damnit. Not this time."

Tank lifted his chin, hoping the men hadn't heard that, and said, "So, about dinner, then. *Please.* And a bed for the night. *Please."*

"Tuh." The shorter one shoved the door open and jerked his thumb toward the opening. "Go on, then. Arrogant little squirt."

Tank kept his back straight and his head high as he went by, senses alert for a surprise attack; but the door shut hard behind them without incident, and Dasin let out a sobbing gasp of relief.

"Are you trying to get us *killed*?" the blond demanded, whacking Tank's shoulder hard.

Tank shook his head, looking around the small room. It was similar to Yuer's home, if rather smaller; the front door led into a large sitting room with comfortable chairs arrayed around a large table. Heavy draperies covered the walls, obscuring any exits other than two large front-facing windows.

The room had no fireplace. Tank found that a relief. And the room was empty at the moment, another good sign; if someone had been sitting in one of the chairs waiting for them, Tank thought he might have bolted on the spot.

"Doesn't do any good to show manners to men like that," he said absently. "They'd take both sides and own the road once all's done. Either Yuer's name is enough protection or it's not, and that's something we needed to know for sure."

One of the draperies moved. A thin woman with long blonde hair emerged, eyeing them cautiously.

"You'll be wanting something?" she said. Her voice carried a heavy northern accent, and her green eyes were watchful.

"Dinner and a bed for the night, s'a, if you please," Tank said.

"You wanting company?" Her gaze flicked to Dasin, assessing. "We only got one girl right now, and I'm off the duty for a few more days."

Tank repressed a grimace of distaste. "No. Just a meal and some sleep."

She nodded and held aside the drapery to reveal a door behind her. "This way, if you please, then, s'es. Bread's done, and chicken's almost ready. I'll show you to your room after you eat."

The kitchen turned out to be a rough-plastered, low-ceilinged room, thick with the aroma of fresh bread, rosemary, garlic, and roast chicken. A trestle table filled most of one wall, easily enough to seat fifteen men. Tank and Dasin sat side by side, their backs to the wall, without a word needing to be said on the matter.

The girl brought them each a hand-sized loaf of black bread and set down a shallow dish of oil. "Test loaves," she said, "but I always like them better myself. And that's walnut oil there; we've a good old tree out back."

"Thank you," Tank said. "You run a good kitchen, s'a."

Her lined face broke into a cheerful smile. "That's kind of you," she said. "Good to hear a friendly word now and again." She turned away toward the stove.

"So you're nice to *her*?" Dasin said in a low voice, tearing his loaf open and dipping it in the oil. "What's the reason for *that*?"

"She's feeding us," Tank said blandly, and grinned at Dasin's scowl. "Never insult the cook, Dasin. That's more dangerous than facing down those men outside."

Chapter Fifty-Eight

"Humans like pain," his mother said.

Idisio blinked out of grey haze and met the warm glare of late-afternoon sunlight. He stopped walking, then realized he hadn't *been* walking and almost fell over from the resulting disorientation.

His mother perched on a tree stump, watching him with uncanny calm. "They like to give pain, and they like to receive it," she went on. "It's one of the things Rosin taught me."

Her eyes seemed colorless in the bright sunlight, except for a sharp dark ring around the outer edge where the white should have been.

Idisio turned slowly, looking around. Tangled scrub brush and feather-fringe trees surrounded them in all directions. The clearing he stood in was barely a weak stone's throw across. The trees, from bark to branch to leaf, looked exceptionally jagged and dangerous. The air felt sharp and hard in his mouth.

Humans like pain. He wanted to argue that assertion: couldn't.

"Where are we?" he said instead.

"Near the next town," she said. "I thought it best to have our talk before we encountered more humans."

Idisio looked at the lines of her face, the coloring in her eyes, and knew he wasn't going anywhere without her permission. That alone raised his hackles. He directed his best imitation of a Scratha-severe stare at her.

She smiled. "You're still a child," she said. "I'm trying to treat you as an adult, son, but I can't do that if you stand there glaring and sulking at me."

He bit the inside of his cheek and reluctantly moderated his expression.

"I understand why you're acting this way," she said. "You were hurt as a child, son; you were taken from me too young and put among the humans. You had to live as a thief and as a . . . ." Her voice faltered. "I found your place. Your den. Your . . . your coins. And I saw—what you had to do."

He looked sharply back to her at that, and found her studying the ground, her face gone a dreadful grey shade. She sucked in a difficult breath, then another; the horrid color flushed into a more normal shade, and she looked up with eyes gone as black as Deiq's.

"It was a long time ago," he said. "It doesn't matter any more."

The words felt hollow in his mouth, like a silver gloss over rot. He was angry, godsdamned right. He was *ha'ra'hain*, he had deserved better than that: and now he wanted anyone who had ever hurt him *dead*, he wanted to feel *blood*. He should have stood beside Deiq and ripped those gate guards apart; nobody could have stopped them—

He bit his lip, hard, as the only alternative to slapping himself back to sense. His mother's dark eyes gleamed with amusement. He'd seen that same murderous laughter in the eyes of those who heard the *voices*, over the years. Tank had been the only one to hear the voices and not develop that peculiar glaze to his smile.

Ellemoa growled, deep in the back of her throat, her eyes narrowing.

She doesn't like that, he thought, startled by her reaction. *Something about Tank—she doesn't like him. He—scares her?* It was a potential weapon. He had to remember that—

"He doesn't frighten *me*," she snapped. "He's a threat. He's trained to kill our kind. He tried to kill *teyhataerth*. "

"I've been having visions of him," Idisio said, and a weight lifted from him, just to confess that so simply.

She showed no surprise, no concern, which added to his relief. "Of course you have. We *see* the future, see in a way the human seers only dream of doing. Only our line can do that. Only you and I, now. That boy is trained to kill ha'ra'hain. He's trained to kill you, son. Of course you're having visions. You *know* he's a threat. You know what he did to *teyhataerth*. "

Her eyes flooded with black for a moment, then reverted to a dark-rimmed grey. Color washed out of her face, seeped back.

"They killed a ha'ra'ha, these humans you think so highly of. They killed *teyhataerth*, and they left. They didn't care that their own kind were trapped in those cells beneath the city. Didn't care that *I* was there, starving, in a cell I couldn't get out of."

That brought to mind the slick yellow walls of a sun-flooded room with no apparent exit: what would have happened if Evkit hadn't let them out? An uneasy shiver ran up Idisio's back.

"Another dishonor, another hurt you've faced without me," his mother mourned. She put a hand over her eyes, her other arm wrapped tight around her ribs, and rocked back and forth, breathing hard.

Deiq cared about status. She cares about me. *Just me.* It made brash dismissal almost impossible. Whatever her flaws, she saw him as a son—wanted to care for him like a mother.

It was a dreadfully seductive thought.

I'm going to start crying. Talk about something else. Fast. "If we're from Arason, how did we wind up in Bright Bay? And how come I never knew I was ha'ra'ha, and Ninnic's—*teyhataerth*—never saw me?"

She drew in a long breath and straightened, folding her hands in her lap. "There were evil men in Arason. Your father tried to save us by sending us to Bright Bay, but he didn't realize that it wasn't a safe place any longer. He had to choose—which of us to protect. He only had strength for one. He chose you."

Her dark grey eyes filled. Tears began streaking down her face, but her breath and voice remained even.

"He put a protection on you that hid you from even my vision, and pushed you somewhere in the city. And *teyhataerth* . . . took me."

In the following silence, the drone of sandbugs seemed very loud. Idisio's heart hammered and skipped in his chest. *My father chose to save me? He threw my mother into the arms of a monster—to save me?* He blinked hard, refusing tears.

"Not a monster. It wasn't a monster," his mother said, her voice shrill, then modulated back down. "It wasn't *teyhataerth's* fault, what it became. It was all Rosin. All Rosin. It wasn't *teyhataerth's* fault. Rosin controlled it."

"But Rosin was human. How could he possibly control a ha'ra'ha?"

"Rosin convinced *teyhataerth* that he was stronger and smarter," his mother said. Her black-rimmed stare bored into him; then she smiled a little, a predatory expression. "That's not important. I've been forcing you along this far because you wouldn't listen to me. I can't keep doing that. It's not the right thing to do. I love you too much to force you to obey me. So I'm going to explain it all to you. Listen: Humans and desert lords are nothing but weak, unworthy insects out to use you for their own gain."

"That's not true!"

"Will you at least listen to my side?"

He hesitated, torn; but it was the least he could do, after all she'd suffered on his behalf. And she cared about him. She really did. This all came from how much she loved him . . . He could at least listen. There was no harm in that.

She's been forcing me along? He looked back over days filled with grey haze and confusion, of odd, velvet whispers that convinced him to keep going, and felt a sharp alarm. *How do I know she's not going to keep doing that? She's lied to get me this far. She'll lie to me again.*

"I haven't lied to you, son," she said softly. "That's one promise I've held to. I haven't given you a single lie—unlike those desert lords you admire so."

"Stop that," he said, shivering. "I don't like you just—pulling thoughts from my head like that."

"You're not very good at being quiet, son," she said. A thin smile flitted across her face, then disappeared back into a deadly serious expression. She leaned forward. "Listen to me. Listen to my side, as you agreed. Listen: Those desert lords used you as bait to trap what they saw as a monster. How is that acting as any kind of *friend*, or even an ally?" She paused, watching his face intently.

"Those men aren't *good people*," she went on. "They left dozens of their own kin to die in the dark and the silence. Do you know what a human starving to death sounds like? I listened to twenty-four humans die that way–after those twenty-four had killed and eaten everyone else in their cells first. I could have given them a better end than that. A *faster* end."

Blood streaming along her hands–slick and hot in her mouth, and the wet crunch of bone–

A thick shock ran through Idisio's whole body. He stumbled a few steps aside, went to his knees, and vomited. Only acidic liquid came up.

His mother said, pragmatic and cool, "Being ill over words doesn't change the past. Why allow yourself such an exaggerated response?"

"I'm not cold like you and Deiq!" Idisio snapped, rocking back to his feet, and came forward a step, his shoulders rounding. "I won't be like that!"

Her eyes cleared to a steady pale grey. "Cold?" she said. "Because I don't endlessly punish myself for what's done and gone by?" She paused.

"And Deiq is hardly innocent," she added. "He's done things that make what I told you look *kind*."

"How do you know that?" Idisio demanded.

Her eyes narrowed and took on a feral glitter; then it faded into a bewildered expression. "Know what?"

"How do you know that about Deiq?"

"Who?" She glanced around, staring at the long shadows creeping across the clearing. "It's getting dark," she muttered. "We should go, son. We have to get to Arason." She sniffed the air like an asp-jacau scenting after a snake. "We have to go."

Idisio couldn't tell if she was faking her sudden confusion or if she genuinely found the shadows so disorienting that she'd lost the thread of the conversation.

She loves me. Whatever else, I have to remember that's real. She wants what's best for me. We may not agree on what that is—but she's honest in that one thing: she loves me.

In the face of that, he couldn't bring himself to call her a raving lunatic.

He said, "What if I say I don't want to go to Arason?"

She raised a clear grey stare to his face. "Are you going to say that, son?"

Images unrolled behind his eyes: using blisters and bindings to make himself look diseased and bring in coin as a beggar; a silver coin, turning over and over between his fingers . . . a hard blow that pitched him nearly the width of a small room, the glares of a roomful of men as they assessed which side of the predator/prey line Idisio stood on . . . the odd look on Riss's face as she turned and left his room for the last time.

"Another slut," his mother said softly. "All she ever wanted was the company of a man powerful enough to protect her and malleable enough to control. Once she saw you for what you are, she couldn't wait to get away from you. None of the humans will ever really trust you. You'll be forever watched like a rabid animal–and put down like one, at the first sign that they don't control you completely, by the very humans you thought of as friends."

Deiq's sharp voice drifted back into memory: *Don't flinch around them.*

In the gathering haze of sunset and shadow, what she was saying made perfect sense.

"Is that the life you want, son?" she said. "When you could live peacefully with your mother in your ancestral home, learning the things the humans won't ever allow you to know? You'll meet your father. You'll speak with him whenever you like."

"My father. . . ." A surprisingly sharp longing burned in his chest at that.

Silence drew down around them, punctuated by the shirring trill of awakening nightbugs.

"Will you come to Arason with me, son?" his mother said, her voice scarcely a whisper. "Will you come and meet your father, and let me teach you the truth of your heritage? Will you come with me, and be loved and honored and respected? Do you really want to stay with the humans, where you'll always be the despised, distrusted outcast?"

He looked up, thinking that over. Vivid slashes of orange, red and purple streaked the early evening sky, turning the scattering of clouds into gilded, feathery puffs: each one so distinct and close that he felt as though he could reach out, pluck one from the sky, and cradle it in his hands like a warm puff pastry.

"Puff pastry . . . yes. I'm a very good baker," his mother said, her voice threaded with silvery longing. "It's been a very long time since I've handled flour and water, salt and oil. I want to put a loaf of my own bread in my son's hands and see him smile as he tears into it. I want to clean up the crumbs and run a comb through his untidy hair and pick up the clothes he tosses on the floor. I want to see him laugh and run through the rain and play with rainbows."

"I'm a little old for splashing in puddles," Idisio said, but the words came out hoarse and thick.

"You're never too old for that. I'd run right beside you. Rain is *beautiful*. Cleansing. Sacred." She sighed deeply. "Please," she said. "Please, come home with me."

She held out both her hands, not moving from her perch on the tree stump; and after a long moment of staring at her, Idisio took three steps forward and laced his fingers through hers.

Chapter Fifty-Nine

Rain rattled over the roof in a short burst that chilled the room further. Tank half-rolled, tugging the blanket up over his shoulder. The bottom corner shifted with the movement, leaving his feet bare. The blanket had gotten turned sideways at some point.

He muttered a curse and sat up, yanking at the thick fabric to sort it out. Dasin had managed to tuck most of the blanket around himself; in one swift movement, Tank shoved him over onto his back and jerked the revealed fold of cloth free.

Dasin gave a sleep-thick whimper and flung up a hand to shield his face, curling into a tight ball at the same time. Tank ducked the unintentional blow, draped the blanket back into proper alignment, then tried to settle down; but the bed was narrow to start with, and Dasin's curled-up form used twice the sideways space he'd been occupying before.

Precariously perched on the edge of the mattress, chill air attacking his bare torso, Tank swore again, then shook Dasin's shoulder lightly.

"Move over, Dasin," he said. "You're about to kick me to the floor."

Dasin whimpered again, still resolutely tucked into a defensible position. "Don't," he breathed. "Please . . . please. Not again."

"Holy gods," Tank muttered. He shut his eyes for a moment, steadying his breathing, and wondered if he could stand a night on the floor after all. A renewed draft of chill air washed across his torso, answering the question immediately.

He sighed and rubbed a hand over his face, forcing himself the rest of the way awake. Dasin didn't seem to have a violent reaction to being touched in his sleep, so Tank gripped the blond's shoulder lightly.

"Hey," he said. "Dasin. *Dasin.* It's me. It's Tank. Tanavin. I just want you to move over, that's all. Wake up a moment, move over, all right?"

Dasin whimpered; the sound turned into a low moan, nearly a growl, as he uncurled–too fast. Tank went backward through pure reflex, landing hard and gracelessly on the floor with a resounding thud. He rolled to his knees, groaning, and wiped his face clear as he squinted through the darkness.

Silence hung thick for a moment. Then the covers shifted and Dasin whimpered again: a sound of complete, disoriented terror.

"Dasin," Tank said hastily. "You awake, Dasin?"

Another moment of taut quiet: then Dasin said, shakily, "T-t-t-anavin?"

"Yeah." Tank hoisted himself back up to sit on the edge of the bed, brushing dirt from his hands. "You had a nightmare, I'm guessing."

"Did I hit you?"

"No." He put out a hand, searching; located Dasin's skinny arm and wrapped his hand around it lightly. "You all right now?"

"Y–" Dasin stopped. "I don't know," he said after a moment. "It's really damn dark in here, Tank."

"Yeah. I know. But there's a half moon, or thereabouts, outside, so think about that." Tank let go of Dasin's arm and stretched out, tugging the covers up around himself again. "Full dark is a good thing, to my way of thinking, anyway," he said. "Means everything's done for the day."

Dasin sat still for a few breaths. "Not how it was for me," he said at last. "Got any aesa? I was so tired I forgot to bring my saddlebags in. They're on the floor by the stall door."

"No. I don't use it. That's your poison, not mine."

"Shit. Hope they're still there . . . ." Dasin hesitated, then moved as though to get out of the bed. Tank put a hand out, wrapping it unerringly around Dasin's arm again.

"You're *not* going out there right now," Tank said. "Not alone. Not with that crew lounging about and more'n likely well past a few drinks by now. And *I* ain't getting up."

"Tank–"

"Dasin." Tank didn't release his grip. "Go back to sleep."

He felt a heavy shiver pass through Dasin's thin body. After another few breaths, Dasin sighed and tucked down under the covers.

Not long afterwards, he said, "You asleep?"

Tank stared at the darkness between himself and the ceiling. "No. Say it."

"Say what?"

"Tell me the nightmare. Or whatever's on your mind. You won't sleep until you do."

There came a long silence. At last Dasin said, voice oddly stifled, "You said the same thing to Wian."

"So?"

"I'm not like–"

"Don't," Tank said flatly. "Don't draw that line. I'll pound it right back down your throat."

Dasin snorted, a frustrated sound.

"Why should I tell you anything?" he said. "You already know what my nightmares are about."

"Say it if you need to, anyway. Or whatever's on your mind."

"Fine, then–give me a straight answer: Why didn't you do it?" Dasin said abruptly. "Wian. When she grabbed you–and I know damn well she did at some point; for all her talk she's a whore from toe to hairline–why didn't you answer it?"

The inflections in Dasin's voice, the silence, and the darkness all combined to demand a deeper response than Tank had given previously. He lay still, thinking about it, then said, very quietly, "Because no matter how it started, right now she *is* a whore, from toes to hairline. And I won't be the one on the other side of that pairing."

Dasin sighed softly. "Yeah," he murmured. "I figured it was something like that."

"Why did *you*?" Tank said, unable to help himself.

"Because–" Dasin stopped, his breathing suddenly gone ragged. At last he said, in a wavering voice, "Because it stops me thinking. Stops me *remembering*."

Tank squeezed his eyes shut, his jaw taut. In the following silence, Dasin stirred restlessly, then turned over to face away from Tank.

"Go to sleep," Dasin said, voice muffled. "No point in anything else."

Tank half-rolled and put a hand on Dasin's skinny shoulder; gripped once, lightly, then shifted to put his back to Dasin and listened to his own breathing until it mapped out a road to sleep.

He half-woke, at one point, to find a knobbly warm back pressed against his and Dasin's snoring filling the room. He thought dimly about pushing Dasin away, but drifted back to sleep before he could decide why that even mattered.

He woke again, more fully, to find a thin hand tracing across his back, and went rigidly still.

"You have a lot of scars," Dasin said, the words barely audible. "I never realized. I just–" He took his hand away. "I woke up with my hand on your back and . . . well. I wondered, when you told Wian you had your own, because I don't . . . I don't have any. Not like that, at least. My village didn't allow–they couldn't leave marks on us." He paused. "You never said anything about being beaten like this," he added, very quietly. "This why you always kept your shirt on in training sessions?"

Tank kept his eyes shut and tried to remember *when* he'd taken his shirt off; he *never* did, and certainly not around Dasin. He remembered feeling cold air on his torso, earlier, but hadn't even been aware of what that meant. He must have been more tired than he thought.

"Say it," Dasin said. "Your own nightmare. This *isn't* like mine, Tank. Not by the hells' width. I never went through–this. And I know you: there's memories you wouldn't have talked over with Allonin, because he–didn't want to know some things. We both saw that, didn't we? But you can tell me."

"You don't want to know it either, Dasin."

Dasin growled low in his throat by way of answer.

Habit insisted that it was a mistake to bring the past out; but Tank felt something reckless and angry stir inside him, as though it had been waiting for the invitation.

"The name I chose when I went to the Aerthraim," he said, not even trying to keep his voice mild. "Tanavin. There were these two boys in my village. Tan and Avin. One of the more brutal regulars came in and wanted Avin–skinny little thing, too scared to ever fight back, got hurt a lot. We all did what we could to protect him. Me and Tan, mostly; we were the biggest. This time, Tan stepped in and went in Avin's place, but Tan was older and tougher and the man didn't like that."

Tank paused, listening to Dasin's breath whistling between his teeth.

"Tan–died that night," he said. "We thought the man would be banned for life, but he came back less than a month later. He brought a bag of pretty glass jewelry and a few bottles of good desert lightning. Banna let him in and he took Avin." He blinked a few times, took a long breath, then went on: "We all liked Tan. A lot. He was the one always stuck up for us. He's the one taught me I didn't have to accept whatever was handed out as my due. He made me start palming the dasta, and going without now and again. I went in–real young. He started older. Knew about the outside world a bit." He paused again. "Avin flat worshiped him. When this man killed Tan, Avin got–real, real quiet. Wouldn't talk to anyone about anything. Went through the motions. Wasn't really there. But when the man came back–"

Dasin let out a faint, distressed sound.

The rest of the words tumbled out, unstoppable: "Meek little Avin went hot-crazy. Killed the man. Then our keeper–"

"*Tank*–gods–"

"–beat Avin to death. In *front* of us. The next night was when Allonin came and bought me away from there."

He paused, but there was one more thing that needed to be said. One of the things Allonin wouldn't have been able to bear hearing about–or might have already known. Tank had never asked; hadn't wanted to know for sure. Still didn't.

He said, voice flaying his throat, "The part I didn't tell Allo–I would have been next. The man had already said he wanted to try me after Avin, and our keeper promised him–free rein. Because I was getting older. Too old for most of the regulars. Like Tan. So she didn't care–"

He stopped, unable to voice the rest; shut his eyes and focused on breathing evenly. At last, Dasin flattened a trembling hand against his back, then withdrew and rolled to set his spine against Tank's again.

Tank stared through darkness, dry-eyed, and said nothing more. But slowly, slowly, the pressure and warmth of Dasin's bony back against his served to melt the rigid tension of bringing that memory into the moment. His breathing eased, bit by bit; and bit by bit, the sting of that fierce hatred began to dissolve. Not entirely: it ran far too deep. But it was a beginning.

"Thanks, Dasin," he said after a while, low enough to avoid waking him.

Dasin pressed a shoulder back and murmured, as quietly, "Go to sleep already, loon."

Chapter Sixty

Moonlight brightened and faded around Kolan. A patter of rain swept across and went away again. Once, there came the faint stinging of hail. The sun rose, and sank away again. None of it particularly bothered him. At least it was *real*. And there weren't any voices here, just the seagulls and the waves and the wind.

Whenever it rained, he tilted his head back and let it run into his mouth; that and the pale moonlight felt like enough to sustain him forever. Now and again, he nibbled on the last of the road food in his pack: a largish chunk of hard cheese and a packet of crackers.

Crabs scuttled across his feet. Sand-flies swarmed around him, then wandered away again. Far out in the water, a plume shot up high: a dolphin, maybe, or a whale. A school of small fish burst from the water in a sparkling, leaping cloud as some unseen predator chased them from below.

A black tern landed on his shoulder and grockled in his ear briefly before flying away.

The sound startled him back to himself, and to a realization that he hadn't eaten in several days. How many? It didn't matter. He wasn't hungry, but without the support of *teyhataerth* he needed solid food. All the crackers and cheese were long gone.

He waded out into the water, stood utterly still until fish came to frolic around his knees; then bent swiftly and snatched a glittering prize into the air. The other fish fled. The one in Kolan's hand writhed desperately–

–begging for life, for freedom, for mercy–

Kolan stared at the fish, his eyes welling with sudden tears: then leaned over again and gently released the small creature into the water.

Wiping his hands on his shirt, he came out of the water and up onto the sandy shore. Turning, he stared out over the vast expanse of ocean for a long time, thinking over that momentary connection with the fish.

A long-ago conversation with Solian went through his mind: *They're just bugs! There are hundreds and hundreds of them, Kolan! They give birth to dozens more every few days. We'll be overrun if all we do is shoo them gently outside. The gods don't care about bugs. They care about us. Otherwise the bugs would be running the world, not humans.*

Kolan stared out over the water and said aloud, "But what if the bugs think they are the ones running the world?"

He staggered a little, abruptly light-headed and weary. Past time to get some solid food. Rainwater wouldn't do any longer, apparently.

Time to face humanity again. At least long enough for a meal.

Dawn had come and gone. Early-afternoon light hazed the air, and a scattering of clouds rode the sky. To either side, the beach ran in a sweep of rumpled white and gold, speckled with shells, seaweed, and storm-cast debris. The sand softened as he went inland, grinding against his bare feet; he stopped and looked down in mild surprise. When had he lost his shoes? After a bit of careful consideration, he recalled taking them off and setting them up near the line of dunes. A cursory search through the grassy hummocks produced nothing but more sand.

He shrugged, not particularly concerned, and went on.

Past the line where whipgrass tussocks and sandseed vines kept the sand from blowing back down into the sea, the ground turned to a silty dirt overlaid with a short, spiky, hard-bladed grass. Kolan winced a little as the sharp edges jabbed between his toes.

Movement to his right drew his attention: two forms, a larger and a smaller, plodding in a large circle a fair distance away. Kolan hesitated, watching them; then, intrigued and hoping that they might have food to share, went toward them.

Closer, the two resolved into a man and a boy, dressed in worn clothes and carrying long forked sticks. They barely glanced up as Kolan approached, all their attention on the large pit they were walking around. The older one stopped, pointing, and said, "There. Push that one over a handspan, it's above."

The boy pushed with his stick. The man grunted approval and signaled him to resume walking. Neither one looked at Kolan, now less than a stone's throw away.

"*S'es?*" he said tentatively.

They ignored him, all of their attention on their work. Kolan stepped in a little closer and looked at the contents of the pit: a mass of long, thin reeds, soaking in water. A faint scum had begun to form on the surface, and now and again the reeds shifted slightly, bobbing above the water. The man and boy shoved each protruding bit back under the water as it arose, with an attentiveness that suggested dire consequences for allowing the reeds to dry out. Nearby, a double-bucket shoulder yoke rested on the ground, empty; not far from that sat a close-woven, covered basket.

"*S'es,*" Kolan said again, "do you have any food? I can pay you." He put a hand to his belt pouch, not at all sure if that were true. It was hard to remember money as a concept, let alone keep track of how much he held.

"No food," the older man said without looking up. "Don't have any ourselves. Go away."

Kolan found himself looking at their feet as they plodded round and round. The older man was barefoot, his heavily callused feet nicked and bleeding; the boy wore shoes too large for him, obviously stuffed with padding to make them fit. Kolan looked at the shoes for a while, blinking slowly, then said, "You took my shoes."

"You wasn't using them," the man said, still not looking up.

"I'd like them back," Kolan said mildly.

"Demons don't need shoes."

"I'm not a demon."

"Then you're a ghost. Nothing human stands and stares at the water days on end without moving like you done. Every time we go to fill th' bucket for the pond refill, we seen you. Same spot. You ain't human."

Kolan smiled, genuinely amused. "I'm very human," he said. "I'm also very hungry."

"Told you," the man said, prodding a bobbing clump of reeds back down under the surface, "ain't got none. Had our bread this morn, we'll have our millet this even. None to spare, not for man nor demon, so move along and find someone else to haunt."

Kolan began to turn away, then paused and came back. "If you think I'm a demon or a ghost," he said, "why aren't you afraid of me?"

The man flickered a glance up at that, his blue-grey eyes smoky with contempt. "You'll kill me or you won't," he said. "No point running away from the only thing as puts food in my son's mouth over a *maybe*." Then, to his son: "Look, there—"

"Got it," the boy said, already prodding with the pole.

The older man grunted and went back to his silent, sour plodding; stopping now and again, scowling at the pool, then moving on again. His gaze never left the reeds, ever attentive for one breaking the surface.

Kolan stood still, watching them; looking at his stolen shoes, and the older man's bleeding feet, and the pool of submerged reeds. At last he slung his pack to the ground, then stepped forward, lifted the yoke, and settled it over his shoulders.

"You walk off with that," the man said without any particular emotion, "you're killing us."

"Just to the water's edge and back," Kolan said, and plodded off.

When he returned, he set the buckets down by the edge of the pit and stepped back out of the way. The older man grunted, set his pole aside, and tipped in the fresh seawater with care; moved the yoke and buckets out of their walking path, and resumed his own steady plodding.

"Piece of bread left in the basket there," he said after two more circuits. "If'n you get another round of water."

Kolan sat down beside the basket without comment. The piece of bread was larger than his fist, and stale. He picked at it slowly, mindful of how long it had been since he last ate. When half the piece remained, he put it back in the basket, stood, and picked up the yoke again without a word.

"Leave 'em," the older man said when Kolan returned with the buckets. "Won't need 'em for a few more hours." He waved a hand at the boy. "Ablo, take him home. Get him a place to sleep tonight, rest yourself. Come back at moonrise. Not you," he added to Kolan. "You've helped enough. By nightfall the retting pit'll be throwing off the gods' own stink."

Kolan squinted at the pit. "That's not flax, is it?"

"No. Blackreed. Rather work with flax, the smell is worlds better'n black-reed, and it don't take so much attention. But it don't pay half as good as this. Rich folk like cloth from this stuff. Say it's softer an' lasts longer. I wouldn't never know; couldn't afford a fingertip's worth, myself." He prodded a float-ing reed back under the surface, scowling.

"I can endure bad smells," Kolan said, smiling.

"Not like this, you can't," the man said dourly. "Smells like a cow with diar-rhea died and busted wide open. I got a mask for me and the boy. Go on. Get my boy safe back to the house; been all sorts round here of late."

The boy opened his mouth to protest, outrage on every line of his face.

"I'll be glad of the protection," Kolan said with a straight-faced earnestness that silenced them both. "And the guidance. I'm not quite sure where I am, truth be told."

"Not far outside Sandsplit," the man said, and spat to one side in bitter commentary. "Where a man of means can be nothing the next day from a word said wrong. Go on, while there's light to go with. Ablo, stay away from the girls, mind–Get back here to help at moonrise."

The boy nodded, blank-faced, and motioned Kolan to follow him. When they were out of earshot, he said, "Man of means, my grandmother's arse. We never been but a drink's price from the poorhouse my whole life."

"Everyone needs their lies," Kolan said peaceably.

The boy looked sideways at him. "Sounds like a soapy's talk, there."

"Yes."

"Oh. So all that standing and staring out at the water–you're on some sort of fasting pilgrimage, then?"

Kolan smiled. "Something like that," he agreed.

"You should have said."

"Does it really make a difference?"

The boy said nothing for a few steps, then: "No. Not really."

They plodded through the late-afternoon light in companionable quiet. Around them, tall stands of feathertrees shook pale blossoms into the steady breeze; long, striped grasses bowed and danced. A large black bird circled high overhead, veering along the air currents with no apparent goal in mind other than to enjoy the moment.

A faint sea-brine aroma clung to Kolan's clothes and hair, and sandy grit squished between his toes, driven into abrasiveness by the sharp grass. He ignored the discomfort and put his attention on other sensations: the wind against his face, the steady glare of the sun from his left, the mournful screech of sea-birds battling somewhere nearby.

The footpath sloped up a high bank. At the crest, a group of young children in tattered breeches ran in circles, pouncing on each others' shadows and on each other, shrieking with laughter. They paused as Kolan and Ablo came over the slight rise, staring wide-eyed; then tumbled back into their game without further concern.

Not far away, a group of equally ragged huts stood around a central fire pit already heaped high with dry and green branches and grasses. Several large logs that looked to have been well-tumbled by the sea sat around the fire. A small girl in a brown shift stitched about with white flowers was walking along the narrowest log, her eyes squinted in concentration, skinny arms out for balance. As she caught sight of Ablo and Kolan, she slipped sideways, stumbling, and barely avoided sprawling on the ground.

Ablo hooted derisively. The girl stuck her tongue out and darted into one of the huts. A few moments later she emerged with a tall, lean woman whose harsh grey hair matched her severe face.

"Ablo," she said, then stared at Kolan with instant distrust. "What's this? Did something happen to Imin?"

"He sent me home to get some sleep," Ablo said. "This one came along and helped a bit. Imin says to get him a place to rest."

The woman glanced over her shoulder, then back to Kolan, her frown deepening. "Just where is he expecting us to find a free bed?" she demanded. "And I'm supposing a meal is expected!"

"*S'a*," Kolan inserted, "I'll be content with a patch of grass free of bloodants, and a bit of bread is more than enough to spare."

She snorted, surveying him with a sharp, assessing stare.

"We're not so poor as all of that," she said at last. "Sit. We'll find you a space and a bowl." She turned and went back into her hut.

Ablo, smiling, waved to Kolan and went off to another hut. Kolan sat down on the log the small girl had been balancing on. Without really thinking about it, he pulled out his marble and began rolling it between his hands. He sat still, staring at nothing in particular, and time blurred as it had while he stood before the water.

Around him, people moved, spoke, laughed; lit the fire, ate a meal, danced around the fire. Warmth washed over his face, someone slapped his back, nudged him, shook his shoulder. He sat still, working the marble from hand to hand, dimly aware of everything but too contented with the moment's experience to respond to anything.

At last he blinked and shook his head, rousing from his dazed contemplation of nothing. A pale half-moon hung far overhead, a thin scattering of clouds trailing across the glowing surface; a bowl of thin millet soup sat at his feet, a few enterprising ants digging through the contents. He lifted up the bowl, picked out the ants with care, then gulped down the soup in three long swallows.

From across the firepit, the grey-haired woman watched him, her face ruddy in the dying light of the fire.

"You're an odd one," she said. "Ablo said to leave you be, that you've had a fit like that before and you would move when it suited you."

Kolan looked back at her and said nothing.

"There's a spot in with me tonight," she said.

"That's kind of you, *s'a*," he said. He studied the lines of her face with care, then shook his head slowly. "I won't impose on your good nature."

"Imin will be staggering in a few hours past moonrise, once he's too tired to mistrust Ablo's capability any longer," the woman said. "The others won't stir nor share, not for gold; they work at trades like charcoal and lime, dawn to dusk, and don't care for company other'n their own sort. The smell, for one; it's no sweetness to one as isn't in the trade themselves." She paused. "I work fields," she added, smiling a little. "Gathering and such. It's a bit nicer at the end of the day; and in the off-season, there's always caring for this lot to keep me busy."

Kolan studied the dying fire without speaking. After a while she got up and came round to sit beside him. He looked at her sidelong, not moving. She put a hand on his knee, leaning in; a dizzying surge of raw desire twisted through him–Gods, how long had it been since someone touched him with any kindness?

Memory turned sharply sideways into recalled agony.

Her skin was gold and red with reflected fire, the air was hot and humid, and her eyes were black, so black, so very very–and the man they'd brought in began to scream–and Kolan wrenched at his chains, screaming at her to stop, for the love of the gods, don't do this, harm none–

With a harsh gasp, he put up a warding hand and leaned away.

He could feel the woman's temper begin to shift even before she said, "What are you, some kind of soapy, then?"

"Yes," he said hoarsely. "I am."

"Oh," she said, dismayed. "I didn't think–I'm sorry, *s'iope*."

He made a faint gesture, not looking at her. She retreated to her former seat.

Kolan stared at the fire, grimly shoving that memory, like a protruding blackreed in the retting pool, safely back beneath the surface. That time, those days, needed to be as dead to him as Ellemoa.

Am I really sure that she's dead? What if–No.

The edges of that thought bore a brutal blackness that warned him not to explore it further. He sighed and stood, scooping up his pack and cautious of his balance until he was quite sure the world would stay steady around him.

"I'll walk along," he said. "I'll manage without sleep for a bit longer."

She stared at him, the severe lines settling back over her face, and said nothing.

He bowed once, both hands to his heart in genuine gratitude. His failings weren't her fault; she deserved what courtesy he had to offer.

"Which way to Sandsplit proper, *s'a*?" he asked.

She pointed silently and gave no return farewell as he walked away.

Chapter Sixty-One

I'm going home. With my mother. I'm going to meet my family at last.

It was a large concept to absorb, and Idisio walked without speaking, trying to take it in. It had been easier to accept that he was ha'ra'hain, that he deserved the respect of all he encountered by that fact alone, that he had *power* where he had always seen himself as powerless.

Family. A community. Arason, according to his mother, understood how to treat ha'ra'hain. There were certain . . . agreements in place that made the relationship a civil one. "Of course, that held while the *chekk* was there," she added, her smile fading. "Once the others left . . . and it was only me . . . they weren't as respectful. But we'll change that, you and I. We'll start a new *chekk*, and they'll return to the proper ways."

Chekk seemed to be equivalent to tribe or community; Ellemoa had trouble translating the concept, and dodged questions about why the chekk had left and she had stayed.

Idisio, still struggling with the basic concept of *I have a family*, didn't really try to pin her down. He had too much to think about already. *My father. I'm going to meet my father.*

She smiled as they walked, hummed often, and stopped to pick bright flowers and wind them into her hair. Now and again she broke into open song: children's ditties, for the most part, few of which he had heard before. One, a lullaby clearly developed in a farming community, she repeated several times:

A flower falls, a drop of rain, a seed in ground, a new life sprouts; a seed to bloom, a bloom to fruit, a plate of food, a stomach full, and off to bed, and off to bed, it's time to rest your weary head . . . A dream of stars, a star of dreams, a journey made, a life complete; a step to home, a home to build, a bed to rest your weary head, and off to bed, and off to bed, it's time to rest your weary head . . . The fire warm, the warmth of home, the ale in hand, the shutters closed; outside the wind, outside the cold, inside the warm and drowsy home . . . and off to bed, and off to bed, it's time to rest your weary head . . . and off to bed, and off to bed, it's time to rest your weary head.

She varied the lyrics sometimes, apparently making them up on the spot; but they always dealt with the pleasantness of family and home, shelter and security. Idisio soon found himself smiling every time she sang it, and even joined in on the chorus a few times: which brought a radiant joy to her expression.

By the time they reached Sandsplit proper, Idisio scarcely remembered that he'd ever distrusted his mother, or seen her as a monster in the least. She was simply his mother, his kin, his family—and he would fight to protect her, and she him, as it should be.

Sandsplit was the same tidy, quiet, sprawling town Idisio remembered; but an odd smell hung in the air, and the back of his neck began to itch as they walked along the sandy paths. His mother appeared completely serene, humming softly, even singing small snatches of childhood lullabies.

"Do you want to stop for the night, son?" his mother asked, pausing at a crossroads.

Understanding that she was offering him a concession to make him happy, he considered declining; but his feet hurt and his back ached from walking, and her constant singing of that lullaby had put him in mind of the pleasures of a good hot meal and a bed. He said, "Yes. Please. I'd like that."

"Is there a place you'd like to stay at? You know this town better than I do."

"I only came through once," he said. "I don't want to stay at the same place as last time—it's too expensive, and we're going to need the money we have to get to Arason."

She smiled at him fondly. "No, son," she said, "we don't need to worry about money at all. But I'll follow your lead."

"Money makes everything easier," he said pragmatically. "I'm not sure what other inns there are here, though. I suppose I'll just ask—"

"You don't need to ask a human for directions, son," she said. "Close your eyes and think of yourself as a bird, soaring high above the city. Wait–" She tugged him to the side of the road as a cart rumbled past. "Now."

He shut his eyes, stared into the multicolored darkness behind his eyelids, and tried to think of himself as a bird. A moment later, he staggered, dizzy, and felt his mother catch his arm in a steadying grip.

Sandsplit spread out beneath him in a hazy patchwork of fields and houses and roads; at the same time he could feel his mother's grip on his arm and the firm ground under his feet. Nausea burned the back of his throat.

"Think of finding an inn," his mother said from somewhere at once near and far. "A cheap place that will treat us well. Someplace nearby."

His stomach steadied. He found his vision drawn to the west, to a small, dilapidated-looking inn; found himself absolutely aware of what streets to turn down in order to reach it.

"Now shut your eyes, blink without opening your eyes, then open them to look at me," his mother said.

Patchwork vision disappeared. He felt a light wind riffling through his hair. When he opened his eyes again, his mother was smiling. The serene expression and the setting sun combined to lend her a fragile beauty.

"Very good, son," she said. "Very, very good."

She sighed, peace fading, and was once more a skinny, exhausted-looking woman with ragged light brown hair and large grey eyes, standing by the side of the road in a dress much too large around hips and bosom. For some reason, seeing that dress sent a sudden chill through Idisio's nerves. He squinted, trying to pick out details in the fading light.

She hissed softly, then said, "The inn, son. We're going to the inn now, like you wanted. Lead the way."

After a few steps, her hand crept into his. He gripped it tightly and grinned, absurdly enthusiastic. Crickets chirred as they walked through the darkening streets. Torches flared into life, casting erratic, flickering pools of shadow. A gnawing unease took root in Idisio's stomach.

The dark splotches of shadow moving across his mother ate away shape and line, turning her strides into a flowing movement of gaunt edges.

Am I really doing this of my own will? Is she still pushing me around? He couldn't tell. He didn't feel hazed—and his reasons for agreeing to travel to Arason with her hung clear and logical in his mind—but there had been a suspicious moment of disorientation when he'd tried to look at her dress more closely. The light was too poor, now, to make another attempt; he'd have to try again in better light, when she wasn't paying attention.

That might take a while. Like Deiq, she didn't seem to miss much.

She squeezed his hand reassuringly. "Not much farther," she said.

They turned down a narrow, uneven street. The houses to either side seemed blank and indifferent until Idisio realized that the back side of the buildings faced them. A distinct stink of rotting garbage and urine hung in the air. He glanced down at his shadow-shrouded feet as he trod in something slick, fairly sure it hadn't been mud.

His stomach clenched and cramped. This was entirely too familiar–he'd spent most of his life in streets like these. All the moment needed to turn into a walking nightmare was–

Someone belched ahead. A large form staggered toward them. Two. Three large men. Idisio blinked, panic rising, and vision cleared into grey clarity: three burly men, one with his arm in a sling. Memory escaped control: sequences that had begun with similar encounters flashed through his mind.

Beside him, his mother began to hiss, like a kettle gathering steam.

"No," Idisio said, fighting to gather his composure. "They're just walking through, move over, let them go by–"

"*Bad men*," his mother said in a low, venom-filled voice. "I won't let them hurt you, son."

"No, they won't, it's all right—these aren't the ones who–"

She hissed and shook off his restraining hand.

"*No*," he said, grabbing after her as she started forward, and missed his hold completely.

"Hey, pretty pretty," the lead man said, grinning. "Two pretties, I'd say."

The reek of heavy drinking drifted from him in a rotten miasma. "How much, sweet?"

"You misunderstand," Idisio said loudly, lunging; caught his mother's arm and dragged her back and sideways a step. "We're only passing through to the inn beyond, *s'es*. We're travelers."

"There's a thing," another man chuckled. "As if I wouldn't know a whore when I see one in the dark."

One of his companions erupted in laughter. The other, darker-haired and older, stood still and quiet at the back. As the laughter died from the air, the older man said, "She's not a whore, Frenn. Neither is he. Let 'em by."

"Aw, what?" Frenn protested, half-turning to glare back at the last man. "You been around Venepe too long, Rat. Or did that wet ta-neka get to you? Angling for that pretty coin now, are you?"

"Step off it," Rat said without visible emotion. "Let 'em by."

"Aw, I know a whore," Frenn declared. "They're just tryin' to up the bid price. Well, look–" He fumbled in his belt pouch.

"Frenn," the first man said, moving to set his back to a wall, "Rat's right. You ain't seeing what you think you are. Let 'em by."

"The two of you are turning into right purse-lickers," Frenn said, and tossed a coin toward Idisio. "Here, now, don't you tell me that's not enough–"

A flicker of silver flashed through Idisio's vision and landed in the muck at his feet.

His mother let out a shivering screech and ripped her arm from his grasp.

He threw himself forward and slammed her sideways up against a wall before she made more than a single bounding step. *"Get out of here!"* he shrieked at the startled mercenaries. They needed no second invitation to take to their heels, dragging their still-protesting friend along.

A stone wall thudded up behind his back a moment later, knocking him breathless and dizzy; his mother's nightmare glare filled his vision with blackness more complete than that of an underground pit.

"How dare you," she snarled, face rigid and white with rage.

He gasped for breath, coughing, unable to answer coherently.

"Never get in my way again," she snapped. "You haven't earned the *right* to interfere, son! And those were *bad men*."

"They were drunk," Idisio choked. "You can't punish them for being drunk!"

"I can do *whatever* I please, to *any* human, for *any* reason, or none at all if that suits me," she said. "Don't you dare forget that. Ever."

He shut his eyes and shook his head, fighting to ease his breath back into a steady rhythm. "No," he said. "No, that's not right. That's not—that's not *right*." He couldn't put any better words to his refusal: had no breath, had no clarity to work with.

"The only reason for us to restrain from violence," she said, "is that it generally causes more trouble than it's worth—not because of some puerile human notion of right and wrong. Their laws and their morals don't *apply* to us, son."

"Maybe they should," Idisio said, catching his breath at last. "Maybe they're something worth listening to."

"No," she said. "Their morals and laws keep *them* from killing one another, nothing more." She blew out an irritated breath. "Never mind. We'll speak more of this later. For now, let's get to that inn."

Idisio eased away from the wall, rubbing the back of his head gingerly; it felt as though a lump were forming where his skull had hit the brick. He straightened and studied his mother with a cold eye. Believing that humans would never trust him because of his heritage: that he accepted wholeheartedly; Deiq had said as much, himself. Believing that he had the right to kill humans at any moment for any reason—no. That way lay chaos on a grand scale; he flinched from even thinking on the potential for disaster if all ha'ra'hain believed as his mother did. But Deiq hadn't acted that way; Deiq had kept a sane view on the matter. Deiq, as he had said, cared about human political and economic stability. The path his mother suggested gave no care for anything human—and regardless of Idisio's own past, that was just too far of a step for him to take.

Some things do not require violence to a lesser form of life. That sounded much more sensible than *We can do whatever we please.*

"Yes," he said. "Let's go to that inn. I think that's a very good idea."

She stared at him, her eyes filled with black, and said, "You're still not understanding, son. We're ha'ra'hain. We do not accept the disrespect or abuse of humans, drunk or sober or witless fools. I thought you grasped that concept already."

"In the south," he said, recalling conversations with Deiq, "I'd agree with you. But this is the northlands. They don't *remember.* Why punish them for ignorance?"

"It is not *my* problem that they are ignorant," Ellemoa said. "They only exist on our sufferance, son. They exist because of you and because of me—because of the agreements the ha'reye have formed with the desert lords. If they've forgotten, then it's past time they're reminded of the situation."

"So you're calling the humans our slaves?"

"Slaves, cattle, insects, whatever term you want to use," she said. "They don't *matter,* son. They're meaningless to us."

"Except when *we* want something from *them.* How is that different from what you accuse them of doing?"

She shook her head, her eyes fading back to pale grey.

"You'll learn," she said. "You'll learn. Let's go to that inn."

He stood still, dissatisfied with that answer, his confidence shaken. She was so *ready* to attack over nothing at all; what was the trip to Arason going to be like? What would she do if he wasn't there to stop her from overreacting?

What would she do if he refused to travel with her at all, come to that? Looking at the chill in her pale eyes, he wondered if that ever had been an option.

"I won't force you to take a single step," she said, clearly tracking his thoughts. "But if you turn aside and leave me to go on alone, your father will be *very* disappointed in you, son. Think on that, before you carry through on any thoughts of running back to the humans. And think on this: you have an *obligation* waiting for you in Arason. A sacred trust."

"Obligation?"

"You are the last of the Arason ha'ra'hain," she said. Her eyes darkened again. "You *must* go back. You must take over protecting the area when your father cannot do so any longer. He *needs* you to come home. *Arason* needs you to come home."

He stood still, shock searing like ice throughout his whole body.

"I didn't want to tell you, because it's such a large burden to bear," she said. "It's a terrible burden for a boy who's barely aware of himself as anything other than a street thief and toy for men like *those* to . . . ." She stopped and visibly shuddered, closing her eyes. When she opened them again, the black had faded to a blurry ring.

He shook his head, barely comprehending her words. His mind, so clear and certain a moment before, was hazed and grey once more: from shock, no doubt. His legs felt strangely weak, as though he were in danger of collapsing.

"I need to sit down," he said. "I need to go–just–sit down. Let's go to the inn. A tavern. Something. Let's go–just–sit."

"Of course, son," she said, hooking her arm through his with tender solicitude. "Anything you want, my love. Anything at all."

Chapter Sixty-Two

By late afternoon, the air had turned chill enough that Tank looked forward to the roaring heat of Yuer's oversized hearth. Dasin tucked his rain cloak more tightly around himself, sullenly silent as he had been all day. Tank let him be. Prodded by the previous night's talk, his own mind kept returning with treacherous clarity to *those days*, and comparing them to today: *This is better*, he thought. *No matter the situation with Yuer–this is better.*

It was a shaky balance, but it served the moment and allowed him to walk between the leering guards at Yuer's door with barely a flicker of terror; allowed him to follow Dasin's lead and offer a grave bow, take a seat, then meet Yuer's hooded stare with a blank expression.

"Tea," the old man said after a moment, motioning. A slender young woman with loose red-blonde hair came into the room with a tray. She knelt beside the low table, set out cups, poured tea, put three full cups in three empty hands, then retreated with the tray and without the least glance at anyone but Yuer.

Tank set his back teeth together–lightly, to avoid his jaw hardening visibly–and kept his blank expression in place. Yuer, watching him, smiled. Tank sipped tea, not quite looking at anything in particular; in the chair next to his, Dasin did the same, breathing evenly.

"This is lovely," Dasin said after a moment. "Mint?"

"It's a combination of Stone Island white and a bit of mint," Yuer said. "It's proving to be a very popular blend along the southern coast and lower northern cities. Sells for a silver the ounce."

Dasin blinked, sleepily appreciative, and finished off his drink. Tank cradled his nearly empty cup in his off-hand and went on staring at the space past Yuer's left shoulder.

"How was your journey?" Yuer said. "Bit of a storm, as I hear it, in Bright Bay."

"Yes," Tank said when Dasin didn't answer. "Rainy. And cold. Windy. Delayed us a bit."

Yuer waited a few moments. The silence stretched. At last the wrinkled old man said, "You're very good at acting stupid, Tanavin."

"Tank."

"Precisely my point." The old man snapped his fingers; the blonde girl came back in, refilled his empty cup, then retreated once more without offering Tank or Dasin any tea. "I can see at a glance that your mentor trained you well past the level of a common mercenary; and you have to know by now that you're in the middle of a deadly serious game. This posturing of *mercenary* fits you like a consumptive man's suit on a blacksmith."

Tank looked at the hearth, watching the crackling, dancing flames, and said nothing. Dasin, slumped back in his chair, began to snore lightly. A moment later, his hand opened, the cup spilling out. Tank lunged and caught the cup before it hit the ground. He set it on the table and eased back into his seat.

"Well past the level of a common mercenary," Yuer murmured. "You have exceptionally good reflexes."

Tank sat back into his chair, realizing that he hadn't let go of his teacup during that hasty grab for Dasin's–and hadn't spilled a drop of the liquid remaining in his own cup. He shrugged and took a careful sip, avoiding Yuer's intent stare.

"Aerthraim is a name to raise significant caution," Yuer said. "Apparently, so is that of *Tanavin*."

He paused. Tank could feel that black gaze boring into him.

"I have two approaches when dealing with such names," Yuer said finally. "One is to recruit them to my side. The other is to be sure they can't damage me. I prefer the former, naturally."

"I'm just a mercenary, trader Yuer," Tank said, and met the withered man's gaze full on for one long, ferocious moment. "Nothing in that to raise any sort of caution. Don't know what people have been telling you. My name's Tank, and I'm a mercenary. Nothing else."

Yuer's thin lips moved in what might have been a smile.

"Indeed," he said. "This will surely be an interesting arrangement; amusing, if nothing else. Well, setting your identity issues aside, do you have my delivery?"

Tank drew in a long breath, set his teacup on the table, and said, "Yes." He made no move to reach for the saddlebags at Dasin's feet.

"Ah," Yuer said softly. "You're not happy about something."

"I won't be involved with delivering whorehouse drugs," Tank said flatly.

Dasin's light snoring deepened to a raspy snorking. Yuer lifted a hand; a husky man came into the room a moment later and scooped Dasin up from the chair. "Take him to the second guest room," Yuer directed. The servant nodded silently and retreated.

Tank watched the man's retreating back and felt a sudden chill. His gaze went to the two small white cups on the table, and his heartbeat staggered in his ears. "He wasn't *that* tired," he said, scarcely audible, and met Yuer's amused stare.

"Neither are you, apparently," Yuer said. "Here you are, wide awake and arguing with me."

Tank sat very still, his hands loose in his lap. "You're going to kill us," he rasped.

Yuer shook his head. "My delivery, please. Put it on the table."

Not seeing anything else to do, Tank leaned over, pulled Dasin's saddle-bags up into his lap, and dug out the bundle of oilcloth and padding. Yuer grinned as Tank unwrapped the box, apparently highly amused by the care Dasin had taken in protecting his delivery.

Tank slid the box onto the table and dropped saddlebags and wrapping to the floor at his feet, and waited, watching Yuer steadily.

The old man said, "Break the seals and open the box. *Carefully.*"

Tank's belt knife took care of the seals in a few moments; lifting the lid revealed a tightly packed mass of translucent white crystals. The smell of the sea filled his nose.

Tank sat back, staring, knife loosely held in one hand.

"Horn salt," Yuer said. He inhaled loudly through his nose, his eyes droop-ing half-shut. "Very valuable, and very tasty. I'm excessively fond of it, but it's difficult to lay hands on without certain connections. I lost many of my former connections over the course of the Purge; I'm not ashamed to say this single item is much of the reason for my alliance with Seavorn." He blinked, lizard-like, at Tank. "No doubt you don't believe me. But then, you're very young, and inclined to be suspicious. And you don't understand the value of good food to an old man. Perhaps I can show you the difference. Are you hungry?"

Tank looked up at that, his hand tightening on the knife. Yuer laughed.

"Ah, you don't trust me," he said. "Well, then—go your way, if you wish. You've done this one thing for me, and I'll give your friend a chance at that caravan he wants to lead." He paused. "I do know my reputation," he added, his face stretching into a leering grin again, "but I'm not nearly so fierce as people think. I've simply found it useful to have a ferocious reputation. Go your way. I won't cause you a word of trouble, and I'll tender your farewell to your friend when he wakes."

Yuer pulled a small cloth bag from one of the folds of the heavy blanket and tossed it onto the table. It landed with a chittering thud and slid across the table to rest in front of Tank, neatly missing the box. A few small salt crystals jolted out to scatter across the table.

"Your pay," Yuer said. "Good day." His grin widened, stretching drooping folds of skin into a savage leer.

Tank slowly slid his belt knife back into the sheath. He stared at that grin for a few moments, then lunged forward.

"What are you *doing*?" Yuer's voice scaled to an unprecedented shrill peak.

Tank dug his fingers into the salt; his fingers brushed cloth. Salt crystals cascaded from the box as he hooked and pulled, lifted out a velvet pouch smaller around than his palm, and tossed it on the table.

"Is that salt?" he asked, staring straight into the old man's eyes.

Yuer was no longer smiling. He sat still as a statue, his black gaze emotionless and icy-cold. "No," he said after a moment. "And you've ruined a good salt shipment as well by digging your dirty fingers into it."

He raised a hand. Tank didn't move or take his gaze from Yuer's face; the blonde girl came into the room, silently handed the bags of velvet and cloth to Yuer, picked up the box, then left without even glancing at Tank.

"You'd have done better to walk out and let me think you fooled," Yuer said.

"What was in the bag?" Tank demanded, his throat tight. "Dasta?"

"It's not your concern," Yuer said. "It could be dried oregano and you'd still have ruined a prime batch of my favorite salt." He paused. "I *wasn't* lying on that," he added. "I generally avoid outright lying. It leads to endless complications." He sighed. "*You* are a complication, Tanavin Aerthraim. More of one than I wanted." He glanced at the teacups and shook his head. "Much more."

"You lied to Wian," Tank said.

"Did I?" Yuer's gaze went hooded again. He looked amused.

"She thought you were *saving* her from Seavorn. If she'd known–"

"You weren't here, Tanavin. You don't know what I said or didn't say. And Wian herself is a phenomenally accomplished liar. She'll admit as much to your face and deliver a masterful lie in the next heartbeat."

"I believe *her*," Tank said stubbornly.

"Then you're an astonishing fool," Yuer retorted. "No doubt she told you about her dreadful childhood, and being forced into a life of whoredom, and you fell right into thinking of her as victim. Don't make that mistake, Tanavin. She's an extremely dangerous young woman. I know for fact she's killed at least once for one of her previous masters. It would be safer for you to feel pity for a nest of blood ants."

Tank looked down at his hands, remembering Wian's own words: *I've earned these bruises and whippings ten times over. Don't feel sorry for me. Don't try to help me. It'll just get you killed, and that's the first truth I've handed out for free in years.*

"You know I'm telling you the truth," Yuer said. "As I said, I don't lie often. It's largely unnecessary when one holds the correct cards."

Tank shut his eyes for a long moment, then opened them to find Yuer watching him with a peculiar expression.

"What now?" he said. "Are you going to kill me, or is that part of your reputation exaggerated?"

"Rumor always expands on fact," Yuer said. "One true fact to consider, in this case, is that I believe you'd be a very useful addition to my staff, for a number of reasons; one of which is currently snoring in my guest room."

Tank's jaw tightened. He endured Yuer's amused survey without flinching.

"You're very attached to Dasin," Yuer murmured. "And he to you. Are you lovers?"

"No!"

"Ah." Yuer's eyes drooped nearly shut. "So sensitive over such a small matter. Well, I doubt the two of you can be parted, whatever your relationship. If you walk out that door on poor terms, or . . . disappear . . . I risk Dasin losing his focus, his edge, his *usefulness* as a potentially brilliant young merchant. He really is a genius, and Stai Aerthraim is no fool herself; to call him her star student means he is, truly, something exceptional. I want him on *my* side, handling *my* business, Tanavin. The Purge left me with a severely thin margin of resources. I need to build that back up, and quickly. I believe Dasin's good enough to do so in short order, whatever his age; but I'm also beginning to see that he may not function properly without you by his side."

"I'm not that important to him," Tank said thinly.

Yuer sat back in his chair more deeply, his head tilting to one side.

"I disagree," he said at last. "And thus I offer you a compromise, rather than sending you to my guards for a brief discussion about proper manners. I do have a legitimate business to maintain. I do need honest merchants to carry my wares. So: I won't ask you or Dasin to carry anything but spices. Everything in your wagon will be completely legal. You'll handle the Bright Bay through Sandsplit run; if that goes well and I see I can trust you two, I'll give you the Isata route in a few months. If you do well with that, I'll let you develop the Assiasan route. Quite a lot of potential for good money there."

"What do you want in return for all this kindness?" Tank made no effort to hide the bitterness in his voice; he already knew what Yuer would ask.

As expected, Yuer said, "You'll keep your mouths shut about . . . this." He lifted the small velvet pouch. "Not much to ask, is it?"

"What's inside that bag?"

"Oregano," Yuer said dryly. He tossed the cloth bag of coin back onto the table. "Not a bribe," he added as Tank stiffened. "Advance wages."

Tank opened his mouth, not sure what to say, and found himself blurting: "Do you supply dasta to the katha villages?"

The silence set in and stayed like hardening mud. Tank couldn't believe he'd asked that aloud. By the expression on Yuer's face, neither could he.

"No," Yuer said at last, his eyes like black flint. "Those places are obscene corruptions of an honorable tradition. Now get out. Go take a room at the Traveler's Rest, and tell them to bill me. If you wish a meal, go across to the Black Horse Tavern–it's near that inn your former employer booked rooms at– and tell them the same thing. I'll send Dasin along when he wakes. You may return to me in the morning with your *considered* answer; until then, I don't wish to see sight nor hear word of you. Get out."

Tank scooped up a double handful of saddlebags and packs, aimed one last long, emotionless stare at Yuer, and said, "Thank you for having that much decency—for not supporting the katha villages."

Yuer's return stare could have set green wood on fire. "*Out.*"

Tank nodded and left without another word.

Chapter Sixty-Three

The closest tavern turned out to be called the Black Horse; Idisio, remembering the glossy, noble beasts he and Scratha had ridden from Bright Bay to Sandsplit, found that name comforting. Remembering that, however, put him in mind of leaving those horses with Yuer; and he wondered whether, if he were to apply to the wrinkled old man very politely, he might gain those two horses back.

Yuer always goes with his highest profit, Scratha had said. Glancing sideways at his mother, Idisio shuddered at the price the devious old man might ask of two ha'ra'hain. No: better to leave that nest unstirred, and go on foot.

They settled at a corner table. The other patrons in the crowded room spared them only the mildest of curious glances before turning back to their own conversations and games.

"Good hope-days to you," the serving girl said as she reached Idisio's table. She smiled with genuine cheer. A garland of pale flowers had been wound into her long dark hair, and bright blue paint streaked her cheeks in a swirling, intricate design. "First drink is on the house tonight, and the blessing-soup is free to all."

"Pardon, s'a," Idisio said awkwardly, "I'm not familiar with your local customs."

At almost the same time, his mother said, "It's that late in the year? I thought the Life Moon was overhead."

"No, s'a," the girl said. "We're under the Hope Moon."

"The weather's going to be turning soon," Ellemoa muttered. "We have to move faster, or we'll be wading through snow. I don't like snow."

The serving girl eyed her curiously. "From above the Hackerwood, then, are you, *s'ieas?*"

"I don't see how that's your concern," Ellemoa said icily, raking the girl with a severe glare.

"What's blessing soup?" Idisio interjected hastily as the serving girl bristled. *It's only polite conversation,* he tried to tell his mother; found a black wall of harsh silence barring the attempt, and withdrew feeling slightly bruised.

"A bit of everything ready for harvest this time of year," the girl said, eyeing Ellemoa with dawning disapproval. "I go by an old custom, and keep a soup simmering from birth to full of the Hope Moon to feed the field workers; we add to it day by day. Right now it's got chicken, eel, apples, peas, rosemary, onions, garlic, and greens. Tomorrow there's oysters going in, and a stack of shucked corn. Not everyone offers blessing-soup these days, but I like to hold to some of the old ways, myself, and I haven't heard no complaints." She dimpled a bit.

"That sounds wonderful," Idisio said. "Two bowls of that, please."

"I don't want any," his mother said flatly. "It sounds *vile.*"

"Something else, then, *s'a?*" the serving girl said with a noticeable chill in her tone and expression.

"Not *here,*" Ellemoa said, glancing around in a way that placed her objection squarely on the tavern itself.

As the girl began to bristle, Idisio said loudly, "Thank you, *s'a,* the soup will be welcome for me. It's been a long walk today." He caught her eye and twitched an eyebrow. "We're both tired," he added in a lower voice, pitching it to her ears alone. "Forgive and forget the lack of manners, please."

Her cheeks tinted in the lantern-light, and a smile washed across her face. "No trouble at all," she said, then hurried into the kitchen.

Idisio blinked, a dull sense of dread settling into his chest: remembering Deiq and a servant with an adoring grin. Had he influenced this servant into forgetting his mother's rudeness?

"Of course you did," his mother said. "You see? You're not above getting what you want from humans, when it matters to you. Although why her good regard should matter I can't understand."

"I was just keeping things simple," he said, and heard it fall flat.

"Really?" she said. "And if she comes back and asks you to take a walk with her, you'll refuse? Do you really think any human would be interested in you except to gratify their own needs, if they knew what you are?"

"That's not—" Idisio shook his head, frustrated, feeling the conversation slipping off track and at a loss for how to bring it back around. "There's no reason to be rude to her," he said finally.

"What's rude?" Ellemoa asked. "What's polite? Why do you keep measuring such matters by human standards?"

"It's all I know," he said through his teeth.

"Obviously. Here's *our* politeness, son: they don't ask after our business and we don't interfere with theirs. They give us what we want when we ask, and we don't hurt them in the taking of it. They can ask us for aid—*after* helping us with what we need."

"That's—" Idisio searched for words to express his reaction to that. "That's very—arrogant on our part, isn't it?"

"Arrogant? They're *insects*," she said, leaning forward. "You keep missing that point. They're barely sentient, most of them, and blind to the secrets of the world. Why should it matter if they think us arrogant or rude?"

"Well, they outnumber us, for one," he said dryly.

She gestured with one hand, dismissing that statement. "No more than a colony of ants does the average human," she said. "It's all easily kicked over and destroyed by one person, son. The two of us could destroy this entire town, if we so chose, before the morning light."

He felt lightheaded for a moment. The taste of blood, hot and copper, ran along the inside of his cheeks; his hands tightened into fists, and somewhere distant there was a *whispering . . . .*

"*No*," he said, as much to the whisper as to her statement. "That's not right. That's not *right*. They deserve better than that. They haven't done anything to hurt us."

"Neither did the ants a human kicked aside to till his fields," she retorted. "It's all a question of whether it benefits us to bother. At the moment, it doesn't. Tomorrow, it might. You *must* grasp this, son. Whether you like the lesson or not, it's the truth: the moment you need or want something badly enough, you'll find justification to take it, whatever the cost to the humans. Better to face that at the front and learn to persuade instead of force, especially if you're going to be this squeamish over necessity."

He stared at her with a grey disquiet. "I don't believe that," he said. "I don't. I won't be like that."

"Son," she said, "you *are* like that."

The girl returned with a large bowl of soup and placed it in front of Idisio. "Anything else, *s'e*?" she asked. She didn't even look at Ellemoa.

"No, thank you," Idisio said, without trying to be nice this time, and watched lines of disappointment briefly etch the skin around her eyes. She flashed him a quick, uncertain smile, and went to tend to another table's requests, glancing back twice.

"If you'd smiled at her the way you did the first time," Ellemoa murmured, "she'd have asked you to take her for a walk after dinner."

He put his gaze on the food and didn't answer. He didn't want to think about her words right now. He was hungry. He focused on being hungry, on the mingling of rosemary and chicken, the sharp bite of garlic and the creamy slickness of shredded greens, the meaty coarseness of red beans, until the bowl was empty.

Sitting back, he belched with unapologetic satisfaction. "Ought to settle in along the Coast Road," he said. "These taverns serve the best food I've ever eaten. Excepting Kybeach, of course." He laughed a little.

His mother said nothing, her gaze on the flickering of the triple-wick lamp on the table.

"I'm sure it's very good in Arason," he added hastily, wiping a sleeve across his mouth. "Didn't mean anything by that."

"I don't know," she said, not looking up. "I haven't been there in a long time. And I never ate with the humans the way you'll do." She lifted a shadowed stare to his face. "You know how to get along with humans. I never did. I never understood them. Not even the few who were kind to me. They all seem like strange, brutal animals to me, son, who lie to one another and hurt one another for no good reason."

"You had no reason to hurt those men in the alley," Idisio said sharply. This latest switch in temper alarmed him more than most of the others: instinct warned that the apparent weakness masked something dangerous.

"No reason *you* knew about," she returned. "You don't understand the half of what you see yet, son."

He opened his mouth, then shut it; her observation was too close to Deiq's own accusation. "So what am I missing, then?" he said finally.

"It doesn't matter," she said. "What matters is that you still don't trust me. You still don't *understand* that I know far more than you do."

"From where I'm sitting," he said, "you're not explaining a whole lot to help me understand that you have reasons for what you're doing."

"Why must I *explain*?" she said irritably. "I'm your mother. I know more than you. I see more than you. I understand more than you. That's simple fact: your business is to *listen* to me, and mind what I say. Understanding the *why* of things comes later, once you've grown into your shoes a bit."

"But—"

His mother shook her head and stood. "Time to go, son," she said. "No need for an inn. I'm tired of coddling you. We need to reach Arason before the cold weather sets in. We won't stop again until we're home."

And the dangerous bit emerges. "What happened to not ordering me around?" he said. "I thought you weren't going to force me to do anything anymore."

She stared at him, her eyes a dark, muddled grey color. "What happened to trusting me?" she shot back. "What happened to hearing my side and being my son? You're treating me like a monster again, son, and I don't much appreciate that, after all I've been through."

He bit his lip, fighting to hold on to a fading certainty. "I—didn't mean it that way," he said. "I just—those men—you would have—"

"I would have done less to them than they've done to others," she said. "They were vicious, brutal men who enjoy causing pain to others. If you'd seen them, truly *seen* them, you'd understand why removing them from the world would be a blessing to every creature in existence. But you don't have that sight yet. You haven't grown into it yet. You're still fighting what you are, fighting what you can do, and I don't have patience for that. Either walk with me, son, or go your own way; but stop refusing to believe the truth because it's unpleasant to your ears."

She turned away and walked to the door; paused there, looking back, and made an imperious gesture for him to follow.

I'll meet my father . . . I'll be respected . . . I'll be . . . I'll be loved. She cares. I mustn't forget that. She really cares. And what if she's right? What if those men were the monsters, and I just didn't see it?

She's not saying anything all that different from what Deiq said, after all.

Idisio rose, dropped a coin on the table without checking to see its color, and followed his mother out of the tavern.

Chapter Sixty-Four

Ellemoa almost purred with satisfaction as she heard the crunch of her son's feet following her out of the tavern. Another of those tedious conversations, perhaps two more, and he'd stop questioning her. She could start teaching him about proper ha'ra'hain ways then, and arrange a safe place for him to learn about feeding; she would guide him through the final changes, keep him from going mad, just as her mother had done for her.

She began turning over possible situations in her head, ways to provoke his human-trained morals to balk so that she could demolish his misunderstandings. Perhaps arranging a show of human violence toward them would do the trick: that was never a difficult maneuver.

The tall torches bracketing the front door had been lit. Even combined, the light didn't reach far against the blackness of full night; Ellemoa felt an uneasy shiver work down her back. *Maybe we should stay the night at a human inn*, she thought. She found herself loathing the idea of traveling in darkness. Perhaps it would be better to stay still, to rest, to gather her strength and allow her son that much more complacency and trust.

She opened her mouth to tell her son that she'd changed her mind, after all, that they would stay at the nearby inn.

A tall young man stepped into the light between the farthest torches. His attention clearly on his own thoughts, he took two businesslike strides closer before raising his head and noticing their presence. He slowed, then stopped, staring.

Torchlight caught in glimmers along his red hair.

A jolt of recognition slammed through Ellemoa's stomach: this was the human who had attacked *teyhataerth*. This was the human who had been trained to kill ha'ra'hain.

Violence built a scant heartbeat later. As she took the first step forward, her son said: "Tank?"

She froze, watching their gazes connect: watching a bond neither was aware of flare into argent life.

"Lifty?" the redhead said, as incredulous as Idisio; then his attention shifted sideways, locking onto Ellemoa, and his side of the argent sizzled into a dangerous shade of red. "Who's this?"

You know who I am, Ellemoa told him.

"My mother," Idisio said at the same time.

The redhead stared at her blankly. Either he hadn't heard or refused to understand: but that searing color wrapped throughout his spirit warned her against taking another step forward.

He'll kill me. But he doesn't want to kill my son. I don't understand! It doesn't make sense.

She eased back a careful step, her stare never leaving his face.

"Go away," she said aloud, scarcely audible to human hearing. His eyes narrowed: he'd heard that clearly enough.

"Mother," Idisio said, abruptly wrapped in the murky blue-orange of alarmed bewilderment as he made the connections. "Mother, don't—he's not a danger."

The redhead's eyes narrowed. "I'm not looking for a fight," he said, which told her that he understood the situation just fine, himself.

"Neither are we," Idisio said, too fast and too loud; the redhead clearly registered that as a lie, and backed up a step, his hand falling to the hilt of his belt knife.

"Go away," Ellemoa said again, unable to resist a prowling step forward in the face of that retreat. "Go *away.*"

He squared his stance, shoulders rounding, and his stare changed to something less amicable. "You don't get to order me around," he said, flat and cold.

Fire rose in her, tinting her vision: her muscles bunched, gathering—

Her son grabbed her arm, hauling her back a step. "*No,* mother!"

She whipped round, rage driving her for a terrifying, blurred moment that ended with her son sprawled on the ground, gasping for breath. Regret set in immediately, but there was no time to offer apologies: she spun back to the redhead and found him two steps closer.

She snarled, driving him back a pace, and said, "He doesn't want you harmed. That's the *only* thing keeping you alive in this moment, *tharr.* I don't like you. I don't trust you. You're dangerous. So *go away.*"

He stood balanced on the balls of his feet for a moment, his gaze flickering to her son. The red turned to a muddied, mottled mixture of white and crimson. "I don't much want *him* harmed, neither," he said at last. "And you seem ready to hand out some hurt yourself."

"He's my son," she said. "I won't harm him. I *will* hurt you if you don't leave us alone."

Behind her, Idisio staggered to his feet. "Mother," he said, a stifled gasp. "*Don't.*"

This was, on reflection, an absolutely perfect opportunity to teach her son one more critical lesson about forming attachments to humans. This human was *trouble*—if not now, then in the future. Being trained to kill meant that he would attack, as soon as he felt threatened; and given what she knew about him, given what she knew about *teyhataerth*, made placing a threat that he would see and her son wouldn't a childishly simple matter.

She narrowed her eyes and sent tendrils of green and gold snaking out to surround him—false tendrils, illusions, of course: that had been *teyhataerth's* family line-gift, where hers lay in visions. The human didn't know that, couldn't sense the difference between illusion and reality; but also didn't react as he should have, by driving forward into a fierce attack. Instead he withdrew without moving, retreating behind a solid, impenetrable wall of *No!*

She snarled frustration: had he sensed the hollowness of her illusion? Impossible—and yet—

Her son, ignorant and more easily panicked than the tharr before them, grabbed her again, his scent thick with fear, howling protests right into her sensitive ears. Nerves already strung taut, reflex took it for an attack: she flung him away again, then pounced on him, screaming into his face as the only alternative to ripping his throat out—

—and a bare heatbeat later something slammed into the back of her head, driven by more than muscle could bring to bear: driven by the same combination she herself had used to bring Deiq down, back in Bright Bay—a flaring of incandescent, needle-focused rage, rock-solid certainty, and physical force.

She wavered, fighting desperately to stay conscious; a second blow, as hard as the first, sent her spinning into depthless blackness.

Chapter Sixty-Five

Tank stared down at Idisio's mother as though expecting her to spring up and attack again–or as though debating whether to kill her while she lay defenseless. Idisio stayed on the ground, gasping for breath, trembling too badly to even think about standing up.

Is he going to attack me now? There was no doubt that Tank *knew*. No doubt that he could have killed Ellemoa rather than knocking her unconscious. *And he can kill me. I don't think I could even get up in time to stop him.* His mother's wild screeching had completely paralyzed Idisio's muscles; at least he hadn't voided himself. There was that miniscule mercy.

As Idisio's breath began to steady in his chest, Tank blinked and looked at him, torchlight catching glimmers of gold into his bright blue eyes.

"You all right?" he said. "Want a hand up?" He held a long, thick chunk of firewood in one hand with careless ease.

"Ah—no," Idisio said. "I'll be—just a moment." He drew in a deep breath, feeling his muscles finally release, and scrambled to his feet. He couldn't help glancing over at the nearby pile of firewood: at the axe still leaning against the chopping block. He sucked in a deep, shaky breath of relief.

"You all right?" Tank repeated.

"Yes," Idisio said, his shoulders relaxing. "I'm all right. Thank you."

Tank tossed the chunk of wood underhand; it landed in the dirt near the axe. "What a complete fucking moon-case," he said, nodding down at Ellemoa. "She really your mother?"

"Yes. She really is."

"Huh." Tank studied Idisio's face, frowning a little. "Want help getting her inside?"

"Not a good idea," Idisio said a bit sharply. "She wakes up, we're starting this all over again. You had the right idea: You go on your way, we go on ours."

Tank glanced at the unconscious woman again. "She's about as stable as a brick balanced on a pin," he said. "Be careful."

"She won't hurt me." Idisio squatted and gathered his mother into his arms. Blood seeped from two spots on her head, matting her hair into a flat, tangled mess. She proved to weigh surprisingly little. He staggered as he came back to his feet, briefly lightheaded.

Tank didn't move. "Lifty," he said. "This is a strange chance of a meeting, and there's no saying I'll see you again this side of the Black Gates–so–I'm sorry. For Blackie, and–all of it. I wasn't myself at the time."

"You were there to kill a ha'ra'ha," Idisio said flatly.

"Well—yes," Tank said, scratching the back of his neck and looking away. "But I didn't *know* that. Look, it gets—really complicated. Someone had been feeding me sedatives without my knowing, and I was all muddled up from that when I met you—and I just wasn't myself. So I'm sorry."

"Are you following us? Are you here to kill us?"

"No!" His protest, shocked, seemed genuine enough. "Gods, I had no idea you were here. I thought you were back in Bright Bay yet. I wouldn't even have whacked her if she hadn't been about to tear you apart."

"She won't hurt me," Idisio said reflexively. Tank's eyebrows arched in clear disbelief.

"Sure looked like it from where I stood," he said.

Idisio shook his head, glancing down at the limp form in his arms. "You headed east?"

"No. West. Back to Bright Bay."

Idisio let out a breath of relief. "Could you carry a message?"

Tank nodded soberly, his gaze on Idisio's mother. "She's more dangerous than you think," he said. "The way she tossed you aside and came after you–she'll kill you next time you cross her, if not when she wakes up."

"I'm her only son," Idisio said stubbornly. "She won't hurt me."

Tank shook his head, openly skeptical, then said, "What's the message? Urgent, I'm guessing?"

"Yes." Idisio drew in a short, sharp breath, then said, "Go find Lord Alyea of Peysimun. Her family mansion is inside the Seventeen Gates. Deiq of Stass will be near her, wherever she is, and he's the one I need right now. If you can't find them, find Lord Eredion of Sessin. He'll know where Deiq is. Probably. You might meet them on the road. I *hope* you meet them on the road." He made himself stop babbling.

Tank regarded him with a cool, appraising stare and said, "Picked up some high company, haven't you, Lifty? I take it you're not on the streets any longer?"

"No," Idisio said. "Times I wish I was. Oh–they know me as Idisio. I've . . . left Lifty's life behind."

That brought a smile to Tank's face for some reason, but all he said was: "What's the message?"

Idisio glanced down at his mother again, then met Tank's intent stare. He drew in another sharp breath and said, "*Help*. And *hurry*."

Tank's weight shifted as though to step back; then he went still and said, "I can help right now." His hand went back to the hilt of his belt knife.

Idisio froze, panic washing through him in a white flood. "No," he said, scarcely audible even to himself.

"I got a good look at her eyes," Tank said. "She's killed before. Doesn't regret it a bit. And she'll kill again–might well be you next time."

"No. She's my mother. She's *kin*. She won't hurt me. All she wants is to get to Arason, and she wants me to go to Arason with her; she won't hurt me." Idisio shook his head fiercely. "You can't understand. Deiq will. He'll know what to do. *Find* him. He can help. I'll stall her, or get her back on the road if she looks to be turning dangerous. Just *go*."

Tank lifted his hand free of the knife with ostentatious care and turned it palm-up, fingers spread wide. "I'll go run the message, then," he said.

"The faster the better," Idisio said huskily, and headed for the inn without looking back.

Chapter Sixty-Six

Ellemoa wandered slowly through a grey haze, listening to the quiet, relishing the stillness. It had been a long time since she was surrounded by peaceful silence: longer since the emptiness had looked grey instead of black.

Ellemoa, someone said.

She shook her head and turned away, recognizing the distorted echo underlying the voice: this was a memory, not a real contact. She didn't want to remember that voice right now, nor ever again. She wanted this to be . . . a fresh start. A new way, a new life. She'd escaped. She didn't have to remember that any longer.

Ellemoa . . . darling. Laughter spiraled through her head. *Mother. How lovely. You're a mother . . . .*

She shuddered, birth pangs wracking through her, drawing her helplessly into the memories she'd been resisting. *My son . . . I'll never leave you alone again. Never. I'll always be there, to protect you . . . always.*

You can't protect him, because you haven't escaped, Ellemoa, the voice taunted. *You'll never leave me. I'll always be here for you, darling, and you'll come to like that. Oh, yes, you'll beg me to come for a visit, before long. I'm the only thing that's real in your life now, Ellemoa, I'm your only source of light.*

No. She'd escaped. She had to believe that. Her son, her only son, was near—she could feel him, could sense him, could see the shape of his mind—

His fear spiked through her: *She's killed before,* someone said. *Might be you next time.* And even as her son shook his head, refusing to accept that, tendrils of doubt coiled through his mind.

He's afraid of me? How could he believe I would hurt him? I would never hurt him. He's my SON . . . .

She tried to reach out, tried to tell him without words how much she loved him: a blank wall of revulsion barred her from contact, a repetitive whisper of *She's killed before . . . doesn't regret it a bit.*

Of course I don't regret it. I did what I had to in order to survive. But my son sees me as a monster for it. I don't deserve that. All I did was take him away from those who would harm him. I took him away from the places where Rosin was. Nothing good can ever live where Rosin stood. Doesn't he understand? Doesn't he see?

She saw a flash of red hair, an intense blue stare, a crackling ache that engulfed her entire skull; thrashed in the grey haze, swamped with sudden terror. Somewhere in the darkness that lay coiled in the back of her mind, bells rang, marking off the endless, infinite, dreadful passage of human-kept time.

Nothing is real except me, Rosin said. *Nothing will ever be real except me. I am all you have now, Ellemoa, and I am all you will ever have again. You have no son. You have no friends. You have no family. You have nobody and nothing except me.*

He said that over and over, in the darkness and in the light–

Skin stripped from her bones and rebuilt itself, flayed away by a thousand tiny, painstaking knife cuts. She screamed and ran from the feeling, racing away into the safety of grey silence. The pain kept pace, circling around her, forcing her back into her body, back into awareness of agony near at hand.

You can't run away from this, Ellemoa, Rosin laughed. *I know how to make you stay here and endure it all. But I'll stop it right now, if you like. You know what to do, to make this stop. You know what to do . . . You know what I want. Give me a child . . . or give* teyhataerth *a child.*

She tried, again and again, wrenching hopelessly at the structure of her body, twisting and wringing every pinprick of her being to produce the desired connection–and failed. Failed. Again and again, failed . . . .

Deep in the mourning darkness, *teyhataerth* whispered: *He has no children. There is no life in his seed. He will not hear me on this. He will not hear that the failure is not ours. I am sorry, Ellemoa, I cannot stop him, I cannot make him hear me.*

Then give me a child yourself, she demanded. *Make him stop hurting me!*

That was met with a deep sadness.

I cannot, the other said. *I have no more to give than Rosin himself. He does not understand: most of the second and third generations cannot produce children; and when we do, they are simply human, not the Elder-born he wishes to have under his control. It is the one fatal flaw in his understanding of our kind. You are rare, to have produced a son, Ellemoa. You are rare. He is rare. If you ever find him again, if he is alive, treasure him for simply being your son.*

Had *teyhataerth* ever actually said that, or was it a compilation of her own frenzied, nightmare-born thoughts? She couldn't tell. She whimpered as the agony of uncertainty wracked her.

Somewhere else in the darkness, Kolan whispered: *You'll find him, Ellemoa. You will. I know it. I can feel it in my soul. He's alive. You'll see him again. And you'll be proud of what he's grown into, over the years.*

That was real. That had really happened. Kolan had never stopped urging her to believe that she would find her son, even as Rosin insisted her only hope for a child was to produce another one for him.

I have my son back . . . I can be proud of him. Kolan was right.

Then the smell of sweetened ginger, the sight of ample cleavage and a whorish smile arose in memory. He'd meant to run; if she hadn't planted the suggestion to delay for a pretty girl, he'd have taken to his heels. He'd argued with her, refused her, rejected her, interfered with her: what was there to be proud of in any of that?

But he's mine. He'll learn. He'll understand soon. And once we get to Arason, I'll find him a good girl to keep him company.

You'll never see Arason again, Rosin said. *You always dream so predictably. You're dreaming now. You're not free, you know. You're still here, with me. Here's proof–*

A burst of sharp pain from her stomach; fingers pinching a tiny fold of skin cruelly hard. Was it a vivid memory, or a moment of reality?

Nobody loves you, Ellemoa, Rosin said. *Nobody but me. Look: even your son hates you. Look at him. He wants to kill you. Everyone wants to kill you or enslave you. I'm your only salvation, Ellemoa. Do what I say and the pain will stop. Do what I say . . . .*

My son doesn't hate me! She fought to remember that she was free, that she was talking to a ghost. Rosin was dead. She'd escaped. Her son stood beside her, and he didn't hate her, didn't want to hurt her–

She looked again at the shape of his mind and recoiled. *He does hate me. He sees me as a monster. How could he? I'm trying to save him. Trying to show him what's rightfully his. He's been among the humans too long . . . He sees them as equals, as allies. He doesn't understand what they're capable of. He doesn't really believe me, that they're only out to use him.*

He doesn't love me. He never will. The humans have twisted his mind. Maybe he's even been in league with Rosin all along. No, no, that's not possible . . . is it? No. Rosin's dead. He's dead. He's dead . . . .

Isn't he?

In answer, cold, cruel laughter echoed through her mind.

Chapter Sixty-Seven

As Lifty–*Idisio*–disappeared into the rickety inn, Tank took two steps in a random direction and realized he was in trouble.

Hurry. Carry an urgent message at speed to a place three day's ride away: and while he could reasonably claim the saddlebags he'd tucked under the bed at the Traveler's Rest, he couldn't claim the *horse*–that was in Yuer's stables, and there was no chance of walking off with it unless he agreed to work with Yuer.

Why do I care? Why does it matter what happens to a scruffy ex-street thief–or, for that matter, to a–a ha'ra'ha? Incredible to believe, impossible to believe–if Tank hadn't seen it for himself. Tendrils of green and gold had flickered in his vision every time he looked at Lifty's mother. And Lifty's eyes had begun to turn a disturbing dark shade when Tank suggested killing the madwoman.

It would have been the second time Tank had killed a mad ha'ra'ha–but it would have been the first time he'd known what he faced.

We didn't tell you because Ninnic's child would have pulled it from your head, Allonin had said, apologetic. *You had to go in blind. Surprise was our only chance. We had to cripple or kill it.*

You didn't think I'd ever walk out, Tank retorted in memory. *You expected me to die.*

Allonin had looked away, a hard, pale cast to his almond skin, and given no answer: which had been answer enough.

This wasn't just about Lifty. Everyone in Sandsplit was in serious danger, if she woke up angry. And after being laid out by a mere human–she'd be *raging*.

I could have killed her easily, while she was unconscious, Tank thought, staring at the inn. *It would have been the safer notion, because figuring out how to bring her back to sanity–I've no damn idea what to do with that. But trying to kill her would put me up against Lifty–Idisio–and I don't think I could handle both of them at once. I don't want to attack Lifty, in any case. He hasn't done anything to deserve that. He gave me shelter during a bad time, whatever the ending to that situation; and he stopped her from coming after me. He's not dangerous. She is.*

I hope Idisio's right that he can handle her when she wakes up. And I really hope that whoever this Deiq is, he knows what to do and can get here in time.

Tank headed back to the Traveler's Rest to collect his saddlebags.

Not long after that, he pushed past Yuer's guards, ignoring them completely. They afforded him the same courtesy and made no attempt to stop him from going through the door. Yuer sat in the same spot, with the same blanket; the table was clean of all salt residue. An ornate teapot shaped like a horse's head sat steaming gently, the topknot-lid slightly askew. The room smelled strongly of oranges and mint.

Yuer regarded Tank with raised eyebrows. "We really do need to have a discussion about your manners at some point," he said.

"What do you know about ha'ra'hain?" Tank said. "Specifically, ones who've gone completely mad?"

Yuer sat forward sharply. Liquid sloshed from the small cup in his hand, darkening a patch of blanket. He stared at Tank, mouth open, then drew a short, harsh breath and said, "Why, exactly, would you ask that question?"

"You know enough, then," Tank said. "I don't want Dasin hurt. Keep him safe and give me the horse; I'm off to fetch someone who knows how to handle this."

Yuer stared another moment, his mouth shaping silent words, then said, "Where is it?"

"The Green Branch Inn," Tank said. "My advice, leave her alone. And her son."

"Her *son?*" Yuer's voice went shrill. "We have *two* of them here?"

"He's not crazy," Tank said, hoping he was right. "She is. He's doing his best to keep her from hurting anyone. Chances are if you stay out of their way and don't provoke them, he'll keep her balanced–" Silently, he prayed he'd guessed right on that as well–"and they'll go on their way without trouble; but keep Dasin safe, give me the horse to carry the word, and I'll sign with you."

"Who are you carrying the word *to?*"

"He said to look for someone called Deiq."

Yuer stared, his face bloodless and still, for a long moment; then let out a sharp bark of laughter. "Set a viper to catch a rat," he said. "Well, *I'm* not getting involved in this one. My people are coming inside and staying out of this mess." He waved a hand. "But since you seem inclined to get involved–go. I accept your proposal. I'll keep Dasin here until I'm sure they've gone. Meet Dasin at the Copper Kettle in Bright Bay once you've completed your . . . messenger duties. If you survive the delivery."

Tank turned and left the room without bothering over farewells.

Riding at night was a new experience for Tank. The road was often hidden in drifts of black shadow cast by the scrub edging the road; the pale light of a half moon gave little to no help. The black gelding seemed unconcerned, and found its way along the road without hesitation; all the same, Tank kept to a walk or trot, uneasy with trusting the horse's vision past that point.

A few miles out of Sandsplit, the horse slowed, then stopped, tossing its head, just before a heavy swatch of shadows from an overhanging stand of trees and brush. It began to back up. Tank squinted into the deeper shadows at the side of the road, one hand on his dagger, and listened to the small sounds around him; paid attention to the shifting of the horse under him, and let it move as it wanted.

"Help me," someone said in a thin, wavering voice, like a lost child.

The horse sidled away from the sound, snorting. Tank felt its muscles bunching.

"Stay where you are," Tank said sharply. "You're about to get kicked in the head, you damn fool. Stay still." He tightened his grip on the reins. The horse snorted again but accepted the cue and backed up some more.

"I'm not going to hurt anyone," the voice said. "I can't stand knowing what he showed me. Please. I've been trying so hard to be good, but the voices won't let me rest. Please, help me."

"The *voices*?" Tank said sharply. Then, as the horse jittered again: "*Stay where you are!*"

The voice rose in a desperate, broken appeal: "Please! I saw a place–in what he showed me–in Bright Bay, there's a place where I can get help. But I'll never make it alone. It's taking all I have to talk this clearly."

"I'm not inclined to take a raving moon-case on a two day ride," Tank said curtly. "Not when my horse would rather kick you senseless than take you on. You'll have to find another way. Now move or get stepped on."

As he spoke the last words, hands grabbed his calf, fingers digging in tight and hard through the leather of his riding boot. "You should have helped me," the voice said, tone shifting to a guttural menace. "Now I'll have to try pushing this off on you instead–"

Time seemed to twist: even as Tank kicked out–drew his dagger–felt the horse go sharply sideways–tendrils of green and gold sliced through the interstices of each moment, wrapping around him, digging for purchase like thorny vines.

In the distance that lay between *now* and *then*, a black screaming began to build. The scars on his back–and other places–itched ferociously, as though newly scabbed over instead of years healed.

A familiar voice said: *You like this . . . You want this . . . .*

The scars began to stretch and burn, as though about to split open into the original wounds once more.

"No," Tank said aloud, in a fractional, fragmented moment-within-a-moment; instinctively, reflexively, gathered up all the shining filaments into a giant, tangled mass and shoved them—not back at the man clutching his leg, but *elsewhere*—

Near at hand, the man screamed and collapsed, convulsing. The horse completed its sideways shuffle and sprang forward into a headlong gallop. Tank clutched frantically at mane and reins, hanging on with what coherency remained, his only thought *Don't fall off, don't fall off.*

Eventually, the horse slowed to a walk. Tank sat up, pushing loose hair from his face, and pulled the beast to a halt; dismounted, went to his knees, and vomited. The horse tossed its head and moved sideways a step in apparent distaste. Tank hauled himself upright, still trembling all over, and after a moment of fumbling recaptured the loose reins. He felt his way along them, patted his horse's jaw reassuringly, then stood leaning against the beast's solidly comforting, *real* bulk until his knees steadied.

The scraped-raw feeling faded, little by little, into a general, weary ache. Moving his shoulders produced an odd sticky feeling across the back of his shirt and along one shoulder, where the aches were the worst.

He didn't need light to know what that meant: he was, or had been, bleeding. From wounds closed over more than six years ago.

As he swung back into the saddle, wincing, he said to the silence around him: "*Mercenary*, godsdamnit. *Mercenary*! Normal! *Ordinary*! Why is that so hard?"

A light breeze riffled through his hair briefly, then dissipated.

Tank swore again and set the horse to a reckless canter, impatient to reach shelter—or sunlight—as quickly as possible.

The sun was cresting the horizon when Tank arrived, bone-weary and irritable, in Obein. His mood wasn't helped by the discovery of a hastily-erected barricade across the road into town. Six sturdy men, three with longbows, three with polearms, and none with smiles, stood arrayed behind and to either side of the barricade. A seventh, the only one with armor—although that consisted of a battered helmet and an ill-fitting hard leather plate across his chest—stood in front of the barricade, squinting at Tank's approach.

"Hold!" the guard demanded, holding up his hand, palm out. "Identify yourself and your purpose here!"

Tank reined in a stone's throw away, studying the scene with weary bewilderment.

"Tank," he said with the last of his patience. "I'm traveling to Bright Bay. What's with the fence? This wasn't here day before yesterday."

That caused an excited murmur among the guards behind the barricade.

"You admit to passing through this town recently, then?" the leader demanded.

"*And* he has a southern accent," another guard said, loud enough for Tank to hear.

"Of course I was here!" Tank said. "I came through with merchant Dasin, under trader Yuer's seal. Now I'm going back to Bright Bay with an urgent message. And what does my accent have to do with anything?"

At mention of Yuer's name, the muttering stopped. The guards all stared at him, white-faced and cold, then began shooting each other surreptitious glances.

Someone said, low-voiced, "We *did* say he might be behind it, with all his odd–" Someone else shushed him sharply.

"Behind *what?*" Tank said. "*S'es*, all I want is a fresh mount to get through to Bright Bay. Merchant Dasin will be coming along and will pick up this one–" He stopped, seeing their expressions go hard again. "*What?*" he snapped with real anger this time.

"We've no horses to spare," the lead guard said. "Someone drove them all off. After killing a tavernkeeper and his daughter."

"Ripped them apart like a wild animal," another guard said. "The way a *barbarian* might. Hid the bodies, too."

"Don't tell him everything, you idiot!"

Tank rubbed a hand over his mouth to hide a smile; sobered completely as they glared at him, closed-off and hostile.

Tank held his increasingly restless horse still with an effort and took a deep breath. "Wasn't me," he said. "I'm a mercenary, not a murderer."

"Don't seem like much of a difference from the ground here," one of the guards behind the barricade called out. There was a nervous murmur of agreement from his companions.

"Holy gods," Tank muttered under his breath. Then, louder, "I'm *sworn*, with the Bright Bay Freewarrior's Hall."

"You work with *Yuer*," the lead guard said. "That's a name as been raising some caution of late. Lots of strange southern folk passing through of a sudden, since Ninnic died; and an awful lot of them are invoking that name as protection. Starting to wear *thin*, round here, and after such a dreadful murder as this, well–" He spat to one side. "We're not allowing no southerners in our streets for a few days, until things settle down."

Tank nearly snarled aloud. He said, brutally, "Half the traders driving along this strip have a heavier accent than I do, and don't come from any more south than Bright Bay itself, or Sandlaen. And whoever tore your people apart–if it *was* a person, and not an animal–is probably long gone up the road and laughing by now. You're doing yourselves no good by this stupid barricade."

They glared, their own tempers rising; polearms shifted to a distinctly readier slant, and the bowmen were fingering through the shafts in their quivers.

"He's got the arrogance of all the barbarians," one of the bowman muttered. "Be just like them to do something vicious and then come back and laugh at us in our misery."

"Be just like Yuer to hire it done," someone else said, and the mood darkened further.

"That's enough," Tank said sharply. "I understand your fears, but you're jumping at shadows, and I'm too godsdamned tired to put up with your idiocy. Let me through to an inn, if you don't have any horses to lend; I'll sleep as quick as I can and be on my way without asking more favors. My message is *urgent*."

"Urgent or not," the leader said obdurately, "we're only bound to let News-Riders through, not southern redling trash."

Tank's temper strained hard at that; he was anxious, and exhausted, and out of patience with these damn fools. But riding over them—or trying to jump the barricade, tempting and showy as that would be—risked injuring the horse and slowing him further. All things considered, the best option was to hang on to the last threads of his self-control and make them deliver the first blow.

When do you fight? When you have no other choice. For once, this really wasn't the time.

"If you're going to attack innocent travelers," Tank said, "may as well start with me. But you'd best kill me in the doing, because one *scratch* and I'll have the lot of you up in front of the King himself for unprovoked attack on a Hall-sworn freewarrior."

He nudged his horse into motion; bows and polearms went to the ready immediately. His jaw taut, he kept his hands relaxed on the reins and guided the beast off the road and around the barricade, leaving a wide gap between himself and the guards.

One of the guards stepped in his way, polearm held at a forbidding angle. Tank stared straight at him and kept the horse moving. As his teeth began to creak from jamming them together and it seemed that the tip of the blade would pierce the horse's neck at any moment, the guard swore and dove awkwardly out of the way. The polearm thudded to the ground, the man rolling to avoid catching up against the sharp edge.

Tank heard the sounds of rapid, muted argument from the other guards; a moment later, in peripheral vision, he saw the remaining polearms and bows waver and droop. He let out a long breath and went on without looking back.

Chapter Sixty-Eight

The narrow-faced innkeeper squinted at the small golden rose in Idisio's hand, pursing his lips. "And for that?" he said.

"Five days' lodging and your silence on our presence here," Idisio said. While the latter request was probably far too late, given the scene at the Black Horse Tavern, Idisio *really* didn't want Yuer to get involved. He thought it more than a little likely that Yuer would find this situation rife with potential.

He rubbed at his eyes, wondering if that was his own cynicism emerging or his mother's paranoia. They felt uncomfortably similar, at the moment.

The innkeeper looked at the unconscious woman laid out on the fireside bench, frowning. The commons room was otherwise empty, as was–Idisio blinked, feeling momentarily dizzy–as was the inn itself. Three other rooms on the ground floor around him had occupants booked in, but all were elsewhere at the moment.

Idisio put out a hand to steady himself against the wall, trying to make the movement a casual one. Fear skittered up and down his spine like a icy-cold spider. *How the hells do I know which rooms are empty?*

It had made perfect sense for him to know things like that at Scratha Fortress: there was a ha'rethe there to feed him the information. Like a whisper in the back of his mind, he remembered Deiq saying: *You're still developing.*

But what am I developing into?

Idisio bit back a whimper, wishing Deiq were around to explain; wishing his own mother could be trusted to deliver reliable information. He'd already tried reaching out to Deiq, in case he could speak to the elder ha'ra'ha over significant distance, and been met with a blank grey haze that muffled and dissolved the effort every time. Whether that came from something his mother had done to him, or whether the distance was after all an impenetrable barrier, he couldn't tell. The effect was the same, in the end: Tank was his only hope of getting a message through that he was still alive–and still *badly* in need of help.

"I don't need no trouble here," the innkeeper said, bringing Idisio back to the moment.

"No trouble," Idisio said. "Just lodging and peace for a few days."

"Someone attacked your friend there," the innkeeper said. "That sounds like trouble to me."

"No trouble. She's been ill. She's not quite herself," Idisio said steadily. "She needs to rest. She's no danger to you." He caught the man's eye and held it. "Just lodging and peace for five days," he repeated softly. "Please. Give us an east-facing room and keep your silence as to our presence."

The man blinked and ran a hand through his thinning, lank grey hair. "Take the room down the right hand hallway there, last door on the right. There's no key. Most of these rooms bolt from the inside, is all you get." His gaze went to Idisio's unconscious mother again. "Sunrise rooms always go first. You're lucky to get that one. If business was better–but it's been a bad stretch. Pack of unsworn been driving regular guests away." He looked to Idisio. "I'd say get her under cover afore they come back from their drinking night," he added. "They're not picky about awake or asleep."

"Which room are *they* in?" Idisio said.

The innkeeper opened his mouth. In the fractional moment between that and speech, words spilled into Idisio's mind: *The west side/hope they leave soon and take broken collarbone with them/mannerless pigs/what they did to Neda/but I'm the only one believes her–*

"They're on the other side of the inn," the innkeeper said. "You shouldn't run into them. Are you all right? You look ill of a sudden."

"Fine," Idisio said through his teeth. He handed over the rose, suppressing a surge of guilt: he would have to send compensation to Alyea for what he'd stolen—no. He had the right to take anything he wanted; she was a desert lord; she would understand—and Deiq would make sure of that, if the issue came up. Still, it put a hard knot in his stomach, to rest on that *right*: he hadn't taken the items as part of his due, he'd taken them as a thief fleeing the premises with filled pockets, and that distinction made all the difference.

A sly line came to the innkeeper's expression as he examined the small metal flower. *Nice piece here/worth more than a few days lodging/wonder what else they have/strange sorts too/bet Yuer would like to know about them/if they're fugitives he might even give a reward–*

Idisio said, sharply, "S'e–"

The man jerked a startled, suspicious glance at Idisio.

Idisio bit his lip, then forced his voice to soften. "Thank you for the room. For your graciousness. For *leaving us alone* for the next five days. For *not telling* Yuer anything about us being here."

The man stared, seeming bemused, then shrugged, sketched a lazy farewell with one hand, and turned away. Idisio scooped up his mother and headed for their room.

Once inside, the door safely bolted and his mother laid out on the single, wide bed, Idisio sat down on the floor and let himself shudder all over for some time. He blinked in and out of complete darkness, his eyes flooding with tears every time the black returned; going dry with each phase of grey clarity.

That in itself was disconcerting enough to make him want proper light. He rocked onto his knees, then tried to stand up: folded back to the floor in a graceless sprawl. He rolled back to his knees and stayed there, hands on his thighs as he tried to calm himself.

"I'm tired," he muttered, not believing it for a moment. "I'll be all right with some sleep. But I can't sleep, can I? Because if she wakes up–"

He rubbed his eyes, swearing under his breath, trying to think through what to do next. Light seemed like a good idea no matter what the other choices wound up being, but he didn't have a tinderbox with him and it was unlikely the room offered one. For that matter, he didn't remember having seen an oil lamp in the room. He glanced around, squinting a little, and found a single fat, half-melted candle on the small bedside table.

"Great," Idisio muttered. "Now I have to figure out how to *light* the damn thing–What did Deiq say? *See it lit–*"

With a sharp, crackling hiss, the wick burst into flame.

Idisio stared, his mouth slightly open; patted the side of his own face a few times to check that he wasn't dreaming, then staggered to his feet.

"Developing," he said under his breath. "Right."

Remembering that conversation with Deiq put him in mind of another trick he'd seen the elder ha'ra'ha pull off ever-so-casually: *Wards, to ensure our privacy. They're fairly simple . . . I'll teach you.* But he'd never gotten around to it, of course. Trying to explain how to light an oil lamp and steady his body temperature had been all the instruction Deiq had really offered; but if it was simple, perhaps Idisio could figure it out on his own.

What had Deiq done, exactly? Idisio remembered him walking around the area, passing his hand along each entrance–pointing when he couldn't quite reach a spot–and an odd shimmer had followed his fingers, settling into the rock and fading away almost immediately.

Idisio began to raise his hand, then stopped and lowered it again. He'd been out on the streets long enough to know that anything dangerous was best attempted with absolute confidence; from picking a pocket to making a chancy jump, uncertainty almost guaranteed failure.

He drew a deep breath, then another, summoning up the old street-thief brashness; sauntered over to the door and traced his hand along the frame, thinking: *Privacy. Leave us alone. Nobody here. Go away.* Idisio had no doubt that Deiq would walk right through, but hopefully those less skilled–all right, *humans*–would be turned away.

A pale blue line ghosted behind his fingers, sinking into the worn, gapped wood so quickly that Idisio wondered if he'd imagined even seeing it. Setting aside doubt, he went to the single wide, low window and traced the frame of that as well. This time he made sure of what he was seeing. The ward line seemed hazy, compared to the hard golden sparkle of Deiq's wards; Idisio set that aside as something to puzzle over later and turned to check on his mother.

She lay still, breathing shallowly but evenly. While blood matted her hair, the wounds beneath had almost completely disappeared. Idisio rubbed his hands together, considering, then frowned and leaned in to study her more closely: the dress she wore looked oddly familiar.

A faint waft of sweetened ginger rose to his nose.

He straightened and backed away from the bed a hasty step, his pulse thundering in his ears. "Oh, gods," he said, one hand over his mouth. "Oh, gods, *no.*"

He looked down at his own clothes, nausea rising in his throat: a maroon peasant shirt and dun trousers, the latter almost more patches than original cloth. He couldn't remember having seen anyone wearing the outfit in Obein, but that dress hadn't been a voluntary gift–and his mother wasn't the type to simply steal a garment.

Unless the shirt and trousers were the serving girl's spare clothing, which seemed unlikely, he had to believe that his mother had killed two people in Obein: the serving girl and whoever was with her at the time of Ellemoa's attack.

She's killed before, Tank had said. *Doesn't regret it one bit.*

Idisio's certainty that his mother wouldn't hurt him wavered like the smoke curling from the candle flame. He looked at the door and the window, considering; thinking through implications. If he could set wards to stop people getting *in*, surely he could set wards to stop someone getting *out*. That seemed only reasonable. *How* was another matter, especially as she, like Deiq, would probably walk right through any attempt of his to hold her.

But then again, she'd admitted he was stronger than she'd expected. She'd used reason to convince him to go with her voluntarily, because forcing him to move along was tiring her. So maybe she would have some trouble, after all; enough that the ward might alert him, wake him, if she tried to pass them.

He had to try. He could feel exhaustion racking aches up throughout his body, and didn't dare risk falling asleep without at least some effort to contain his mother from seeking out another victim–or unleashing her frustrated rage on her own son.

Please, gods, let Deiq get here soon, he thought, and began tracing ghostly blue lines around the bed.

Chapter Sixty-Nine

Tank paid a half silver round for the stableboy to take care of his horse, flopped down across a line of hay bales and fell asleep instantly. Before noon he was awake and saddling the horse again; it stared at him with what might have been reproach but proved energetic enough for a steady canter once they cleared town.

He had to admit he missed the grey mare he'd left with Venepe; while this beast was definitely the equal of any King's Rider's mount, it lacked the mare's sassy attitude. Tank couldn't imagine this proud horse ever biting its rider or groom; that would be far too undignified.

He laughed at himself. "Now I'm putting personalities on horses," he muttered. "Next I'll be hearing them talk."

He wondered if he ought to give the horse a name. It hadn't seemed important up to that point, but with a long road ahead, it was a usefully trivial thing to think about, with endlessly amusing possibilities. By the time he reached Kybeach, he was trying to decide between Snake and Sin.

He'd also ridden through a sharp rainstorm that appeared out of nowhere and left as quickly, leaving him sodden and cursing. His temper hadn't eased by the time he dismounted in the shabby stableyard, and the horse seemed as irritable; it jerked its head and stomped a hoof perilously near Tank's foot.

"Knock it off," he muttered, swatting it on the side of the neck. "I'm not happy either." It snorted and stamped a back hoof this time.

A skinny blond boy peered at them from the open stable door, apparently unwilling to emerge into the cloud-weakened sunlight. Tank stared back, scowling, and waved, beckoning the boy out into the open.

The boy sidled out a step, another, his narrow-eyed gaze fixed on the horse; then, abruptly, scuttled back into the stable.

Tank swore under his breath and led his horse forward. It balked, tossing its head, a few steps before the threshold; Tank's efforts to persuade it forward only made it back up.

"Come on," he said aloud, half to the horse and half to the rapidly clouding sky. "Come *on!*" The horse only backed up another step, lashing its tail.

The temperature dropped, fast enough to prickle Tank's skin with foreboding: he glanced up at the darkening clouds and redoubled his efforts to wrestle the horse forward into shelter. It snorted and reared; he ducked aside as a heavy hoof swept past his right ear.

"All right, damnit," he said aloud as the beast thudded back to earth, "that's enough of that!"

His breath plumed in the air as he spoke. He stared at that, horrified and realizing that the horse's breath was coming out in heavy clouds now; his skin was burning from frost, not fear. The horse danced sideways, dipping its head and tossing it high as though trying to fix on the source of its own unease.

Something small and sharp smacked against the top of Tank's head, hard enough to make him yelp. Tilting his face to look up, he caught a dozen frozen missiles full on against his cheeks and forehead before he managed to duck into a protective hunch.

The horse let out a rumbling neigh of complaint and bolted for the barn. Tank held onto the reins for the first three steps, then gave up and did his best to at least flip them over the saddle before they were completely torn from his hand.

Ice rattled down in thickening sheets as he followed the horse into shelter. Someone shouted incoherent protest. Tank caught up with the restlessly turning horse in a few swift strides and grabbed the trailing reins, thankful it hadn't stepped on them during its flight.

"Easy," he said, slapping it on the shoulder. "Easy, easy."

It slowly quieted, glaring at one of the stalls, its ears pricking forward, then slanting back sharply. Tank grinned and led the horse forward; yanked the unlatched half-door open fast and said, in false surprise, "Oh, hey, sorry about that, didn't know you were in there."

The blond boy, nearly plastered into the back corner of the stall, glared at him sullenly. "Keep that devil-beast away from me," he said. "Get it away!"

Tank looked at his horse, back to the stable boy. "You know this horse, or you don't like black horses in general?" he asked.

"It *bites*," the boy said; a heartbeat later, the horse lowered its head and extended its neck, snakelike, teeth bared.

"Whoa," Tank said, pulling the horse's head sharply sideways. "None of that! So much for dignified," he added under his breath as he turned the horse around and aimed it toward another empty stall two doors down.

The stable was empty, no question; he hadn't had much hope that Kybeach would offer anything by way of a remount to begin with, but it seemed that there weren't even any travelers passing through who might be willing to loan their horse out for a price.

His legs, back, and shoulders ached as though he'd been dipped in fire. He needed a rest before going on, and his horse's slowing pace and irritability on the road told him the gelding felt the same way.

"Gods, I hate this place," he muttered as he began unhooking saddlebags. "Be happy never to stop here again." Raising his voice, he called out, "Feed and water, please!"

"Gold round up front," the boy retorted, appearing at the stall door and glaring in at them. The horse, head toward the far end of the stall, kicked out at the sound of the boy's voice; a heavy back hoof thudded into the stall door, cracking one of the boards. The boy yelped and dove aside; Tank swatted the gelding's shoulder hard.

"What the hells did you do to this horse to make it hate you like that?" Tank said. "And a gold round is absurd. Half a silver and you're lucky at that." He dropped the saddlebags near the stall door, then began on the bridle.

The boy said, from considerably farther away now, "Didn' do nuthin'. It's evil, that beast. Come through here once afore, under the hand of a couple outsiders as thought themselves better'n everyone local here. It's a gold round because it's the last good feed we got left. Witch came through and took up all the rest, sayin' it was hers by right."

"A *witch?*" Tank said. He leaned over the stall door to hang the bridle on the outside peg; the boy was squatting across the aisle. Tank squinted at him. "There's no such thing as witches."

"That's all you know," the boy retorted. "We've a witch not a half-day's walk from us, I'll have you know. We usedta run supplies up to her—well, Kera did, anyways. But now Kera's dead, and nobody else dares go out to the witch, and so the witch sent a servant out to collect her due. And part of that due was all the winter feed we had. Don't have no money to buy more, not with no travelers stopping of late; and without feed we don't *get* travelers, if you see. So I want a gold round, or you can use your own stores, or go hungry for all I care."

Tank shook his head and started on the saddle.

"Give him the feed, Baylor," someone else said: a world-weary child's voice.

The boy yelped again; there was a scrambling noise, then he said, panting, "Stop sneakin' up on me, witch-brat!"

Tank moved to the stall door and looked out. The boy was facing off with a familiar young girl: the street thief Tank had picked up in Bright Bay. She was considerably cleaner now, and with her hair tightly shorn, her eyes seemed unusually large under a widow's peak hairline. Her dress, while worn and patched, was respectably fitted and clean: so she'd found someone to take care of her.

She flicked an amused glance at Tank, then returned her attention to the boy. "There's more feed left than you're saying, Baylor. I watched what she took, an' it wasn't all your stores. Besides, this ain't *your* stables. You don't get to set the price. You just work here, for as long as the village master lets you stay."

"Bitch," the boy snarled. "*You* ain't got no say here neither, so get out afore I put a pitchfork up your skinny arse."

"Be the first time you did anything with a pitchfork," she taunted.

"Stop it," Tank said mildly. "Go get me the feed. Half silver. Or I'll show you what *I* can do with a pitchfork."

The boy glared at him and sulked off. The girl laughed and came over to the stall door, peering in at the horse.

"He rid that beast out to Sandsplit once," she said conversationally. "Doesn't know how to ride worth a damn, and the horse knew it was bein' stolen, is my guess. It remembers. Horses is smarter than people think."

Tank went back to unbuckling the saddle and didn't say anything, but his stomach sank at the confirmation that he was riding stolen property.

"I was wrong," she said, sounding not in the least embarrassed about it.

He heaved the saddle up and over, brought it to the stall door, and balanced it on the rim of the door, staring down at her. "About what?"

She wouldn't quite meet his gaze. "About–the demon. I didn't realize until I got to Kybeach–that she was already on the road, with Lifty–*ahead* of you. I woulda warned you, if you'd kept me along with you." She cocked her head and shot him a fast glance, unsmiling. "I can see you've already run into her. I–I'm sorry for getting it wrong."

"So much for *sight*," he said a little sourly.

She shrugged, her gaze sliding aside again, and said, "I don't *always* get it right, do I? Otherwise I'd be making a living at tellings, wouldn't I? Pays better'n begging, for sure."

"With more risk of your head in a noose for witching."

She ignored that. "I see one thing clear and no mistake to it–you got ghosts trailing around you that need rest." Her eyes searched the air around Tank's head, and she gave an uneasy shudder.

"Ghosts," he said, his voice flat with skepticism.

She shook her head. "Not dead spirits, not always," she said a little impatiently. "Sometimes just–things you got to do, things you're hanging on to that you can't let go of–I ain't got fancy words for it. But you're *weighted* with 'em, and some of 'em are near burning you up. You ought to be on the road. Longer you wait, worse things'll be."

The pattering of ice turned to a thunderous downpour of rain; the already-dim light inside the stable darkened further. He brushed away the chill her words put along his spine and said, pragmatically, "Nobody's going anywhere in that."

She shut her eyes and cocked her head.

"It'll clear by evening," she said after a moment. "Get a rest, then. I'll watch your beast for you."

"You?" he said, unable to help a snort of laughter. "You'll watch it right out the door."

She stuck her tongue out at him. "I can't ride," she said, "an' I ain't likely to put all that tack back on the beast of my own self, now, am I? Couldn't lift that saddle, f'r one thing, an' I *told* you–that horse ain't stupid. It knows who its rider ought to be. It wouldn't go nowheres with me. It only went with Baylor because he hit it hard enough to make it run."

"Did not," the boy said sullenly as he returned with a bucketful of grain. He set it down, lifted the saddle out of the way and onto the stall-side saddle tree with a grunt of effort, then handed the bucket up to Tank.

"That ain't what the horse said," the girl said.

Baylor rolled his eyes and said, "Half *silver*, if you *please*."

"So now you talk to animals?" Tank asked, amused, as he dumped the bucket into the feed trough.

"Not usually," she said. "This one's different. He's got stories behind him."

Tank shook his head, dug out a silver round, and flipped it at Baylor.

"Go on, then," he said. "Thank you."

Baylor slunk away without answering.

"The inn here ain't worth the walk through the rain," the girl said. "You already know that, I'm guessing. There's a cot in the box stall two down, though–usedta be a pregnant mare there, an' they had the stableboys watching her day an' night."

"What happened to the mare?" Tank took out the currying kit and set to work.

"Witch's servant took her and the foal," the girl said. "Probably better off with her, anyhow."

"The owner didn't argue that?"

"Owner's dead. Gerho merchant, killed himself."

Tank stood still, staring out at her with a vague feeling of disquiet in his stomach.

"Yeah," he said. "I knew about that. Saw him dead, my first trip through here. That wasn't but a few days ago."

"She came through the same day as he died," the girl said with relish. "Some around here are wondering if the man really killed himself or if she witched him into it, to get her own back. Working for a witch, after all, she's bound to have picked up a few tricks. I heard as she was his wife, and she left to serve the witch; some are saying she came back to get her daughter, and found her daughter had died, and killed her husband as a punishment."

Tank shook his head and resumed his work.

"Not my business," he said. "Where's that cot?"

"Funny thing," she said, not moving. "The merchant's daughter was killed, and some think it was another servant–the one as rode in on that same horse you're brushing down now."

Tank straightened and glared through the murky light at her.

"Stop it," he said. "Now I *know* you're trying to spook me."

She laughed and went away. Tank stood still, listening to the rain thundering down, mixed with the occasional patter of ice chips, and felt a chill that had nothing to do with the drafty air of the stables.

He woke to a scuffling sound and a savage grunt; rolled from the cot to his feet and vaulted over the stall half-door in what seemed, to his sleep-blurred senses, like a single fluid movement.

Dim afternoon light filtering in through the open doors showed him two figures rolling on the floor, scratching and clawing at one another. He went forward, grabbed the larger form and hoisted, turning, and threw–the way he'd once tossed another skinny blond boy across a training room floor–and this one landed with the same undignified yelp, which brought a grin to Tank's face even as he turned to the smaller form.

"You all right?"

The girl scrambled to her feet, glaring at him.

"I had it handled!" she said indignantly.

He laughed, resisting the impulse to reach out and brush chaff from her hair and clothes; turned to survey Baylor, who was climbing to his feet as sullenly as he did everything else.

"What was that about?" he asked the blond boy.

"You gotta sleep, witch-brat," Baylor said, ignoring Tank entirely. "You won't always win. An' you won't be so quick to run if you're outnumbered, neither. Remember that; I can get a half dozen as would be willing to hold your skinny little arse down for a proper lesson–"

Tank's smile faded. He took three fast steps and swung. Baylor shrieked, trying to dodge: wound up sprawled across the floor again, this time with a bleeding mouth.

"I'm not afraid of him," the girl said, but her voice shook as she said it.

Tank knelt over the boy, letting enough of his weight down to keep Baylor pinned, and put a hand round the boy's skinny throat. "I ever hear word this girl's been touched," he said, "by you or another here against her will, whether it's by a fist or otherwise–I'll take you to pieces. You hear me? You and anyone else involved in holding her down for a *lesson*. You'll look like a godsdamned disjointed chicken by the time I'm done. *You hear me?*"

Baylor gurgled, eyes wide. The sharp, sour stench of urine rose into the air. Tank released his hold and stood, grimacing; backed away to give the boy room, and spat on the floor near Baylor's feet.

"I'll be coming through here regular," Tank said as the blond scrambled to his feet. "And I'll be wanting to see she's been left alone."

Baylor glared, one hand to his bleeding mouth; spat violently at the floor himself, then ran from the stables.

Tank drew in a long breath and let it out, calming himself. He turned to face the girl. She was staring at him with an odd mixture of surprise and fear.

"You move fast when you're mad, don't you?" she said. "Didn't expect you to get all that upset over–well, me."

Tank shook his head, the aftermath of anger souring his mouth, and went to collect his saddlebags. Further sleep wasn't likely to happen now; and the rain had stopped, in any case.

He emerged into the aisle to find the stableboy nowhere in sight and the girl scratching the gelding's nose. She grinned, no longer in the least afraid of him, and moved out of his way.

She hung half over the stall door, watching him work, until he was securing the saddlebags. Then she said, "I'll give you sommat, in return for–just now. It ain't stolen."

"What?"

"Your horse. It ain't stolen. You're worried about that, but it ain't. There's no taint to it, and it's happy with you; that means you're rightful."

"You said Baylor stole it."

"He did. I'm guessing your horse got back round to the right owner somewhere along the way after that, and the right owner gave the horse over to whoever gave it to you."

"That's a wild stretch of coincidence," he said.

She shrugged. "I know what I see."

"You know what you can spin out of thin air," Tank retorted, caught between annoyance and amusement, and led his horse out into the aisle.

She shook her head, blinking. "Remember what I said, ghost-rid. You got to settle those ghosts out, or the demons will always find you, wherever you go. That kind of weight *draws* them. You won't get clear of the demons until you're clear of your ghosts; and that means anyone traveling alongside you is in danger, sooner or late."

Tank stared at her, his mouth open; then drew in a sharp, harsh breath and said, "Stay away from me and keep your delusions to yourself. I'm not interested."

As he led Sin into the weak, rainwashed sunlight, he could feel her silent, intent stare boring into his back: but when he risked a glance back, she was nowhere to be seen.

Chapter Seventy

Ellemoa woke in the grey light of dawn and sat up, raking her hands through her hair as she looked around. Idisio shook out of a light doze at the motion and rubbed a hand over his face, then scrambled to his feet as she focused on him.

"Idisio?" she said. "Son, where are we? What happened?"

He studied her for a moment, weighing the innocence of her tone and the blank bewilderment of her expression against instinct. Deciding to believe it was genuine, he said, "We're in Sandsplit. You've been ill, so I took a room for a few days."

"I've been ill? I'm never ill." She ran her hands over her face and throat, as though checking for swelling, and shook her head. "I'm not ill."

"It's not that sort of illness," Idisio said. He hesitated, then took a chance and added, "You haven't been yourself."

Her roving hands paused on the back of her head, and her eyebrows lowered into a frown. "There's a lump here. How odd. Did I hit my head?"

"Yes," Idisio said, relieved at that easy of an explanation. "You fell and hit your head. It made you a bit odd, and I thought it best to let you rest for a while."

"That was kind of you," she said. She drew her knees up to her chest and wrapped her arms around them, then looked around the room vaguely. "Are we close to Arason?"

"We're in Sandsplit," Idisio said. "I'm not sure how far that is from Arason."

"Have we crossed the Hackerwood yet?"

"No."

"Then we're a long ways away yet." She sighed. "We should go on. But I'm so tired." One hand went to the back of her head to explore the lump there once more. "I don't remember falling."

"Sleep until you're not tired anymore," Idisio said, putting all the persuasion he could summon into the words. "We'll have the room for days yet. There's no hurry. This is a good place to rest. It's a safe place to rest."

She blinked at him, frowning a little. Finally, she shrugged and stretched out on the bed once more. "So tired . . . ." she murmured, her voice trailing off into a mumble. Moments later, her breathing evened out.

Idisio leaned against the wall and steadied his own breathing. Was it really possible that he'd *persuaded* his mother, as he'd done on occasion with humans? If so, she must have really wanted to; he had no illusions that his strength exceeded hers. Then again, Tank had delivered a solid blow. It had obviously weakened her. Idisio was a bit surprised it hadn't caved in her skull completely. And, he admitted ruefully, a little disappointed, as dreadful as he knew that thought to be.

Please, gods, he thought again, *let Deiq get here soon. I don't know if I can handle her once she's fully rested.*

And I don't know what she'll do to me when she remembers Tank.

His mother stirred and rolled over, whimpering a little.

"Kolan," she said. "Kolan, I'm so sorry. I'm so sorry, I didn't want to, they made me . . . ." The words trailed off into a guttural, growling sound, then to silence.

Idisio slid to sit on the floor again, leaning against the wall, and watched her as the air brightened with sunshine.

"I can't do it," she whimpered after a time. "I've tried. I've tried. I only have one child, and I lost him. He's dead . . . I'll never see him again . . . and I'll never have another. I can't. I'm *trying,* Kolan, but I *can't* . . . ."

Idisio's breath stuck in his throat for a moment.

"They're hurting me, Kolan," his mother breathed, then rolled over again, her face into the pillow, and muttered a long string of words Idisio couldn't hear well enough to understand. At last she rolled clear and went back to deep, even breathing.

Idisio sat very still, barely breathing himself, the hair standing up all along the back of his neck and arms. As the prickling faded, a thought occurred to him: if he was able, by some miracle, to influence his mother–if she really was that weak–he might be able to plant suggestions in her mind to turn her from her casual disregard of human life.

And whoever Kolan was, that sounded like a name she'd listen to.

He put a hand to his throat, thinking through what to say and how; again, instinct told him that confidence would be the key. He had to really believe he could do it, because if he tried and failed . . . She'd already shown raw fury over him simply stepping in her way. If she ever suspected he'd tried to control her the way she'd done him . . . .

Idisio rubbed his throat gently, cleared it twice, then gathered breath and nerve and said, very softly, "Mother? Are you awake?" Her breathing remained steady and deep. He listened carefully for a few moments; then, reassured, whispered, "Sleep, Ellemoa. Stay asleep."

It seemed best, for some reason, to use her name instead of calling her *mother* again; he trusted intuition and went with that approach. But something felt off, all the same. He didn't sense anything happening. He tried again, focusing on *wanting Ellemoa asleep, deeply, deeply asleep* as he spoke, and felt a shivering vibration underlying the words this time.

She sighed a little and turned her head. It seemed to him that she relaxed even further; a sort of peace came over her narrow face, and a faint smile hovered on her thin lips. He let out a silent breath of relief, then said, as quietly as before, "Kolan wants you to be kind, Ellemoa. Kolan wants you to stop hurting people. Stop hurting humans," he corrected himself hastily. "He wants you to respect life."

His mother rolled her head from one side to the other, frowning slightly; he held his breath until she sighed and relaxed again.

"He loves you, Ellemoa," Idisio said, not sure why, intuition leading him once more. "Kolan loves you very much. He wants you to stop hurting humans. He wants you to trust . . . trust your son, and listen to what your son says. Whatever your son says to do, listen to him. Do as he says. Trust your son. Trust Kolan."

She sighed, a more distressed sound this time, and turned on her side to face away from him, curling up into herself. He bit his lip and let her be, afraid of pushing further; not at all sure if his efforts had worked, or that she wouldn't know, on waking, what he'd tried to do.

At least, he reflected ruefully, if she did spot his attempt at controlling her, he'd know about it very quickly.

He sat back again, steadying his own breathing into an aqeyva trance, and waited.

She woke again later that day and sat up, leaning toward the sunlight visible through the open window.

"How are you feeling?" Idisio asked after a few moments of quiet.

She turned her head, blinking at him as though surprised by his presence; stared at him with a frightening lack of recognition for a moment before breaking out into a broad smile. "Idisio," she said. "My son."

"Yeah," he said, uncomfortable and embarrassed all at once. "How are you feeling?"

"Tired," she said. "Sore." She rolled her shoulders and rubbed her neck, yawning. "Where are we? What happened?"

"We're in Sandsplit," he said. "You've been ill. You needed to rest, so we're staying a few days while you rest."

"And you stayed with me?" She smiled. "Thank you, son. It's good to know you won't abandon me when I'm ill." She looked back toward the window, closing her eyes, and purred a little.

Idisio drew in a long, careful breath. "You've been talking in your sleep a bit," he said casually. "Who's Kolan?"

She opened her eyes and stared at him. He froze, his heart tripping into a hammering rhythm at the sharp blackness of her stare. Then she blinked, and the black washed out of her eyes, returning them to a pale, mild grey.

"Kolan?" she said. "I don't remember." She stretched out on the bed again, rolling to put her back to him, and said nothing more.

He left her alone, too shaken by that brief, ferocious glare to pry further; but when her breathing deepened and evened again, he repeated his attempt at persuasion. This time he provoked no reaction at all, and wasn't sure if that was a good sign or not.

As sunlight dimmed toward late afternoon shadows, she stirred and sat up, wrapping her arms around herself; her face looked pale and bruised, her large eyes sunken in her too-thin face.

"Idisio?" she said. "Son, where are we? What happened?"

"We're in Sandsplit," he said. "You've been ill. I booked a room for a few days to let you rest."

She stared at him, frowning. "I'm never ill," she said. "What happened?"

"You haven't been yourself," he said. "I thought some sleep would help you recover."

She shivered, looking around the room. "I don't like it here," she said. "I want to get back on the road. Why do you say I haven't been myself? What have I done, to make you say I'm ill?" She looked back at him, her eyes a clear, pale grey, and waited for an answer.

"You've hurt people," he said steadily.

"Have I?" She cocked her head to the side and appeared to be thinking about that. "I suppose I have, haven't I. Why does that make me ill?"

"They didn't deserve to be hurt, mother," he said. "They didn't do anything to deserve what you did to them."

She smiled at him with fond indulgence and said, "You really don't understand very much, do you, son? Well, I won't argue with you. You'll have to learn your own lessons on that." She sighed and looked out the window again, her expression wistful. "I'd like to watch a sunrise or a sunset with Kolan again," she murmured. "Just once more."

He hesitated, then said, tentatively: "Who's Kolan?"

She didn't look at him. "He's dead. It doesn't matter who he was."

"Sounds like you cared about him."

She shrugged, still staring out the window. "Maybe I did," she said. "But as he's dead, what does that matter? Nothing. No more important than those humans you're so upset over. They're meaningless. Insects. You'll outlive the oldest of them without noticing they're gone."

"I was *raised* as a human," he said.

"I know." She turned her head to look at him with mild grey eyes. "It's a shame. I'm beginning to think it's ruined you."

He sat still, afraid to move in case that sent her into a rage. She studied him for a few moments, then smiled and slid to sit on the edge of the bed.

"Why do they matter to you?" she said. "They've hurt you and lied to you and disrespected you. They do worse to each other than anything you have ever endured. I've seen it, son. I've seen into their minds, over the years; I've seen what lies behind the polite smiles and the false promises. Of all the humans I've faced, I've never seen one with honest motives. They're like a pack of rabid cats, tearing one another apart."

"Not even Kolan?" he said recklessly, and this time she was the one to go motionless, her eyes wide and almost colorless for a long breath.

At last she blinked and said, "Kolan told himself plenty of lies; he was just better at believing his own lies than most humans. It made him harder to break, because he *believed*. But it didn't save him, in the end. Belief in a lie never really works."

"How do you know he's dead?" Idisio pressed. "You escaped. Maybe he did, too."

She shook her head, smiling, and said, "No. He's dead. I know he's dead, because I killed him." Her smile abruptly faded to an anguished expression. She tilted her head back and let out a low, keening sound that pierced Idisio's ears and chest with identical sharp pains.

He scrambled to his feet, shaking all over, and said, "So you care. You *care* about Kolan. You're *sorry* you killed him! Aren't you?" It seemed terribly important, in a blurry sort of way, to force her to admit to feelings; to prove that ha'ra'hain could love as fiercely as any human.

"Yes," she breathed, her eyes colorless again, and scooted back onto the bed, drawing her knees up to her chest and hugging them. "Oh, gods, yes. I miss him."

Idisio pressed his back against the wall, breathing hard, and tried to think of what to say next. Intuition rose, unexpected and sharp: *Deiq's not coming. I'm on my own.* He bit his tongue against the urge to swear aloud, and wished he could doubt the knowledge; but it held the odd, echoing certainty of a true vision. To give himself time to think, he crossed to the single window and stood looking out. A draft of chill air, scented with night-blooming flowers, swirled into the room, dispersing the thickness he felt in his chest. His mother breathed deeply, clearly enjoying the sweet floral aroma; he turned to find her smiling.

"Tell me about Kolan," Idisio said, encouraged by that smile. "Tell me why you liked him. What you found good about a human."

"He was kind," she whispered, closing her eyes. "When nobody else would speak to me, he did. He treated me as an equal. He wasn't afraid of me–at first–even though he knew what I was. Even though his own father thrashed him for coming to see me. Even though the Elders disapproved of him seeing me. He was *kind*."

"And you killed him," Idisio said. "And you regret doing that."

She raised a tear-streaked face toward the ceiling and keened again. The sound put chills up Idisio's back and raised the hair on his arms.

"Yes," she mourned. "I killed him. The only one who was ever good to me." She buried her face against her knees and let out a choked sob. "You're right, son," she said, the words muffled. "I've done bad things. I've hurt people who didn't deserve it."

"Yes, you have," he said, his own breath thick in his throat.

She sat up straight and blinked at him, her eyes watering. "What do I do?" she said. "How do I make amends for doing such bad things, son? Tell me what I should do."

"You stop *doing* those things, for one," he said sharply. "You stop killing humans just because they annoy you."

She wiped the back of one hand across her eyes and said, unsteadily, "It's not that easy, son. Not after so many years of being told to kill, being *made* to kill . . . it's like breathing after a while. It's hard to see anything wrong with it."

"Well, it *is* wrong," he said. "And you have to stop."

"What if I can't?" she said, cocking her head to one side. "What if it's a part of me, son; something I can't help any longer? I know I'm not what you'd consider sane; I'm not sane by human standards, certainly. What if that's what I am, now, and it's not ever going to change?"

"I believe you can," he said. "If you want to. Because you loved Kolan, and you regret killing him."

She considered that for a time, twisting her fingers into the skirt of her dress. "I don't know," she said. "I'm not sure I could do that. I don't know how."

"I know someone who can help you," Idisio said. "If you'll come back with me, there's an elder ha'ra'ha in Bright Bay–"

"Deiq?" She laughed, genuinely amused. "No, son. He's not someone to trust. He planned to kill me, when they set you out as bait."

"No–" Idisio said involuntarily.

"What did you think they were going to do, once they caught me?" she demanded. "Tie me up and lecture me? Feed me drugs to calm me and bring me back to sanity? Then what? They'd never have let me leave their custody, son. Not after what I've done. They'd never have trusted me to walk free. No. They would have killed me, in the end. That was the only path they had in mind."

Idisio scrubbed both hands over his face, shaking his head. "No," he said again. "Stop that. I know what you're doing. Stop it."

"I'm telling you the truth," she said.

"You're twisting the truth," he retorted. "Deiq didn't want you to die. He wanted to save you. To bring you back to sanity. That's what they all wanted."

She smiled, tilting her head a bit. "You're a romantic," she said. "You're a human-raised romantic. But I won't go back to Bright Bay, so what will you do when I slip again?"

Idisio stared at her, appalled by her matter-of-fact tone. "You can fight it," he blurted.

"No," she said. "I can't." Her grey eyes flooded with tears. "It hurts," she whispered. "What Rosin did to me–I'll never be free of that pain. I'll never be able to control that rage."

He swallowed hard, his own eyes damp. "Then you have to stop it," he said. "You have to end it. The pain, the anger, all of it."

She cocked her head to one side, frowning at him. "How do I do that?"

He dropped his hand to the hilt of the long Scratha dagger; drew and tossed it, in a careful, underhanded lob, onto the bed beside her. "This is the only way left that I can think of," he said.

She stared at the dagger as though she'd never seen one before, then looked up at him. "This is another vision, isn't it?" she said, her voice eerily flat. "This is another trick of Rosin's. I almost believed it, do you know that? But my son would never do this to me."

Idisio shook his head. "This is real, mother," he said, the words thick in his throat. "Rosin is dead. You're out in the real world now. No visions. No games. No tricks. It's true. I'm really here, and–"

"And you really want me to kill myself," she said. An unsettling dark ring formed around her pale grey irises. He found himself sitting on the floor again, and fought the urge to put an arm up as a shield against that fierce glare. "After all I've explained, after all the effort I've put into making you understand what we are, you think suicide is the best option for me? Because I hurt a few stupid *humans*? Son, as fast as they breed, they won't even notice the loss. In less than a hundred years, they'll have forgotten all about it."

"What about Kolan?" he said, desperate.

"What *about* him?" She swung her legs to sit on the edge of the bed again, then rose, ominously slow, to tower over him. "He's as meaningless as the rest of them. Do you think your stupid little whispers affected *me*? I'm not that weak, son. Not after what I've been through. I let you think you'd influenced me only because I wanted to see what you would do. I wanted to know what kind of son I have. Now I know. You're no better than Rosin. You want to control me to what you consider righteous. And when you can't bend me to your will, you'd have me kill myself for being what I truly am, what you won't allow *yourself* to be."

She stood over him, a chill in her colorless eyes that had nothing to do with her usual raging madness.

"I survived Rosin," she said softly. "I'll survive this. Oh, I won't kill you. I won't break the Law. Go on your way, little boy, and I'll go on mine. I don't need you, and neither does Arason; you wouldn't be up to the responsibility after all. Better that you never go there. Better that your father never finds out what a failure you've turned out to be."

She began to turn her back on him, then paused and swung around to look him in the eye.

"But before I go," she said, "you're going to learn something from me that you'll never learn from those friends of yours. Something your precious Deiq is far too afraid to show you. I'm going to give you a glimpse of who you really are; of what you really are, and of what *freedom* ought to mean to you."

"Oh, gods–" he said involuntarily. "Don't–"

"There are no gods, little boy," she said, her eyes darkening rapidly. "There never were any gods. There's only ever been the ha'reye–and us."

A heartbeat later, the world around him went sharply away, swallowed up into the solid black of her eyes.

Chapter Seventy-One

Tank rode through the token gate at the eastern edge of Bright Bay well after dark without challenge: the single, sleepy guard perched on a stool by the road barely glanced up as he passed. But the easternmost of the Seventeen Gates, not surprisingly, had been shut for the night, and the guards there were wide awake and less than helpful.

"I've a message for Deiq of Stass," Tank said, dismounting so as to stand at an even level with their stares. "For Lord Alyea. I'm bound for the Peysimun residence. Urgent."

They looked at him sideways, taking in the sweat, dirt, and exhausted horse. "Can't wait for morning?" the tallest asked, skeptical.

"*No*," he said. "Send a messenger to tell them I'm here. Tell them I've a message from Idisio. *Urgent*. I'll wait. Just *tell them*."

"You're not a News-Rider," the man said slowly, pondering. "They've got rights to go through any time of day or night. But you–"

"Send the damn messenger!"

"I'd be more inclined to help if you showed any couth at all," the man said stiffly.

"I'd be more mannerly if *you* showed any wits," Tank retorted.

They glared at one another.

"I'll send a runner," the tall guard said at last. "But I'll warn you–if he comes back with word that you're not welcome, you'll find yourself in a cell for the night as a reminder to cool your temper when speaking to your betters."

Tank managed–just–to refrain from observing that he didn't see where the guard was in any way his *better*. "Send the runner," he said instead. "I'll wait."

Shaking his head as though he'd heard or guessed at the unspoken bit, the tall man motioned to his companion and said, "Go wake one of the runners."

Tank stood beside his horse, ignoring the dark glares the tall guard kept aiming at him. His entire body ached; the nap in Obein and Kybeach hadn't done much against his overriding exhaustion.

At last, a messenger sprinted toward them.

"Let him through," he panted. "Hurry, Lord Eredion said, let him through. I'll take him back."

Tank hauled himself back onto his weary horse, pulled the messenger up behind him, and left the damnfool gate guards behind as quickly as Sin could manage.

The streets stretched too long, too dark, and far, far too quiet. The clack of Sin's hooves echoed. The few people moving about cast disapproving glares as he went by. Once, a patrol of white-garbed guards moved into his path; the messenger leaned around Tank and waved something that fluttered in Tank's peripheral vision. The guards stepped aside.

The Seventeen Gates made a vast circle, and the streets inside the majestic fence echoed that form. After that observation, details and time alike blurred into an incomprehensible mass of movement and pressure.

"Hey," the messenger said out of the haze, and delivered a sharp prod to Tank's ribs. "Don't go pitching off on me, we're coming to the Peysimun gates. Wake up!"

Tank shook his head and forced the world back into its proper shape and size as they rode through a set of tall black metal gates and across a wide courtyard.

A fountain splashed, nearly invisible in the torchlit darkness, and the scent of jasmine and night-blooming roses drifted through the air.

"Ride over there. That's it, stop here." The messenger slid off the gelding before it had even stopped moving. Tank followed more slowly.

"Up there," the messenger said, taking the reins. "See, he's waiting for you, that man there on the steps. That's Lord Eredion."

One look warned Tank to go more rather than less formal: while Lord Eredion's clothes were rumpled as though he'd been sleeping in them, still the cut and material were finer than anything Venepe had sold, and the man's broad, dark face–and title–spoke of southern nobility.

"My lord," Tank said, "Lif–Idisio sent me."

Lord Eredion's face tightened: confirmation that the name meant something to him.

"Idisio," Tank repeated, knees weak with relief, then fought to remember what he had to say to this elegantly dressed man. "He's in Sandsplit. With his mother."

Another deepening of the fine lines etched into Lord Eredion's stern face.

Words ran past his control and turned to babble. The world began to spin around him. He drew in a sharp breath and forced himself steady.

"She's going to hurt him," he said, trying for clarity. "I know she is–" and exhaustion turned his words into a meaningless slurry in his own ears. He hauled himself silent, not at all sure what he'd just said.

His legs–and his consciousness–gave way underneath him a moment later.

He awoke to cream-pale walls and the shifting of early morning sunlight through fine glass windows. The scent of gardenias hung in the air, and the bed under him was softer by far than anything he'd ever rested on before. He lay still, disoriented; at last, memory sorted itself out, and he sat up–too quickly: his head swam, and he nearly pitched off the bed before he caught his bearings.

A moment later, the door opened and a familiar figure slipped into the room. Wian stopped, biting her lip, on seeing him already awake and sitting up; then, shyly, advanced and set a neatly folded stack of clothes on a chair near the bed.

"They might be a little large," she said, "but they're clean. I–guessed at the size." Her face tinted, turning a palette of relatively fresh bruises into a mottled mess. "Your clothes are being cleaned, and I thought you'd like something–a little nicer. While you're here."

Tank glanced down, realizing for the first time that whatever servant had put him to bed had stripped off all his clothes in the process. He looked up, already wincing. Wian was studying the floor, her face bright crimson.

"There's a–shortage of servants here, just now," she said. "I've been–helping out." She ducked her head, backing up two steps, then turned and left the room.

Tank let out a long breath, not sure if he should be relieved. At least she wasn't likely to gossip over what she'd seen. Unless it gave her a benefit, he corrected himself wryly; and realized that her embarrassment had been entirely feigned. He sighed and reached for the clothes.

Someone–probably, again, Wian–had made an effort to wipe most of the trail dirt from his riding boots, but they still clashed with the more elegant trousers and shirt. The shirt hung a bit loose over the shoulders, and the trousers ran generous in the leg, but they'd do for a day. His belt and pouch didn't look entirely idiotic against the outfit, as far as he could tell. He didn't particularly care if others disagreed–he never went anywhere without his belt pouch near to hand. Just in case.

That done, hair brushed out and secured into a triple-bound tail, he looked around, uncertain as to the next step. If his clothes were being cleaned, that implied an invitation to stay at least for another day; and he didn't have enough spare sets to abandon any lightly. Dasin wouldn't catch up with him until tomorrow at the earliest, and while there were other things he could do in Bright Bay, none, at the moment, seemed as appealing as climbing back onto that wonderfully soft bed and going back to sleep for a while longer.

His stomach suggested other ideas.

He cast a wistful glance back at the bed, then shrugged and opened the door. Wian–of course–stood in the hallway, waiting for him. As he stepped out of the room, she cast her gaze to the floor.

"*S'e* Tank," she murmured.

He regarded her with a mixture of bemusement and annoyance, and said, "Wian, stop it."

She straightened and met his gaze, but her shoulders shifted as though uncomfortable with that directness.

"Sorry," she said. "I want you to think well of me."

"Putting on fake ways won't do that," Tank said. "Something to eat around here?"

She hesitated, then nodded and said, stiffly, "This way."

Very probably she'd wanted or expected him to ask after how she came to be here, and whether she'd escaped Seavorn's tender care. Tank grinned at her back as they walked and kept his silence.

"You saved my life, you know," she said over her shoulder after a few steps.

Tank deliberately misunderstood, hoping to keep things dry. "By kicking Dasin off you? Naw, he wouldn't have gone that far–"

She turned to face him, real color flaring in her face. "No," she said. "By listening. By–by caring. It was the first time someone treated me–*right*–in a long time."

She paused, as though expecting a response. He shrugged, not sure how to steer her away from the maudlin speech he could sense coming, particularly as he suspected it wouldn't be entirely genuine.

"I've been thinking it over," she said, crossing her arms and not, to Tank's relief, in the least soppy. "And it wasn't only that you were decent. It was–like you *knew* me, knew all about the worst of me, and you accepted it. Like it didn't matter to you. And I thought about the nightmare, and how you listened to me tell it, and I remembered you said something. I got stuck on a word, and you said it for me. But you couldn't have known."

"It was an easy guess," Tank said, glancing away.

"No," she said. "See–I know how to spot a lie, myself. You didn't guess. You *knew*. As though you'd–seen–the dream. And it seemed to me that I'd–felt–someone beside me, during that nightmare, that night; someone watching alongside me. And I think it was you."

Tank glanced along the hallway, suddenly anxious–and not only because her tone had begun to waver from matter-of-fact to emotion-laden. "Not so loud–"

"There–see?" Wian said. "It *was* you!"

"Was or wasn't, doesn't matter," Tank said. "Talk like that and you'll get me hung as a witch."

She laughed. "Not so much, these days," she said, her tone steadying back to dry cynicism. "Not in King Oruen's court, and with all the desert lords parading about Bright Bay these days."

"It's not all that safe out on the Coast Road yet," he said, "and gossip flies faster than a horse gallops. So if you don't mind, drop that talk. I don't see where it matters, anyway."

"It matters because it changed me," she said. "It made me realize that you were right. I can change *my* part in the world. I can change *my* life. *You* did."

She paused again, her dark eyes searching his face for reaction: he gave her his best blank stare in return.

He wasn't about to explain how he'd done it. He had no intention of telling her that Allonin had bought him out of a katha village and invested considerable time and effort in breaking him from that mindset. Had no interest in pointing out that it had taken a team of ketarch healers and the teachings of an old woman who wasn't, in Tank's retrospective opinion, nearly as simple as she'd seemed at the time—in short, if not for the hard work of a number of dedicated people over the course of months and years—*he* wouldn't have changed one bit.

Except in the strictly physical sense: because by now, he'd have been dead. So it wasn't at his feet that the change ought to be laid, but to Aerthraim efforts, much as he hated to admit it—and he wouldn't, to her. It wasn't any of her concern, and her efforts to change herself weren't any of his.

She went on in spite of his lack of reaction: "I begged sanctuary from the king. He granted it. And now—well, Seavorn's dead, and Kippin's on the run, and I have a chance at starting over. Because of you. Because you *listened.*"

Tank shrugged, deeply uncomfortable. The only thing he could think of to say was *So what do you want from me now, then?*; which seemed tactless at best and an invitation to emotional ranting at worst.

In the distance, something smashed. Wian jerked, her attention focusing on that noise, then grabbed Tank's wrist and cried, "This way!"

He let her drag him into a dead run; managed to jerk his wrist free after the second turn, but by then he was so hopelessly lost that following her seemed the safest course.

Gaudy, intricate decorations caught Tank's eye as they ran: a spray of long, crimson feathers, their quills dipped in fine silver, arced along one wall. A mosaic of moon-silk shell pieces, each smaller and thinner than Tank's littlest fingernail, glittered along another. He slowed to take a second, astonished glance at that as he went by, unable to believe not only the intense amount of craft that had gone into that decoration, but that someone had spent so much time building something so useless.

"Come *on,*" Wian called. She'd stopped at the last door in a long hallway and was waving him forward.

"This isn't the kitchens, is it?" he said, knowing it for a stupid comment. She ignored him and pushed through the door. Moments later, someone screamed from within: a woman, tortured and fierce.

"She's awake!" Wian cried.

Something else crashed. Someone swore. Wian yelped.

Tank went through the outer room, compelled, impelled by something he had no words for. Not Wian—no. There was a *smell* in the air, tantalizing, vague, *demanding*—

The door to the inner room of the suite hung half-open. Tank saw glimpses of movement through it, and heard another heartrending scream. Sense said *Walk away* and *Not my business*; something more reckless and primal drove him to peer through the doorway.

A tall, dark-haired woman marked by a horrifying array of bruises, cuts, and weals stood, naked, in the middle of the room. Lord Eredion and a strange dark-skinned man, both fully dressed, stood against the walls to either side of her. Glass fragments were scattered across the floor by their feet.

Wian knelt before the woman, dazed, hand to her head; surrounded by more broken glass and shards of pottery. Blood trickled down her neck.

"Gods damn it, Alyea!" Lord Eredion said. "We're not going to hurt you! Deiq, can't you–"

"She's too fragile," the other man said. "There's nothing for me to grab hold of. She's still raving with dasta."

Dasta–the word set off an unexpected cascade of connections and memories. Tank's vision went hazy, tremors rippling through his muscles; he fisted his hands, fighting the all-too-familiar feeling: the beginning of a fit.

He couldn't move. Couldn't even reach for the belt pouch with the all-important *chich* sticks. A sharp whine began to build in the back of his head, emerged as a broken whimper: somewhere distant, someone cried, "Get out of here, you idiot!"

Another voice said something about *helping* and *Tank*.

He tried to shake his head, not understanding: *Tank* meant nothing to him, *helping* was a word without a meaning–all that existed was the *pain*, the *fear*, the *anger*–

The dark-haired woman turned and looked at him, looked *through* him, looked *into* him.

I see you, she said.

Her mouth didn't move. The words unrolled directly into his mind, a series of language-images that wove through the mist, pushing it aside, locking his attention wholly onto her.

I see you. I can't see anything else–where am I? What's happening to me? Why am I so angry? Why are **you** *so angry?*

He opened his mouth to say *I don't know* to at least one of the questions. Before he could form the first breath of sound, he felt her shove aside the mist for a better look at his anger–

Glass crunched under his knees. A howl ripped from his throat. His childhood rose behind his eyes in a flurry of images he'd worked for years to forget. Defiance and rage shoved her back with feral strength:

GodsdamnitIdonotwanttolookatthat–and you have no right–*no! Enough. Stop. Get* out!

She sucked in a shattered-sounding breath and cried out without words: images unrolled into his mind, a series of crystalline moments from her own memories–

–her head snapped to one side so hard she saw stars . . . He'd almost broken her neck with the blow–

–Cabe, kill them . . . A sharp blade, a gout of blood . . . Thick perfume, sweet-sick, the world going black . . . Waking to blue and white curtains and a familiar stare–

He didn't know the man she showed him, but he knew that stare, oh gods yes, he knew that look: the look of someone who was *curious*, gods help him, *curious* as to what would happen if he bent a boy's pinky finger *just so* or laid a hot iron *just there*–

Ohholygodsno–Idon'twanttoseethis–no–please–

The images rolled on, unstoppable as a sandstorm, eroding the boundaries he'd built between past and present, destroying his self and turning him into an amalgamation of *alyea/tank/littlered*–

–her defiance: *Just kill me . . .* dryly amused answer: *Oh, no, no . . . That's silly. And no fun at all . . .* her temper, blazing back: *Go fuck yourself! . . .* a sentiment *littlered/tank* empathized with completely–

–*branded . . . I've got my own scars . . . so what?* Only it wasn't *so what*, not now, not with her pain ripping open the closed doors he'd long ago, with Allonin and Teilo's help, locked tight and sealed, so he'd thought, forever–forever *safe*, forever *normal*, forever *notthatpersonanymore*–

Pressure. Warmth. She was in his arms now, weeping uncontrollably; he'd come to his feet at some point. Something tickled his knees with a feathery touch. Ignoring that, he wrapped his arms around her, even as his own pain/ rage screamed *Throw her across the room, get her away, get clear, run, run,* run–

–then his rage was subsumed in her own, and the pain-memories kept unrolling–

–*she tried to punch out . . . to spring, to claw,* anything–

–*littlered, limp, helpless against that different face wearing the same detached, amused stare . . . You don't have to take the dasta every time,* Tan said. *Palm it. Dump it on the floor and kick dirt over it . . . But then what they do will hurt more,* littlered said . . . *So?* Tan said. *You'll be awake. You'll be yourself . . . Pain isn't that important. Being awake, being alive,* is.

–*hold her, Tevin*–

–*a thick miasma of rosemary and garlic*–Tank gagged on the memory of that smell, staggering back to a dizzying awareness of the room around him: from the boots on his feet to the dawn light frosting the drapes to the severe glares of two men nearby, at least one of whom raw instinct demanded he run from *immediately*–

–and back into the swirling maelstrom of shared/tangled memories once more–

One thread of the agony, at least, he understood, could do something about, could *grasp*: dasta. He worked a trembling hand free and pawed into his belt pouch until his fingers wrapped around a thick stick of *chich*; pulled it out, heedless of spilling anything else from the pouch, simply not caring about anything but getting some fraction of their shared pain to *stop*.

He nudged her chin with a knuckle–*Trust me, trust me, this will help*–slipped the chich into her mouth, told her to chew, keep chewing, *keep chewing*–

The trembling, sharp urgency faded. She sagged, locked muscles releasing all at once. He staggered as he scooped her up. The weight brought the tick-ling in his knees to a flare of bright, new pain, finally identifiable: he'd landed on the broken glass earlier. His knees were badly cut.

But pain didn't matter. It never really had.

There was a soft bed a few steps away, one she attached a sense of *safety* to; he lurched the short distance and let the mattress take her weight from him. Tried to back away, to regain a separation of self, head still spinning: *No, don't leave me alone,* she said, fiercely commanding.

With no defenses left against her, he gave up and let himself press into the mattress, her warmth solidly tucked up along his torso and legs, her hair in his nose. Her scent was thick with pain-sweat and old blood and–*other*–odors. If he could have moved he would have rolled away and bolted from that alone, but his body simply refused to so much as twitch, every muscle exhausted, every old scar and bruise and brand aching, and her pain writhing through him—

    —a knife, sliding under the skin, delicate, twisting, lifting, peeling—

    Stop, he said, summoning everything he had for that command. *Stop. It's over. No point going back over it. Let it* stop.

    She pulled in a long, shuddering breath; let it out; slid, unstoppable, over the edge into complete black unconsciousness, dragging him along into the relief of oblivion.

Chapter Seventy-Two

Idisio walked in a grey haze, only dimly aware of his surroundings: evening had melted into true night, blurring shadows into solids and solids into uncertainties. Sandsplit seemed a place of ambiguities and mystery; bushes became mystical shapes that spoke of hidden secrets, the chill air bristled with intriguing aromas, and the ground underfoot seemed less a definite surface than a convenient suggestion.

He wondered if he could sink down into the ground, walk through dirt and rock as though they were as permeable as air.

Of course you can, someone whispered; it sounded almost like the familiar voice of his intuition, but seemed much clearer—and carried an oddly feminine tenor. *But not right now. That's not important right now. Keep going . . . .*

He obeyed the prompting, trusting the voice as he'd always trusted his intuition. A stately cottage with a brick path curving around it seemed familiar: he paused some distance away, studying it with interest.

I've been there before, he thought hazily. *With . . . with someone else.* A sensation of chill damp, the smell of mud—a ripple of darkness and fear—flittered across his mind, then faded into irrelevance. That didn't matter either.

He circled the cottage, the intuition-voice steering him in a steadily narrowing spiral; found himself reversing as gradually, until he stood well away from the building once more.

So someone here knows about our presence, the voice said. *Look closely—right there, and there—*

Idisio focused: a thread-thin, shimmering line traced along the ground all the way around the cottage.

That's a ward-line, the voice said. *It's a general one, to turn away all our kind.*

It's drawn with foul substances and no real skill; I could break it easily. I should punish this fool for his impertinence—barring us! He has no right to stop us going anywhere we wish to walk. But that can wait. Right now, I have an important lesson to teach you. This way . . . .

Idisio moved through night-quiet streets. Humans passed by, oblivious to his presence; guided by the voice, he let them be. Common laborers, shop-keepers, housewives: they weren't what he was after. They weren't . . . *interesting* enough.

This way . . . .

At the edge of Sandsplit, a small cottage stood alone, separated from its nearest neighbor by a wide border of garden rows and hedges. Smoke came from the chimney, firelight and lanternlight limned the shuttered windows: it was a tidy house, a quiet spot, a respectable place.

Here, the voice said. *Listen. Listen closely . . . .*

Idisio put his hand to the whitewashed brick of the wall and closed his eyes, focusing: a swirl of motion, the faint scrape and splat of footsteps, a kettle being stirred, a fire being prodded brighter.

One human. A woman. Young.

Alone.

Listen, the voice said again. *Listen, more closely yet. Listen to her.*

Idisio blinked and splayed his hand out more widely across the brick, then shut his eyes again.

Satisfaction: she could take care of the house, as her mother had taught her. *Mother would be proud of me.* As her father would be, when he came home. *When will he be home? It's been so long. I hope nothing's happened to him on the way.* She wouldn't worry over it. Each day brought what each day brought, and there was nothing to be done about it. *Turn the lantern up a bit, there's mending yet to be done—always something to keep busy with, have to keep busy.*

Wistful: The hope-day dance last night. *I wish I'd gone.* But her father had said to stay away from such things unless she had a chaperone along, and cousin Behe was off to Sandlaen Port for something or another, and Father was off to Bright Bay for his business—*He said he'd be back by hope-day. He promised. I shouldn't worry. I shouldn't. But . . . he's never been this delayed before.*

Lonely: Nobody to talk to. *I'd so like to go walking out with someone. Even Nenea has that young man from Obein who visits her on occasion. But everyone is too busy . . . and I'm not so interesting or attractive as to make up for our lack of money or status. Nobody will look my way—certainly not when I'm hardly allowed to go out and meet anyone! If Father's business does better this trip, perhaps . . . I wonder where he is. Oh, I shouldn't worry over him. But it is so very, very quiet here. What I'd give for someone to talk to . . . .*

Idisio felt a sigh ghosting through his mind. *Yes,* the intuition-voice whispered. *This is what you're looking for. This one will do. Knock on the door.*

As he approached the door, an odd *shifting* took place inside him, a sensation like a pin being slid from the hinges of a gate. He paused, blinking: the world around him seemed, infinitesimally, different. Sharper. Louder. More . . . *real.*

Never mind, the voice told him. *Knock.*

The wood trembled under his knuckles; he winced and lightened up on the next few raps.

The door opened. The girl stared out at him, more attractive than she saw herself: long brown hair, neatly plaited back into a heavy braid; hazel eyes; a northern-sharp nose and high forehead. She had just enough by way of curves to show gender but no more, and her plain blue dress made no attempt to draw attention to what was there.

"Good evening, s'e," she said, polite and wary all at once, one foot casually wedged behind the door.

"Good evening, s'a," he said, bowing a little, and found himself caught in a dizzying moment of confusion over what to say next. Then words spilled out: "I have news from your father. He's been delayed somewhat in Bright Bay, and asked me to stop in and speak to you on my way through Sandsplit."

She smiled but didn't move, her gaze still watchful. "That's kind of you, s'e," she said. Her thoughts came through as clearly as speech: *So he knows I'm alone; but Father would never send a young man to our door while he was away. Not without giving him the pass phrase we've arranged.*

The pass phrase came to Idisio with the faintest nudge: *chachad bird feathers.* Something about that amused him, but he couldn't think of why. He said, smiling easily, "He's doing very well with his business, he'll be bringing back a fine profit, and he'll be bringing back some of those chachad bird feathers you asked for."

She stared a moment, then her smile relaxed.

"Come in, s'e," she said. "I've a kettle on for tea."

"Thank you, s'a, that would be a treat," he said, and followed her in, careful to leave her plenty of space. *Careful now*, intuition-voice warned. *Don't scare her. You want her trust.*

A strange, stifled voice asked *Why? What am I doing here? Why am I lying to her?* —then damped into silence as Idisio settled into a ornate, stiff-backed, and thinly padded chair.

He sat with his eyes half-closed, listening to the girl's movements as she filled the teapot and brought a tray to the sitting room table in front of him. A vague impulse to study the room passed through him and faded: his surroundings weren't important at the moment. Only the girl mattered.

She sat on the edge of the couch, a matching piece to his chair that looked just as uncomfortable, and poured tea with a trembling hand; a tiny tremor, but he saw it clearly. She was nervous and excited by the odd situation, trying to act very adult against a surge of adolescent anxiety.

Perfect, intuition-voice purred.

"You keep a lovely home, s'a," Idisio said, smiling. He leaned forward to take the proffered cup of tea from her hand before she had a chance to set it on the table and slide it toward him. He put his hand palm up a handspan under the cup, then curled his fingers to grip the small vessel from beneath. Flustered and confused by the impropriety, she nearly dropped the cup into his hand. He held still, allowing her to retreat, before leaning back into his chair and taking a measured sip of tea.

She grabbed up her own cup with a rattled lack of grace, managing—just—not to spill the entire thing onto herself in the process of getting it to her mouth.

Idisio sat very still and waited for her to recover her poise, his expression neutral and his gaze aimed at his knees. After a few moments, she cleared her throat and said, "I'm sorry, *s'e*, I've been rude. No doubt my father told you my name–" She paused, one eyebrow arching: another test.

"Of course, *s'a* Enia," Idisio said easily. "And I'm Idisio. I met your father at the Copper Kettle; we breakfasted together, by chance, and when he found out I was headed this way he asked me to carry the message to you that he was delayed. Said it would save him the cost of a News-Rider message."

The stifled voice nagged at him, asking what the hells he was doing; he shrugged it off. It was simple to pick what he needed from her topical thoughts and a fascinating game to adapt his tone and pacing to the tiny cues she didn't even know she was sending.

She smiled, relaxing again. "That's my father," she agreed. "Always looking to save some money. But they've been hard years of late, so it's hard to blame him for watching the bits."

"That's likely to change, from what he told me." Idisio leaned forward and set his empty cup down on the table; flattened his hand over it when she reached to pour him another. "Tea's not really my drink of choice," he said. "This was lovely, *s'a* Enia, but it was enough."

"Oh–" She glanced at the sideboard. "We've wine . . . ." He gave no reaction. "And . . . well, I don't know, it's a bit rough for a gentleman, but my father always keeps some desert lightning to hand . . . ."

Her thoughts ran through Idisio's mind: *I hope he doesn't ask for that. I'd have to drink it with him: the host drinks what the guest drinks. But Father never lets me drink anything stronger than wine . . . . Oh, dear. I wish Father was here. I'm not at all sure I'm getting this right.*

"Desert lightning sounds perfect," Idisio said, then put contrition into his tone: "But surely it's too strong for you, *s'a*?"

Color flushed along her high cheekbones, then faded. "I'll cut it with a bit of tea, for myself," she said. "If you've no objection, *s'e*."

"Of course, and I'll do the same," he said. "And I won't trouble you past the one cup, at that. I wouldn't want to outstay my welcome. But let me pour this time, if you would, *s'a*." He rose, collected her cup and his own, and went to the sideboard. "I'm guessing it's this white jug, here?"

Narrow-necked and tall, the glazed earthenware vessel hardly deserved to be called a "jug"; but Enia's thoughts put that as the proper name for any vessel holding hard liquor, no matter the shape. *This bottle is teyanain-crafted*, Idisio thought, and felt momentarily dizzy. The world steadied around him quickly enough that he gave no external sign of his disorientation as he poured the clear liquid into the cups. The fumes made his eyes water.

Good gods what am I thinking ran through the back of his mind, then dissolved like the vapors rising from the cups.

As he wrapped his hand around her cup, he delicately strengthened the potency of the double spoonful of liquor he'd poured. Not so much as to incapacitate her; just enough to relax her more than such a small amount normally would.

You don't want her unconscious, intuition-voice said. *That's no fun at all.*

He set the cups down on the table and retreated to his chair without making eye contact; allowed her to pour the tea, and picked up his own cup properly this time, after she'd sat back away from the table.

They sat in silence for a few moments, sipping their drinks: Idisio could sense Enia's anxiety returning as she tried to think of something socially appropriate to say to this strange visitor her father had sent as messenger. She didn't want this handsome young man to think her an unschooled bumpkin, but what passed for manners in Sandsplit might be entirely different from what Bright Bay nobility considered acceptable. And surely this young man, with his considerable poise and courtly mannerisms, must be some sort of noble. It would make sense for her father to trust someone of note as a messenger, after all . . . .

They do so much of the work for you, the intuition-voice whispered, dark with amusement. Enia's mind was so filled with ticking over points of proper behavior that Idisio had a wealth of information to draw upon.

"Enia," Idisio said softly. She blinked, shivering a little, and stared at him with wide eyes. "You don't have to say anything at all. It won't offend me to sit in quiet for a bit. You're very good company, without a word spoken."

She swallowed, her eyes going even wider, and seemed to have trouble breathing. To cover her confusion, she gulped down the rest of her drink without pause.

He sipped his more leisurely, allowing her to realize her mistake on her own: *the host never finishes a drink or meal before the guest.* She sat gripping her cup, blinking hard, visibly trying to decide what to do; he smiled at her, then rose and moved around the table to take her cup from her hand.

"That's all right," he said. He set both cups on the table and sat down on the couch a careful arm's-length from her. "I'm not so easily offended. Why don't you stop worrying about propriety? It's really not so important, after all."

Each sentence carried a slightly stronger persuasive nudge; that, coupled with the enhanced desert lightning swirling through her, brought her shoulders down into a more relaxed pose and a flush to her cheeks.

"Oh, I suppose I am being silly," she said. "It's only that I'm sure Father expects me to set a good example for a guest."

"I'm sure he does," Idisio said. "But you are setting an excellent example, s'a. You've nothing to worry about. Nothing at all."

He put a hand out, palm-up, with the last words; she laid her fingers across his without hesitation, then flinched a bit. He held still, keeping his smile gentle, and she slowly relaxed; just as gradually, he curled his hand, enclosing her fingers, pulling her toward him with the lightest possible tug.

Even a young human male would have difficulty staying faithful, someone said: a masculine voice amid an echo-vague memory of distress and confusion. It faded before he had a chance to grasp it properly, and instantly seemed irrelevant.

Enia leaned forward by fractional angles. He eased himself closer by tiny increments.

Are you saying I'm some kind of animal? That I won't be able to control–his own voice, this time, laden with rage and panic.

"S'e–" Enia drew in a deep breath. "I think–I'm sorry–" Her face was flushed and her eyes bright with a conflicting mixture of nervousness and liquor; she began to lean away from him.

"Call me Idisio," he said, his grip firm around her hand. "And you have nothing to be sorry about."

"Idisio," she said, pausing in her retreat. "I don't feel quite–right, I'm afraid. I should really–"

He brushed the fingertips of his free hand against her forehead. "You're a bit warm," he said, "but I don't know that you're *ill*, exactly." He caught her eye and smiled. This time, he made it powerful instead of reassuring.

Color flushed all the way down her neck. Her breathing went ragged.

"Idisio," she whispered, and came the rest of the way into his arms.

Once more, there came a strange shifting sensation in his mind, as though another pin were being slid from the hinges: and a thick heat began to fill his lower stomach.

Some kind of animal . . . .

No, the intuition-voice said. *The physical desire is nothing. It's easily controlled. It's only useful as a way to distract her while you reach for what you really want.*

A distant part of his mind shrieked in horror: *What the hells am I doing?* The growing heat scorched the cry into a dried-out, faintly crackling shell of itself. Enia's increasingly loud and rapid breathing drowned out any remnants of his own inner protest.

His hands moved across her body. She moaned and tipped her head back, all defenses gone: thinking of nothing, open to every sensation he evoked in her. He hooked a finger into the neckline of her dress and tugged lightly. The fabric seemed to simply unravel out of the way of his finger, leaving her sprawled across his lap in nothing but a pale linen shift.

She had no thoughts of resistance or impropriety left; lay with eyes half-shut, breathing hard, waiting to see what he would do next.

Look closely, intuition-voice whispered. *Look very closely. Not at her physical body; that's a shell. See what's inside and beyond the physical.*

His vision shifted: now he saw a writhing network of multicolored lines laced throughout flesh and bone, swirling, pooling, streaking in hypnotic chaos. In the midst of that chaos lay a single steady, unmoving dark spot; a tiny, dense blotch that seemed, in this new vision, like a keystone in an arch. Or a pin in a hinge.

At that thought, Idisio felt another shifting, sliding sensation inside himself: one last pin pulled out of the final hinge. His vision flared white, broken only by a single dark, immensely *solid* point of importance.

Reaching that spot, touching that spot, *possessing* that spot, was the only thing that mattered now. The heat of physical desire was spent ashes against this overriding, overpowering need; and the spot was so close, so easy to just–grip–

He closed himself around the spot and found it to be at once tiny and vast, thin and wide, flat and depthless. Touching it ran liquid sunshine through his veins and a heat beyond belief blasting through his entire being. He pulled the spot into himself, engulfed it, drank it in, bathed in it, rolled it around himself like a blanket–

Somewhere, someone was screaming, shrill and agonized and piercing. He barely heard it, lost in the explosive ecstasy of the experience: beyond the joy of any physical encounter he'd ever had, beyond any sensation even Riss's best efforts had been able to–

Riss.

The name set off a cascade of suppressed memory, shattering his fierce joy into a steadily rising mountain of horror. A heartbeat later, the piercing shrieks cut off into a broken, gurgling hiss: a death rattle.

He slammed back to his senses with the force of having fallen off a Horn cliff; choked, gagging on his own breath, his vision swimming and blurred.

Now you know, son, his mother said, icy and distant. *Now you understand what it is to be ha'ra'hain. So go back to your humans and see if you can look any of them in the eye without thinking how good it would feel to do that again.*

His vision cleared as her presence faded from his mind. He looked down at Enia's limp body, still sprawled across his lap; at her sightless eyes, a trickle of blood working its way from each one. Another thread of blood ran from her nose, and her mouth was filled with blood, her tongue nearly bitten in half.

Idisio sat still, staring at her, his mind comprehensively blank with shock.

Deiq's voice rose in memory: *We're not so different, Idisio. Not nearly.*

Deiq's dark sarcasm, his thinly restrained temper, took on a whole new significance. *He's fighting against–doing this–all the time–Holy gods. Why didn't he tell me–no. I wouldn't have understood or believed him. Not without–this–Oh, dear and merciful gods.*

I killed her. I killed her.

His vision sharpened: he watched as the colorful lines laced throughout Enia's body died away to a vague grey tracery. Dust motes sparkled across his vision. He saw the tiny diamond patterns in the skin of her hand; narrowed vision and watched cells dying one by one, blood settling slowly to the lowest point, muscles relaxing and relaxing into complete flaccidity.

Shuddering with abrupt revulsion, he jerked himself out from underneath her, toppling her lifeless body onto the couch like a discarded rag doll; yielded to panic and bolted from the cottage.

Chill air struck his face, slapping him from panic into an unexpected rage: *My mother did this to me. She made me into a killer, into a monster. She did this to me.*

She has to pay for what she's done. She has to be stopped. If she can do this to me–to her own son–no. No more. Never again.

He lifted his head and sniffed the air: her scent hung clear and strong. She hadn't bothered to hide her trail. He'd find her easily.

And when he did–he wouldn't use whispers to settle what now lay between them.

He checked to be sure that the long Scratha dagger was in its sheath at his side—he must have picked it up before leaving their inn room on that horrific, deadly quest—then broke into a hunting run.

Chapter Seventy-Three

Tank moved through a mixture of dream, memory, and trance: walked through the halls of a world his/not his, engulfed in a bizarre, blurry-edged clarity. Alyea walked at his side, her hand in his: that firm grip served as his one solid point of reference, the one reassurance that he wasn't completely lost to reality yet.

Sunlight spilled across a stone-flag floor; the air was warm and humid, and sharply scented with the fierce spices Banna had used in the breakfast dishes. The plates still sat on the side table, contents reduced to crumbs: littlered's mouth still felt warm and greasy from the meal. Across the small in-room dining table from him, a lean man with kind dark eyes smiled, watching littlered with a fond possessiveness . . . .

Tank turned sharply away, pulling Alyea with him. *No,* he said. *No. I won't look at that. Please. No.*

Perception spun, another room forming around them: a room with blue curtains, flooded with sunlight as the other had been—but the smells here had nothing to do with kindness and everything to do with pain.

The bed rolled under Alyea, the room spun—then it settled, and she sat up, dazed and shaking; accepted the small cup of tea a dark-haired man handed her, and drank it down, thinking of nothing but the dryness in her throat and the tremors in her stomach. Where am I? she said, barely a whisper, hoarse and cracked: and he smiled. You're where you need to be right now, sweet, he answered. You're where you want to be right now.

Something stirred in her at the sound of his voice: a blind, unreasoning defiance. I don't want to be here, she said. I don't need to be here. Let me go.

Oh, sweet, he replied, we'd miss you so terribly if you left us. I don't think we're ready for that. You're entirely too much fun. And you're having fun, aren't you? You're enjoying this. Admit it . . . .

She glanced down at her naked body: saw a horrifying array of weals and bruises patterned across skin from chest to toes, and knew that more decorated her neck and face. You're insane, *she said, looking back at him, but no emotion came into the words, no conviction, no anger at all: and he laughed at her.*

Alyea stared at that scene with a frozen intensity. Tank pulled her away, pulled her around to face him, to lean against him, intending to shut both their eyes to the madness swirling around them and *rest*—but the motion turned them both around into another sunlit room and a sour smell, this time: sweat from summer's heat, and from a beginning fear:

You're growing up, *the man said, stroking a hand across littlered's bare scalp; he sounded sad, and littlered tried to think of ways to make him happy again.* I won't grow up, if it makes you sad, *he said, but the man laughed a little and said that wasn't possible.* I'll miss you, *he said.* You've been so wonderful. But you're growing up, and Banna doesn't have anyone else that I like right now; so I won't be back here again. You'll have a new friend soon, don't worry. You won't miss me at all.

Littlered cried then, and fear brought a sour sweat to his skin: Tan had said last night that this would happen soon. Littlered hadn't believed it. Hadn't believed the man would ever leave him. But now it was happening. Don't leave me, *he begged.* Take me with you.

The man shook his head, sad and smiling all at once, and pulled littlered into his lap once more . . . .

Alyea's presence pressed against Tank, turning his attention away from the horrified recognition of the reality: he'd allowed himself to remember the pain, because that fueled the rage the Aerthraim had awoken in him, but had comprehensively blocked the earlier times.

The—gods help him—the *good* times.

Yes, Alyea said, close enough to be a part of him now. *That was part of it.* Memory of Kippin laughing, taunting: *You're enjoying this—see? There, and there, you like that, you're not above enjoying yourself—see?*

Tendrils of green and gold laced through their shared vision, bringing a prickling pressure against Tank's chest and groin—*no,* he said, and struck out with everything he had, rage funneling into a tremendous blow—but this time it swept through mist, ineffective, the force spinning them both around into an overlapping weave of memories.

Kippin laughed as Banna glared at littlered; Pieas's sour breath mingled with the reek of a room considerably smaller and less attractive than the sunlit haven of the day before. *Can't pass you off for that crowd any longer,* Banna said. *Time for you to move to the next set.* Her sharp disappointment mingled with Lady Hama Peysimun's sour expression on hearing Alyea's tale of being attacked by a young, drunk southern nobleman. *You shouldn't have been out on your own,* Hama said, even as Banna spoke: *You growing up so fast lost me a good customer.* Littlered didn't understand. Alyea didn't understand. The man had been his *friend*—and she'd been *hurt*—why didn't mother/Banna seem to care?

I'm your friend, Kippin said, stroking the side of their shared face. *I want to make the pain stop, sweet, I truly do. It's so much more fun to watch you enjoying yourself*. And they wanted to ask, desperately wanted to ask, what they had to do to earn the pleasure instead of the pain, because they would do *anything*– but they said nothing, fury cascading into a molten white-out of vision, leaving only raw defiance.

Breathe. Tank rolled sideways into the inner stillness Allonin had drilled into him and Teilo had reinforced with her witchery and her drugs. Allonin– but that was another pain, another shame, another horror: he pushed it away and focused on *breath*. Alyea, unresisting, went with him; *aqeyva* murmured through her mind, along with a similar flinching away from some painful memory of her own. Her discipline melded with his, bringing them into an utterly silent void. They rested in the emptiness, listening to the soft rhythm of pulse and breathing, and little by little the world aligned itself around them in proper tracks. Memory unraveled and faded safely into the past.

Can't change the past, one of them said. *But it doesn't have to matter in the now. And it wasn't your fault, or mine: drugged senseless for the one, never knowing better for the other. That's not who we are now. We have a choice. We can let that go. Let that section go.*

Tank resisted: anger and shame writhing through him, sharp and raw. Alyea resisted, drenched in self-loathing and fury.

Aqeyva. Breathe.

The void soothed away emotion again. They faced one another, drawing in close, closer: *I understand*, they said together; and having one other who truly saw, who truly accepted–was enough. That particular corner of the rage dissolved, slowly, into a grey ash and blew away, dissipating into unimportance.

There was more anger. There always would be. But that one small piece– was gone: and that was enough, for now.

Privacy returned, tiny corners of thought held apart from one another. In one of those solitary pockets ran, very quietly, the thought that this was what Wian, in her inarticulate way, had been striving to say: that Tank had stood beside her in nightmare and accepted, and released her from one small piece of her pain. But he hadn't shared his own, or trusted her in the least. He'd only watched. Not because of her profession: because she hadn't *wanted* to see beyond herself. She'd only wanted to *get*, not to give; while Alyea had brutally yanked out the guts of his agony, laid them beside her own, and forced them both into a bizarre augury: telling the future through the echoes of the past.

Alyea stirred against him, returning from some private contemplation of her own, and said: *Enough. For now, it's enough. Let the next moments take care of themselves.*

Twined together, they descended into the healing peace of true sleep.

Silence and darkness surrounded them, took away emotion, took away fear and pain; after some endless time, they surfaced together into a brighter level of slow-rolling, shared memory-dreams. In a wordless conversation, they shared visions of first times and best times and worst times and unmet needs; began to press together, seeing what would please the other most–

A sharp sound jarred Tank from the relaxed haze of anticipation. Alyea sighed, the moment lost, and slid back toward the deeper void once more, unwilling to follow him to full awareness. Aches returned, along with the pressure of a full bladder: he rolled, eyes barely focused, to seek out the chamberpot that habit insisted would be nearby–*No chamberpot*, Alyea said in a dim haze, *bathroom*–and retreated completely into the obscuring dark.

Tank began to push up on one elbow, surroundings clarifying: a large room, curtains drawn back to allow late-afternoon sunlight through, and a stifling heat barely eased by the open window. *There was an icestorm in Kybeach yesterday*, he thought, baffled by the sharp, prickling sweat he could feel slicking his body; and turning his head to look at the other side of the room, met a gaze as cold as that storm had been.

Dark and depthless, that stare, set in a fine-boned, almond-brown face; sable hair pulled back into a neat, tight triple-bound tail caught close at the base of the skull. The man sat still, solidly placed on the light chair, but in a way that suggested a readiness and capacity for explosively swift movement.

Deiq of Stass: a flurry of images braided through Tank's forebrain as the hindbrain shrieked at him to run. He stared back at the man, frozen like a rat before a riddler-snake, his only conscious thought *Please gods don't let me piss myself–I'll get it all over Alyea–*

"Bathroom's that way," Deiq said, his tone underlaid with a distinct growl of displeasure. Faced with a plausible escape from that increasingly savage glare, Tank nearly bolted for the indicated door.

He stood shivering for some time afterwards, welcoming even the heated stink of the indoor toilet room as more pleasant than returning to face Deiq. The residue of shared memory marked him as simultaneously *dangerous* and *safe*; how Alyea could live with such sharply opposite perceptions of the man, Tank didn't understand.

One thing he could tell without resorting to Alyea's memories as a guide: it would be a bad idea to let Deiq know that Tank had any idea who and what Deiq was. That knowledge would necessarily mark Tank out as far more than a common mercenary; and while the previous–night? day? How long had he slept?–while his encounter with Alyea might have made it difficult to pull off *ordinary* around this man, there was no sense driving the nail further into the block than it already stood.

One thing he *didn't* want to be around this man was a perceived threat. Deiq was the type to simply remove a threat . . . permanently. And while Alyea was still blind to it, Tank could see clearly from her memories of the man that he was more than friendly in his intentions toward her.

Man. Tank breathed deeply and tried not to think of Deiq as anything but that. It wasn't safe to think of him as–

Another segment of Alyea's memories clicked over in his mind. *Idisio. He is ha'ra'ha. So is his mother.* A stark and vivid image of shredded bone and a cottage drenched in human effluvium filled his mind. *Dear gods! And I attacked her with a stick . . . .*

But he couldn't stay in the piss closet forever. Tank drew another breath, settled his pulse and his thoughts into steady order, and returned to the bedroom.

Deiq didn't seem to have moved, but Tank's boots stood beside the small table now, not by the bed. His dark stare tracked Tank's approach, and he tipped his chin in a barely visible gesture toward a second chair.

"Sit," he said.

Tank obeyed without hesitation, deeply grateful that at least there was a table, however small and flimsy, between them. He tugged on his boots with a strong sense of relief; he liked being barefoot, but it felt like a needless vulnerability at the moment. Straightening up, he first perched on the edge of the chair, then, realizing that being anxious was worse than pointless with this man, settled more firmly into the seat, straight-backed. He met Deiq's black gaze squarely.

The man's thin lips twitched: in amusement or irritation, Tank couldn't tell.

"My name," he said, "is Deiq. And you are Tanavin of the Aerthraim."

So much for *ordinary*. Knowing that much meant Deiq knew–everything relevant. And everything dangerous. Tension threading along his muscles, Tank kept his expression blank and said, "I'd rather be called Tank, *s'e*, thanks all the same."

Deiq tilted his head to one side, eyes narrowing: not a hostile expression, to Tank's relief, but a surprised, curious one.

"Tank," he said. "Why would you discard a name of note for a lowly drunkard's tag?"

Tank opened his mouth, shut it again, startled by the man's genuine interest.

"I . . . I don't know," he said, fumbling; then surprised himself further by offering raw and dangerous honesty. "I didn't want to be Tanavin any longer. Or . . . of the Aerthraim."

Deiq's mouth stretched; a smile this time, albeit a dark and sardonic one.

"Yes," he said. "I can understand wanting to distance yourself from the Aerthraim. They weren't entirely honest with you, were they?" He paused. Tank said nothing; any response would drag him irretrievably past any attempt at *ordinary*. "I don't blame the Aerthraim for lying to you, either," Deiq added, more quietly. "The only mistake they made was allowing you to live afterwards."

Tank sat perfectly still but not frozen this time, his muscles gathering into the same coiling readiness to move that he had sensed in Deiq. "Are you looking to correct that?"

Deiq stared at Tank for what seemed a small eternity. Then his gaze flicked to the bed, to Alyea's curled-up, sleeping form. He stared at Alyea for a while, unblinking; finally turned a much milder gaze on Tank.

"No," he said. "I should. But I won't. Not after–what you've done." His gaze went to Alyea again, as though compelled. "What was that thing you made her chew on? It looked like a stick."

"Chich," Tank said, his chest loosening with relief. "It's more like a very hard jerky. The Aerthraim ketarch developed it to help with . . . with dasta fits." He ducked his head, flinching away from all the implicit admissions about himself in that statement, never mind that Deiq very likely already knew about it all; he couldn't endure seeing that knowledge in the man's eyes. Couldn't take the chance of seeing pity there.

When he looked up again, Deiq's expression was completely blank and his gaze on his hands.

"Interesting," he said in a muted voice. "Leave us a few, if you'd be so kind. If you can spare any."

"Of course," Tank said, already fumbling with his belt pouch. He sorted

392   *Leona Wisoker*

out four; ticked over the count of the remainder with his fingers, grimacing a little. He'd have to find a way to get more soon. He couldn't go through Dasin. Any request from Dasin for chich would be tantamount to admitting that Tank was traveling alongside him, and while that news reaching Aerthraim Family might be inevitable in the end, Tank wanted to put that day off for as long as possible.

He didn't want to be found; he wanted to disappear, like the Aerthraim Lost: that group of engineers and inventors who had fled Bright Bay during the Purge, gone north, and vanished from all knowledge. Even if that was an impossible dream, he intended to try.

He set the four sticks on the table, pushed them to midpoint. He kept his gaze on the chich as he said, "Don't use more than two in a day. Send to the Aerthraim ketarch for more. Don't–" He stopped, biting his lip, and tried to think of how to say *Don't tell them it was me* without sounding like a fool.

Deiq let out a grating chuckle. "You were never here," he said.

"Thank you." He glanced over to Alyea, smiling a little: she'd curled up like a child lost in the depths of a dream. Deiq made a soft, growling noise; Tank looked back, startled, into a sharp, hostile blackness. "I should go," he said, the only rational response to that glare.

Deiq tilted his head, agreeing. His unblinking, unwavering gaze turned heat to chill along every bit of Tank's exposed skin.

"You were never here," he repeated, more definitely this time.

Tank sat still for a long moment, breathing difficult; cast one last, deliberate look at Alyea, then rose from the chair. "No," he said, looking down at Deiq. "I came here–"

Deiq's face hardened, muscles tensing toward motion.

"–to tell Lord Eredion about Idisio and his mother," Tank went on unhurriedly. Deiq's expression shifted, lines drawing a different tension now. "Idisio asked for you, *s'e* Deiq. He needs your help."

He endured the man's cold stare without flinching. At last, Deiq said, tone muted again, "I've heard. We'll do what we can. Thank you for the message, and for–your help."

Tank nodded and turned away.

"Tanavin," Deiq said before Tank had gone two steps.

Tank turned, cocking his head, and waited. Deiq's expression had gone thoughtful. He said, "Why become a mercenary?"

Tank sorted through answers, finally settled on honesty again. "Lets me beat the shit out of folk as deserve it," he said. "With my hands, or with a big damn knife if I need that to help. Nothing fancy or–strange. Just like anyone else would do in a fight."

Deiq's mouth moved into a real smile.

"May your gods hold you gently, Tank," he said. "Teth-kavit."

Tank blinked, his eyes swimming with sudden relief: that was close enough to a declaration of truce to suit him. "Teth-kavit," he said with care, and left the room without a backwards glance.

Chapter Seventy-Four

Sandsplit proper lay a good hour's walk from the outskirts; the group who had fed Kolan lived farther out on the fringe than he'd thought. Not surprising, given that their assorted trades were those that carried the vilest odors and social stigmas.

He didn't mind. The walk gave him time to solidly bury his thoughts of Ellemoa, the disturbing memories, the agonizing ache of wishing she had survived. He could have saved her, once away from Rosin. He was certain of that. He *knew* her, he understood her so deeply that—

"Never mind," he muttered, and shoved that longing behind the barrier. Today, now, *move on*—He had a road under his feet, and a destination, finally, clear in his mind: Arason. He'd go back there, and see if the Arason Church had survived the troubles; would petition to be accepted back, as novice or junior—whatever they allowed him. He would stay within the walls of the Church and revel in the safety of those chill stone walls, in the silence and the space for prayer.

He walked, barefoot and uncaring of it, recalling every last detail of the rooms and courtyards and furnishings of the Arason Church, concentrating so intently that when grass changed to sand and then to laid stone underfoot he barely noticed. The buildings and trees looming around him slowly drew his attention from his reverie. He stopped, looking around him in appreciation of how the patterned night-shadows of human architecture mingled with those of ivy-draped featherpalm trees and stone pines.

A vague breeze wandered over his feet, sending an odd shiver of uncertainty up his legs like a message, a warning, a whisper of dread. He stood still, blinking slowly and listening to the quiet darkness. Crickets chirred. Night-frogs sang their creaking songs. A cat yowled, somewhere far away; a human laughed, high and shrill.

Doors opened and closed. Feet went this way and that.

Human sounds faded away, leaving only the night animals to disturb the quiet. Kolan shrugged a little, dismissing his unease, and walked on.

A ripple of sound, more sensed than audible, stopped him three steps later: a tortured, dying scream. Not nearby–well to the northwest of him–but it carried that peculiar, despairing resonance that only came from one kind of death.

Kolan stood, fixed in place as surely as though he'd been chained again. His first thought was of Ellemoa–but that was foolish, she wasn't here, she couldn't be–

But that had been a death caused by a ha'ra'ha feeding. Which meant there was another one moving about here, in spite of the barrier laid down across the Forest border.

Good gods, how many of them are there?

It occurred to him that Arason had once hosted an entire community of ha'ra'hain; and suddenly he felt much less certain in his plan to seek sanctuary there. If *sionno* Hagair had really understood what the creatures could do, Kolan had a feeling he would have been considerably less tolerant of their presence and more sympathetic with Captain Kullag.

"But we never killed any humans," someone said from the dark shadows of a stone pine to his right. "We took what we needed from the Lake, and left your kind alone."

Kolan's heart thudded into a rapid, shocked rhythm; he spun to face the voice, his lips already, silently, forming an impossible name.

"Rosin taught me to hurt the humans," she said, emerging from black shadow into the dim starlight. "Rosin taught me to enjoy the pain I caused."

She went sideways, circling him like a stalking cat examining its prey. He stood still, eyes shut, too stunned and breathless to even speak.

"I thought I killed you," she said from somewhere behind him.

"Not quite," he answered, dry as old bones, then broke into a laugh, unable to help himself. He turned to face her, heedless of danger. "I thought they'd killed *you*. Gods–Ellemoa!" He put out a hand; withdrew it quickly as she startled back.

They stared at one another in mutual wonder. Slowly, she advanced a step, another: paused, one hand at her mouth, worrying at her lower lip. A sudden cascade of aches wracked across his body, as though every old wound she'd caused was flaring to life, reminding him of what he faced.

Flames tracing along his arms; her eyes gleaming gold and red in unholy reflection, laughing as he screamed . . . .

She backed up another step as he yelped in reawakened agony. He caught himself to silence, clenching his jaw to keep the whimper contained, and waited until the aches faded somewhat.

"It doesn't matter," he said then. "It's over. It's over. And Rosin's dead. *Teyhataerth* is dead. They can't force you into that any longer–"

She laughed, straightening into more assurance, and said, "You and my son! You both think I should go by *human* standards of behavior."

"Your–He's alive!" A grin stretched Kolan's face wide. "That's *wonderful!*"

"No," she said flatly. "He's a coward and a disappointment."

Joy faded. He stared at her, unable to believe her cold demeanor. "Ellemoa," he said, despairing. "He's your *son*."

"And he thinks like a human."

"Is that such a bad thing?" he said softly. "Is it, truly? We're not all like Rosin, Ellemoa."

"No?" she shot back. "You were just thinking that your precious Head of Church should have exterminated the lake-born, not encouraged tolerance of us!"

Breath hissed between his teeth–but of course she'd be able to see his every thought, with or without him knowing about it.

"I was thinking about what *you* did to me," he said, low and fierce. "Are all ha'ra'hain like you, Ellemoa? Or are you the Rosin Weatherweaver of your kind?"

She came forward two fast steps at that, and ghostly blue flames flickered along her fingers for a heartbeat, then went out. He held his ground, entirely unafraid all of a sudden; what more could she do under the open sky, after all, than she'd already done in the depths of the earth?

He deliberately brought the encounter with Fen to mind; she smiled a little, then retreated.

"You should have killed him," she said. "You would have enjoyed it."

"But I didn't," he said. "And I won't kill for enjoyment, nor to save myself pain. That's based in weakness, not strength, no matter what Rosin told you."

"I don't know why I never killed you," she said, amusement vanishing into a sneer.

"You were never *told* to kill me," he said. "And you took orders, didn't you? Anything Rosin ordered, you jumped right into doing."

"I didn't have a *choice!*" she snapped. Starlight caught golden flecks from her eyes. "I was trying to survive!"

"What price survival?" he retorted. "*I* took the pain for refusing to do what *you* wanted."

In a blurred leap, she stood right up against him, her eyes streaked with luminescent gold now; a bare finger's breadth from actual physical contact, she paused: rigidly still, glaring like a maddened asp-jacau.

"Your refusal cost *me* pain," she snarled. "Don't you throw that in my face as though it makes you godly! You saw what he did to me–every time–"

"Yes," he said, unflinching. "I saw. And I saw what *you* did to the humans he brought you afterwards. Didn't it ever occur to you–Rosin set you at me *knowing* I'd refuse to follow your least wish, *planning* to punish you for my obstinacy, and then giving you victims to vent your rage and frustration on–in front of me, every time. Supposedly to teach me a lesson, wasn't it? To make me obey your commands. Only it had nothing to do with *me*. It was all about bringing out the worst in *you*. Didn't you *see* that? Didn't you see what he was doing? You must have, by the end."

Her eyelids slid over dimming gold in a slow, measured blink; when her eyes opened again they were a flat, whiteless black.

"Yes," she said, low in the back of her throat. "I saw."

She stepped back and turned away, then knelt on the ground, hands splayed out across the stone. He waited, watching the line of tension working through her back and shoulders; he'd seen her in enough versions of agony to know when staying very, very still was the only safe course.

At last she rose and turned to face him again, features composed and eyes human-normal.

"You're a fool," she said. "You ought to be trying to kill me."

He laughed. "Why? So that you'll be able to call killing me self-defense? No. I won't make it that easy on you, Ellemoa. I've never raised a hand to stop you from hurting me, and I won't now."

"You swore you wouldn't let anyone hurt you ever again," she said. "Hypocrite! You'll attack a helpless thief, but not someone who overmatches you."

"I'll defend myself," he said, "but not against you. Never against you. That would make it too easy for you. I intend to keep your actions on your own conscience, not mine."

"You think I have a conscience?" she said bitterly. "Again, you put me among the humans."

"If you didn't have a conscience," he said, "you wouldn't have sought out your son. You wouldn't have simply walked away when he disappointed you." Something in the way her head moved just then made him ask, sharply, "You didn't kill your *son*–?"

"No," she said: a truth with a lie attached. He could feel it, even in just one word. "He's alive."

Kolan exhaled hard, debating whether to push for the details of the matter. Her head moved again, in slow negation. She wouldn't answer. He shrugged, letting that go, and said instead, "You have a conscience. You could have killed me before I knew you were behind me, just now. You still could. But you're–"

Once more the golden eyes glared into his, the heat of her body a bare hands-breadth away. "Don't presume," she said. "Don't dare think you understand me. It's not your place."

"You didn't answer my question," Kolan said, shifting tactical ground with the ease of long practice. Keep her off balance, keep her confused, keep her *intrigued*: that strategy had kept him alive so far.

"*What* question?"

"Are all ha'ra'hain like you? Is this how you were taught to behave by your mother?"

A stretched, fragile moment of stillness followed that; then she was gone, silent as she'd come, ghosting off into the darkness.

"Ellemoa," he said, not moving: he knew this game, too. But this time she didn't have the constraint of stone walls bounding her movements. "Come back here and face me. Answer my question. Or are you afraid of the answer?"

"You're deliberately provoking me," she said, low and hoarse, from somewhere behind him. "Do you want me to kill you, Kolan?"

"I want you to come back and face me," he said. "I want you to tell me the truth about yourself. Were you truly born to maim and kill? Is what Rosin taught you the way all ha'ra'hain aspire to behave? Is this the way you want your son to act–seeing humans as beneath you, as slaves and animals to slaughter and torture for your own enjoyment?" He paused, then dropped his volume to a scant murmur, knowing she'd hear it clearly: "Do you really *want* to treat humans the way Rosin treated *you*?"

"You've said that before."

"And more. Were you listening? Under Rosin's control, fine—you were compelled. I've always understood that. That's why I never fought back: there was no *point*. But those days are over. You don't have that lash on your back any longer. It's your *choice* to hand out pain, now; your *choice* to follow the path Rosin set before you." He paused, then said, with carefully measured inflection, "Your choice to be *just like him*."

Silence. A long, dark silence; after a time, he began to wonder if she'd ghosted off completely, freed from the boundaries that had always forced her to return before.

"No," she said from close by his right side, very quietly. "No, I'm still here."

He put out his right hand palm up, slowly, without making any other move at all, even to turn his head; then waited. After another long, long stretch of listening to nothing but crickets and frogs, there came a faint scuffing sound, like a heel kicking lightly against stone.

"I can't, Kolan," she said, nearly a whisper. "I'm not—stable. Not sane. I'm still so *angry*—I so desperately want to pass the pain along." She paused. "My son told me I should kill myself. Maybe he was right—"

Kolan sucked in a distressed breath.

"Oh, gods, Ellemoa," he said, understanding her pain and her son's point all at once. He bit his lip before he could blurt out something unwise.

"I was so angry," she said. "So *hurt*. My own son . . . All I wanted was to protect him. To save him. And he . . . he can't get past seeing me as a monster. He doesn't want to understand."

Kolan closed his eyes, steadying himself. "The Creeds tell us," he said unemotionally, "that within every man is a monster and within every monster is a man; and that before we pick up our knives to attack one another we ought first to look within to excise our own evil."

"You and your Creeds," she said, wearily. "Don't you ever stop reciting those washed-out pieties? What's your own evil, then, Kolan? What's *your* monster within?"

"You are, Ellemoa," he said, a little surprised at his own ready admission of it.

"That's nonsense," she said, sharp and hostile. "I can't be your inner monster. I'm out here, not inside you! Stop trying to confuse me."

He smiled, his eyes still closed, and said, "No, you're not inside me, Ellemoa. Not literally. I'm sorry; I wasn't clear. I didn't mean to confuse you."

"What did you mean, then?" she demanded.

"I mean that in spite of everything you've done—to me, to others, to yourself—Ellemoa—" He opened his eyes and stretched his left hand out into the darkness, so that he stood with both arms outspread. "I still love you."

She hissed and spat; he could almost feel her bristling with outrage. "Your stupid little human notions of love are meaningless to me!"

"Are they?" he said. "So it means nothing to you that I understand you completely—"

"You *don't*—"

"No?" He reached into memory for a trick she'd shown him long ago, before their shared captivity.

Pale orange flames flickered along his fingers for several heartbeats, then faded away.

She hissed briefly: he couldn't tell if she were angry, amused, or startled. Then she said, in a burst of raw agony, "*Why*? If you'd only done that–even once–for me–to show Rosin that I wasn't lying, that I could teach him–I tried so hard to give him the abilities he wanted. He called it *my* failure–just like my failure to give him a child–He wouldn't understand, wouldn't *listen*–"

Kolan shuddered at the thought of Rosin Weatherweaver learning how to summon flame to his hand, or any of a dozen other tricks Ellemoa seemed to regard as trivial. Bright Bay wouldn't be torn up; it would have been *leveled*.

"*You* listened. You learned. I gave you–so much–you don't even know. Even now, you don't really understand what I gave you, back then. You think your strength comes from your gods!"

Kolan sucked in a sharp breath, shaken by the implications of those words. She'd never spoken of that time, in the darkness; talking of moments spent under sunlight had been too painful for both of them. Before he could think of a response, she went on:

"But then–you ran away." Her tone turned distant, hazed with recall. "You ran away from me for showing you what I could do–and that you could do it, too. That humans weren't so very different from the lake-born."

"No," he said, seizing the chance to press his point, "we *aren't* all that different, are we?"

She was silent.

"You're a fool," she said at last. "You truly are. I know what you're trying to do, Kolan; but it isn't going to work. I'm not that–that *foolish* any longer. I'm a monster; my son had it right, and I'm *slipping*–"

She stopped, her breathing harsh and labored.

"Go, Kolan," she said suddenly. "Please. Go. Walk–don't run, never run, but go. Get away from me. I won't remember–who you are. *Please*."

"There's that conscience you keep saying you don't have," he said. "Come back here and face me. If you're going to kill me, have the grace to come at me from the front. Look me in the eyes while you do it."

"*Kolan*."

"Come here."

She stood before him, eyes more white than black, and shivered all over as she stared at him.

"You're being very strange," she said in a small voice. "Why aren't you afraid?"

He brought his arms around with infinite caution and pulled her into gentle contact: torso, hip, and thigh just touching. He waited until her shivers faded to an oddly relaxed stillness, then said, "Because there's nothing to be afraid *of*."

She stirred, then leaned slowly forward against him, her own arms wrapping around his waist, and rested her head against his shoulder.

"Your faith again," she murmured.

"Yes."

She sighed, a long exhalation that seemed to draw a heavy weight from her thin body with its passing. "There are no gods, Kolan," she whispered. "Your faith is a lie."

He smiled ruefully, recalling years of agonized doubt while writhing in the dark and the fire: asking himself that very question, for if the gods existed, how could they possibly allow Rosin Weatherweaver to exist alongside them? The answer he'd arrived at, in the end, had been astonishingly simple.

"It doesn't matter if the gods truly exist or not," he said. "At the end of the day, gods are just a convenient hook to hang right behavior upon. My faith, these days, is in *that*; not in invisible, voiceless forces I can't prove or disprove the existence of."

"You'll get yourself hung for heresy one of these days," she said, then broke into sudden laughter that washed over Kolan like the clear, cold waters of a snowmelt-thick stream. He joined in; something twisted and black inside of him loosened and let go, drifting away on the wave of their shared laughter.

"Oh, it's been so long since I laughed," she said after a while. "So long."

"Stay with me," he said into her hair. "Stay with me, Ellemoa."

She shivered again; he kept his hold light and loose and himself very still. At last she said, "Would you obey me, if I stayed? Now that Rosin's gone?"

"No," he said. "Never. But I'll do what you *ask* of me, if I see it as right."

She was quiet for a while, evidently thinking that over. At last she said, "And if I kill again?"

"I'll stand in your way," he said. "You'll kill me first, before you touch another. If you can live with that—well, *I'll* be beyond caring at that point."

She broke out laughing again, a wild sound that rolled over into more honest amusement. "You're as mad as I am."

"Yes."

Her arms tightened around him. "All right," she said. "For as long as I can."

She straightened, pulling away a little. He loosened his embrace, his fingers barely touching each other behind her back now, and let her choose to come to him.

Chapter Seventy-Five

Night's blackness didn't exist: Idisio moved through an oddly lit world, as though an amber sun shone across everything at just the right angle to remove all shadows. There were no secrets under this new, hard-edged vision. Corners angled sharply enough to cut, walls bulked strong as mountains–and at the same time, it all seemed fragile as a child's dollhouse made of thick paper and fingernail-thin sheets of wood. He felt he could walk through anything in this new world without pause, and leave behind only as much damage as he cared to show in his wake.

On that thought, he turned and walked straight through a thick-trunked stone pine: suffered only a momentary blurring of vision and a brief itchiness across his entire body. Three steps clear of the tree, he stopped, turned, and studied the unmarked stone pine with a deep satisfaction; then walked back to it, sank his fist into the wood, and withdrew a thick chunk. The gaping hole began to weep sap instantly. He stuffed the broken piece back into the hole, where it sat crooked, like a squashed cork in a bottle neck too large for it. Sap coated his fingers; he held his hand out in front of him and *willed* the sap to slide off like water from oilcloth.

A series of thin splats rattled against the ground before him as the sticky tree-blood simply melted from his hand, leaving no residue behind.

This is what it means to be ha'ra'hain. I can do . . . anything.

Exultation filled him. He broke into a loping run and found the ground whipping by as though he were back in the teyanain's *clee* trance; leapt, and landed halfway up a tall tree without effort. Too fast; he twisted sideways to avoid slamming into the very *solid* trunk approaching his face, intuition warning that it wouldn't yield to him this time.

Holy gods–

Thrashing and falling through densely-needled side branches, he grabbed for purchase. Every branch he managed to grip snapped instantly. His feet caught on a wider limb; he staggered sideways from the impact and slid through something damp and sticky. *Godsdamn birds–*

He began to fall again; kicked out at the trunk, shoving himself clear of the tree, and tumbled backward, managing–just–to land in an upright crouch, hands splayed on the ground. He stayed there for some time, panting a little in reflexive shock. *That'll teach me to be arrogant . . . .*

He hauled himself back to his feet, aches flaring across his body in another reminder of unexpected consequences. Apparently, being able to do anything didn't mean it wouldn't hurt . . . But even as he had that thought, the pain faded away into a ghost-echo, then a memory.

Wide-eyed, he stared at the amber-tinted, shadowless world around him. *This is what my mother was trying to explain. This is . . . incredible. I'm practically invulnerable.* A moment's attention dispersed the sap and needles clinging to his clothes and skin; as he watched, the assortment of small scratches and larger cuts closed over, the blood from each wound seeming to simply absorb back into his skin.

How in the hells did Tank lay her out with a chunk of wood?

That brought recent events to mind, though, and the dying scream of an innocent girl: rage flared, quick to catch as a long-dry torch. The edges of his vision turned an odd, hazy white. His mother had taught him to find an inn simply by thinking of it; now he turned his attention to finding *her.*

Southeast. Not far away. He set off again, more slowly, a stalking pace now. For whatever reason, she wasn't moving. There was no hurry.

In a matter of two dozen steps, he could smell her: a distinctive aroma of rot overlaid with pungent spices. He'd never noticed it before, but he had no doubt that was her scent; it *belonged* with her, the way *sour* belonged with an unripe sunfruit.

Another scent wove through hers: a soft, deep note that somehow conveyed *male* and *malnourished.*

Idisio slowed even further, placing each foot with the intense care he'd used when stalking Deiq in the ruins–it seemed so long ago! But he'd proved his point, back then: he could sneak up on Deiq. He'd be just as capable of surprising his mother, especially if she was distracted with a new victim.

He had no intention of giving her a chance to get in a blow of her own before he struck; and as he would only get one try, he'd have to make that one *count.*

He eased his thoughts to utter blankness, aligning himself with the shadowless clarity of the world around him: flowed through space as translucent and silent as the air. He didn't exist; he was a floating particle in the midst of other specks . . . .

Idisio came to rest behind a large tree and stood still, eyes closed, listening: discovered he didn't need to *see* her to see her. It was very like his visions of Tank, but in the moment and under his control.

The stranger had his arms loosely around her, and he was, incredibly, *smiling*–a beatific expression as though he'd never wanted anything more than to embrace a murdering lunatic. And she–leaned up against him, her entire body relaxed, her arms around his waist. Idisio had never seen her so–so *calm*. So motionless.

He withdrew into the protective haze of an aqeyva trance to think it over: comparing what he knew of her to this moment, going back over everything she'd said. In the dispassionate calm of trance, he tried to see if, after all, his perceptions of her had been skewed somehow. He searched for any indication that he'd missed a vital clue along the way.

I'm better at lying than you are, son . . . Humans . . . they're meaningless. Insects . . . After so many years of being told to kill . . . it's like breathing.

No. She was lying. Playing. Taunting the man with her apparent submission. Any moment now she would laugh, and he would scream, and–*no. Not again. Never again.*

Rage broke him out of the trance and into a sharp hunter-focus: she remained still, unsuspecting–relaxed–*vulnerable*. Gods only knew why she was choosing to play the role that convincingly, but it was a lie. She'd said it herself: she was a very, very good liar. And he would never understand the first quarter of anything she did, kind or cruel.

His hand rested on the hilt of the long Scratha dagger for a moment; but he understood, now, that a simple knife wouldn't do nearly enough damage. A moment later, his vision narrowed in on something that *would*.

Yes. There.

Apparently ha'ra'hain also possessed that dark, compact spot of *self-ness*. Hers was larger and somehow *heavier* than Enia's had been–which made it an easy target. In the white-edged mist of his rage, the irony of hitting her just *there* seemed incandescently appropriate.

Not willing to waste the only chance he might ever get, hoping desperately that he didn't need to be in physical contact to get to that spot, he *reached*, fast and sure and hard; she thrashed upright in startled reflex a fraction of a heartbeat too late. He engulfed the dense mass like water flowing around a sinking stone, gathered himself around it like a net, and yanked it into himself with a brutal cruelty he hadn't known himself capable of until that moment.

Her scream went past the human-audible range in moments. He savored the vibrating agony as it swept through the air; shame tried to get a foothold, lost, and faded away.

Apparently I'm not only capable of intentionally killing, I'm entirely capable of enjoying it, Idisio thought hazily. Then the orgasmic rush hit, as it had with Enia–but *more*, infinitely *more*, ecstasy doubled then tripled then quadrupled– and he howled, utterly lost to anything but that all-encompassing *heat* . . . .

As the staggering intensity began to dim, memory of Deiq's sardonic voice drifted into awareness, dragging the traces of shame along with it: *We're not that different. Not nearly* . . . .

I believe I might owe Deiq an apology or ten if I ever see him again. Gods . . . .

A window shattered somewhere nearby. The disruption of sound, slight as it was, served to pitch Idisio sideways into awareness of the real moment. He was on his knees, leaning against the tree for support, and panting as though he'd run from Scratha Fortress to Bright Bay. The man was on the ground, whining wordlessly, his hands over his ears.

Ellemoa still stood, rigidly stiff.

Idisio hoisted himself sideways, too dizzy and disoriented to even think about rising from his knees, and stared, unable to believe his eyes. *She's* standing. *Oh, shit—*

Her eyes had turned a lambent white; her hair was heavily streaked with pale grey and paler silver. She stared right at him. Her mouth moved, but no sound emerged. After a few moments, he realized that she had no voice left to speak with. He watched her lips shape words, over and over; he'd never been particularly good at reading lips, but intuition moved in to help this time:

Finish it. Finish it. Finish it . . . .

She's crippled, Idisio thought, horrified. *I did this. I don't think she can heal—not from this much damage—she's blind, and mute, and gods know what else.*

Oh, gods. What have I done?

Her mouth kept moving: *Finish it. Finish it. Finish it . . . .*

He stared at her, and thought of a dead girl in a cottage less than a mile away. Thought of the smell of sweetened ginger, and of her conviction that humans were insects; thought of his own accelerated healing abilities, and of the risk he took if he let her live: because if she did ever recover her strength . . . .

He shut his eyes and opened *other*-vision; found what was left of that blackness and wrapped it in a tight grip—gently this time—and softly, softly, drew it from her, little by little.

She offered no resistance. Made no sound. Slowly, slowly, sank to her knees—graceful, swaying, as though this were nothing more than a dance in the rain—and folded to the ground beside the still-whimpering stranger.

She reached out one bone-thin hand, as she drooped into a final sprawl across the cold cobblestones, and gripped the man's hand tightly. Just for a moment. Then her hand, along with the rest of her, went limp.

Lifeless.

Oh dear and holy gods—I did it. I really—I really— Thought shredded into incoherence.

A moment later, the stranger groaned and rolled to his knees, leaning over Ellemoa's body; his hands caressing her in a vain, desperate attempt to shake her back to life.

"Oh, no," he moaned. "No. No—gods!" He twisted to stare at Idisio, his face white as the stars and streaked with tears. "What have you done? *What have you done?*"

Before Idisio could answer, the man turned back to the corpse and dragged it up into his arms, hugging it against him, rocking back and forth and muttering; the words stifled both by his wracking sobs and by his mouth pressing against her hair.

"Saved your life," Idisio said, rather drunkenly. He tried to stagger to his feet. The world spun in strange and unpleasant new ways around him, and he decided to stay close to the ground after all. "She was going to kill you."

The man shook his head and sat back on his heels, still cradling Ellemoa's body in his arms. "We all die sooner or later," he said, ducking his head to draw the back of one hand clumsily across his face, wiping away tears and liquid snot. "She wouldn't have killed me. Not right away. We had some time. Gods only know how long—but we had *time.*"

Idisio began to say, "You're *entirely* mad, do you know that?"–and stopped as something occurred to him. "Oh, gods," he said instead. "You're *Kolan*, aren't you?"

"Yes," the man said. He shifted the limp form to rest against one arm and used the other hand to gently stroke Ellemoa's tangled hair from her face. "And you're her son. I'd like to say *nice to meet you*, but–" His voice choked off into an ugly mixture of cough and sob.

"I think she loved you," Idisio said helplessly. "She tried to say you didn't matter, but I think–I think she really did care. As much as she could care about–anything."

"I know," Kolan said. "If she didn't, she would have killed me years ago."

He sighed and stood, cradling Ellemoa's body in his arms; looked down at Idisio for a long moment, then shook his head and turned away.

Idisio made no effort to stop Kolan as he walked away with the body of a madwoman finally at peace. The world was still spinning erratically around Idisio–and his eyes were suddenly too blurred with tears to allow him to see much of anything at all.

"Goodbye, mother," he whispered as the vague outline that was Kolan faded from his watery vision. "Goodbye."

The faintest breeze wandered across his face, carrying a whisper that might only have been his imagination: *Goodbye, my beloved son . . . Goodbye.*

Chapter Seventy-Six

She could have killed me.

Kolan laid Ellemoa's limp body on the grass where leaf began giving way to sand and set about gathering what driftwood he could find.

When her son attacked her—she could have drawn strength from me. She could have killed me, to save herself. I wouldn't have fought. She knew that.

He built a carefully layered square out of the largest pieces of driftwood; arranged the rest neatly inside, tucking tangled nests of dried grass into the inner layers.

She didn't even try to save herself.

Searching through the plants along the dune-line, he found wild lavender; after a moment's consideration, he shook his head and passed that by. Instead, he gathered armfuls of sweet thistle and sea-oats, sand roses and morning spice-weed, and worked those, along with an armful of well-dried seaweed, into the bier, leaving plenty of clear space between the branches for airflow.

By the time he managed that much, the stars were turning toward morning. He went along the lower beach, gathering the whitest, least broken assortment of shells he could find; gathered a number of largish rocks and shellrock fragments as well, and slid those latter carefully through the lattice of branches to rest in a rough pile at the bottom of the bier. The shells he set aside.

Returning to Ellemoa's still form, he knelt beside her, tracing a hand along the side of her cool, slack face. His eyes blurred with tears.

"You only thought you knew how much you gave me," he murmured; dashed his vision clear with the back of one hand and scooped her up before his nerve could fail him entirely.

He laid her out across the low bier, arranged her with hands folded and eyes closed; set the most beautiful shells he'd found across her brow, chest, and stomach, and set the rest in random patterns around the edges of her body, framing her with the bones of the sea.

He tucked his flawed blue-green marble under her hands, put a single, perfect white sea-rose over them, then stepped back to survey his work.

Someone coughed, not close by but near enough. Kolan turned without haste and found the blackreed retter standing a hefty stone's throw away, watching him without expression.

"Won't be enough," the man said. "That's hardly enough to heat water, what you got there. Won't do for putting a body to ash."

"I know," Kolan said. He turned back to the bier. Kneeling to pray seemed– pompous, somehow, and out of place for the situation. She hadn't believed, hadn't lived by any of the Creeds; hadn't, by any stretch of human standards, been a good person.

She didn't even try to fight.

He sighed. "At least you saw the sun again," he said aloud. "Even if you died in the dark, the way you always feared–at least you walked through sunlight once more, before the end."

He raised his hands. Red-orange flame rippled along his fingers. Behind him, the retter grunted. Kolan read a dour satisfaction in that small sound, and his own mouth twisted in a bleak smile for a moment; then he stepped forward and thrust his hands deep into the pile of sticks beneath Ellemoa's body.

Closing his eyes, he drew in a long breath: collected every memory of every day since their shared imprisonment began, every moment of rage and pain and fear and frustration, and blew it out along with his breath.

Burn, he commanded: wood, stone, shell, and flesh obeyed.

He pulled clear and staggered back, as lightheaded and breathless as though he'd just blown out a thousand candles at once. His hands itched. Looking down, he found a fiery rash of blisters spreading from fingertip to elbow on each arm. Heat hammered at him, a yellow-red glare searing across his vision. He backed up several more steps, gasping, whimpering a little as the pain of scorched flesh registered; but he'd suffered worse, in the darkness under Bright Bay–and usually at her hand.

Why don't you want to kill her? the woman outside of Kybeach–the gerho merchant's renegade wife–had asked, furious with bewilderment. *After what she's done to you–why don't you want her dead?*

As Ellemoa's flesh began to char and melt in Kolan's summoned fire, Kolan murmured, "She never really wanted to do those things to me. For all that she enjoyed hurting me–she hated it, at the same time, and couldn't ever let anyone know; it wasn't safe. But I knew. I always knew . . . ."

From a few steps away, the retter cleared his throat and said, quietly, "My boy says you're a soapy?"

"Yes," Kolan said. He wiped a hand across his face. "I was, anyway. What I am now . . . I don't entirely know."

"Well, you're human enough to grieve for your dead," the man said pragmatically. "And caring enough over one as you just admitted hurt you to set her up with a fair pretty bier and light the gods' own blaze for her pyre, however you managed the trick. I figure you're holy enough yet to be praying over her in one form or another."

Kolan stared at the fierce flames. The heat had grown so intense that it dried the tears leaking from his eyes as they emerged. "Yes," he said. "You're right. Thank you."

He drew a deep breath, then began reciting the Creeds: every single one. It wasn't hard; he'd said them over and over, in the darkness, a reminder of what he clung to, a circular path to keep him within the bounds of sanity as madness hammered at his soul.

Harm no living creature, from beetle to boy; all have their place and purpose in the eyes of the gods . . . .

The retter murmured each one along with him, missing a word or phrase now and again, or hesitating as though he'd learned a different version. Kolan kept his gaze on the flames and his attention on his recitation, focusing as tightly as though he were trying to copy a line without blotching the page.

Obedience to the gods requires a clean heart and a dedication to one's given tasks . . . .

The sky beyond the flames paled as he spoke, and a vibrant orange blush began to build to the southeast, as though the dawn had chosen to reflect the conflagration before him.

Seek not the chaos of the world outside, but be content with the inner truth and strength the gods will always give to those who truly seek it . . . .

As he reached the fiftieth of the Creeds, a ghostly whisper arose, circling his inner ear with a familiar bleak humor: *You and your Creeds . . . .*

He smiled, and went on regardless.

Within every man is a monster and within every monster is a man. Before you pick up your knife to attack another, use that knife first to excise your own flaws . . . .

She whispered the words along with him, far from devout but not as mocking as she'd been in life, either; and from that point on, her voice, faint and fragile enough that it seemed a hefty sea breeze would dissolve it, followed along with his, word for word.

As the heat of the fire faded and dawn grew around him, his eyes remained dry and his voice steady. He finished the hundredth and final Creed as the bier sank into a pile of glowing coals and ash:

Those whom the world sees as the least worthy of love, the gods always place first.

"May the gods hold her soul gently," the retter said quietly, then bowed to Kolan with profound reverence and turned away.

"They will," Kolan said, not caring if the man heard him. "They will."

Sunlight streaked the air. A dawn sea breeze, rising, blew the ashes out to sea: leaving behind only a single, clear glass marble.

Chapter Seventy-Seven

The closest gate to Peysimun Mansion turned out to be the Red Gate; and that turned out to be closed and heavily guarded, even under daylight. Four guards faced the outer city, their attention roving along the stretch of iron fencing to either side of the gate. Two more stepped out from the thick-walled guardhouse to face Tank as he led Sin toward them.

"Morning, s'ieas," he said, smiling at them with false cheer. Not showing his true feelings was a lifelong habit, the more so when his mood was as brittle and dark as the remnants of a fierce fire; and guards, especially, weren't safe to show that kind of anger around.

He wanted *out* of this place. Away from anything to do with nobles or people with power; away from any chance of encountering Wian, who he'd managed to avoid on his way out of Peysimun Mansion. Walking to the East Gate, while it would have put him closer to the Copper Kettle and been a shorter walk overall, meant going through noble-held territory for most of the distance.

Tank wanted to walk among *ordinary* people for a while, and remember what *simple* meant. It might ease his thundering headache and black mood.

The guards nodded at him, surveying him with care. The taller, a lean woman with a round face, said, "Morning, s'e. Planning to travel through this way, are you? Not something I'd recommend, myself."

He looked at the four guards and the long stretch of fence: open iron fencing for a goodly distance to either side of the gate, and thick, spear-tipped stone from there on. He looked at the blank, dirty back walls of buildings beyond the bars, and the drifts of trash caught against fence and buildings alike.

A shift in the breeze brought a foul smell wandering past his nose.

"Not a good area, I take it," he said dryly.

She shook her head. "Not these days," she said. "Most of the rat-chaff blew up along this stretch of town over the past few years. I'm imagining King Oruen will send us through to clear it at some point, but that's not today. And if you'll pardon the boldness, s'e, that horse and that sword will be worse than useless out there."

He looked through the bars of the fence, a slow smile working across his face. "Sure to be a fight on the way through, is that it?"

"No question. Your boots alone–" She stopped, her own expression creasing from dour to amused. "Huh," she said.

"Any chance you could spare someone to walk this beast over to the East Gate, and I'll come round the long way to collect him?"

She pursed her lips and looked sidelong at her companion, who was openly grinning. "You don't show up by sunset," she said, "we keep it all."

"Done." He handed her the reins, then passed the other guard his sword, harness and all.

"You registered with the Hall?" she asked, practical, and scratched Sin's nose fondly. "Nice fellow you got here."

"Yes. Name of Tank."

"We'll let the captain know, if you don't show up."

"That's appreciated," he said. "But you won't need to."

"Huh," she said, shaking her head, and "Huh," again; then called for the other guards to open the gate. "We won't open it for you from the other side," was her parting warning. "Only one way through these doors, s'e."

"I'll see you at the East Gate," was all he said; and didn't look back as the gates clashed shut behind him.

He was limping a little when he collected Sin, a solid two hours before sunset; the guard captain at the East Gate, eyebrows raised, handed over a thick, cloth-wrapped bundle along with horse and sword.

"Bandages and salves and such," he said. "Kina said you'd likely need 'em, if you showed. Looks like she was right."

Tank touched one corner of his mouth gently; his fingers came away spotted with blood. "Yeah," he said. "Thanks. Which way to the Copper Kettle from here, s'e?"

He listened to the directions as he strapped on his sword harness, wincing a little; hoisted himself clumsily into the saddle, nodded farewell, and turned Sin's nose east and north.

The only room available at the Copper Kettle was a single-bed; but it was a largish room, with proper chairs and a writing-desk, along with a small in-room dining table and wardrobe. The bed itself was wide and soft enough for three to rest in comfort.

A servant in immaculate and starched white livery escorted Tank to his room, then insisted on staying to tend the various small injuries.

"It's what I get paid for, *s'e*," he said when Tank tried to send him away. "Whatever the guest requires. And we've merchants and half-nobles here who stay days and weeks at a time; some of them go out for a night of drinking and come back in far worse shape than this." He grinned, exposing crooked and gapped teeth.

Too exhausted to argue, Tank sat docile after that, allowing the man to gently strip off the stained and ripped clothes; the servant showed no reaction at all to the old scars, and his tending of the new wounds was brisk and professional.

"There, now," he said at last, gathering up the ruined clothes and blood-stained washcloths. "You ought to be safe enough to get some rest, *s'e*. Blood on the linens always upsets the cleaning maids . . . Dinner's served just past nightfall. I'll come by and advise you when the dining room opens, if you like."

Tank nodded slowly, his head and eyes feeling weighted and thick.

"Thanks," he mumbled. "Be sure Dasin knows what room. He'll be in–another day, maybe two. Skinny blond. Merchant."

"I'll be sure of it, *s'e*," the servant said.

Tank hoisted himself to his feet and stumbled to the bed. The soft, flat surface welcomed him. An unmeasured stretch of time later, someone drew a light blanket across.

"Damn loon," a voice said some time after that. "What did you get yourself into this time?"

Tank rolled over, blinking back to awareness, and focused on Dasin with some difficulty. "Whah?" The room was warm and humid and grey with twilight. "You got here fast."

"You've been asleep over a day straight," Dasin said tartly. "I'm told you staggered in here yesterday before sunset, looking like all the hells had a pass at you, and went out cold."

"Uhhrr." Tank rubbed a hand over his eyes and sat up slowly. "That's still a fast bit of riding." He squinted; Dasin looked as grey as the room around them. "Your horse alive?"

"Don't be stupid," Dasin said. "I wake up with you gone and Yuer all but laughing in my face over having drugged me, and I get told I'm to meet you in Bright Bay–What do you *think*? And Yuer wouldn't tell me *anything* other than that we're to gather supplies for a run back to Sandsplit, and there's a merc here I'm to meet with and hire, name of Raffin, and you're waiting for me at the Copper Kettle–If you're still alive, that is, he says, and won't tell me *why* that's a question at all! And then I hear, as I go through the village, about a girl dead out by the edge of town–raped, by the sound of it–and everyone's glaring at outsiders as though I'm in Kybeach instead of Sandsplit–Obein was no better, I had to *bribe* my way through, if you can believe it–some stupid damn barricade over the road, and they got mad when I said that was stupid as aiming to get milk from a snake–"

Tank laughed and put up a hand to stop Dasin's rant.

"Enough," he said. "Gods, take a breath!"

Dasin turned away sharply and set about lighting the large oil lamps on the desk and dining table. When the room was bathed in a soft glow, he said, "They're serving dinner. Roast chicken and greens."

Tank ran his hands through his hair and swung his legs to sit on the edge of the bed. "Not really hungry," he said. "You?"

Dasin shook his head, not quite meeting Tank's gaze.

"Tired," he said. "Tired and–scared." His face was pale and weary in the yellow light.

"Scared?"

"Didn't know if you'd be alive. Looks like you nearly weren't." Dasin flicked a glance at the array of bandages and sticking-plaster in which the servant had left Tank swathed.

"Oh–this isn't–" Tank stopped and drew a breath. Explaining that the cuts had nothing to do with why he'd left Dasin behind would involve explaining too much else afterward. "This isn't anything," he said instead. "A few scratches. Nothing important."

Dasin snorted. "What you think of as scratches," he began, then shook his head and fell silent, turning away again.

Tank sat still, frowning at Dasin's skinny back, and said, "You were really that worried? Why?"

Dasin took a restless step toward the door, then went to his pack instead and dug out a pipe and a small leather pouch.

"Dasin," Tank said, a little sharply.

"Shut it," Dasin said without turning. He filled and lit the pipe; the sweet, earthy aroma of aesa drifted through the air. Dasin took two heavy draws, exhaling clouds of grey smoke, then turned and held the pipe out to Tank.

"No," Tank said.

"Take it," Dasin said, eyes bright and clear. He walked over to stand before Tank and offered the pipe again. "I know it's my poison, not yours–but damnit, trust me for once. Just the once. Take it."

Tank looked at Dasin's fierce expression, then shrugged, wrapped his hand around the pipe and drew. Once, then again: his hand shook, and Dasin's closed round for support. Smoke swirled through him, dragging clarity away with surprising speed. He pushed the pipe back at Dasin and hoisted himself onto the bed. Leaning against the headboard, he shut his eyes and let the world sway in silence for a time.

"I went looking for a fight," he said at last, eyes still closed. "Found one.

Won it."

"Yeah," Dasin said. "I figured it was something like that."

He settled on the bed beside Tank, leaning back in companionable quiet. They passed the pipe back and forth for a time, not speaking.

Eventually, Dasin set the pipe aside, resting it carefully in a small dish on the bedside table. He said, "I was scared. I get scared easy, Tank. I–count on you being around. Didn't realize it until I woke up alone in Yuer's guest room, and had to ride from Sandsplit to Bright Bay not knowing if I'd find you on a burning slab at the end of the road."

Tank sighed and ran his hands through his hair. *Sorry* didn't seem the right thing to say, somehow.

"I'm harder to kill than all of that," he said instead. "You spook too easy, Dasin."

"I just said so, didn't I?" Dasin said, irritated now.

Tank put out a hand, intending to grip Dasin's near shoulder; the angle turned out awkward, and he wound up putting his arm across Dasin's shoulders instead, gripping the far one.

Dasin sucked in a short, harsh breath and sat very still, head tipped back.

"Ah, damnit," Tank said, and began to withdraw his hand. Abrupt tension gathered in Dasin's skinny body; he bit his lip and left his arm where it was. "Dasin–"

"Shut it," Dasin said, scarcely audible. "Just–damnit–shut it."

Tank let out a long sigh, wondering if the aesa had anything to do with the heat gathering in his groin; experience told him that was unlikely. While dasta prompted one to act outside normal behavior, aesa . . . dismissed the masks and blew open the secrets.

"Dasin," he said, very quietly. "You never said. I thought you went–the other road."

"I walk both," Dasin said, voice dry and thin. "That's what *I* was taught to think normal." He turned his head, just a little, to glance at Tank sidelong. "I know you don't," he added. "So I never said."

"You never *asked*," Tank said, as dry himself, and felt a shiver run through Dasin's skinny frame.

"You told Frenn and Breek–"

"Well, what else? I wasn't looking to get in a fight at that point."

Dasin hesitated, then said, barely audible, "And I thought, after–" His hand crept, tentatively, to touch one of the scars across Tank's bare stomach. "I figured the memories were bad enough to turn you away from . . . any reminders."

"That was–then. And different." And Dasin's wiry strength had no chance against Tank's own, but Tank knew better than to say that aloud. "It's the past. It's over."

Aesa haze forced him to admit to himself that without the moment of crystalline understanding he'd shared with Alyea, he wouldn't have been nearly as comfortable making that statement, relegating the past to the past and allowing the moment to be enough. Even under an aesa cloud, he wouldn't have been willing to face his real reaction to Dasin's presence so close at hand, wouldn't have allowed his true response to Dasin's admission. Gods knew he'd refused to see Dasin's interest for long enough.

He tightened his grip and drew Dasin against him. A few moments later, he pulled away a handspan and muttered, "Careful, damnit–I bite back."

Dasin laughed, color flooding his face; and said, fiercely, "*Good.*"

Chapter Seventy-Eight

Idisio moved through nightmare. The crisp amber edges of the world had blurred into a bloody halo, and his inner ear rang with screams. He barely felt the ground under his feet as he stumbled back to the inn. Laughter paced his steps, a voice he'd never heard directly before: *You haven't escaped me, you know. This is all a dream . . . You dream so predictably.*

Escaped *who* didn't matter under the rising tide of crimson and white filling his vision. *Escape* was the important word, the part that made sense; if he ran fast enough, if he got back to the room at the inn—the last place where everything had been *normal*—quickly enough, he might be able to escape that mocking, smug, twisted voice.

It didn't work. If anything, the voice was stronger there, in the small, dilapidated room laced with his mother's scent. *You'll never really escape me . . . You'll certainly never forget me, sweet. Even if you do get away, I've marked you forever. You'll never really be free. You're safer with me . . . I'm the only one who understands you.*

Idisio gagged on black, scabby hatred and flung out a hand. The lone, stubby candle on the nightstand table flared to life. It produced more shadows than light and only disrupted what amber clarity was left to him; he willed the flame out and sat, shivering and bewildered, on the edge of the bed.

What was happening to him?

I killed my mother. He was paying the price for matricide. *I didn't have a choice.* But that was an answer the new, blood-edged darkness inside himself wouldn't accept.

He wondered what Deiq would have done. Probably nothing so very different . . . except, somehow, hitting Ellemoa very hard with something very sharp would have been more Deiq's style; he would have left her in several pieces, too small to heal the way a scratch did.

Could I have done that? It hadn't even occurred to Idisio to try; a belt knife, however long or well-crafted, still seemed like an absurd weapon against a ha'ra'ha's strength and speed. And he wasn't so much an expert with knife-fighting, either; he'd always run away from fights, by choice, or used his fists when a scrap was unavoidable. Perhaps with years of training and a long, sharp sword, he might have been able to–

Laughter spiraled through his mind again. *You like thinking about killing, don't you? I can see it in your eyes . . . .*

Idisio shut his eyes and put his hand over them, shivering again. *I'm losing my mind.*

How would Cafad Scratha look at him if he ever found out what Idisio had done? It wouldn't be a fake glare at that point. He'd wear the same look as the other desert lords had–and now, now Idisio understood why.

I'm dangerous. Gods, I can't believe I was so blind. He realized that he'd always suspected most of the respect Deiq garnered was human foolishness. He'd seen the fear of the desert lords as nothing more serious than fear of the un-known, and he'd seen Deiq as little more than a masterful showman who took advantage of the credulous to build a fearsome reputation.

But if anything, they didn't fear Deiq *enough.*

Get used to it, Deiq had said, his expression fierce.

How the hells do I do that? Idisio thought as the room around him slow-ly streaked with red, the amber dissolving under the flood of detached fury coursing through his body. He *liked* that rush he'd felt from killing the girl and his own mother, oh yes he did. It was far better than even the best sex he'd ever experienced. *How the hells does Deiq keep from slaughtering everyone around him?*

Breathe, Scratha said in memory, his voice severe. *Look at your breath. Shut out everything else.* And Deiq's voice chimed in: *Will you just drop into a full aqeyva trance already? Block everything out. This isn't over yet. I'll pull you out when it's safe.*

He's not here to pull me out this time . . . but I don't really need him to, either, do I?

Staying submerged in an aqeyva trance, in that safe grey nothingness, seemed infinitely preferable to being overwhelmed by the hideous hunger ris-ing in him.

He dropped down into the grey, twisting himself round and round until he'd worked himself into that tiny, private part of his mind where nothing existed but the steady flow of breath and pulse. Even there, tendrils of red and white snaked after his attention; he ignored them. The grey dissolved them, dispersed them, distanced murderous rage into insignificance.

After what seemed a handful of heartbeats and forever all at once, the ten-drils stopped trying to prod him into action. He sensed the flood of fury drain-ing slowly, steadily away: going from a torrential icemelt river to a muddy puddle. Intuition told him it wouldn't get better than that. He sighed and un-wound himself with fragile care, stepping around that slickness as best he could.

So aqeyva worked as a method of controlling the vast anger he'd somehow absorbed from his mother. That was a good thing to know, as was the new understanding of what happened when he drew–whatever that had been–from another creature.

He could feel Enia's memories swirling through his mind too, now, but they were fragile and easily shredded things, scarcely strong enough to see clearly. But his mother's memories–

Don't look at that, he told himself, and retreated into an aqeyva haze until the temptation to see into her agonized darkness, to understand why she'd done the things she'd done, went away. He wasn't strong enough to look at that. He'd already begun to crumble under the least fringes of it.

She'd been right. He was a fool and a child, without any real understanding of the world he walked through. But even if he had understood entirely, he probably wouldn't have done much differently. Whatever Kolan believed, Ellemoa had been—as Tank put it—stable as a brick balanced on a pin. The risk of her losing all restraint had been too high; and now that he understood how strong the pressure inside her had run, he knew his decision had been the right one.

Kolan was human. Like the desert lords, he only thought he understood what he'd been dealing with.

Idisio rubbed his eyes clear and looked at the open window–and into a flood of bright, warm sunlight. His overloaded eyes flooded with tears for a moment, then adjusted and dried out.

Sunlight, his mother said, desperate, whining, *needing*–

He checked to be sure he had belt pouch and knife–the only things he owned, now, as there was no point even trying to go back to Bright Bay–then went out into the warm daylight. The inn stood among a stand of thick featherpalm trees and stone pines, heavily draped with ivy; the side of the inn on which Idisio's room had been was the only spot receiving direct sun. The front door lay bathed in cool purple-grey shade.

Idisio shivered and started for the sun-striped road beyond the inn yard, then stopped, staring.

Kolan stood on the road, watching him without any particular expression. The sunlight caught glimmers of silver from his brown hair, and he had lines on his face that belonged to a man much older than the age at which Ellemoa's memories placed him.

For some reason, Idisio thought of Yuer; he put that aside as a distraction and focused on Kolan instead. He took a tentative step forward and said, "Kolan?"

Kolan only looked at him, gaze steady and clear and grey. Kolan didn't speak. Kolan–*waited*, as though to see what Idisio would do now.

Had his eyes been that color before? Idisio couldn't remember, and the uncertainty put another chill up his back. But the fastest path to get to the sunlight was to approach Kolan, and the inner pressure was growing–whining, nagging, pleading, *demanding* that he leave the cooler shadows. The *darker* shadows.

He walked forward, slowly, watching Kolan for any indication that the man planned an attack. Kolan stood still, his smoky gaze amused; his only motion to tilt his head to one side a bit. As Idisio neared, the man turned and walked east along the road a few steps, then stopped and looked back at Idisio, one eyebrow raised.

Idisio stared, speechless and bewildered. Kolan stared back, waiting with apparently infinite patience.

At last, Idisio took a step, then another; stood at the man's side without ever quite meaning to do so. Kolan nodded and began walking, Idisio beside him. After a while, Idisio noticed the man angled his path to walk through sunlight whenever possible. Something taut inside him relaxed; he loosened his stride, and even grinned as a flock of starlings wheeled overhead, grackling their hoarse, strident cries, the sun catching iridescent patterns out of their black feathers.

Kolan watched the birds too, smiling as though at some fond memory, but remained silent. Idisio, not knowing what to say, settled willingly into the companionable quiet. As they neared the eastern edge of Sandsplit, Kolan finally spoke.

In a voice that belonged to a much younger man, he said, "I want to start by telling you about the bells. There were always the bells . . . ."

Bells of the Kingdom
Glossary and
Pronunciation Guide

A number of the words in the southern language include the glottal-stop, which is rendered here as ^. A glottal stop involves closing, to some degree, the back of the throat, resulting in a near-coughing sound when released. Sometimes this sounds as though a hard "H" has been inserted.

Aenstone (ayn-stone): An Aerthraim Family-created stone composite; they hold the process secret. In sufficient quantity, aenstone blocks psychic communications, inhibits the use of psychic abilities, and weakens ha'ra'hain.

Aerth (ay-erth): Rough translation: *feathers, freedom, flight*. Exact meaning dependent on dialect and context.

Aerthraim lanterns: Any lamp filled with the peculiar green oil produced only by Aerthraim Family; gives off an unusually white light and little to no smoke when burned.

Aesa (ay-sah): A common plant whose leaves, when dried and used in a pipe, produce a mild euphoria. Illegal in the north; legal south of Bright Bay.

Ahnn (awwn): There is no direct northern equivalent to this word; an expression of gratitude for one's host's honor, patience, generosity, and grace, with overtones of *Thank you for not killing us while we sheltered under your roof.*

Alli (ahl-lee): **1.** The number *two* (southern). **2.** A simple two-pipe instrument, usually wooden, occasionally metal, common to the southlands.

Ana-ha, va'bit (**ahhnah**-hah, vah-**beet**): Rough translation: *Service/apology accepted.* A very old and out-of-use phrase: ha'ra'hain accepting apologies or submission from a human.

Aqeyva (ack-**ee**-vah, alt. ahh-**keh**-vah): A combination of martial-arts training and meditation disciplines. The combat training is often referred to as a 'dance' as it involves smooth, flowing motions that have no apparent resemblance to any fighting mode.

Asp-jacau (**asp**-jack-**how**): A slender canine with long, thin snout and legs. Its short-haired coat tends toward fawn or brindle coloring. Its excellent sense of smell is primarily used to detect dangerous snakes and (in some cases) drugs. In Bright Bay, only royalty or King's Guard patrols may own an asp-jacau, but below the Horn the asp-jacau is a common companion animal.

Athain (ath-**ain**): Lit. translation: *spirit-walker*. Teyanain specially trained to manipulate energy and psychic forces; extremely dangerous people, and very rare. Athain are considered holy by the teyanain. While they have elaborate outfits for ceremonial purposes, in "ordinary" clothes athain are distinguished by a unique manner of braiding their hair: beginning as one braid, then dividing further into three smaller braids, usually laced with tiny beads.

Ayn (**ain**): Chabi piece representing water. Cylindrical in shape, the ayn moves like a crooked stream: two spaces in one direction, three in another. It is one of the most versatile pieces on the board.

Bene (**beh**-ne): 1. The number *three* (southern). 2. A relatively simple three-pipe instrument common to the southlands. Like the *alli*, it is most commonly made of wood.

Cactus-flute: A long, thin flute made from minor branches of the same hard-skinned cactus used for making shabacas. Produces a thin, piping sound; sometimes tied together in sets of three to produce a wider range of tones.

Calcen (**khal**-czen): The title teyanain use for their leader; not permitted to outsiders. It is considered a gross offense for any non-teyanain to use that term.

Callen (**call**-en): One sworn to the service of a southern god.

Ceiling tube: A skylight in the form of a wide tube lined with mirrors; developed by Aerthraim Family. The secret of their manufacture is tightly controlled; they must be installed and repaired by Aerthraim craftsmen.

Chaal (**chawl**): A southern servant's term for people of high southern status; generally refers to desert lords.

Chabi (**chah**-bee): A desert game whose underlying principles, moves and strategies reflect the principles of survival in a dry, hostile environment. In chabi, different types of pieces represent wind, water, goods, and money; different areas of the board represent compass directions, fortresses, fire, air, and water.

Chekk (check): A community of ha'ra'hain openly living above ground. Extremely rare, as the genetic deterioration generally turns any such group into a human community within three generations—and the combative nature of many ha'ra'hain makes creating a balanced community a tricky process.

Chich (chihch): A substance developed by the Aerthraim to assist with various drug addictions, notably dasta. Generally mixed into a tough, extremely spicy fruit or meat jerky carrier.

Chichi (chee-chee): A small, hand-held clapper style of drum; generally a lightly hinged or tied striker and a metallic or wooden "head".

Clee: Three athain working together; extremely rare and extremely dangerous.

Coming or going: Street-slang inquiry about a relationship; "is she coming or going" means, more or less, "is she your girlfriend or a temporary amusement?"

Comos (Cohm-ohs): One of three gods honored in the southlands. Represents the neutrality/balance/questioning energies; also linked to the season of winter, the colors white and brown, and curiosity. Callen of Comos, if male, must be castrated; women must be past menopause to be allowed out in the world at large.

Dahass (dah-hahs; alt., dah-hass): Nomadic tribes that roam the uncharted and unclaimed southlands and follow no ruler but their own leader. They are likely the source of many of the wilder tales of southern barbarism that circulate in the northlands, as they find spreading such rumors amusing.

Daimaina (day-may-nah): Southern version of "housekeeper"; generally but not always shares the Head of Family's bed. Holds considerable power in her own right, but in a sharply limited sphere. Male version is *daiman*.

Dasta (dah-stah): A drug originally developed by the ketarches, whose use has altered significantly over the years.

Dashaic (dash-ache): So-called dasta tea is dasta powder turned into a thick, potent syrup. Dashaic travels better than the powder, as it runs less risk of being ruined by damp conditions, but is more difficult to produce and thus far more expensive.

Datda (Dat-dah): One of three gods honored in the southlands, Datda represents the negative/death/change energies; also linked to the season of high summer, the colors red and black, and the emotion of anger. Commonly called "the Sun Lord"; saying the name aloud is held to be bad luck. Only Datda's Callen may safely pronounce the holy name, but they tend to be reluctant to advertise their affiliation; everyone knows that most Callen of Datda have trained extensively as assassins and spies.

Dathedain (dath-heh-dane): Followers of the god Datda.

Desert sage: A tree-sized plant resembling ordinary garden sage, which has adapted for desert life; the leaves curl up during the day's heat into thick, needle-shaped rolls, and spread out in damp weather or at night. After a long drought, even a slight breeze will stir the dead leaves into a shivery, rattling sound. The dry wood gives off a pleasant aroma when burned, but the leaves are not edible. Often holds large nests of blood-spiders and micru.

Desert truce: An agreement to work together for mutual survival in a hostile environment; ends immediately upon reaching safety.

Devil-tree: A tree largely found in southern wastelands, with deeply fissured bark, wildly twisted branches, and semi-soft needle-style leaves; cones are bright red and poisonous to humans, but attract a variety of wildlife. The wood does not burn easily and gives off a nasty smoke.

Druu (dreww): Master drummer. Must understand and be able to use each of the numerous percussion instruments known in the south.

Eki (eh-key): One of the Four Gods of the Northern Church pantheon; represents Wind. She is considered to be the most evil of the Northern gods, and her good nature is rarely appealed to, for her favors carry a heavy price. Her strength is that of the air and clouds. She is deceitful and often malicious. Thieves often call on her for protection.

Esthit (ess-thitt): A drug originally developed by the ketarches, whose use has altered significantly over the years.

Estiqi (est-**eek**-ee): A liqueur made from esthit; lowers boundaries and dulls the senses. Used, in theory, to help "stuck" desert lords (i.e., desert lords resisting the transition to their altered natures) open fully to their new abilities. Tends to have an aphrodisiac side effect. The actual effects of estiqi vary by individual and can be unpredictable.

Fii (fee): The teyanain (and thus vastly more complicated) version of *thio*.

Four Gods: The pantheon of the Northern Church; Eki (Wind), Payti (Fire), Syrta (Earth), and Wae (Water). Each has a dual nature (good/evil), and the Church teaches that mankind must ever be careful not to provoke the "evil" side.

Fours: street slang term for devout followers of the Northern Church.

Furun (fuhr-root): Chabi game piece representing money. Shaped like a coin, the furun may move one square in any direction once unlocked; it may only be unlocked by a grey shassen jumping over it.

Gods'-glory flower: A common vine in the humid areas of the southlands; sports large, funnel-shaped flowers in an infinite variety of colors and blooming patterns (morning, evening, middle of the night).

H'na (heh-^hna): A teyanain-peculiar word (generally only pronounceable by the teyanain, as well), of obscure derivation and meaning, even to loremasters. Ties into an old story about a woman who worried herself into one crisis after another until at last she married a man who could calm her nerves.

Ha'bit vanaa (hah-**beet** vah-**nahh**): Rough translation: *Forgive your servant's offenses*. A very old and largely abandoned phrase, once used to indicate total submission/apology for wrongs done to a ha'ra'ha.

Ha'inn (properly: hah-^**inn**; more commonly: **high**-inn): Lit. translation: Hon-*ored One*. Reserved for ha'ra'hain. The glottal stop between *a* and *i*, always difficult for humans to manage, has fallen out of favor over the centuries.

Ha'inn-va (high-**inn**-vah): Very old and abandoned phrase indicating total submission to the will of a ha'ra'ha.

Ha'ra'ha (hah-^**rah**-^hah); plural **ha'ra'hain** (hah-^rah-^**hayn**): Person of mixed blood (human and ha'rethe).

Ha'ra'hain (hah-^rah-^**hayn**): Plural of **ha'ra'ha**.

Ha'rai'nain (hah-^**ray**-^nayn): Plural of **ha'rai'nin**.

Ha'rai'nin (hah-^**ray**-^nin); plural **ha'rai'nain** (hah-^ray-^**nayn**): One who has dedicated his or her life to serving the ha'reye.

Ha'rethe (hah-^**reth**-ay); plural **ha'reye** (hah-^**ray**): Lit. translation: *golden eyes*. An ancient race, predating humanity.

Ha'reye (hah-^**ray**): Plural of **ha'rethe**.

Ha'reye-kin (hah-^**ray**-kin); alt. **true-ha'rai'nin** (hah-^**hray**-nin): 1. A human who has spent so much time around the ha'reye that he or she has changed physically; no longer human, a ha'rai'nin more closely resembles a lesser ha'ra'ha. 2. A lesser ha'ra'ha who has spent so much time among the ha'reye that it is growing into greater powers. Both are extremely exceptional; at this time, only one human qualifies as the first and only one ha'ra'ha qualifies as the second.

Hai-katihe (high-kat-**tea**): Rough translation: *those who serve (intimately) a ha'ra'ha*. No longer in common use.

Hanna-aerst-yin (hah-**nahh** ayrst **yin**): Rough translation: *binding a bird in a cage of chains*. A rare and powerful teyanain marriage ceremony, only performed for people of extreme importance among the teyanain. Both *aerst* and *yin* are words peculiar to the teyanain dialect, and their exact meanings vary by context.

Hask: Lit. translation: *cast out*. Implications of dishonor, of betrayal, of irrevocable shame.

Hecht (hehkt): trator; oath-breaker.

Hopam (hoh-pahm): Literal translation: *dream house*. Generally used to refer to establishments that provide various illicit but relatively minor narcotics and hallucinogens, such as aesa and esthit.

Iii-naa tarren, iii-nas lalien, iii-be salalae (eee-nah tar-ren, eee-nahs lah-lee-en, eee-beh sah-lah-lay): Rough translation: *We serve the gods, the gods smile on us, we survive under the glory of the gods*. Implications of submission, sacrifice, loss of selfhood in service of the divine.

Iishin (eee-eee-shinn): Master acrobat; prominently used as a frontman in southern parades and processionals.

Ish (isshh): Prefix indicating feminine/female aspects.

Ishrai (Ish-wry): One of the three gods honored in the southlands; represents the positive/feminine/birth energies. She is also connected to the season of spring, the color green, and the emotion of love.

Ishraidain (ishh-wry-**dane)**: Women serving penance for various crimes, under the protection of Ishrai.

Ishrait (ishh-**rate)**: High priestess of Ishrai.

Itibi (ih-**tih**-bee): A small, high-pitched drum; generally held in one hand and struck with a light striker.

Itna tarnen, itnas talien, itnabe shalla (it-nah tahr-**nehn, it**-nahs **tah**-lee-en, it-**nah**-bay **shah**-lah): Rough translation: *We empty ourselves into the gods, the gods pour themselves into us, glory be to the gods.* Implications of partnership, gods and man giving to one another in service of building a better world.

Jacau-drum (jack-**how** drum): A large drum, generally stationary, with a wide head; produces a deep, booming tone. Originally covered with the skin of unusually large asp-jacaus, thus the name. Today these drums are usually made with cow, deer, horse, or goat skins, depending on how rich the owner is. Also called a *shaska drum*; only experts make a distinction between the two styles.

Jii (geee): Gifters; part of southern processionals and parades, *jii* toss candies and small coins to the watching crowds. Catching a *jii*-flung gift is considered a sign of good luck for the rest of the day.

Jungles: Also called *Forbidden Jungles*. An area of tropical rainforest far to the south where the majority of the surviving ha'reye and their human deevotees live; outsiders are not permitted to enter.

Justice-right: The right of a desert lord to intervene in a situation and see it resolved according to his own opinion of justice.

Ka (kah): Honored (generic term).

Ka-s'a (kah-ss-^**ah)**: Honored lady (generic term).

Ka-s'e (kah-ss^**eh)**: Honored gentleman (generic term).

Kain (cain): Rough translation: *servant's child*; honorable connotation, able to formally claim the relevant bloodline, and even inherit if more direct heirs are no longer eligible/available. The similarity between this and *kaen* makes the pronunciation, in this instance, very important; and yet, because kaens were seen as servants of their people, there is a certain blurring here as well. While it is not exactly *polite* to pronounce *kaen* as *kain,* only a person looking for an insult will take exception to the mispronunciation if it is an honest dialectic error rather than a deliberate attempt at offense.

Kath (kath): Rough translation: *servant*. Used with a variety of modifiers to indicate occupation and status; *s'a-dinne kath* indicates a kitchen or dining hall servant; *s'a kathalle* indicates a cleaning servant. When used in conjunction with *kath*, the female gender indicator (*s'a*) does not imply a female servant, but rather the concept of serving. The term *katha village*, while in common usage, is grammatically incorrect: it should properly be *vaa-kathe*, "village of intimate services".

Kathain (kath-**ayn**): Personal servants to a desert lord; generally offered to visiting desert lords as a courtesy, and considered an essential part of a new desert lord's staff for at least the first two years. Duties range from amusing their lord with playful games to more intimate services. This peculiar word is the same in both singular and plural forms, (i.e.: *Tanavin was a kathain*; *The four kathain left the room*; *The kathain's room was small*.)

Katheele (kath-**eel**): Rough translation: *spy through seduction*. An honorable profession, in the southlands; katheele are generally trained as spies and assassins as well as two or three minor specialties such as herbalist or etiquette master. They must maintain a keen understanding of current politics. They never act alone, but serve a specific Family or individual. Toscin Family trains the bulk of katheele, but at some point in their training, katheele decide whom they wish to serve; for their chosen master to refuse their service is nearly unheard of and incredibly rude.

Katihe (kat-**tea**): Rough translation: *honorable intimacy*; obscure term rarely used in modern times.

Ke (keh): Prefix or suffix indicating masculine/male aspects.

Ketarch (**kee**-tarsch): Organized groups of healers in the south who focus on preserving old healing lore and researching new ways of healing.

L'chin (lee-^kin): A teyanain-peculiar word (and generally only pronounceable by a teyanain, as well) of obscure derivation and meaning, even to loremasters. Ties into an old story about an opely welcomed guest who turned out to be less than honorable, was not what he professed to be, caused a major disaster, and yet redeemed himself by saving the day in the end.

Loremaster: Combination historian, genealogist, and researcher; as a group, one of the major political forces behind the scenes in the southlands. Every Family has (or is supposed to have) a group of loremasters resident.

Louin (loo-**een**): Lit. translation: *honored representative*. Largely used during transitional periods, when a newcomer has not yet taken his new station but must be granted some formal title for the sake of status.

Loremaster: Combination historian, genealogist, and researcher; as a group, one of the major political forces behind the scenes in the southlands. Every Family has (or is supposed to have) a group of loremasters resident.

Mocker: The lead figure in a southern drum line; usually female. She finds anything and everything to make fun of during a procession, then creates songs (called *mokoi*) afterward and spreads them far and wide.

N'sion (nn-*sigh*-on): The supreme leader of the Northern Church; previously referred to the head of the Bright Bay branch of the church. Since the banishment of all Northern Church priests from Bright Bay, a new n'sion has yet to be selected.

Nu-s'e (noo-ss-^eh): Honored man of the south (female is *nu-s'a*); generic honorific in the absence of specific indicators.

Numaina (noo-main-ah); plural numainiae (noo-main-ay): Proper title for a Scratha Family ruler.

Oamver (ohm-vehr): Rough translation: *negotiation table*. Ceremonial item of furniture, brought to all southland meetings; what is on the table at the beginning of the meeting has tremendous symbolic value. (During Scratha Conclave, the central table served as the oamver, and the fact that it was empty reflected a state of temporary truce among those normally at odds).

Oiu (ooh-ee-ooh): 1. The number *four* (southern). **2.** A complex, and usually rather large, four-pipe instrument common to the southlands. Like *alli* and *bene*, it is normally made of wood.

Pahenna (pah-hen-nah): Rough translation: *Stay out of my business, I know what I'm doing.*

Payti (pay-tee): One of the Four Gods of the Northern Church pantheon; represents Fire. Payti's "kind" incarnation is usually pictured as a short, plump man, with ruddy cheeks and a contagious cheeriness. In Payti's "dark" incarnation, the form is that of a tall, beautiful woman with a seductive gaze that bewitches all men who gaze upon her to their destruction. Payti's strength is that of the sun and the flame.

Peh-tenez (pay-tehn-ehz): A negotiation ceremony held over tea in which only truth may be spoken and the conversation may not be disclosed to those not a part of it. Largely a teyanain protocol, but some other Families use it when they wish to seem very serious about a political arrangement. Only the teyanain, ironically, can be fully trusted to hold to the original, sacred nature of the ceremony; to outsiders, it's largely a show, but teyanain will be absolutely honest during a true peh-tenez, and consider any deceit or breach of protocol a killing offense.

Protector: Not all fortresses are protected by full ha'reye any longer; some are occupied by first or second generation ha'ra'hain. Those aware of the distinction tend to use the term 'protector' to refer to those lesser ha'ra'hain bound to serve a particular Fortress.

Qisani (key-sahn-nee): A rocky cavern complex in the southern desert, which was given, under a Conclave decision, to the Callen of Ishrai many years ago as a haven of their own. All the desert Families contribute to supporting the Qisani. The followers of Datda and Comos also have central havens, but they are more secretive about the locations. Blood trials conducted at any of the havens are considered the hardest of all possible.

Ravann (rah-van; alt., rah-vahn): Similar to lavender in appearance and scent, but tends towards a darker leaf color, white flowers, and a slightly more acrid odor; only found south of Water's End, largely around the Aerthraim Fortress lands. Adapted for desert living, very hardy, but does not transplant well.

Reeven (ree-vehn): A ghost that seeks to possess living humans whenever possible; most dangerous during the dark of the moon, and generally driven away by (regional variances in the tale) the scent of lavender, rosemary, or pine. Usually strong-willed people, especially women, are seen as potential reeven after their death; the theory being that such people are be more likely to fight off the final journey into the afterlife, so as not to lose their earthly power.

S'a / S'e / S'ieas / S'ii: Respectful address designators, analogous to sir and madam; specific to gender, and frequently parts of complex and highly specific expressions of relationship between the speaker and the person being addressed.

> **S'a (ss-^ah):** feminine
>
> **S'e (ss-^eh):** masculine
>
> **S'ieas (ss-^eh-ahs):** a group of mixed gender
>
> **S'ii (ss-^ee):** neuter; generally used to address a eunuch.

Sa'ad hii (sah^had hee): Rough translation: *blood hunt.* Indicates that the one hunting will not be turned aside except by his or her own death, and that the prey will likely not survive being found.

S'e-kath (ss^eh kahth): Personal servant to the lord of a fortress; the best are highly trained in scholarship, politics, and combat. Extremely well respected and dangerous.

S'iope (s-^igh-o-pay): Lit. translation: *beloved of the gods;* implications of being neuter, all energy devoted to the gods. Term used to refer to the priests of the Northern Church. Disrespectful nickname: soapy.

Saishe-pais (say-shh-paws; alt. **say-she-pays):** An expression of heartfelt gratitude, indicating that the one so addressed has shown great honor in his/her actions.

Sanahair (sahn-ah-hair): Lit. translation: *shit boy.* The word ties into an obscure southern joke about kicking the person ranked just below you until there's only the chamberpot contents left to kick.

Sannio (san-nee-yo): A novice of the Northern Church.

Sayek-teth (say-hek-tehth): Rough translation: *Blood oath.* A term unique to the teyanain. Means an agreement which, once sworn, gives an outsider limited claim to be treated as a teyanain himself, including gaining the absolute protection of the teyanain—for as long as he continues to protect/serve the terms of the agreement.

Sessii ta-karne, I shha (Sessy tah-**carney,** ee shh-**ha):** rough translation: *You noxious, useless (castrated) little prick!*

Setaka, senaca (seht-tah-kah, sehn-nah-khah): Lit. translation: *Like father, like son.*

Shabaca (shah-**bah**-kah): A large dried gourd or cactus filled with pebbles or dried beans to make a rattle; common musical instrument in the southlands.

Shall (**shawl**): A temporary, portable desert shelter.

Shaska (**shass**-kahh): A large kettledrum, occasionally used in processionals, but mostly placed on tripod stands for in-place use. Also called a *jacau-drum*; only experts make a distinction between the two styles.

Shassen (**shass**-sen): Chabi game piece representing goods. Cubic in shape, the shassen moves one to three spaces in a straight line; it may never move diagonally or jump another piece, with the singular exception of unlocking the furun.

Shay-nin (**shay**-neen): Rough translation: *honored master spy*. Used to indicate a person who has achieved remarkable skill in the various arts of subterfuge, assassination, and intelligence-gathering, and who may be trusted to act with the highest personal and professional honor at all times.

Shennth: Rough translation: *domain*. Used to indicate the sphere of influence/power of a specific individual.

Sheth-hinn (shethh-**hnn**): Assassin.

Shivii (shee-**vee**): Formal wear for many southern men; resembles an ankle-length skirt, usually silk, slit on each side up to just above the knee.

Sio (**see**-oh): The familiar address for a full priest of the Northern Church. Outsiders (non-priests) should use *s'iope*.

Siolle (sigh-**oh**-lay): The familiar address for a junior priest of the Northern Church. Outsiders (non-priests) should use *s'iope*.

Sionno (see-**oh**-noh): Respectful term for a priest of the Northern Church, generally used by fellow priests or devotees, rather than the *s'iope* that "outsiders" use.

Split, The: A time of great chaos and dissension, during which humanity and the ha'reye renegotiated the Agreement and much knowledge was lost.

Stibik (**stih**-bic): A substance developed by the ketarches that temporarily weakens ha'ra'hain and ha'reye. Usually found in the form of a white powder, but sometimes as a concentrated, corrosive oil. It is illegal to bring stibik onto the land of an active ha'rethe; an even greater offense to use against a ha'ra'ha. Stibik was banned and ordered completely destroyed years ago; the ketarches, ever independent-minded, disobeyed the order.

Su-s'a (sue-ss-^ah): Northern lady.

Syrta (**seer**-tah): One of the Four Gods of the Northern Church pantheon; represents Earth. In his "good" incarnation, he is described as a leafy tree in spring or summer; when provoked to evil, he takes the form of a twisted, winter-stripped tree. He is credited with creating mankind and placing them in dominion over all beasts and growing things.

Ta (**tah**): Prefix implying masculine aspects; usually involved in insults (see ta'karne).

Ta feth kii (tah fethh **key)**: Rough translation: *stop shitting around; cut the crap.* Reference to bodily functions is a particularly effective insult against the teyanain, who consider something like this a far worse insult than being called, for instance, bastards. (Especially since most of them know their lineage six generations back on both sides.)

Ta-karne (tah-**carn**-ay): Insult. Rough translation: *asshole.*

Talloi (tah-**loy**): Flamboyant southern dance in which the dancer's shoes contain a small "clacker", making for a noisy and attention-getting performance.

Ta-neka (tah-**neek**-ah): Insult; female version of *ta-karne.*

Tas-shadata (**tahz**-shah-**dah**-ta): Rough translation: *fool, coward, idiot.*

Taska (**task**-ah; alt. **tah**-skah): Courier and guide.

Tath-shinn: Rough translation: *ghost of a female madwoman/assassin/murderer;* implies that a woman who would kill is insane, overly male, and impossible to handle even after death. Probably originated in the lower southwestern coastline region, among the Shakain. In the upper northlands, a similar creature is called a *shia-banse*: the ghost of a woman who died while under the influence of evil.

Te (teh): Prefix indicating formality and honor; no gender.

Telabat-nia-tabalet (**tehl**-lah-baht **nee**-yah tahb-ah-**leht**): Rough translation: *Play the game that is on the table.* Like many southern sayings, it involves a play on words; in this case, *telabat*, the game one is playing at the moment, and *tabalet*, the table one at which is currently sitting. *Nia* is a linking verb that has no real definition in and of itself; it simply puts the words to either side of it into harness, as it were.

Telle (**tel**-lay): teyanain word for "holy" or "sacred".

Teth-kavit (tehth-**kah**-vitt): Lit. translation: *Gods hold you, and blessings to your strength.*

Teuthin (**too**-thin): Rough translation: *meeting place.* Any agreed-upon neutral ground where all are seen as equal and violence is forbidden. Generally implies the presence of nobles of some rank.

Tewi va neesa (**tuey** vah **knee**-sah): Teyanin saying; loose translation: *you spit into the wind/you attempt something pointless.*

Teyanin (**tay**-ah-nin); plural: **teyanain** (tay-ah-**nayn**): A very old, small tribe which retreated to the mountains of the Horn after the Split. Originally the judges and law determiners of the desert, they're now considered the guardians of the Horn.

Tey-b'tibik (tey-bah-^**ktih**-bick): Rough translation: *binding powder.* A long-banned formula for a substance that significantly weakens ha'ra'hain and seriously injures ha'reye.

Teyhataerth (tey-hat-**aerth**): Literal translation: *Child of Earth and Air*: The mad ha'ra'ha controlled by Rosin Weatherweaver who resided under Bright Bay during the Purge.

Teyn-shatha hadinn (**teyn-shah**-thah hah-**dinn**): Lit. translation: *justice's cold bite*. Specifically refers to the teyanain preference for serving up revenge long after the offending party has forgotten the insult.

Tharr (**thahrr**): Rough translation: *the invisible ones*. A derogatory term used by the ha'reye and ha'ra'hain to indicate those humans who do not directly "serve" them (in essence, everyone but desert lords).

Thass (**tass**; alt. **thass**): A person with great status, beyond even noble rank.

That in it: Street-slang for *involved*; politically, not personally.

Thio (**thee**-oh): Status.

Thopuh (**thoh**-poo): Lit. translation: *blood of victory*. Also the name of a style of tea production currently monopolized by F'Heing. Thopuh tea grows stronger, more complexly flavored, and more valuable with proper aging.

Tibi (**tee**-bee): a shallow oval bowl usually carried by travelers in the south; food is scooped from a communal bowl into one's own tibi.

Tine (tyne): Rough translation: *whore's child*; implication of dishonor.

Toi, te hoethra (**toy**, teh hoe-thrah): Lit. translation: *I swear to you I am speaking truth*.

Tvit (**tvhit**): Typical Stone Islands parting; derived from *teth-kavit*.

Tvith (**tvitth**): Rough translation: *circumcised*; often used, in some of the rougher areas of the southlands, as an insult to a man's masculinity.

Ugren (**oo**-ghren): a very rare universal bonding mixture; also used in the southlands to imply unbreakable permanence in an arrangement or situation.

Va (vah): a rigid frame covered with a thick, stretched hide, partially filled with grit or sand; a *va* is generally held in the hands and rocked back and forth to produce an ocean wave-like, *shhhh*ing sound.

Vaa ha'inn-va ne (vah-**ah** high-**inn**-vah **neh**): Rough translation: *Master, I am yours*. Formal phrase of total submission from a very old version of the southern tongue. Almost entirely forgotten in the modern era.

Wae (**way**): One of the Four Gods of the Northern Church pantheon; represents Water. Wae can take any form; in his kindly incarnation he is often drawn as a great, wavering blue horse made from the coldest water of the deeps. His dark side is depicted in forms with a dark, shiny surface, like treacherous black ice—often a snake is drawn for this. Wae's strength is that of the waters, both still and quick, and the mountain glaciers.

Wailer: Street-slang for the tath-shinn.

Ways, the: A series of passages linking areas with an active ha'reye or ha'ra'hain presence. Travel through these passages generally requires the active cooperation of a ha'rethe or ha'ra'ha, and is essentially instantaneous regardless of intervening distance.

Yin: Rough translation: *unbreakable commitment, cage,* or *permanence of spirit.* Teyanain word; its meaning changes depending on context.

About the Author

Leona Wisoker's debut series, *Children of the Desert*, launched in 2010 with *Secrets of the Sands*, published by Mercury Retrograde Press. Her short stories have been published in *Andromeda Spaceways Inflight Magazine*, Michael Hanson's *Sha'daa: Pawns*, and the Dark-Quest anthology *Galactic Creatures*, among other places. She teaches writing classes, writes and edits for the *Sleeping Hedgehog*, and blogs about living a creative life at *The Writing of a Wisoker on the Loose*. Past and current careers include, in no particular order, filing clerk, CAD jockey, graphic designer, massage therapist, editor, computer teacher, and clothing retail. Current fixations involve  a search for the perfect cup of coffee and a hopeless quest to keep the garden weeded. She lives in eastern Virginia with her husband and two large dogs, all of whom routinely try — and usually fail — to drag her away from the computer for long, rambling walks.

For more information on Leona and her current projects, visit one or all of the following:

Children of the Desert series page:
http://www.MercuryRetrogradePress.com/Worlds/ChildrenoftheDesert.asp

Leona's web site: http://www.leonawisoker.com

The Writing of a Wisoker on the Loose: http://leonawisoker.wordpress.com

Free eBook

Whether you're traveling across the desert or just taking the train to work, sometimes you want the convenience of reading electronically. At the Mercury Retrograde Press website, readers who purchase the book in Trade Paper format can download the eBook version of *Bells of the Kingdom*—for free. Just enter the code SIONNO on this form:

http://www.MercuryRetrogradePress.com/eBookform.asp

and we will email you a download link for *Bells of the Kingdom*, in whatever eBook format you choose.

Want More?

Visit the *Children of the Desert* page on the Mercury Retrograde Press website:

http://www.MercuryRetrogradePress.com/Worlds/ChildrenoftheDesert.asp

for even more background on the world of *Bells of the Kingdom*.

Author updates

For information on appearances and new releases, visit

http://www.MercuryRetrogradePress.com/Authors/LeonaWisoker.asp

for announcements and news, or to register for updates by email.

CPSIA information can be obtained
at www.ICGtesting.com
Printed in the USA
EDOW021228110113
382ED

9 781936 427222